NEW YORK NIGHTS

Books and stories by T. Lee Harris

Twenty-Seven Cents of Luck (Short)
Cat in the Middle (Short)
Sweet Water From the Rock (Short)
Muddy Waters (Short)
Winter Wonderland (Novella)

In the Miller and Peale Series
San Francisco at Night (Short)
Chicago Blues
New York Nights

In the Josh Katzen Series
Hanukkah Gelt (Short)
The Pecan Pie Affair (Short)
The Case of the Moche Rolex*

In the Sitehuti and Nefer-Djenou Bastet series
To Be a Scribe (Short)
The Scribe Vanishes (Short)
Wanting the Fish (Short)

* Coming Soon

NEW YORK NIGHTS

T. LEE HARRIS

Per Bastet

New York Nights

Published by Per Bastet Publications LLC, P.O. Box 3023 Corydon, IN 47112
Book designed by T. Lee Harris

ISBN 978-0-9899711-5-7

Cover photo by Dmitry Avdeev through Wikimedia Commons

Cover design by T. Lee Harris

For Dale

Who believed it could happen.

NEW YORK NIGHTS

PART ONE

"Between two worlds life hovers like a star,
'Twixt night and morn, upon the horizon's verge.
How little do we know that which we are!
How less what we may be!"

~ ~ Lord Byron

"Yet, as only New Yorkers know, if you can get
through the twilight, you'll live through the night."

~ ~ Dorothy Parker

ONE

Now, I have nothing at all against the city of New York. In fact, I've had some very good times there. I wouldn't have minded being sent there this time if it hadn't smacked so much of "Let's toss the hot potato to someone else for a bit." Okay, I know that wasn't the actual reason, but knowing in your head and knowing in your heart are two vastly different things.

It isn't that there wasn't a good reason to ship my partner, Galen Miller, and myself off. There definitely was. My name is BC Peale. I'm a special agent for Sentry International and the case my partner and I had been working on in Chicago had blown up in everyone's faces. Big time. Shrapnel expanded on a near-cosmic scale and a very large whack hit New York when associates of Eddie Michalson, one of the principals in our Chicago case, started dying in rather spectacular ways.

Still, New York City was not where I wanted to be.

For one thing, Galen and I were still on the ropes emotionally. Most of the Chicago SI branch was. A colleague of ours, Deputy Director Miguel Marquez, had been brutally murdered a few days back. To make it worse, Marquez was one of Galen's childhood friends. To make it exponentially worse, the killer was Francesco Borgia, my own sire.

Notice I did not say "father." The person in question is not my father. He is my sire. I'm a vampire. He made me as I am.

I suppose I should be grateful for that because I enjoy being a vampire, but the way it happened was not my choice. For a long time — about two centuries, in fact — I had no idea who my sire was. That was part of the vengeance extracted by Maeve Donal, the woman who arranged my change. It brings truth to the phrase "ignorance is bliss" because my sire, Francesco Borgia, is one of the vilest beings on the face of the planet. If I had known, if I had been given a choice. . . ? Oh, I don't know what I'd have done, honestly. I'd be mouldering bones at best had I not been changed, and I would have missed so much. But to know whose blood made me what I am, to know I am forever tied to such a creature of evil?

Well, it's all moot isn't it? I ticked Maeve Donal off, she sicced Francesco Borgia on me and here we all are.

Oh, yeah. New York. It happened like this:

***

BC Peale stepped through the leaded glass door of the funeral home and shut it against the unseasonably chilly night wind. Murmuring voices from the big room to his left reached him, an indecipherable jumble of sound even to his enhanced hearing. Too many people were speaking at once to be able to single out a given one, but he already knew his partner, Galen Miller, was among them. He'd likely been there all day. In many ways Miguel Marquez had been more like a brother to Galen than his own flesh and blood.

He, himself, hadn't been that close to Lt. Marquez, but he'd have been there, too, if he could. His vampiric condition bestowed many benefits, but like anything else, there were trade-offs. To Peale, the biggest downside was lying dormant, as if dead, until the sun set. As spring moved into summer, that time was coming later and getting shorter. There'd still be enough time to pay his respects, though, and this would be his last opportunity. The funeral and burial was slated for the next morning. He'd miss the final goodbye, but that couldn't be helped.

Moving down the softly lit corridor toward the splash of brighter light that spilled over the carpeting through open wood-paneled double doors, he stopped just short. He didn't like modern funeral homes. The smell of death mixed with chemicals set him on edge and the pink-tinted light from inside the room was little too bright to his sensitive eyes. He wondered again why so many places used it. Was it to mimic candlelight or to give the deceased a more natural look? It failed at both.

It did make the crucifix over the casket and other accoutrements of religion scattered throughout the room gleam, though. There certainly were a lot of them. He was glad he didn't have the classic vampiric reaction to such things — unlike his sire, Francesco Borgia. That brought to mind Jasmine Miller's explanation for the difference. According to Mrs. Miller, Borgia reacted strongly to such things because he was so unreservedly evil, while BC, himself was . . . what was her exact wording. . . ? Ah yes, a royal pain in the backside. That made him smile in spite himself, awakening pinprick discomfort from the residual burns left by the magic unguents Mrs. Miller had used against Borgia the night Mick Marquez was killed.

At the time, BC had been grappling hand-to-hand with

his enraged sire and was in too tight a clinch not to be splashed by the sticky, fiery magic thrown on his opponent. The burns were healing more slowly than normal wounds, probably because of their magical nature. Maybe that was a good thing. It was common knowledge that he'd been injured trying to save Mick. If he healed too quickly, it might raise questions. Questions he didn't feel much like answering. It didn't help that the healing process was requiring a lot of blood. Even more than he'd expected. The worst part was that the lingering injuries left him less able to guard his senses than normal. This was a dicey thing in a room full of pounding human blood.

Abruptly, the sounds, emotions and scents of the crowd hit him hard. He closed his eyes and resisted the mismatched urges to spring on prey or run like hell.

He could control this. He *could*.

Come on, the Inferno Jazz Club was regularly more crowded and much more noisy than this group. Still, there were an awful lot of people jammed into that room. It wasn't that big a room and the Marquez clan was large.

A gentle touch came from behind, startling him. Someone ran a hand lightly over his shoulder. He knew who it was without turning. Even through the confusion of scents in the room, this one stood out, spicy and vital as the lady herself.

"Hullo, Jay," he said, looking down into her smile.

"Hello, yourself. How long you been standing here? You *can* go in, you know."

"Just got here, actually. Taking a bit to adjust to the light and all."

Jay said nothing, but squeezed his arm. Her sympathy washed over him, surprising him yet again. She was the one who had suffered the loss, it was her own brother who lay in the casket. Worse, she'd even witnessed his murder. Peale ought to be consoling her, not the other way around.

He answered her smile with one of his own and said, "Jay, I can't express how sorry I am—"

Her expression changed and she swatted him. "Don't you *dare* go there again, Byron Cyrus Peale! Ya did everything ya could to save Mick. That asshole Borgia ain't got no more claim on you than . . . than . . . a *sperm donor*."

He couldn't stop the laugh and she joined in, resting her forehead companionably against his shoulder.

"Thank you," he said after a moment. "That's just the kind of ludicrous image I need to deal with this."

"Well, it's true, ain't it?"

"I suppose it is, at that," he said after a moment of consideration, and offered his arm to her with a courtly bow.

With a triumphant look, she took it and steered him through the doors.

As soon as they entered the crowded room, Jay started talking. "I hope the flowers ain't too much for ya. There's even more of 'em than last night an' they even get to me sometimes. I was sneezin' my head off this afternoon. They started comin' before Mick's body was even released by the Medical Examiner and they just keep comin'. The funeral director even borrowed shelves from another place to hold 'em all," Jay chattered. "I like it better when people give to charities in Mick's name, though. We had a buncha those. Somebody even sent a wind chime. I never heard of that before. It's real pretty, though."

Byron recognized the symptoms. Emotional upset and stress triggered all kinds of things in different people: some people cracked their knuckles, some chewed their nails, Jay chattered — which made what happened next all the more curious.

"That one over there is from Mick's old detective squad an' that one is from the whole Chicago PD," Jay said pointing across the room. Abruptly, she stopped talking and tugged at his arm, pulling him in another direction. "Ummmm. We don't wanna go that way."

"What's wrong with that way?" he asked, balking slightly.

"That's where Mama and my oldest sister are."

"But I like your mama and Bonita."

"Yeah, they like you, too," she said with a sigh. "Too much. They're puttin' a certain kinda spin on our friendship if ya get me."

"Ah. Matchmaker noises. Don't worry, I'm an old hand with those."

"Me, too, but — dammit! Mama spotted us."

Over his shoulder, BC saw Mrs. Marquez rise from her seat, looking in their direction. Before she could move, however, she was blocked from view by the bulk of Benny Glissen, the Inferno Jazz Club's bouncer. The club's manager, Phil Quinlan, and Jump Veron, the Inferno's owner, joined him.

Veron's unmistakable Cajun accents rose over the background babble, "Mrs. Marquez, we mus' go, but we wanted to express our sorrow to you once more before we leave."

Relief flooded from Jay in palpable waves. "Those guys are great. Don't think I could have made it through this without them. Especially Jump, I owe him big time."

"I hear you. I owe him a lot of big ones, myself."

Nodding toward the group, he said, "Why don't you go on over and be with your family for a bit? I have no doubt I can find Galen on my own."

As BC watched Jay thread through the clumps of mourners, Quinlan winked at him. Peale smiled his thanks and turned to find his partner. It wasn't hard. A retired football linebacker, Galen Miller stood out in a crowd much the same way Glissen did. After a moment, he located him sitting in a corner near the casket with Jim and Liza Nelson, — and Mick's widow, Vera. A fresh wave of guilt washed over him.

It didn't matter what anyone else said or how often they said it, it was his own sire who brutally murdered Mick Marquez. That made *him* guilty by association.

As if alerted by a sixth sense, Vera Marquez looked up and caught sight of him. Smiling graciously, she motioned him over and patted the empty spot on the couch next to her.

Pasting on a smile, he joined the group and took the offered seat.

***

Peale paused at the top of the steps leading down to the Inferno Jazz Club and listened to the music leaking around the ornate door. Unless he was mistaken, that was Ray Niello on the piano. Jump must have asked the local quartet Classified Jazz to cover for Nosferatu, the house band. Wise decision. Most of said house band was fresh from a funeral. That didn't lend itself to light improvisation. He wished Jump had seen fit to let him know, though. If he'd known, he wouldn't have rushed to get to the club. On the other hand . . . he chewed his lip thoughtfully, a vague recollection niggling at the back of his mind. On the other hand, Jump *might* have told him and it just didn't sink in. He hadn't exactly been tracking well since the night Marquez was killed.

Pushing the old-fashioned oak and brass front door open, he noted that the brass was especially gleaming. Benny Glissen was taking Mick Marquez' death badly and when Benny was upset, he tended to focus on minutia and the club's glass and brass fittings often benefited. Benny also had a monumental crush on Mick's sister Jay, so it was especially bad this time. He wondered how that would work out. It wasn't a match he'd credit, but history had proven him a dismal failure at romantic relationships.

"Hey, Peale! Didn't expect to see you so early tonight," Phil Quinlan called from his post behind the Please Wait To Be Seated sign. He grinned and added, "If at all."

BC squared his shoulders and said, "Just because I'm not at the keyboard doesn't mean I can slack off."

Quinlan's grin got broader. "Forgot that Jump hired Classified for the rest of the week, huh?"

"Busted," Peale sighed. "More like didn't even hear him tell me. I haven't been exactly on top of things these last few days."

Quinlan's grin disappeared. "Who has?"

Peale surveyed the crowded nightclub. "Good house tonight."

"It's a little jarring, isn't it?" Phil said, following his gaze across the busy floor. "Come from that floral-scented funeral parlor into a carnival. It's like a different dimension or something."

"Exactly what Jump wants," Peale said. "I remember when we first opened the place. He pointed at the front door and said, 'See that *mon ami*? That is where the real world stops and magic begins.'"

"He still says that," Quinlan said with a chuckle. "Too bad the real world doesn't pay attention."

"Thanks for the save tonight. With Mrs. Marquez."

Phil shrugged. "No problem. She means well, but . . . I could see the room was getting to you — hell, it was getting to *me* and my senses aren't anywhere near as acute as yours. Hey, while we're on a supernatural subject: have you found someplace else for *her*, yet?" he asked jinking his eyes upward to indicate the upstairs apartments.

It took a moment for Quinlan's meaning to sink in. "Ah. Maeve."

"Who else. In case you missed it, we don't exactly get on like a house afire."

"Yeah, I noticed."

"I mean, I totally get having to hide out here with the Big Bad on the loose and everything. But that's over." After a pause, he added cautiously, "It *is* over, right?"

"I surely hope so," Peale answered fervently.

Phil shook his head. "How you two were ever an item is beyond me. You don't seem to have a thing in common."

BC was spared trying to respond by the arrival of a large group of regulars. Grateful beyond words, he exchanged greetings with them as Phil busied himself gathering menus. His pleasant smile faded a little as Quinlan guided the patrons to a booth. Unwilling to resume the uncomfortable conversation, Peale took the opportunity to retreat to the relative safety on the other side of the Employees Only door.

Truth to tell, he wasn't sure there *was* a response — not an easy one at any rate. Back in the 1700s, he and Maeve Donal had a lot in common. Sure, they had a tendency to row, but the making up had always been the sweeter for it. That was until the final row that ended with his becoming as he was now. The intervening centuries had taken the two of them along very different paths; neither of them was the same person who met and fell in love so long ago.

He understood what was bugging Phil, though. He didn't really blame him, either. Maeve had always been intensely curious. That was a trait that hadn't altered with the passage of time and when it was sparked, she was like a terrier with a rat. Maeve had never met anyone like Quinlan before and she was fascinated. Phil, on the other hand, being an intensely private person, viewed her interest as prying. Recipe for disaster. He didn't envy Jump's task of keeping their odd little household running on an even keel.

He peeked into Jump's cluttered office. No Jump; must be upstairs. A glance at the small elevator wedged into the space next to the darkened stairway confirmed the theory. Yep. Upstairs.

At the base of the stair, he stood motionless, hand resting on the railing. A few beats more and it became obvious that he was stalling. Interesting. It seemed that Phil Quinlan wasn't the only Inferno denizen having a problem with their visitor — although, for him, it wasn't exactly a new experience. He and Maeve had been at odds with each other ever since the night he awoke chained to the wall in her root cellar. *Not* the optimal way to break the news he'd been made a vampire. It *was* pure Maeve, though.

However, this resistance was subtly different. Try as he might, he simply could not make himself walk up to where he knew Maeve would be waiting for him. Well, not exactly waiting for *him*, but that's how it felt. Actually, it felt more like she was lying in wait for him.

Why?

Good question.

It wasn't that Maeve had been unpleasant. In fact, she'd been anything but. Ever since Mick's murder, she'd been nothing but solicitous. Why did he find that a bigger problem than an argument?

Anger. Yes, that was it, but it was a different sort of anger than the indignation he'd felt on his first night after his change. Odd that he'd think of that after all this time. Then again, maybe not so odd. That was the night that Maeve had brought Francesco Borgia into the equation.

The thought of his sire triggered an intense backwash of emotion that left him sick and shaken in its wake. The intensity surprised him as did the echoing words in his mind, *How could she?*

Ah, yes. That was the crux, wasn't it? He was finding it hard to reconcile how the woman who once loved him could also love someone like Francesco Borgia.

Again, he didn't know why. The past had proven that Maeve was perfectly willing to throw in her lot with anyone who could entertain her — oh, and shower her with gifts. Hell, when he met her in 1777, she was the mistress of one of the British Army officers in charge of the occupation of Philadelphia. That was bad enough, but Francesco Borgia dropped that to a new low. He didn't give a rat's ass that the man was his sire; he was also unrelentingly evil. There was no finer point to be put on it.

He chewed his lip and stared at the closed door at the top of the stair. He'd best move his ass. Emotions as intense as the ones that gripped him were bound to cause fireworks to Jump's precognitive gift. If he delayed much longer, he'd—

The door at the top of the staircase swung inward, spilling light and the familiar scent of old books and vinyl records onto him in a wave.

Jump Veron leaned down and called, "Why you standin' down there blockin' th' hall?"

Leave it to Jump to break the cycle of self-doubt. Laughing at himself, he took the steps two at a time.

The large, airy room with its floor-to-ceiling shelves of books and recordings usually had a calming effect on him. This night the magic was only partially effective. Maeve was nowhere to be seen, but he could sense her presence. He scanned briefly, then nodded toward the closed guest bedroom door questioningly.

"*Mais oui*, *mon ami*, I believe she freshen up a bit. She have been busy today helping in the club."

"Uh huh." Peale's skepticism was palpable.

Jump made a disgusted noise and waved his friend to the chairs. "I do not pretend to understand the two of you. You each expect the worst from the other. Tonight Maeve spend hours in the kitchen to teach Cal how to make the real Irish stew and the soda bread."

Peale dropped into his favorite chair and sat back with eyes closed, listening to the quartet playing downstairs. "Best check it for poison."

"No customers have drop dead yet." Veron didn't move from his place by the door, but watched his friend with concern. Finally, he said, "How you do, *mon ami*? You look a little rough at the edges tonight."

Eyes still closed, BC gave a self-deprecating chuckle and waved the worry away. "Fried around the edges more like, but don't worry about me. I'm fine. Things have just been moving a little faster than I can follow these last few days."

"You still blame yousel' for Marquez' death." It was a statement, no question to it.

Peale remained silent.

Sighing, the little Cajun lowered himself into his own favorite chair, a worn, faded, but comfortable relic — rather like its owner. "I can see it do no good to tell you once again that it is not your fault, so I will not try. I only hope that time will heal this as it heals most things."

BC lifted his head, about to reply, then sat forward and abruptly changed the topic. "Y'know, Classified Jazz sounds great tonight. Especially Ray." He grinned wickedly. "He's almost as good as me on the keyboards."

Jump was puzzled until Maeve emerged from the guestroom trailing a hint of her signature perfume. He regarded his friend with amusement. "Ah, yes, but Ray has not had quite as much time to practice as others." Turning, he said, "*Bonsoir*, Maeve. I hope this evening find you well."

The Irish woman treated both men to a dazzling smile. "Very well, thank ye, Jump. I didn't hear ye come in. Either of ye." She grew serious. "How was Mrs. Marquez this evening? She seemed a bit tired this afternoon."

Jump nodded, "She is still tired, but she is holding up."

"Jay's afraid she's going to have a meltdown after the graveside service tomorrow," Peale said with a frown. "From the pent-up emotions I felt rolling off her, Jay may well be right. I wish I could be there. I might could siphon a little off and—"

"Byron Peale! Don't ye dare go beatin' yerself up over this."

Peale looked up at the Irishwoman in surprise.

"I know ye only too well. Ye've always been one to hold the guilt to yer heart." She waved a finger at him. "AND I know I'm not the only one sayin' so, but Francesco Borgia is t'blame here and no other."

Met with more sullen silence, the Irishwoman waved in dismissal and turned away toward the apartment's galley-style kitchen. "Enough of this. I've better things to do than hammer at yer hard head all night. The electric kettle ought to have the water hot by now. I'm for a cup of tea, would y'like one, too, Jump?"

"It is inviting, but I fear I mus' ask for the rain check." Veron said, pulling himself to his feet. "If I do not put in an appearance in the club before the evening is spent, some of the regulars, they worry."

Maeve headed on to the kitchen and Byron stood to help Jump with the elevator door. Just before he pulled the brass grating closed, he leaned in and whispered, "Deserter."

Veron's only answer was to smile and push the down button.

***

From where Gwen Isendamer sat, the city of Chicago looked like a handful of jewels scattered over a black velvet background. She suppressed a smirk. Quite a beautiful image for a city as grim and grimy as Chicago. She'd never liked the place and still didn't understand why Francesco had chosen it for the main offices of the Este Corporation. Sometimes she wondered if Francesco did, himself.

She shifted her gaze away from the nighttime illusion and onto her lover/employer, Francesco Borgia. What she could see of him, anyway. Halfway through the conference call with their Colombian associate, Francesco had fallen silent, leaving her to deal with his South American counterpart.

Instead, he had turned away to stare out the floor-to-ceiling window that comprised the farthest wall of the office. He hated dealing with the man the Colombians had put in charge. She didn't blame him. For all the man's pretended courtesy, he was crude and ignorant of the subtleties of business.

All she could see of Francesco now was the elbows of his well-tailored suit. Even that limited view told her he was angry. He had every right to be. Their business partners were overstepping their bounds. Again.

The call concerned part of their drug importing operation in New Orleans. More to the point, the Colombians wanted to express concern over the behavior of their main runner for the area. A man named Cruz. As if they needed to be reminded that the man was a loose cannon. His incessant tweaks to the New Orleans import operation never made the runs any easier. Instead, he seemed to be adding layer upon layer in order to make it more complicated. It was almost as if each operation was some sort of test for his machismo; each run increasing in difficulty like an insane video game.

Personally, Gwen believed he'd been sampling the merchandise. That was never a good thing and even worse for a man as unstable as Cruz. He'd always been an idiot, now he was a *stoned* idiot. She'd warned Francesco at the outset that he was a risky hire, but they'd had little to choose from at that point. Things were different now. The drug side of the Este Corporation was ticking along very smoothly now. It would be simple to replace him with another, more reliable operative.

She frowned at the ornate chair back. That was the surface subject matter. In truth, there was much more being discussed than a problem with the New Orleans conduit. It seemed to be more about the recent series of disasters that had befallen the Este Corporation — the ones the Colombians were aware of, anyway. They did not know — and did not *need* to know — that Francesco Borgia was a vampire and somewhere in the vicinity of five hundred years old.

What they did know, however, was that someone had been targeting the Corporation's Chicago couriers. They also knew that a lakeside warehouse had gone up in flames. They had no clue that it was Francesco's own scion, Byron Peale, who had been behind those incidents. Well, it was true that they had lost a lot of valuable merchandise in that fire and it wouldn't be easy to replace some of it, but that should be no concern of the Colombians. The only business they conducted with those people was drug-related. If they wanted to talk arms deals, that would be a completely different thing.

Francesco hated to even speak to the South Americans, regarding them as little more than thugs with delusions of grandeur. Even though entering the drugs business was originally her idea, Gwen was inclined to agree with him. Those idiots! All sides were making money in the partnership, why interfere with what was none of their concern? Did they really think a simple telephone call would rattle Francesco Borgia? All they'd managed to do was make him angrier than he already was. They'd had the nerve to ask, "Is the Este Corporation still on solid ground after all these losses?" She'd had a hard time keeping a straight face when she answered that one. Not that he could see her, but it was better to maintain a business-like attitude.

They'd mentioned the attacks on Eddie Michalson's people in New York, too. She allowed a slight smile. The Cartel representative seemed to think the current attacks were linked to the earlier attacks on the Este Corporation's couriers. If he only knew. Well, if he kept this attitude, he might find out the hard way. She'd never been to Colombia before—

Without turning, Borgia spoke from his place by the window. His words were so soft, she had to lean forward to catch them. He said, "You must go to Louisiana and take care of this problem. I would like it solved before I return."

"Of course, Francesco. I'll head to New Orleans immediately." She paused. "Where will you be going, Darling?"

"I will travel to the compound north of Edmonton. I may be there some time."

"The Canadian place?" she asked, unable to hide her surprise. "But . . . that's in the middle of nowhere!"

Francesco Borgia swung the throne-like chair around, letting the full light fall on him.

She gasped in spite of herself. Jasmine Miller's magic potion had done tremendous damage. Angry red welts crisscrossed his face and neck. The skin between alternated oozing blisters and pale patches where blisters were healing. Even though she had seen the injuries at their worst, right after they happened, the sight of the ravages always caught her by surprise.

He smiled at her discomfort, breaking open one of the blisters. He dabbed at it absently with a handkerchief. "Yes, it is, Cara. My wounds are such that I require more fresh blood than I can safely acquire in this city. I must hunt to heal. And to hunt and heal effectively, I must have complete privacy. I cannot achieve that here."

***

BC Peale pulled the curtain slightly aside and stared out into the night as Captain Jim Nelson fired questions at Galen Miller. For obvious reasons, they'd delayed this debriefing and a very large part of him wished they could skip it entirely. From the somber look on Galen's face and the stoic silence from Lt. Emily Hu, he knew he wasn't the only one. He didn't have to look hard to see that Captain Nelson wasn't too happy, either.

Well, why should they be? Rehashing the events of the weeks and months leading up to what was now considered the conclusion of the Borgia investigation could only aggravate still-fresh wounds — for all of them. Hmmmm. "The conclusion of the Borgia case." Was it really over? Just the night before, he'd assured Phil Quinlan that it was, but it felt like a lie as soon as it was out of his mouth. Certainly, the Este Corporation was severely crippled, but Francesco Borgia had escaped and they'd lost track of Gwen Isendamer and Eddie Michalson. That didn't read as much of a conclusion to him.

On top of that, one of their own had been brutally murdered by Borgia. It seemed like the whole world was making a point to assure Peale that Peale himself was blameless — but was that true? How could they *not* blame him? Hadn't Francesco Borgia been looking for *him* when he held Jay Marquez hostage and beat her brother to death in front of her?

His eyes slid away from the window to watch Lt. Hu efficiently taking notes at her place beside Captain Nelson at the end of the conference table. He wasn't the only member of the Special Ops team feeling conflicted. Calm exterior notwithstanding, Emily's warring emotions battered him from all the way across the room. Em was a classic over-achiever and she'd made no secret of her intention to move up in the Sentry International hierarchy. Now she had — at the expense of a friend and colleague. He wondered if that was why she'd made a point to talk with him before the debriefing. She'd told him that the SI brass felt that he'd . . . how did she phrase it? Ah, yes. "Comported himself in an exemplary manner in spite of the extraordinary circumstances." In spite of the bureaucratic jargon, she'd been sincere. That had been unexpected, but oddly reassuring. Especially so because he knew that not all of his new teammates were as accepting of him; of knowing what he was.

Frank Tidrow wasn't a problem. After a moment's consideration, his response to the revelation was "awesome" with a double thumbs up.

Kim Zoeller was an entirely different story. Zoeller was a practical person who prided herself on a no nonsense approach to the world. For her world to work, there was no such thing as magic and vampires didn't exist. It shook her to her core to be told that vampires were real and Byron Cyrus Peale *was* one. She'd been giving him a wide berth ever since. It wasn't that she was afraid. No, he'd smell that a mile away. She was just . . . distant.

Thank heaven none of them were angry. That was Marquez' original reaction and that had been very hard to deal with. Toward the end, his overt fury had lessened, but a tinge of it had remained, flavoring the background.

On the whole, he preferred neutrality.

"Earth to Special Agent Peale."

Oops. Realizing with a start that Captain Nelson had been addressing him, he turned with a ready apology on his lips, but Nelson didn't wait for it.

"I asked how your injuries were healing. I understand they aren't healing at your normal rate because of the magic behind them, but they *seem* to be better." He pulled his half-glasses farther down his nose and gave him a critical squint. "They look pretty good from here. I can still see where the goop hit, but I have to look for it."

Unconsciously stroking the most painful spot, Peale said, "Yes, it is slow, but at least it's steady. The herbal infusion Mrs. Miller used afterwards helped a lot. Damnable stuff didn't want to come off any other way — not without taking some skin with it."

Emily Hu winced in sympathy. "I gather most of the mixture landed on Francesco Borgia?"

Galen chuckled. "Sure as hell did. It splashed all over the sonovabitch. Smoked every place it touched bare skin too. Face. Neck. Hands." The chuckle gave way to a wide grin. "My mama is a good shot."

Lt Hu nodded. "Glad to hear it. Hope it's hurting like hell. He deserves even worse than that."

Jim Nelson sat back in his battered armchair, removed his reading glasses and massaged the bridge of his nose. His voice was slightly muffled as he said, "Emily has already mentioned this to BC, but you two are getting a commendation for bravery above and beyond. From what I saw that night, I don't think a commendation is enough."

"Aw, *hell* no!" Miller sat forward abruptly. "I don't do that 'I want to thank my fill in the blank' any more, Jim."

"Don't worry, Gae," Jim said. "There won't be any monkey suits or rubber chickens. This will go straight into your records. You're still undercover."

"Well, as undercover as you can manage," Hu said with

her first genuine laugh in days. "I've seen tank brigades who left less wreckage in their wake than you two."

Smiling, Jim shook his head, then opened another folder. Sliding copies of the report it held to the other three, he said, "Next item of business."

Peale abandoned the window and took his place at the table, eying the thick sheaf of paper. "Ah, no rest for the wicked, I see."

"None for you, anyway," Nelson said, then sat back, entering mission-brief mode. "The problem we have, folks, is that activity associated with the Este Corporation has calmed down in our own back yard, but seems to be hotting up in New York. Over the last few weeks, NYPD has been investigating a series of bombings. I'm sure you've seen the news coverage."

After a moment, Galen said, "Yeah, there was a car blew up outside a mob guy's house just a few days ago."

"And at least one nasty surprise through the post," Peale added scanning the pages. "Yes. Two. Both victims with links to organized crime. Methods of delivery were different, but the devices themselves were similar."

"Mmmmm," Hu agreed. "I don't see a Borgia connection, though."

"That would be Eddie Michalson," Nelson said.

"Wait," Miller said jabbing the reports with a forefinger. "Is this suggesting that Michalson is behind the bombings? That doesn't sound right, he's more a gun-in-your-face sort of guy."

"You're right, Gae, but Michalson isn't the perpetrator. He seems to be the target in a roundabout way. Turns out that the victims of the attacks have all been lieutenants in

Michalson's branch of the Este Corporation," Nelson said.

Peale frowned. "That's odd. Do we have any idea who's behind it?"

"My money would be on Gwen Isendamer," Miller said flatly.

"She *is* awfully fond of things that go boom." Peale said. "Could she be making a move to push Michalson out?"

"That's one of the current theories." Nelson paused and looked uncertain. Finally he said, "With all the overlap, NYPD and SINY have agreed to a joint investigation into these attacks." He paused again. "You guys maybe aren't going to like this next part. Since you two were the agents working the case here in Chicago, you're being assigned to this one. As of tomorrow noon, you'll be reassigned to the New York bureau. Your flight leaves tomorrow night and you'll report to Captain Joseph Stallings as soon as possible."

Peale was stunned. He barely heard Galen's bellow or Emily Hu's even louder expletive. After a moment, he came to his senses and joined the chorus.

TWO

I've had a lot of jobs and sampled several professions, but the one I've liked best is police work. It's the one that's held my interest the longest, anyway. I'm Detective Sergeant Tyler Taylor from Homicide. Living in New York, I get more practice than I like at my chosen profession.

Having a good partner helps and I lucked out when I got mine. We're both overachievers, which makes us misfits in the eyes of the hierarchy. I suppose it was natural that when Stroud Girion and I landed in Captain Dennis Brannaugh's lap five years ago, he put us together. We clicked, and to many folks' disgust, became the best detective team in the city. No lie.

Stroud's an impressive lady, holds the regional marksmanship trophy eight years running, black belt in karate . . . all that physical shit. She stands about 5'11" and says it's nobody's damned business where she weighs in.

Me? I'm more cerebral — I'm in good shape — 6'2" and 180, but I've got this thing called a 'high IQ.' It got me into college at fifteen; med school at eighteen and my MD with specialization in forensic investigation by twenty-three. Add in being born in the states but raised in Australia, you come up with a few elevated eyebrows. Call it stubbornness on my part, but after years in New York, I'm still refusing to work out the accent — makes me *memorable. Besides, the ladies love it.*

It isn't all roses, though. We're undeniably the best detective team in our district (we think in the city), but we're also the most abrasive. When Brannaugh called us into his office that Monday night, we searched recent history for who we'd offended this time. We hadn't a clue, but stepped into the Captain's office expecting to be royally chewed, anyway. It was unanimous, though; better chewed out than busted down to the Public School Safety Lecture detail — again.

Imagine our surprise when he explained we'd been selected for special duty. Relief lasted precisely fifteen seconds. That was how long it took him to utter the words 'Sentry International' and 'Captain Joseph Stallings.' Sentry spelled international trouble and Joseph Stallings spelled bureaucratic overload for any officer unfortunate enough to be assigned as liaison with his Special Ops unit. I suddenly understood why we got the job. So did Stroud.

***

Dennis Brannaugh slouched behind his desk passively watching the shapely redhead storm around his tiny office. It was a damned impressive display if you weren't used to it. Stroud Girion wheeled, jabbing her forefinger into her partner's face. "We *have* pissed somebody off. Somebody big by the smell of this. You're the one with the fabulous memory; *you* figure out who it was!"

Tyler Taylor straightened indignantly. "What good will that do? Somehow I don't think posies and chocolates are gonna help here."

Brannaugh shifted. "Come on, people, this isn't punishment! This assignment came from so high only the

Almighty knows where. Probably someone the commissioner does lunch with. Doesn't matter a rat's ass anyway, because it's tied in to those mob hits you guys are working. They link up with something Sentry's working on in Chicago. . . ."

Girion reentered orbit. "Has to be somebody high profile. . . ."

"The mayor, maybe?"

She rebutted scornfully. "Neither of us have *met* the new mayor!"

"Yeah, y'have. Only he wasn't mayor then."

"Oh, yeah . . . I think I remember that. . . ."

Brannaugh roared, "Ten seconds! If both your asses aren't peaceably settled in those chairs in front of this desk by then, I'm calling the commissioner to say that the request came one hour after you'd been kicked down to traffic!"

Gauging the threat sincere, the pair seized straight backed chairs. Brannaugh appraised them. At various times and for various reasons, members of the department tried to pair the two romantically. He for one, was glad it never jelled. They were both exceptionally attractive people, but both could be as exceptionally disagreeable — like now. Refolding his arms across the desktop, he spoke levelly, "Better. You oughta be glad I'm a laid-back kind of guy. Otherwise, I'd have your asses kicked outta this unit no matter *how* good you are."

Girion snapped, "Easy for you to say, *sir*, but we're the ones who'll get splattered when the international crapola hits the fan — it always does when Uncle Joe is involved. Why can't those James Bond wannabes keep their noses out of ordinary police work?"

"I hear what you're sayin', but this time *they* were working the case before we got involved. These bombings you're investigating trace back to a case the Chicago guys have been working for better than a year. You saw a piece of it —

that lakeside arms dump that went up a while back. It's big and it's their baby, we're lucky they haven't pulled some political shit and yanked it out of our hands." He added silently, *"On the other hand, taking Joe Stallings into account, maybe we'd be luckier if they had."*

Taylor interjected, "So we overlapped their case. I can buy that and I got no trouble with it, but why liaise with them? Why not swap information then all go our merry ways?"

Brannaugh hitched his massive shoulders. "Sounds fine t'me, but all I can tell you is what I was told, and I quote, 'NYPD is endeavoring to establish an atmosphere of cooperation with our sister organizations.' Personally, I think you could spread that on a garden and get ten-pound tomatoes, but that's what the commissioner said."

The groans barely faded before he continued, "Do what you can, okay? That's all I ask — be pleasant if you can manage it. Let Taylor do the talking, especially if you have to deal with Stallings. He's an officious, bureaucratic bastard, but he's got more clout than all of us put together. The sooner this is wrapped up, the sooner we'll all be able to get back to normal and chase axe-murderers to our little hearts' content." Lifting a thick file folder from his desk, he flung it at them. "These are hot off the fax from Captain James Nelson of Chicago Sentry. This is all we got on the special agents you'll be working with; the good news is they're out of Chicago and aren't Uncle Joe's handpicked — the bad news is (although they might not know it yet), they have to report to him as their New York commanding officer. One's named Miller, he's some kind of ex-jock. The other guy's named Peale, don't know a helluva lot about him, but he sounds

English over the phone." The thickset captain eyed them, remarking, "Miller's got a good set of lungs, too. I got to hear both of them real good; there was quite a ruckus going on in the background when Nelson called to verify arrangements. Made me feel right at home."

He glared at his top detectives pointedly. They ignored him just as pointedly. Taylor skimmed the pages, unmindful of Stroud's familiar lean as she read over his shoulder until she stabbed a finger onto a page and announced with subdued gravity, "Oh, man! Says here they just lost a friend in the line of duty — their Deputy Director of Special Ops, no less. They must be *real* serious about breaking this thing. The memorial service for Lt. Marquez was just yesterday morning."

Brannaugh nodded somberly. Every police officer, no matter who or where, understood that loss. "Yeah, apparently both Miller and Nelson went way back with Marquez, but according to Nelson, Peale is taking it harder than anyone. Seems to be blaming himself for not getting there in time to save his fellow officer."

As he spoke, he watched Taylor for any sign of recognition. There was nothing on the sergeant's face other than intense interest in the printed words he absorbed. Brannaugh didn't buy it. Six years was more than enough time to purge self-imposed guilt, but a man like Tyler Taylor didn't follow normal time tables.

Perplexed, the Australian looked up from the pages. "What's this notation on Peale's sheet, 'only works at night?'"

Brannaugh's lips quirked. He'd asked the same question. "Nelson says the guy has an allergy to sunlight and a sensitivity to bright light. Maybe he's one of those English eccentrics, maybe he's that goddamn Chicago vampire that's been terrorizing druggies all winter. Who knows?"

Girion muttered, "If he is, I'd like to give him a medal."

The warning growl was instant. "Sergeant Girion! Vigilantism in any form—"

Taylor interrupted, "An *allergy*? Granted that's not unheard of and not my realm of expertise, but it's odd, don't you think?"

"I don't *think* anything, Taylor. All I know is what the man's Captain—"

Stroud pounced, snatching one of the sheets from the folder. "HEY! This is *Galen* Miller! He used to play for the Rams! Wow! The way he used to plow the other guys under was great — I knew he'd retired, but I never heard he joined—."

Brannaugh, tired of being interrupted, gleefully returned the favor. "Look, save the questions and adulation for tonight; NYPD and SI have mutually agreed to give you two the honor of picking these two up at Kennedy around eleven o'clock this pm. There'll be plenty of time on the drive to the hostel to pump for personal details — if you ask real nice you might even get an autograph. Now clear the hell outta here before I change my mind and kick your asses down to Traffic anyway!"

***

Harbored from the frenetic tide of humanity by a concrete pillar, Tyler Taylor snugged a Yankees cap over his unruly mane and scanned the influx of passengers from the Chicago flight. It was the height of irony he and Stroud were tapped to liaise with SI — or was it? Brannaugh said the order came from high up, but who could say the request didn't originate with Stallings. That was the kind of machination the man was infamous for. Taylor knew that too well. Not so long ago, he'd turned the man down cold, and Stallings wasn't one to take no for an answer.

Back when the charter of Sentry International dominated both the news and conversation at the station, the biggest buzz was that New York would be the United States headquarters. No surprise, since Sentry International was United Nations sanctioned and that was where the U.N. itself was. Taylor was shower-damp and gulping a quick meal before bolting out of the apartment for his shift when Joe Stallings, flanked by two Mack trucks disguised as recruitment officers, paid him a visit.

The dossier the brand-new Director had in his hands was complete, flattering, and more than a little daunting. In retrospect, Taylor's unusual background and his distressingly high profile career, made the offer inevitable. Still, it left a bad taste. He'd flatly refused, insisting that it wasn't the U.N.'s job to get into law enforcement. He still felt that way. So okay, relations between established police forces and the new organization were, on the whole, good, and to date SI hadn't become the international monster he'd feared . . . but, the shiny hadn't worn off yet, had it?

They were well-orchestrated from the start, too. At the same time he'd been approached, another team was talking to Stroud. She was more ambivalent than her opinionated partner, and while she didn't accept, she kept the door open. He understood. Taylor had innumerable advantages in life — Stroud had anything but. Anything she'd gotten, was hard fought and hard won. It made her tough and determined to be the best at what she did, but did little to ease the bitterness underlying the drive. Having an organization like Sentry International court her was both flattering and satisfying.

He'd be careful how he greeted the Chicago agents, though. It was unfair to lay his suspicion and anger about SI and Joe Stallings on their shoulders. They knew more about Miller than Peale, who was a relatively new agent, but, by all accounts, they were good cops and deserved better than to be prejudged because of another's actions. Maybe he ought to extend sympathy — if they were as good in reality as they looked on paper, they weren't likely to get along with their new boss, either.

Stroud jostled him. "Heads up, Mr. Surly, I have a visual on our party. That's *got* to be Galen Miller — I'd hate to think there were two guys that size on the same itty-bitty plane. Bingo, there's Peale coming up alongside him. Hmm. Peale's even better looking in person than in his picture." Grasping his elbow firmly, she towed him into the oncoming rush. "C'mon. Let's welcome them to the Big Apple."

Crowds meant nothing to Stroud. Growing up in a small house with a big family and the busy streets of Brooklyn made plowing through a mass of people second nature to her. Taylor gratefully dropped into her wake as she relentlessly cleaved the tide of humanity.

***

The flight from O'Hare was neither long nor rough, but Galen Miller was bone-tired anyway. Doubtless, an emotional hangover from Mick Marquez' memorial service. Was it yesterday? Seemed like years ago. A good part of him still hadn't accepted that Miguel Marquez, his childhood friend and newly appointed Deputy Director of Special Operations and Investigations was dead. He wondered if he ever would.

Forehead wrinkled in concern, he stole a glance at the pale man walking beside him. Peale was uncharacteristically silent and had been throughout the flight. Galen guessed BC's inability to attend the early morning service gnawed at him. It shouldn't, Mick would have understood perfectly. Byron Cyrus Peale was a for real vampire and vampirism had its own set of problems to offset the benefits. Besides, Peale more than paid his respects by spending so much time at the funeral home with Mick's sister, Jay, that the Marquez family was making interested noises about 'the nice Englishman' even through their grief. The comments amused Jay and relaxed her enough to crack a few jokes about hiding BC from the mortician. That was a good sign she was healing already, but the horror still lurked behind her smile. Considering she'd been involved in the fight that took her brother's life and had seen the elder vampire, Francesco Borgia, all but tear Mick limb from limb, the horror would be there for a while to come.

Ironically, BC was astounded that nobody held him responsible for the tragedy. Galen was sure he wasn't being so easy on himself — like he controlled what that bastard, Borgia, did. So what if Francesco Borgia was Peale's vampiric sire? Peale had never asked for the change — that had been arranged more in the nature of a supernatural contract hit than anything else. Hell, until recently, he didn't even *know* who his sire was! Mick himself once observed that Peale was probably the only decent thing Borgia ever did. High praise coming from a guy who'd been looking to bust Peale's ass for the Vampire Vigilante business back home in Chicago. Gae agreed, though. BC had never heard that comment; maybe he should. Eying the teeming masses of travelers, he decided to let it ride until they settled into their new digs — wherever the hell *that* was.

Reminded of the unwelcome transfer, he hunched farther into his overcoat as if against a draft. The thing had been done in such a hurry that there were no accommodations lined up for them in New York. Instead they were being bundled into overnight lodgings at the S.I. hostelry for transient agents. Better arrangements would be finalized by morning. Miller thought this was a bad idea. They were supposed to be under deep cover. He was supposed to be visiting the Big Apple to check on business interests there and Peale was his jazz musician pal coming along for the ride, on the lookout for crowded clubs and all-night parties. Like that was a stretch for BC. Fine. But why the hostelry? What was wrong with a hotel? Sure, it would be a little difficult with Peale's special needs to consider, but . . . Oh, well, it was only for one night — and night was almost over, at that.

The thing that really grated was the transfer, itself. On the surface, the reasons for shipping them off to New York were solid, but the slapdash execution made him wonder if they were merely being hustled out of town. Or out of Borgia's reach, now that the sire had become obsessive about his fledgling? He knew that was what BC thought. Worse, though neither voiced it for fear it would become truth, was that the change was permanent.

Alternatively, there might be another simpler and less sinister explanation. Maybe Colonel Black, the head of Sentry International, U.S.A., just wanted a closer look at SI's newest and most special Special Agent. It was possible, but he wouldn't mention that one, either. With all the other guilts his partner was suffering, it was sure to sound like *he* held BC responsible, too. Given the other knocks they'd had recently, almost anything could be viewed as an accusation. BC and Jim were right: after a while, paranoia *does* become a way of life.

If only they had a solid idea of who they were looking for at the gate — oh, they had names and verbal descriptions, but that was all. No photos. Nothing. The problem with verbal descriptions were that they could fit a lot of people . . . take that pair elbowing their way against the flow of the crowd. . . . Eureka! Give 'em points for the direct approach. Pulling up abruptly, and ignoring the outraged diatribe from the harried businessman who rear-ended him, Gae nudged his preoccupied partner. "We got company, pal."

Stopping in front of the mismatched set, the woman produced a personable smile and her NYPD identification. "Galen Miller and Byron Peale, I presume? I'm Detective Sgt. Stroud Girion. This is Detective Sgt. Tyler Taylor. We're your NYPD branch of Welcome Wagon and tonight's taxi service."

The stationary group (Miller in particular) were disrupting the flow of passengers and becoming the object of a great deal of verbal abuse. Peale's indigo eyes flicked over the surrounding throng, examined the pair of detectives and lingered a moment on Girion, before he remarked, "*Very* pleased to meet you." Grinning mischievously, he jerked a thumb toward his hulking companion. "D'you suppose we might get out of the crush and head to the baggage carousels? If we don't move soon, the townspeople may well tar and feather one of our number, and it's a trifle difficult to conduct a conversation around waving pitchforks and torches."

Miller glowered at his partner, then treated the detectives to his brightest smile. "In spite of the questionable logic, BC has a good idea. I doubt it'll be quieter by the carousels, though. Why don't we stop someplace on the way over to the hostel and grab some kind of take out? That plastic crap they served on the plane wasn't even a good appetizer."

The male half of the NYPD team's distinctive cadences further cemented his identity. "Fine with me. If nobody objects to Chinese, there's a great little Mom and Pop place on the way to your digs."

Peale smiled at Stroud. "Wonderful idea. I'm not hungry, but I have no objection to conversing while the rest of you eat."

Galen eyed his partner dubiously. "It's a plan, then. Hey, I hope you guys don't have a subcompact or anything. Most of our stuff is being shipped, but there are a couple good-sized bags coming off the plane."

Taylor watched his own partner watch the Brit as he responded, "No worry. We knew you were staying for a while, so we nabbed one of the unmarked sedans. The thing's a bloody tank; there ought to be room for anything short of a matched set of steamer trunks."

As Sgt. Taylor stowed the last over-sized hard-sided suitcase, Galen mused that the man might have been being conservative with his earlier statement. From where he stood, it looked like there was *plenty* of room for a matched set of steamer trunks. Presently, the detective straightened, and slammed the lid with the sense of a job well done. "That's the lot. Let's roll, people."

Breaking off conversation with Stroud, Peale twitched uneasily and declared, "I'm not ready yet, there's something at the commercial freight dock I need to pick up. Look, I have the address of our flat. If you three want to head on out, I'll catch you up there . . . ."

Oozing suspicion, Miller whirled. "You have something else to pick up? What is it and why the hell didn't you say something *before* the car was packed??"

Regarding his inquisitor placidly, BC responded, "Well, it doesn't go in the car, does it?"

With a slight smile, Peale headed back into the terminal. Miller called after him, "*What* do you have at the freight desk?" The penny dropped and he howled, "It's that damn motorcycle! I heard Jim tell you specifically to leave that thing in Chicago."

The reply was tossed casually over the retreating shoulder. "I like to have my own transportation. Besides, *I'm* paying for it, not Jim Nelson or anyone else, so that makes it a strictly personal decision."

Growling apologies to the overtly amused cops, Gae plunged into the crowd in pursuit of his partner. "Personal decision my ass!"

Taylor guffawed. "Think I'm gonna like those two. Maybe we ought meet them at the pickup since our orders were to stick with them for the duration and see them safely tucked in."

Speculating after the retreating duo, Girion replied, "That's what the Captain said — and here we were afraid this would be a dull assignment." Sliding behind the wheel, she said, "Y'know, Taylor, this could turn out to be a *very* interesting assignment."

Taylor scanned her with a practiced eye. He hadn't seen that look in a long time, and it didn't take a detective to see Peale was equally interested. He wished he knew enough about the man to decide whether or not he was glad of a budding relationship. Oh, well, there'd be plenty of time to find out. Regardless of what the mysterious high mucky-mucks planned for this collaboration, he sincerely doubted this result was anticipated. Closing the passenger door with a thump, he said, "Interesting is one way to define it, I s'pose."

***

Access to the freight dock was partially blocked by a grimy white panel truck, and the quartet of overall-clad men busy stuffing packages into it pointedly ignored the idling sedan. Skillfully, Stroud threaded the car through the tight squeeze between truck and high chain-link fence, punctuating her maneuvers with colorful observations concerning the truck driver's parentage. By the time the car was positioned for easy exit, Peale and Miller had the motorcycle on the ramp, doing a final inspection.

Muttering curses, she set the brake and cut the ignition. The truck driver idled behind the wheel apparently enjoying the show as the attractive (and irate) motorist exited the car. She strode for the van with purpose. Grinning, Taylor followed. It had been weeks since he'd witnessed an expert vaporization and he didn't want to miss a second of it. To his astonishment, his partner halted short of the target and gave a low, appreciative whistle. Curiously following her gaze, he saw Peale — back view — bent over the saddlebag of the motorcycle. Oh, really! This was too much, he opened his mouth to protest, then closed it just as quickly as she breathed, "Get a load of that *bike*!"

He mentally rebuked himself. He should have known, Stroud Girion might be an avowed rump woman, but she was an absolute sucker for a handsome motor vehicle with an especially soft place for motorcycles.

She continued, "I think maybe I was expecting a crotch rocket or something, but *that's* a Harley-Davidson Softail! It's in good shape, but not new — one of the early ones — maybe even an '84. My guess is it's seen serious road travel. Nice custom leatherwork." She leered and added, "Pretty good leatherwork on the rider, too."

Knew she wouldn't miss the rump. She veered for the motorcycle, vengeance forgotten — or at least postponed. Following his partner up the ramp, Taylor silently agreed with Captain Brannaugh's earlier observation — these two *did* have a haunting familiarity about them. He'd never admit it to Brannaugh, though.

Miller kvetched, "I know what's gonna happen. Jim is gonna call up as soon as word gets back and take a big chunk of *my* ass! He won't go after *you* — Nuh uh! No it'll be *my* ass, because I'm the senior member of this chicken shit team."

Peale grinned and said quietly, "Well, it all depends on how one defines *senior*."

Miller growled unintelligibly, then spat, "Look at you mooning over that thing! I don't think you're worried about transportation at all, I think you're so in love with that damned machine you can't bear to be parted from it."

"You're only saying that because I take it to bed with me." Over Gae's shoulder, he saw their liaison officers ascending the ramp and added, "But only when it's cold — and no-one else is available."

Stroud patted the saddle and said with mock seriousness. "I'm sure you and the Softail are very happy together."

Grinning devilishly, Peale reached into the saddlebag, extracted a well-worn motorcycle jacket, and, shucking his leather duster, stuffed it into the pouch. On the sidelines, Galen hovered like a thundercloud, wondering at himself. It wasn't like he hadn't expected Peale to bring his precious Harley. He'd more than half expected to find it waiting for them — Jim had, too.

The real reason was the restlessness crackling under the slender man's self-assured exterior. In light of past experience, that was worrying. BC's habitual reaction to emotional stress was to throw himself into the nearest all-night jazz spot and come dragging home just before dawn, looped, bone-tired, and barely able to crawl into his room. Not that Gae didn't understand the need for catharsis; it was his partner's self-destructive methods he objected to. *He* was looking forward to locating a gym close to their new quarters and working himself into exhaustion. It had much the same effect as his partner's method, except Gae awoke stiff and sore, but still functional.

It could put a serious crimp in their plans if BC slipped away now, only to rise the next evening with one of his legendary hangovers. The amount of fresh blood required after one of these bouts was phenomenal. The most astounding thing of all, was that with all the wonderful abilities his condition promised, according to Maeve Donal, one of the first things BC had worked out was how to get stoned. Unbelievable.

The combination of Peale's hedonistic nature and recent emotional turmoil gave him pause over the instantaneous flirtation with Sgt. Girion. Flirtation was a way of unlife with BC. He'd bantered with almost every female he'd encountered since Galen met him, but something about this was subtly different. All of Galen's internal alerts were flashing caution mode. Not that he worried about Sgt. Girion; even their superficial briefing made it clear she could take care of herself. Under normal circumstances, anyway, but he deemed it unlikely she'd been confronted with a vampire before.

Miller watched Girion descend the ramp and rejoin her partner by the car. Sgt. Taylor appeared none too sanguine about his own partner's responses, either. It wasn't jealousy, more like concern. It so closely mirrored his own feelings, it gave him pause. Frowning, and unwilling to tire his shocky brain by further analysis, he turned back to Peal and said in a voice pitched to his partner's sensitive ears, "Listen, we've got a lot of ground to cover tonight, both figurative and literal. You stick close to the car. I don't want you taking off on your own until we've reported in."

Slowly donning his jacket, Peale treated Miller to a narrow evaluation.

Not liking the look, Miller said, "I *mean* it, Peale! No bars. No jazz clubs. Not until we've reported in to Captain Stallings. Both Jim and Emily gave us the Asshole Alert before we left and I refuse to handle everything by myself. I want your word or we aren't leaving this spot."

Peale raised his hands in mock surrender. "Okay! Message received and understood. I will not make any detours. In fact, I'll follow so closely, you'll think the Harley was chained to the rear bumper."

"It's an idea."

Peale threw a leg across the saddle and gave the fuel

gauge a final critical examination. The play of supple leather across the firm butt, was doubtless a calculated display, but Stroud proved an appreciative audience, anyway. *The trouble with a man like Special Agent BC Peale*, thought Sgt. Girion, *is that he* knows *he's good-looking and is fully aware of his impact on the healthy, average human female.* So what? Just because a peacock knows it's beautiful, what's wrong with enjoying its plumage? He did seem awfully intent on displaying the merchandise. Could he really be interested . . . *Oh that's infantile. There's no such thing as love at first sight.* Reexamining the muscular curves against the motorcycle, she amended, *Lust* at first sight was a definite possibility.

She'd tread lightly. A relationship with a fellow officer could be dangerous, even if the parties belonged to different organizations. They'd be working in each other's hip pockets for the next few weeks, she'd better consider carefully before moving farther into the pants. Assuming he was interested in a relationship — a guy like Peale flirted like he breathed — it was an autonomic function.

Peeking from the corner of her eye, she considered Taylor; he acted cool, but he'd noticed her interest. Tough. She'd sat through plenty of romantic crap on his part. He could return the favor. Her face darkened as her mind brushed the cases that brought them there. Cases. Such a nice, impersonal word for the horrible deaths of five human beings. Okay, so they were criminals, actively engaged in selling drugs, but *nobody* deserved to die the way these guys did.

Just thinking of the killings made her nauseous. Earlier that morning, she and Taylor were roused from their respective beds to poke through what a letter bomb left of an office. There wasn't much to investigate — of the office or the guy who'd occupied it. Maybe she was worrying too much about Peale. Once they got down to business, there wouldn't be much romance to be found.

Rousing herself, she realized her companions were preparing to leave. Taylor was asking Peale, "I take it you've driven in our little burg before — it can be pretty hard to deal with if you haven't."

Peale answered with a sidelong glance at Sgt. Girion, "It's been a while since I spent much time here, but I can find my way around pretty well — *however,* if someone volunteered to act as tour guide, I wouldn't say no."

Detective Sgt. Girion responded sweetly, "In that case, we'll see if we can line you up for a bus tour tomorrow."

He grinned and gunned the bike's motor. Yeah, she was going to enjoy this. As she returned to the sedan, something about the van still blocking the road niggled in the back of her head. She leaned on the roof of the car and watched. With the changed angle, she could see directly into the back, and what was previously feverish activity now appeared swift, but exceedingly careful — like they were loading cartons of eggs. Curiously, the men were selective which parcels they took from a pallet bearing the logo of a nation-wide trucking firm. Only about every third one was going into the truck and most of those from deep within the stack.

Lingering long enough to draw inquisitive looks from her companions, she watched a man in rumpled coveralls search the pallet, locate a specific parcel, and hand it off to another man in the back of the truck. This man . . . *Damn.* She knew that imbecilic rodent; there were at least two outstanding warrants on him for trafficking illegal arms.

Suddenly, the reason for careful movements became chillingly clear. On the heels of that came the realization that whatever this temperamental material was, it was sitting at a busy loading dock at a crowded airport. Well, it was a wrenching concept, but for someone who regularly supplied terrorists, what would a few more innocent casualties matter? Gritting her teeth and forcing herself to stroll casually to where the others waited, she twitched her head slightly toward the truck and, loudly enough for Taylor to hear over the rumble of the idling motorcycle, said, "It's Rattner. Let's take him."

A slow, predatory smile lit the Australian's features as he followed her gesture. "Oh, this is sweet. ATF has been after him for months with no sign of him and tonight, he crawls out of his hidey-hole right into our laps."

Sidling over to the Sentry agents who'd caught enough to look interested, he hurried an explanation. Miller rumbled, "If the guy is supplying that kind of shit to terrorists, then let's take him right now."

Alerted by an innate, but belated sense of danger, a small, wiry man poked his head from the back of the truck. Alarm contorted the sharp-featured face as he riveted on Tyler Taylor. Shit. If that was who he thought it was, the woman had to be 'Shroud' Girion. He neither knew nor cared who the other two were — the first two were bad enough by themselves. Without waiting to confirm they'd seen him, he bolted around the truck and vaulting into the cab, hissing to the driver, "It's the cops! Leave the rest and get us the hell outta here!"

As one, the others piled into the van and the driver tore away from the platform, leaving the smell of burning rubber in his wake.

Girion grabbed a handful of the nearest coat (Miller's) and dragged its occupant toward the sedan. Diving behind the wheel, she hit the lights, giving Miller just enough time to close his door before tire-squealing after the van.

Taylor spun to shout for Peale, only to find the Harley screeching to a halt beside him. Peale called, "Pile on, and hold tight, I think we have a better chance to head them off than the sedan, but we'll have to pour it on to do it. Extra helmet's on the back."

Taylor crammed the helmet on and anchored himself as Peale tore into the night as the no-longer bored freight clerk frantically dialed security.

Miller watched the motorcycle headlight increase in size and intensity as it closed the distance between itself and the car. Even with his partner's enhanced reflexes, he was *very* glad it was Sgt. Taylor riding behind rather than himself. Just then, the sedan whipped around a tight turn and he experienced the sickening sensation of wheels lifting off the asphalt and jolting down again. At least he was used to the shit BC pulled.

With a smooth flick of her wrist, Stroud unhooked the radio mike from the dash and tossed it to Galen. He caught it as the Harley roared past them.

Galen groaned, "Oh, God."

"Peale probably made the mistake of letting Taylor drive."

"I doubt it."

Stroud redoubled her efforts at the wheel. "Really? Peale knows how to handle that bike, doesn't he?"

Galen decided he was in for a *lot* more trouble than he'd counted on.

The idea was to stop the truck while causing the least amount of distress to its cargo. That in mind, Peale accelerated around the unmarked car and pulled abreast of the van, edging in to impinge on the driver's road. The hope was that the driver would also be reluctant to damage his cargo — unfortunately, the plan was better than the driver. Seeing the motorcycle heading him off, the man jerked the wheel too sharply, and the van veered onto the shoulder of the road. The already strained rubber of one rear tire gave up the ghost with a loud bang, making the driver lose what remaining control he had. The van crashed onto its side into the weed-choked drainage ditch, skidding, and spraying sparks, gravel and sod before grinding to a halt several yards away from its point of impact.

BC braked alongside the wreck and Taylor slid off, weapon drawn as a precaution, calling, "Police! Come out with your hands on your heads."

The detective advanced on the silent truck, praying he wouldn't have to shoot. God only knew what Rattner had in those packages. What ever it was, Taylor was certain it wouldn't take kindly to being shot. The bad guys didn't have the same qualms. As he neared, doors flew open and the van's shaken occupants poured out, weapons blazing. Taylor flattened against the pavement and crab-crawled for the back of the truck hoping Peale had done likewise.

He had. With bullets sparking around him, the vampire dived and rolled. What was it with thugs and explosives lately? Gripping his own .45, he noted return fire from where Taylor crouched at the rear of the van. Drawing a bead on the thug waving the biggest pistol, he squeezed off a round that took the man above the knee, dropping him writhing to the asphalt.

Too easy, he reflected. *A vampire with a pistol is a*

deadly sniper. He became aware of the sound of an oncoming engine rising above the keening of the injured man. It sounded close. It sounded . . . he dived for the ditch as the car carrying Girion and Miller skidded to a sideways stop inches from the Harley and right over the spot he'd just vacated. Flinging themselves out of the car, Galen and Stroud joined the fusillade, using the sedan's doors for cover.

Rattner extracted himself from the truck swearing through blood pouring from a split eyebrow. With speed born of terror, he flung himself over the embankment, and ran. Girion vaulted the embankment and quickly closed the gap between them. Rattner cast a white-eyed look over his shoulder, gave a strangled squeak and, scrabbling frantically for something at his back, ran harder. Stroud didn't wait to discover what the surprise was. She launched herself in a flying tackle Gae Miller would have been proud of and carried them both to land hard on the gravelly dirt. With an ooomph, Rattner went limp under her weight. The frantically sought item proved to be a Heckler & Koch P7. Such an unfriendly rodent.

Dragging her cuffed prey around the wreck, she noted with relief that the gunfire had stopped. There was still an odd sound, though. As she neared, the sound became the agonized wails of a wounded animal. Peering over the berm, she saw the combatants frozen as the last two coveralled thugs stared in dismay at a writhing figure on the ground from whence the sounds came. Gee, who would have thought a human being was making that noise? Then again . . . .

Peale's slender figure rose ominously from the ditch. "Drop them," he commanded.

As one, the men tossed their weapons and clenched the backs of their necks. Stroud dragged her burden a few feet more, and Peale gestured regretfully toward the gyrating man. "Amazing. I appear to have winged Pavarotti."

She regarded the spectacle. "Too bad he doesn't know a few more lyrics." Then with a sidelong glance she said, "You're pretty good with that motorcycle. How are you in a car?"

The tall man smirked. "Front seat or back?"

She snorted as the Special Agent bent to assist Taylor in cuffing the injured prisoner and dragging him out of the roadway.

Miller straightened from the inadequate cover of the sedan door and holstered his unfired weapon with a nervous chuckle. Situation defused (pun intended), and here he'd been afraid something would go wrong. With disaster averted, he rested against the unmarked car. The sound of approaching sirens became audible even to him; after all the hullabaloo, it was probably about to tear the top of Peale's head off. Glancing around, he located him astride the Harley revving the engine, no doubt to make more room for the emergency vehicles. By the car, Stroud was on the radio requesting the bomb squad, while Taylor cuffed the docile men sprawled on the pavement. He allowed himself another deep breath before something not quite right vied for his attention. What? A funny smell. Place was full of funny smells . . . he scanned the area for an anomaly, and on the other side of the overturned truck, he found it. Smoke curled against the distant lighting of the runways. Panic seized him, and pointing, he screamed, "FIRE!"

In a flurry of motion, everyone standing dived into the ditches; all who were prone rolled in. Miller dived and rolled, dragging BC's vocalizing thug with him. BC gunned the Harley, grabbed Stroud as she wrestled with the unconscious

Rattner, and raced a fair distance from the wreck before tipping them all over into the wet bottom of the drainage ditch.

For a moment the universe consisted only of nearing sirens and scuffling from the ditches as Stroud wondered at the agility and strength required for what Peale did — wondering further if he *had* done what she thought he did. Before she could marshal her thoughts into anything resembling logical order, the night was rent with an explosion. She pressed herself flat into the gravelly mud against the rest of the blasts.

Debris, suitcases and toiletries rained from above. Stroud became aware that Peale had thrown himself on top of her at the last minute. Sheepishly, he rolled off and helped her up. She grinned at him, and vigorously dug a finger into her ear in a vain attempt to relieve the ringing. Remembering Rattner, she searched in alarm and found him lying a few feet away. He was still unconscious — leave it to the little rat to sleep through his own spectacular capture.

As one, they peeked over the edge at the hulks of the van and the remains of the police car. They were burning merrily, but giving no indication of further pyrotechnic displays. Stroud winced. Scratch another car. Brannaugh was gonna *love* this.

A distance away, Taylor whooped, and slapping Galen soundly on the back, shouted through the sirens and the din in their heads, "Welcome to New York, Agent Miller!"

Galen sucked at a scraped knuckle, muttering as how it didn't look like they'd left Chicago.

THREE

Stroud Girion blew on her too-hot coffee and tried to ignore the chaos outside their temporary refuge.

Dammit. It almost worked. On the up side, there were no fatalities, and the only casualties were Rattner and the driver — *if* you didn't count the evidence, truck, car and luggage. Most of Rattner's injuries resulted from not wearing his seatbelt. She wondered if they could cite him for that, too?

Special Agent Peale dropped the driver with a leg wound. It was an impressive shot — and as far as she was concerned, not a fraction of the pain the guy deserved. Most of the trouble centered on that particular moron. Not had he been the first to shoot, but if he hadn't blocked the road, she wouldn't have given their truck a second glance. She supposed she should be grateful that Rattner only bought the good stuff. If the explosive had been a lower grade, it was unlikely any of them would have survived the blast. As it was, the stuff simply burned and the only thing that blew was the gas tank — and ammo boxes under the seats — oh and the frag grenade one of the morons had in the glove compartment. Let's not forget that act of brilliance.

Things screwed up, but it could have been worse. *All* the evidence didn't go up with the van. As soon as Rattner and Company made Taylor, they high-tailed it without all their merchandise. Currently, a special unit had the loading platform cordoned off and were very, very carefully removing the remaining packets. God only knew what would have happened if they hadn't stopped the stuff where they did. For some reason, she found it especially despicable that the creeps had shipped it disguised as children's modeling clay.

She took a gulp of the coffee. It was awful and still too hot, but it stopped the cycle of memories that threatened to engulf her. She'd worked the aftermath of the Trade Center bombing. Vivid memories all too frequently haunted her dreams. Before 9/11, she'd spent many hours and lit many candles praying that the terrorism plaguing the rest of the world would stay away from the US. Then, like a bad dream she couldn't wake up from, it happened anyway, right in her own back yard. There were other, more personal consequences for Stroud. Before the attack, she'd felt the anger and abhorrence of the law officer toward those who perpetrated acts of terrorism and the unmentionables who made it possible for them to do it. It was a solid, but somewhat detached sense of moral indignation toward those who broke the law. But, that day in September and the days following, the things she witnessed slowly and inexorably edged that vague anger closer and closer to unreasoning hatred. That was a bad thing for a police officer.

Stealing a sidelong at the two Special Agents, she wondered how they handled it. Ordinary police work had more than enough stress to go around, but terrorism was in Sentry International's job description. It was part of the reason the organization was formed. She didn't envy that. She *did* like the way the two men worked together. They meshed superbly, and more to the point, worked well as part of a larger team. The unplanned re-pairing didn't cause so much as a hiccup. That was important. It said the four of them could operate with a minimum of toe squishing. She was also impressed that neither one shrank from the problem with the wanted felon. Given their orders, they could have — and possibly *should* have, but they dived in anyway. To disastrous effect, but who could have foreseen that?

Even that wouldn't be so bad if SI wasn't bent on keeping their cover deep and complete. The reasons were legitimate, but the practicality was difficult at best. Especially considering their choice of agents. The detonation of smuggled explosives at a major US airport was big news by itself. Media crews of all descriptions materialized almost before the last bits of debris settled on the tarmac. And there they were with the famous face — and bulk — of Galen Miller to hide from people who made their living from finding things out. So far, they'd succeeded, but while the majority of the invaders were making life hell for the crime scene investigators, a few lurked like hungry sharks in the corridor outside this borrowed office.

Airport security was a godsend. Led by a competent ex-Marine, Dave Kelly, they mobilized and rolled onto the crime scene like a platoon of steamrollers. The daunting efficiency probably stemmed from the awareness that the stuff came into and almost got out of their facility undetected. That also explained why Security Chief Kelly had been quick to volunteer his office as a refuge for the undercover team. At least they got Peale and Miller off the field before the camera crews arrived.

She stole a glance at the big man trying to look small in the corner. Frankly, she didn't see how Galen hoped to remain undercover. He'd retired from pro sports some time ago, but a player of his caliber stuck in the memory. It was even more surprising he'd chosen law enforcement as a post-football career. With his looks, her money would have been on show business like so many other former jocks before and after him. She loved her job, but the unglamorous life of police work was an odd choice for a man like Miller. Just proved that no matter how many times you saw a person on TV, you couldn't know an individual from sound bites.

Joining Peale at the Venetian blinds, she eyed the milling media. Where had they all come from? Maybe they simply hung around airports on slow news days hoping a plane would crash or a truckful of illegal armaments would blow up. Sneaking a look at her companion, she watched him warm his hands on the mug of coffee from Security's prehistoric machine. The regular profile gave no hint to what lay behind it, and the anorexic dossier faxed by SIChi shed even less light. There'd been pages on Galen Miller, but *page* on Byron Peale.

Accent notwithstanding, his birthplace was listed as Chesterton, Maryland — wherever the hell that was. She wondered if his parents were college students in the States at the time of his birth, like Taylor's. Taylor took perverse pleasure informing people in broad Australian tones that he'd been born in Princeton, New Jersey. Where Taylor was raised in Australia, Peale's file merely stated he'd spent a great deal of time abroad, predominately in England and Europe. That explained the accent and mannerisms, but where was the rest of it? Schooling? Nothing even about training and he *had* to be trained somewhere, he handled that pistol too expertly. The lovely little hole in the driver's thigh attested to that. That would have been a difficult shot for *her* to make, but Peale took it like he did that kind of thing every day of his life.

There'd be time to puzzle about the Mysterious Stranger later. Right now she was more interested in getting these guys safely tucked into their temporary lodgings at the hostelry. Those were Brannaugh's standing orders and the just-ended phone call didn't change it. She'd hoped that once they were out of sight, they could just lay low and wait for the dust to settle. No joy there. Since ducking into the office, she'd been on the phone so much, that when she finally finished, it felt like a part of her ear came off with the earpiece. The one bright spot was that Brannaugh volunteered to handle Joe Stallings. Unless she was mistaken, she wasn't the only individual cheered by that. The two Special Agents had never met their new CO, but they'd been briefed well. She'd heard the horror stories, too, and felt for them. Just thinking about Joe Stallings gave Stroud the warm fuzzies toward Dennis Brannaugh, Terror of the Five Boroughs. Sipping again from her own mug, she winced and concluded Peale had the right idea. Use it as a liquid-filled ceramic hand-warmer; this drek was never intended for human consumption.

Flashing yellow lights drew her attention to the distant tarmac where the cindered vehicles were slowly being towed away. There'd be more than one detour on the way to the agent's temporary housing seeing how most of their luggage was blown to smithereens. Due to the heavy duty nature of Miller's luggage, some clothing was salvageable, but anything glass was history.

From the corner of the room, Galen asked, "What's it

look like out there?"

Without turning, Peale replied, "I've never seen so many chaps in nylon jackets sporting such an amazingly large portion of the alphabet. Let's see . . . there's our lot, SI, right over there with the NYPD and NYFD gang. As for the rest, they appear to be mostly three-letter combinations. If you can think of it, there's probably at least one out there."

The big man chuckled sourly. "A regular alphabet soup."

His slender partner snorted and turned to Girion. "It appears a group of NYPD have broken off and are starting our way. Any of them familiar?"

She frowned into the night beyond the window, unable to make out the group let alone recognize any of the components. Before she could say so, the sharp burr of the desk phone interrupted. As the only person there who officially existed, it fell to her to answer it. Abandoning the alleged coffee on the windowsill, she lifted the instrument, "Girion."

"Hey, Girion," the gravelly voice of the security chief came across the wire. Dave Kelly here. Thought I'd better warn ya, the NYPD guy in charge of the scene is headed your way, and . . . if the guy's a personal friend, you got my apologies. He's a real prick."

She laughed, "From that description, it could be one third of the force. Does this human detritus have a name?"

"DuVall. Kenneth DuVall."

Smile evaporating, she said, "Nope. Not a friend. Thanks for the heads up, Kelly. I owe you one."

Dropping the handset, she pulled out her cell and hit a programmed button. She jiggled nervously from one foot to the other waiting for the other end to pick up. Glancing back at her companions, she said, "In case you guys didn't catch that, we got company on the way and it may or may not be a friendly. Kenny is an okay guy most of the time but he suffers from an overdose of self-importance—" She broke off and spoke into the cell, "Hey, Taylor. Bad news, somebody made DuVall Officer In Charge. He's on his way here right now. No I don't know who assigned him. We can find out, but I think. . . ."

With only a quick tap as warning, the office door was flung wide open. A thickset figure muffled in a standard issue overcoat hove into the frame, stomping vigorously. A voice from under the scarf announced to all and sundry, "*DAMN*, it's colder 'n a witches bazoom out there. Girion! Can't you and that smart-ass partner of yours ever blow anything up when it's *nice* outside?"

Without allowing a reply or stepping into the small room, the officer began to divest himself of the heavy coat and muffler, taking the opportunity to scan the room. He didn't know the two guys who ducked away from the open door, but the big black one looked familiar. He leaned against the doorframe and demanded, "Why the hell did you leave the scene anyway? We could use some help against all the bureaucrats crawlin' around out there. Who're these jokers? Witnesses or somethin'?"

Over Ken's shoulder, Stroud saw a swarm of cameras and microphones had followed in hopes of getting a comment, swelling the ranks of the group in the hallway. All of them were vying for a clearer view of the room like some kind of multi-headed beast.

Three swift steps brought her into grabbing range, and tugging at DuVall's arm, she said quietly, "Ken, Please. Step into the room so we can close the door."

Irritably, DuVall pulled away. "Dammit, Stroud, I'm too tired to play games. I just wanna go home to rediscover warmth. I need all the personnel I can get at the party outside. Detectives count as personnel."

A ripple of outrage disrupted the corridor beyond as someone bulled through the ranks of reporters. Breathing heavily, Taylor appeared at DuVall's elbow and tried to shove him inside. "Lay off, mate. I could hear you all the way down the hall. This lot is SI. . . ."

That was the final straw. "Shit. More Sentry? Those guys are as bad as cockaroaches. See one, you got 'em everywhere!"

A babble erupted from the hall behind him. Aware too late that he'd made a serious mistake, DuVall stood blinking and dazed in the sudden flash and glare of lights. The leather-clad man by the window was at the door in an instant, and with unexpected strength, pulled the officer inside and shut the door against the rising tide of microphones.

"Well," he said with a wry smile. "So much for deep cover."

***

Dennis Brannaugh exited his car, scratched fitfully at the graying stubble on his neck, and gave a jaw-creaking yawn. In a way, he was grateful for the call that pulled him from his bed. At least it lent a reason for the wakefulness that had plagued him since his wife died a few months back— He cut the thoughts off. No. Don't go there. Gravel crunched beneath thick leather soles as he trudged toward the bright portable lights marking the crime scene.

Squinting against the brilliance, he slowed, nonplussed by seeing Taylor and Stroud standing under the lights. Bewilderment gave way to a knowledge that excrement would soon be hip-deep when he IDed the pair beside them as the SI Special Agents. The ones who were supposed to be staying out of sight. Upping his pace to a light jog, he made for the group.

As he neared, the uniformed officer talking with the quartet whipped around. At the sight of the approaching Captain, the officer darted back toward the buildings. Too late. *DuVall. Shit. Of all the people to assign to a sensitive situation . . .* the jog changed to an angry stride that ate up more ground than a run.

***

Capt. Joseph Stallings, Director of Special Operations and Investigation, New York was cranky. He preferred to think of it as "hyper-vigilant" but to his staff, it was simply "cranky". He'd barely gotten home from the office and shucked his jacket when the call came through about an explosion at the city's major airport. That was bad enough. Learning that his newest agents were in the middle of it? There were no words. He didn't even want to think about the paperwork he'd have waiting when he returned to SI headquarters. Someone was going to pay for this and he knew just the pair of cowboys he was going to hang for it.

Flashing his badge and ID at the uniform controlling access, he guided his BMW into the indicated spot grumbling at the inconvenience. He should have been on site twenty minutes ago. No, scratch that. He *should* be at home in bed. There was no earthly reason for the Chicago agents to be involved in a high profile snafu like this. For that matter, there was no earthly reason he should be dealing with agents from Chicago. It was a serious breach of etiquette for Chicago to send agents to New York. As National Headquarters, New

York was the senior entity. *I should be sending people to Chicago*, he fumed as he killed the ignition.

Punctuating his thoughts with a door slam, he fumed, "*Special Agents*! *Just another way to say prima donnas as far I can tell. Look what they send me: an ex-football player and an English guy who thinks he's a two hundred year-old Colonial American vampire — what next?*"

They could have at least waited until they'd checked in before running off on a tear! He'd hoist them by their balls if they tried to tell him Rattner was linked with Borgia. Various agencies (SI included) had watched that individual for months now, and from the accumulated dossier, it would have been a major break for Borgia to hire him. This was a worm with a price; nothing would remain secret for long with Richard Rattner in the mix. Considering that Edgar Michalson was recently linked with Borgia, that was probably the precise reason Rattner was out of it. Rattner and Michalson were local boys who came up together on the streets. Nobody would know Ratty's tendency to live down to his name quite as well as Eddie. Intelligent man, Michalson. Pity he went the way he did. He would have made a wonderful agent.

A set of flashing police lights broke away from the gaudy mass around the cordoned-off pavement and headed his way at high speed. Cursing fluently, Stallings leapt aside as the unmarked car and accompanying motorcycle whizzed past him. Brushing the dust off his tailored overcoat, he stepped back into the lane, muttering bitterly. It was becoming impossible to tell the police from ordinary motorcycle punks. Bestowing a final glower upon the rapidly disappearing taillights, he stomped toward the brightest lights to find the Officer In Charge. As many agencies as were involved here, finding *one* OIC would be a trick. Maybe he'd better sniff around until he came across his own unit or someone he knew well enough to get good answers from.

At the edge of the parked-up lot stood a small knot of policemen. In the midst of this cluster was a familiar figure, Captain Dennis Brannaugh. Perfect. Brannaugh's people were responsible for the collar in the first place, so Denny would be on the business end of ATF's official ire and not him. He could quite justifiably argue that his agents were incidental to the affair. As he neared, it became clear that Denny was angry — as usual.

The red-faced police captain was sweating even in this cold weather. He'd better be careful; a fleshy man like Brannaugh needed to mind his heart and blood pressure. Joe wondered which of the hapless officers erred this time and what infraction he or she committed. Smirking, Joe Stallings flashed his ID at the young officer who stepped forward to stop him, and insinuated himself through the blue cordon to await the end of the tirade.

Stallings' thoughts froze solid from a chill that had nothing to do with the ambient temperature as he heard, ". . . and when a fellow officer tries to tell you said agents are incognito, you do not, I repeat, do *not* turn and scream about agency rivalries in front of TV cameras! Am I making myself understood, DuVall?"

Before the mortified officer could manage so much as a nod, there was a shriek not unlike that of a wounded cat from the sidelines: "WHAAAAAT?"

Brannaugh whirled to face the klieg-lighted apparition of Joe Stallings, overcoat billowing like demonic wings, cutting a swath through the assembled personnel. Turning to DuVall, he said, "Get the hell outta here *now*! I want to see you first thing when I get back. Go back to the station and wait in my office." Without a backward glance, DuVall beat a grateful retreat as ranks of uniformed police closed over his wake and Dennis Brannaugh stepped in front of the charging DSOI.

Brannaugh called, "Joe! I'm glad you're here. We gotta talk!"

***

"Hey!" Peale said happily. "They've got a special dim sum menu — do they have pot stickers and fried Won Tons?"

Galen Miller regarded his partner like he'd suddenly sprouted wings.

Stroud observed, "I figured you'd change your mind about not being hungry as soon as the aromas from the kitchen hit you, BC. It does rotten things to my will power, too."

Peale looked guilty. "Oh, it isn't for me. In spite of all promises to the contrary, I'd like to make a detour on the way to our flat. I missed an appointment due to the . . . Ummmm . . . unexpected circs surrounding our arrival. As late as it is now, I may well need a bribe to get back in good graces."

With an almost imperceptible snort, Stroud returned to the menu, seething with self-directed scorn. Hypothesis proven. He had a date lined up before he even hit the city. There was no more thought behind his attentions than an alley cat gives to scratching an itch.

The alley cat's partner wasn't taking it so calmly. "What the hell . . . did you set up some sort of midnight rendezvous at a club or something?"

Peale waved it away. "No, no, no! It isn't anything like *that*, it's purely business. I phoned Prometheus before we left Chicago and asked him to run a couple data queries for me — kind of on the side. I'd like to have that in hand before we start our joint inquiries."

Growling, but mollified, Miller returned to his perusal of the Chinese restaurant's overhead menu. "One of these days you're going to let me in on what you're planning and I'll drop dead from shock right on the spot."

In a lighter mood, Peale turned to their liaison officers and said, "If you guys don't want to make an extra stop, I understand. It's been a dreadfully long night and this promises to make it longer still. I'm afraid, though, that the Sentry Data Center wasn't here the last time I was. I'll need directions to find it."

Taylor grinned. "No worry, it's simple to get there from here, but it'll be closed for the night. Why not wait until morning when it's open for business?"

"As much as I hate to say it, from what I've heard about our new CO, waiting might be a bad idea," Miller said. "Anyone with the nickname 'Uncle Joe' worries the hell out of me. If we wait, we might be under too big a shit pile to go later."

Peale hummed assent, then said, "Yeah, and Emily Hu warned me the man has even less of a sense of humor than his namesake, Joseph Stalin, did. Definitely worrisome."

Girion looked uncomfortable. "I wasn't going to bring this up, but that scenario is a definite possibility. That guy we passed on the way out? The one with the NATO overcoat that dived out of our way? *That* was Joe Stallings."

"Yeah?" BC grinned evilly. "Wish I'd known. I'd've buzzed him closer."

Galen rolled his eyes. "You would, too. Once a punk always a punk. But, I agree, it sounds like a good idea to make the run now — providing we can get in."

"No problem. Prometheus practically lives at the place and he's expecting me—" Glancing at the wall clock, the Special Agent winced. "Make that 'was expecting me two hours ago'. You guys put in the orders and I'll ring Brendan to let him know we're coming. From our past chatroom conversations, dim sum should be an acceptable offering."

***

Breath rasping, Mills Cutter stopped long enough to be sure no one was behind him, then turned and broke into a run again. He'd almost made it to the road when his foot caught on something hidden beneath the leaf litter, sending him headfirst through a wall of bramble and into the ravine beyond. Thorns tore at skin and clothing as he and what seemed like half the hillside landed in the slow-moving creek at the bottom. Painfully, he pulled himself to his feet and froze, alert for any sign of his pursuer. Nothing but his own heart pounding in his ears.

He'd lost his bearings in the fall, crouched low into the shadows of the creek bank to figure out where he was. If he was right, his truck was parked along the nearby road just a bit south of the creek. If he could reach that, he'd floor it all the way back to Edmonton without stopping for anything. Damn his luck. All he'd done was come up for a little hunting, and camping. Things had gone great until night fell and this guy who looked like he'd been in some kind of fire walked into his camp and snapped his rifle in two. Honest to God. In two pieces. All he'd said was, "Run."

Mills ran.

When he'd caught his breath, he made a break for it, scrambling up the hillside using saplings for handholds. At the top, he climbed part-way out — and stopped cold at the sight of the stocky man standing motionless in the clearing. Who the hell was this guy? How did he get in front of him and not even be breathing hard?

The man closed the distance between them with terrifying speed. A hand like iron gripped the front of his jacket and lifted him effortlessly out of the gully. The dim light glinted off the white streak in the otherwise black hair and made the angry red marks he'd seen earlier on the square face look like black stripes.

"I am very disappointed, *signor*. I had hoped that an outdoorsman such as yourself would present more of a challenge."

Without warning, the stranger's free hand entangled his hair, yanking his head back. Lips so cold they seemed to burn touched his throat and the moonlit Canadian wilderness faded to black.

***

"Side door," the vaguely female computer-generated voice reported.

Brendan Grant, Senior Information Analyst for Sentry International, New York, looked up from his dog-eared science fiction paperback toward the wide screen monitor that displayed the low light camera feed. Four people stood there. Hmmm, he was only expecting one. — and unless he was mistaken, that one was in the front. Pushing his glasses farther up his nose, he squinted at the slightly grainy image. Yes, that was definitely BC Peale and the large individual directly behind him had to be Galen Miller. He didn't know the man and woman flanking Miller, but given the communications that had been flashing through the center over the last hour— His chain of logic was disrupted as Peale lifted a large, slightly grease-soaked bag up to the supposedly hidden camera. The words "Food Bribe Enclosed" were scrawled across the sack.

"Ah, White Fang, I presume?" Brendan said as he swung wide the reinforced steel door.

The answering grin flashed in the darkness giving the odd illusion that there really were fangs as Special Agent Peale replied, "Prometheus! Unchained, I see."

"Still chained, unfortunately." Stepping back, he gestured the visitors inside. "However, since my chains are mostly electronic, I get to move around some."

The handsome man in leather that he knew from the SI chatrooms as Whitefang made quick introductions, then held the big bag up. It exuded enticing smells. "We come bearing dim sum and other Chinese delicacies. Got an out-of-the-way place we can feed a horde of ravening law enforcement officers?"

"My office is about as out-of-the-way as you can get. Come on, I'll clear a space and you guys can give me the hard data on what happened at Kennedy tonight," he said as he led them down a narrow, book-lined corridor toward a splash of light painting the carpet near the end. "Radio chatter, text messages and sketchy news reports only get me so far."

"Ouch. Heard about that already, did you?" BC grimaced. "Why do I think that augurs ill for us?"

"Ordinarily, that might not be the case, since this data center is the hub for local SI communications. But tonight . . . ? I'm afraid so. The lines have been burning up since the explosion. I gotta admit, I'm real glad you folks decided to stop by here anyway, I was afraid you'd be too busy dodging fallout to come. Oh, before I forget: I just forwarded a message to Elaine (She's the agent handling the security desk at the Sentry hostelry, by the way.) that will be of particular interest to Special Agents Peale and Miller. What it boils down to is Captain Stallings wants you both under virtual house arrest until he can drag you into SIHQ for a reaming first thing in the morning."

Peale's reaction was curious. He stopped dead in his tracks and whirled toward his partner as if he'd been struck. Miller gave the smaller man a gentle shove to get him moving again. "I know. I'll take care of it."

Noting the exchange with carefully concealed interest, Brendan added it to the already impressive heap of data he had on Byron Cyrus Peale a.k.a. BC a.k.a. White Fang. His curiosity glands were working overtime in regard to this Special Agent. Data Analyst Grant had a talent for research and a high security clearance, two things that had won him the task of checking the background of one Byron C. Peale for ChiSpecOps. There were tons of interesting stuff, yet, with all the information passing through his hands, he'd been unable to reach a definitive conclusion about what he was dealing with. BC Peale was not a normal person, that was the most obvious interpretation. If he was, there were a helluva lot of coincidences about him and his ancestors. Brendan didn't believe in coincidences.

What that meant was, the dim sum was welcome, but not strictly necessary. The IT wizard was far more interested in meeting his unique cyberpal face-to-face. Tossing in New York's most infamous homicide detectives was spicy sauce for the potstickers. All in all, it promised to be an interesting evening.

With economy of motion born of long habit, Brendan

cleared enough desk space in the cluttered office to spread out the feast. He was unsurprised when BC excused himself from eating and slid cross-legged onto the floor with his back braced against the doorjamb.

"I have something you might be more interested in," Grant said, dropping a ponderous stack of printouts onto the carpeting next to Peale. "There's what you asked for last night. Scary thing is, it's not all in. That's the bulk of it, though. The rest should be in hand sometime tomorrow."

Peale dived on the printouts with the same eagerness his companions were attacking the food. Riffling the pages, he glanced up, concern carving a deep line between the indigo eyes. "I know you've reassured me time and time again, but I worry you'll catch serious flak for running this stuff outside normal channels."

"I'll tell you what I always tell you, BC. As long as the email gets to its proper destinations and the nets don't crash while I'm on duty (They never have, by the way.) nobody gives much of a damn what I do otherwise." He shrugged and helped himself to another steamed dumpling. "Besides, none of this stuff was classified and some of it, the detectives here have already seen."

"Yeah?" Tyler Taylor glanced down at the text, and swallowed his Egg Roll with an audible gulp. "Hey! I recognize that! *I* filed that stuff on the letter-bombing this morning."

Stroud Girion peered over her partner's shoulder, then her eyes widened. "Brendan, tell me you haven't been hacking the police system."

"I gotta admit, I have. It isn't a real complicated system; no safeguards to speak of. You guys should do something about that — I can help, if you like . . . ."

Stroud grabbed a handful of papers from Peale, scanned them and groaned, "Oh, man, Captain Brannaugh is gonna go Chernobyl."

Taylor grinned. "How's he going to find out? You gonna tell him? I'm not. Other than to say that a systems analyst advised an upgrade to our security measures, I think we can keep this among ourselves. Providing said systems analyst doesn't mind exchanging . . . ahem . . . other professional courtesies."

"A real pleasure, Sgt. Taylor — and I mean that!" Grant beamed. "I've been following you guys' work for years. Wish I could be a part of it."

BC chuckled and reached through, repossessing the printouts. "Rather looks like you already are. This is good stuff, Bren — but no surprise there. It's more complete than I hoped to have this early on. Also no surprise, the stuff on Francesco Borgia is kind of spare."

Around a mouthful of General Tso chicken, the data analyst declared, "The word you're searching for, BC, is *nonexistent*! Only way I got what you see, I had to send a special request to Aladdin in Seattle to get. If Aladdin can't find it, it doesn't exist *anywhere*."

Puzzled and interested, BC asked, "Aladdin? That's the first I've heard that handle."

"Doesn't surprise me. Not many have heard of him. His real name is Michael Sakady; he's almost a secret weapon for the West Coast Ops. Rumor has it that he's some kind of electronics whiz who escaped from an Eastern Bloc country before the Soviet Union self-destructed. I met him in a math discussion room on the SI private chat and I gotta admit, he knows his stuff. Kinda scary, really."

Taylor was interested. "Scary math? How so?"

"Well, we were discussing mathematical concepts versus engineering principles and Aladdin launched into a dissertation on the concept of the square root of negative one." Glancing around at the furrowed brows, he promised, "It's complicated and I'm not sure I got it myself, so I won't go into it, but suffice it to say that by the time he finished, there was only me and Saint Patrick from Houston left in the chat room. I think Aladdin got kind of embarrassed 'cos he finished by saying that maybe you had to be Czech, Russian or Polish to deal with it adequately."

"I can pretty much guarantee Australians aren't dealing with it at all. This one isn't anyway," Taylor said.

Stroud nodded. "Brooklynites are out of that loop, too."

"Aladdin's the best researcher I ever worked with, though," Grant said. Turning to Peale he added, "He's the one who found most of that stuff on Occupied France and Berlin during World War II. You know? For that report I sent to Chicago a while back. I gotta admit, the bulk of what we're waiting on is a similar background report he has running on Francesco Borgia."

Everything inside BC froze at the mention of his own dossier Jim Nelson had Brendan compile. They'd never talked about it online and until then, he'd all but forgotten Prometheus was the author of that damaging document. Taken individually, the bits of information included in the report meant little or nothing, combined they screamed, "This is the trail of a vampire." Not a very careful one, either, as Jim was wont to point out. For the first time, Special Agent Peale wondered uncomfortably how much Brendan Grant had pieced together for himself.

Alarmed, Brendan noticed the already pale face go pasty under the glare of the fluorescents. That was not what he'd intended. He added casually, "By the way, I hear since that earlier case is closed to everyone's satisfaction, that earlier body of work has been nuked."

White Fang relaxed visibly, and Prometheus, checking to make sure nobody else reacted, continued, "What it boils down to is, if you have anything kinda tricky to look for in the future, you might go directly to Aladdin. You're on S.I. Net, leave him e-mail; he always responds. If you want, I can introduce you to him."

Willing his friend to know he *was* a friend, Brendan's eyes locked with BC's for a moment before the latter's face split with a wide grin. "I might do that — but, I think I'll steer clear of negative one. I'm more Fine Arts oriented myself."

An electronic rendition of Hail to the Chief sounded from Stroud's pocket. She rolled her eyes. "That'll be Captain Brannaugh. I wonder if Uncle Joe killed Kenny. Sorry, folks, I gotta take this." She stepped over Peale and into the hall as she pulled the device out and tapped the screen. "Hey, Captain, did they have to tie Stallings down or just tranq him?" There was silence, then her voice changed as she asked, "Where? Okay, no problem, we're close. Tell Brown we'll be right there."

She ended the call and leaned in the doorway looking infinitely tired.

Taylor closed up the remains of his meal. "What's up?"

"Another hit, double one this time. About fifteen minutes from here. Sgt. Brown is handling the scene and expecting the four of us ASAP."

"Another bomb?"

"Yeah. A car this time. The guys hadn't gotten in before it blew, Still took 'em out, but at least there's something for the Medical Examiner to work with." She stuffed her phone back into her pocket. "Looks like you got your wish, BC. You got your information before we started our investigations — just."

BC treated the group to a lopsided smile as he said, "Yeah, but looks like Uncle Joe won't get his. No way we're going to go to the hostel to be put under house arrest until *after* we've been to the crime scene."

***

With the green-shaded accountant's lamp off, the only light in Joe Stallings' private office spilled through the open doorway of the receptionist's area. He rechecked his militarily neat desktop by the dim glow. Everything of a sensitive nature was locked in the wall safe, and all memos carefully shredded and disposed of properly. Others found amusement at this residual habit from his days with the CIA, but he found it strangely comforting, he was a man who hated clutter.

He was also a man who was done in. The idea of simply crashing on his office couch rather than driving home only to come right back to face the inevitable morning media deluge was becoming more inviting by the second.

Rubbing the knotted muscles at the base of his skull, he groaned and for the hundredth time and hurled mental invective at the concept of time zones. That always gave him a kink, especially when he was tired and angry, and someone he badly needed to talk to — Colonel Black in this case — was in Japan. He smiled with satisfaction at the knowledge that time zones didn't stop him from phoning Jim Nelson in Chicago to apprise him of what his two star agents managed to do before they'd been in New York a full hour. Maybe Dennis Brannaugh didn't hold the pair responsible, but *he* did.

Why on earth were those two dropped on him, anyway? He didn't like cowboys, and everything in their past performance said 'cowboy' in flaming letters. If tonight's brouhaha didn't prove him right, nothing would. The Colonel had to listen to him this time.

Oh, dammit anyway! Half his trouble was that the Colonel *did* listen to him. It was his personal request that secured Tyler Taylor and Stroud Girion as liaison for the Chicago agents in the first place. He was so busy looking for a way to entice them onto his team, he failed to take their own cowboy tendencies into account. The astonishing thing was that Colonel Black jumped on the suggestion, declaring it a wonderful idea to team the four operatives up. Oh well, whatever flak came his way because of it, he'd have to smile and take it.

Fate was out to get him. That's what it was. Why else did this supernatural folderol keep popping up? This time it's an agent who thinks he's a vampire, the last time it was a guy pretending to be a werewolf. It was beyond belief that two normally rational men like Brian Black and Jim Nelson were willing to believe such poppycock. Worse, Black believed it even though he hadn't *met* the man. Well, neither had Joe, but past experience told him there were no such things as vampires. The Romanian Werewolf debacle was proof of that.

He winced at the memory. His one consolation lay in the fact he'd been so very young and the man perpetrating the hoax so very clever. It didn't help that the murders were so horrific, it was hard to imagine a human being committing them. The biggest consolation was that Stallings had been the first to notice the discrepancies in the "werewolf's" story. Looking into those eventually revealed the murders to be an elaborate smokescreen to cover the real motives of the agent in question. The Vampire Vigilante crap that Peale pulled in Chicago reminded him of that. A lot. Oh! Pardon the mental slip . . . SIChi were *now* calling it 'Lake Shore Robin Hood,' especially now that Robin was working for them. VV fit better. If Peale went off on a tear like that in New York . . . well, the man ought to be hospitalized or in counseling at least, not working as a top security agent. That really stuck in his craw.

Orders or no orders, he intended to take a hard line with Special Agent Peale. Black and Nelson were cutting him a lot of slack because they believed he was such a good operative. Joe didn't see any justification for that in the record — what there was of it. The only remarkable thing he could see about Peale's record *was* the lack of information in it.

No. He'd suffered great humiliation because of the werewolf case, and wasn't about to let that happen again. Yawning widely, he glanced at the time, swore mentally and flipped off the rest of the lights. Looked like the couch won the toss.

FOUR

"Ten good people! TEN!!"

Jaw muscles rigid, Eddie Michalson whipped the third spoonful of sugar into his first cup of the day. Despite every precaution, two more lieutenants were dead and the police were all over the scene before his people even heard about it. He didn't know how the hell they did it, but it proved one thing: NYPD was just as upset as he was. Well, he knew that. He'd know that even if his department informants hadn't been telling him that since before he even boarded the plane from Chicago.

Gwen Isendamer was behind it. There was no proof, but he knew it. He knew it just like he had pictures. His guys started dying — *messily* — right after he ruined her last bid to get the Boss to make her a vampire. The woman gave him the heebie jeebies! Francesco Borgia crawls in looking like the losing side of a war and Gwennie's first thought was that he'd be so weak, he'd do what she wanted. The scariest part was it almost happened. It would have happened if Eddie hadn't shown up in time.

The Boss was glad for the save, though. So was Eddie. But, glad wasn't the same as comfortable. It was sheer luck that his man, JD, was on the door that night. The next morning, Eddie slipped him an under-the-table bonus for calling him right away. Then he'd shipped both JD and Dirk to a remote place to lay low until further notice. They were his last people in Chicago and he knew they weren't safe. The move was so hush-hush, even the Boss didn't know where they were. That was a *good* thing.

The idea of Gwennie as a vampire petrified him. It would petrify any person with half a brain. As long as he could prevent it, he would — no matter what happened afterward. The Boss must agree, because when he recovered, his attitude changed toward her. It was subtle, but she'd noticed. It never occurred to her she could be to blame; instead she accused Eddie of poisoning Borgia against her. Michalson suspected if anyone other than Gwen herself was responsible, it was the kid.

The kid. Listen to that! Imagine thinking of a two hundred maybe three hundred-something year old vampire as "the kid." Couldn't help it, though. It fit.

Regardless of whose fault it was, Gwen was on Eddie's case for any little thing ever since. That was the long and the short of it. Taking a vampire's empathic nature into account, he wondered if the volcanic hostility was another reason the Boss decided to disappear into Canada. Wouldn't blame him. *He* wouldn't want to know what everyone else was feeling all the time — especially with a headcase like Gwennie. If he were an empath, there wouldn't be an exit close enough or a plane fast enough to suit him once that shit hit the fan.

On second thought, maybe one thing did matter. If his suspicions were on the money, he'd be coming to the top of Gwennie's list pretty soon. Any time, she could waltz in and ace him without looking like she had anything to do with it. All she had to do was trot out the righteous indignation number and play the "I was in New Orleans" card. Sure, the Boss would know better, but that wouldn't do Eddie much good. Worse, with Eddie gone, Borgia'd need Gwen's expertise more than ever. That would be bad.

Okay, what could he do about it? Not much. Running to the Boss was a no-go. This was strictly between him and the Ice Empress. Eddie understood that. He didn't like it, but he understood it.

Reclining his easy chair as far back as it would go, he willed muscles to unknot. Unhappy reasons for the homecoming aside, he was glad to be back. He was a New Yorker born and bred, and while Chicago was an okay town, he couldn't get used to it. Ah well, time for his news fix. Maybe he could get his mind off his own troubles by seeing what problems the rest of the world was having. Flicking the remote power button, he reached again for the coffee pot. The newscaster was in the middle of a story as the set came on, and Eddie brightened, recognizing the face of Rick Rattner. Just like that butthead to get caught that way. Blew up part of the airport and brought everyone and their uncle down on his head. What an idiot! The man was careless and stupid. That was the reason he was blackballed from any operation sponsored by the Este Corporation. . . .

He halted mid-chortle and mid-slurp as another familiar face filled the screen. It was outdoors at night with emergency lights glaring in the background. The reporter shouted over the wind as she demanded, "Mr. Miller! We understand you're here in the capacity of Special Agent with Sentry International. How long have you worked for SI and what was your part in tonight's incident?"

The soft voice was almost lost to the microphones as the unwilling interviewee replied, "I can't comment on anything at this time."

Without another word, Galen Miller ducked into the crowd and made a successful escape. His companion wasn't so lucky. As he turned to follow Miller into the crush, the reporter slipped into his path. "How about you, Special Agent Peale? Can you give us a comment?"

Bestowing a charmingly apologetic smile, Borgia's only scion answered, "Awfully sorry. This is ATF's jurisdiction, perhaps you'd have better luck interviewing them?"

Sidestepping the insistent reporter, the vampire melded into the crowd, leaving her to give a solo precis of the events. Eddie carefully deposited his cup into its saucer and thumbed to another channel. He watched with growing interest over the next hour.

Later, Michalson sat frowning at the dark and stilled television. So, the kid was in New York, too? Coincidence? Like hell. How long had they been here?

More important, did the Boss know the kid was here? God, he hoped not! Borgia refused to have newspapers sent to the Canadian lodge and he never watched the tube unless forced to. It wasn't that the Boss didn't care what was happening in the world, he simply hated watching television. Eddie wondered if the light hurt the ultra-sensitive eyes, or if maybe the idea of TV was still too foreign. Whichever, it was part of Eddie's job description to keep his employer abreast of important happenings as they broke.

Not today, though. For one thing, this was the *morning* news, and the Boss wouldn't care less until evening. He might have to tell him then . . . when *was* sunset in that part of Canada, anyway?

Well, that gave him a little operational latitude. Good. The longer the Boss was in the dark about Peale's whereabouts, the better. He was getting nutzo where the kid was concerned. Besides, Eddie was in no hurry to hear the order that the news was bound to trigger. The current plan involved spiriting Peale away from his companions and forcing him to "listen to reason." Eddie disliked that plan on two counts.

One: That kind of stunt never worked. And:

Two: *He* didn't want any part of putting the snatch on a pissed-off vampire.

No, the Boss needed time to get his head together. —And he would — Borgia was too savvy to be knocked permanently off track by something like this. His frown deepened. It seemed that making a fledgling was a more serious thing than Eddie'd thought at first. Lately, the Boss kept kvetching about something called a "bloodbond". Whatever that was, it was causing a hell of an uproar.

Wait. What if Gwen saw this? This was big. He'd seen coverage on all the networks and while she wasn't the news-junkie Eddie was, she watched regularly. Mostly for the stock market stuff, but— Oh man. That would be an even bigger problem. He'd better cover his ass and call New Orleans like it was business as usual.

He wished there was a way to come at her out of left field. Knock her off balance. If he could take her out before she got to him . . . . There had to be a way to do that and keep his tracks covered. *The kid*!

Sure! Aiming Peale and Miller at her wouldn't be hard — it was their job, right? Yeah. From what Maeve Donal said, that was his best bet. According to her, Peale had a warped kind of honor that could be depended on. Come to think of it, Miller looked like a good risk, too. If a vampire trusted a guy with his secret, he must be pretty good at keeping them. He wouldn't last long, otherwise. Funny about guys like that being cops — or was it? Weird as they were, they might be better suited to it than most.

Still, they wouldn't go for it unless it looked to be useful. Just made sense. Any deal has to have benefits on both sides. What could he offer that wouldn't screw Este Corp. over? Chicago. That part of the business was scuttled, anyway.

He glared at the telephone. First the bad medicine.

***

"I wasn't *watching* the news, Eddie, but I was reading all about how Francesco's little boy and his pal Friday tried to blow Kennedy airport off the map. They're both so wonderfully photogenic, don't you think?"

Ignoring that, Eddie launched into his spiel, "Glad ya seen it, saves me the trouble of explanations. Look, d'ya mind sittin' on this a few days? You know how wound up the Boss is about Peale; I sorta wanna nose around some before I spill it to 'im. I wanna know what the kid and Miller are doin' in New York the same time all hell is breakin' loose."

Stretching luxuriously, Gwen savored the "hell" before answering, "I don't mind holding off, at all. Francesco deserves a little peace and quiet after everything that so-called son of his has put him through. I agree you should find out why Peale is there. Even Francesco at his most stressed won't grudge you time for that."

"Great, but, I don't mind tellin' ya, seein' him and his pal put the wind up me this mornin'."

"But, Eddie, it might have nothing to do with us. They *are* with the US branch of Sentry and that's New York based — it could be a coincidence. Maybe Chicago wanted to be rid of them."

"Maybe so, maybe no. I'll like it a lot better once I know for sure. Look, I gotta get on this, so I'll get back with ya soon as I know somethin' solid."

Shutting off the cell phone, she ran a sensuous fingertip down the warm plastic, musing, *"Don't be too long about it, Eddie, I'd hate to have to get your input through a seance."*

No need to worry, though, she'd give Eddie plenty of time to collect his information. He was *so* good at what he did in spite of the slow-moving street tough front he assumed for public consumption. Her prime task now was to get her hands on the intel before Francesco did. Hopefully, there'd be something juicy on Peale. If the father refused to give her what she wanted, then maybe what she needed was a younger man.

Lips pursed, she re-examined the photo from the morning newspaper. Byron lacked the aura of raw power Francesco exuded, but he was very handsome. That was a plus. She wondered if he'd let her watch him feed? She loved it when Francesco did, especially a kill. That was better than any aphrodisiac.

Hmm. If the plans with Peale worked out, should she bother to eliminate Eddie? Good question. After she and her new lover disposed of Francesco and took over the business, they'd need his talents. No. Eddie would never switch sides — especially not for her. A pity in a way, but on the up side, she'd been so looking forward to his death, it would be a shame to cancel it. Hmmm. That might mean she'd have to push up her timetable, after all. If she missed this opportunity, she might never get another. Too bad she couldn't video tape it, but having solid evidence floating around wouldn't be wise.

Amusing how Eddie's chief worry appeared to be that she'd be smoking the phone lines to Canada. Hardly. She had plans she didn't want Francesco interfering with, either. Oh well, she'd better put in her own call to Tony DeLuca and Vinny Crawford. They were already in New York and it was time to serve up another slice of "hell" to Mr. Michalson. Hmmm. Who should it be this time?

***

There was so much paperwork required to run a business, and even with special cushions, sitting for long periods became excruciating for Jump Veron. When he and BC had entered into partnership all those years ago, paperwork was the farthest thing from his mind. Back then, he'd been enthralled by the prospect of having his own stage, and being able to do things the way *he* wanted. Nothing else mattered. He'd been so young then, and life seemed such an adventure. Hell, it *had* been an adventure. Quite a few of them, truth to tell.

Soft footfalls intruded on his desultory efforts with the tax forms littering the tabletop. Maeve was wandering again. She was so beautiful, it was no surprise that this sensuous creature and his oldest friend were once lovers. After a stint in close proximity to her, even less surprise that the affair ended in a fiery collision of wills. She and BC shared too many characteristics — mostly the bad ones. So far, Jump's relationship with her was comparatively smooth. Perhaps it came of practice in dealing with her male counterpart.

This behavior was also familiar; he'd seen it whenever something or someone forced BC to go to ground. The blessing with BC was, Jump only had to live with the aimless meanderings at night. With Maeve, it was all day, too. He commiserated, though. He hated forced inactivity, too, although his inactivity was usually health-related. He sighed. That was becoming all too common lately.

She'd cooperated admirably with her benign jailers until her spells revealed Borgia was leaving the city. With the threat removed, so was her patience at captivity. However, the real reason for her dissatisfaction lay elsewhere. BC had visited frequently before he and Galen were transferred to New York. Now that he was also far removed, her unrest grew daily.

How sad Maeve had so few friends aside from BC. Jay Marquez and Benny Glissen tried, but neither were comfortable with the formidable Irish woman. She terrified and irritated Phil Quinlan in equal parts. At least Emily Hu and Jasmine Miller got on well with her. True Jasmine's were working visits, but the two women found many common interests, amusingly like suburban housewives swapping "recipes." For himself, he was pleased Jasmine was coming over at all, although the forces she and Maeve wielded so casually made him uneasy. Such things were dangerous; but on the bright side, by working together, they were able to keep track of the enemy. A more important thing than personal preferences.

Though subtler, he knew Emily's visits weren't strictly social, either. He found SIChi's new DDSOI a strange mix, and sensed a deep loneliness in her. Darker still, was the inevitable guilt she felt because her promotion resulted from of the death of a friend. She shared his concern over Maeve's restlessness, too. Perhaps she could convince Captain Nelson to ease the restrictions. With Borgia out of the city — out of the *country* — it should be possible to restore some liberty before Ms. Donal broke free on her own. That could prove disastrous to all concerned. Surely the Captain saw that?

Glancing at the wall clock told him that he had two hours before the club opened and several more before Jasmine arrived. He groaned, and twisting arthritic hips into a slightly less painful position, turned back to the less romantic, but just as necessary IRS forms.

***

Joseph Stallings glowered at the gratifyingly uncomfortable agents standing inside his office. Inwardly, he was as angry with himself as with them. After Brannaugh's warning, he'd foolishly believed himself prepared for the worst. He should have known better. From the aerie of his office windows, the media assault morning brought on SIHQ was incredible. Thank God he'd slept over at the office. If he hadn't, it would have taken a Special Forces retinue to make the entrance. Later in the day, the horde dispersed, mollified, but not entirely satisfied by the prepared statement read by Special Agent Irene 'Gilly' McGillicuddy. His jaw dropped as he'd watched the live feed of the question and answer session. Society today seemed to have its priorities turned on its ear. An explosion of smuggled armaments paled beside the notion that an ex-football player was now a Sentry Agent? Good Lord! All because one of the investigating officers had once put on padded gear and done bodily harm to himself and others in the name of sport. . . .

Black's official decision was the only option — short of firing them, which was the one Stallings lobbied for. They'd simply have to adopt a higher profile, although the Colonel worried it might endanger Peale's secret. Secret. Right! The Director just kept going on about the fluke that blew the cover as high as the debris. Joe responded with the proper noises, but as far as he was concerned, there was no fluke, just stupidity on the part of two cowboy agents who should know better. At least it saved the organization the trouble of getting them different accommodations, as their original cover story called for. The transient hostelry would serve very well from now on.

The late hour made him unhappier, still. Originally, he'd ordered them to be in front of him first thing this morning, but they demurred, using the dodge that Peale couldn't do that seeing how he was undead and all. Gut instinct said to send a contingent of security officers and have them *escorted* in at sunrise. He would have, too, if not for the early morning detour to investigate a killing actually linked with their case. Then there was the difficulty of the media horde laying siege to the building. Now, well after nightfall, the problem children waited to find out how big an axe was going to fall on them. It was nowhere big enough. Still, as Director of Special Operations and Investigations for New York, he needed to take a hard line from the first, lest these Chicago prima donnas get the idea they could jerk him around like a wet-behind-the-ears rookie.

Instructing Peale to shut the soundproof door, he evaluated their physical condition. From Denny Brannaugh's precis, he'd been afraid he'd end the dressing down by sending them to the docs — specifically Peale. Reportedly, the man took a nasty spill from his motorcycle while pulling Richard Rattner and Detective Girion into cover, but oddly, it was Miller who looked the worse for wear. Peale looked fresh, not at all like a man who'd skidded into a gravel-lined ditch with two bodies and a heavy machine. Come to think about it, he *was* pale, and . . . oh come off it, Joe! Stupid thought. He began, "Good evening, gentlemen. So glad you could finally find the time in your busy schedules to join me."

Peale flinched. "Sir, we understand your displeasure. . . ."

Stallings cut the slim Briton off, flinging a bundle of newspaper clippings at him. The bundle was snapped from the air with a neat flick of the wrist, as Stallings snarled, "You understand my *displeasure*, Peale? I don't think so. You two have caused this organization more trouble with one incident than it's had since inception — and it's had plenty! I've never known undercover agents so hungry for publicity. If I'd been told you wanted international coverage for your arrival, I'd have saved you the trouble and notified CNN personally."

"No need. They were there anyway, sir."

Galen winced. He had an uncomfortable feeling his partner's penchant for flip comments wouldn't play well in this venue. A quick look at their new commander confirmed this. Stallings ogled the bland-faced vampire like a wild bull who'd just spotted a man in a red suit jogging across his field.

Stallings exploded, "I find humor inappropriate to the situation, mister! You *will* understand I do not like my orders to be disregarded at the whim of people who are supposed to be subject to them. When I call a meeting for first thing in the morning, I expect my operatives here at the crack of dawn. I neither want *nor* appreciate being told one of said operatives is 'unavailable' until nightfall. It makes me testy, Peale, and when I get testy, I tend to take it out on the person or persons who made me that way!"

Deep furrows appeared between Peale's dark brows, he ventured, "Sir, when I accepted this reassignment, I was given to understand that my records were forwarded in their entirety. Was I misled?"

Joe had been waiting for this. Hands splayed on the

desktop, he slowly leaned as far over as he could without losing balance, hissing, "You were not misled, Peale. They were sent, and I read every word. Now, I'm only going to say this once, mister, so if you think you might have trouble remembering it, you'd better take notes. I don't care what your personal delusions are, but here in SIHQ we do not humor them. Especially when they interfere with the job we're here to do. While you are in my unit, you will behave like any other individual working for this agency and make yourself available twenty-four hours a day. If you have problems with this arrangement, you can discuss it with one of our resident psychologists. They'd be happy to make an appointment to suit you — but *I* won't. Do we understand each other, Peale?"

The vampire's face was stony. A jaw muscle twitched dangerously at the repressed emotion building behind it. The backwash slammed into Galen like a hurricane. Hurriedly, he stepped forward. "Captain Stallings, maybe we ought to take this up with Col. Black. Jim Nelson assured us that he was apprised—"

"Can it, Miller. The Colonel is in Japan and engaged in conferences about jurisdiction — a concept you and your partner seem to understand little of. He will be unavailable for a small piece of domestic friction. And I warn you, I resent the attempt to pull strings, Miller. I was led to believe you were more professional than that."

"I wasn't trying to—"

"I said *can it*, Miller. I'm addressing your partner."

The words were an annoying jumble to Peale as he swayed, eyes squeezed shut, attempting to ignore the veins visibly throbbing in the Captain's neck. Reason argued against the fury that triggered the bloodthirst. Okay. SINY's

Commanding Officer had a valid complaint about the Rattner fiasco. He expected to be reamed for that, but *this* was unexpected and unwarranted. Not to mention dangerous.

When he joined Sentry, he'd revealed a secret, and in return received assurances it would be handled carefully. Now, blind-sided by a breech of trust, the anger and anxiety from the other occupants of the confining walls assaulted his senses and shattered his defenses. Hot blood pounding in nearby throats struck like rhythmic sledgehammers at his self-control. The stockyard 'dinner break' dulled the impact, but if that asshole didn't get out of his face, he couldn't be responsible — a sharp bang startled his eyes wide open and shoved the surging Hunger to the background.

Confused, he homed in on the source of the sound: a large book, square in the center of Stalling's desk blotter. Slowly, Stallings' shouts resolved into human speech, ". . . I *said* perhaps you would like to explain this, Peale? We're waiting for enlightenment."

Numbly brushing fingertips against the fine-grained leather binding, he read the gold lettering, and answered in a voice closer to normal than he'd hoped to produce, "Other than the obvious observation that it appears to be a rather expensive edition of Bram Stoker's *Dracula*, and in view of your previously stated objections concerning the possible other connotations, I have no explanation, Captain. Should I have?"

A startling alteration came over the Captain. Collapsing in on himself, he sank into his chair, saying, "Well, since it was addressed to you care of this department, we'd hoped you would. In light of the letter bombs used in several deaths you two are investigating, the unit mobilized and the thing was rushed straight to the lab. They still have the wrappings for future comparisons, but other than smudges that were probably from latex gloves, there was nothing. Well, there was the damned book, of course — oh! And this. Don't know how I could have forgotten it; maybe I was trying to." He drew a piece of paper in a Mylar sleeve from the drawer and slid it atop the book. Miller scooped it up.

Stallings continued bitterly, "Also don't know why the lab boys wasted the Mylar, we've been all over it and there's nothing there except more smudges. Laser printer. Probably Hewlett-Packard, but then again how many aren't? The content is as inexplicable as the rest. Does it make sense to either of you?"

Peering around his partner, BC read,

"I know your father. If you would like to learn more about him, be at the top of the Empire State Building tonight at eleven pm.

Bring a friend if you like."

The room swam, and as he caught himself against Galen's solidity, he heard Stallings crow triumphantly, "At last! Something means something to someone! What is it, Peale, is it the reference to your father? The present tense had me confused. I was under the impression your father was deceased."

"My true father is indeed gone, Captain Stallings. I think this is an unpleasant reference to Francesco Borgia."

"Oh, *that* again." Seeing the lean face darken, he waved it away. "Let's not get into it. I accept that Borgia believes himself to be your . . . sire, is it? How I feel about it is irrelevant in the face of that. The important thing is that this would appear to be from someone close enough to Borgia to know about you."

BC answered simply, "That's the only face I can put on it, sir."

Miller dropped the laminated sheet back onto the blotter. "Me, too."

"Then it appears, gentlemen, we have a problem." Two pairs of wary eyes met his as he continued, "I intended to restrict your movements for the next few days, but this might be the inside break we've been looking for. Talk to Sgt. Myre about whatever backup and equipment you need."

Peale demurred, "I don't think backup is a good idea. We should keep this as small as possible. Anything more than Galen and myself might frighten our informant off."

Miller spun, "What? You mean you *want* to go?"

"You don't?"

"By our lonesome? With our cover blown sky high?"

"Whoever wrote this knew who we worked for and in what capacity — that wasn't on the news. Neither was any mention of Francesco Borgia. I don't know why you're upset; you never insisted on backup in Chicago."

"And look what happened in Chicago."

"Okay, then, I'll go alone," Peale said. "Gae, I need to know who this joker is — I mean he/she/it obviously knows *something*! Why that book? The references to my 'father' has to mean Borgia — and I doubt it's him. According to what Jump, Maeve and your mother tell us, he's in Canada."

"I dunno, I keep remembering what happened the last time someone said he knew something about Borgia. That was Hernandez' dodge, too. I'm betting you won't forget what happened then for a long time."

"This is different. Hernandez is dead, and the Empire State's observation deck is not a deserted place. Besides, you've been invited, too — not much of a trap if one is allowed to bring the cavalry, is it?"

"I'm nuts for listenin' to you. There's probably twelve guys with crossbows up there waitin' with stakes for *both* of us."

"ALL RIGHT, GENTLEMEN!" Smacking the desk for emphasis, Stallings snarled, "Get out of here, I'm sick of looking at you! You're here to work — get to it. Requisition whatever equipment you can both agree on *and* get your asses right back here as soon as the meet is over. I'll want a full report immediately."

***

Gwen Isendamer sat alone in the rented bungalow's living room, the door slam that rattled the windows still ringing in her ears. She walked over to the couch where the lone lamp cast a circle of yellow light against the Louisiana night, and eased herself onto the cushions. Swirling the freshly mixed White Russian, she waited. She didn't have to wait long. The door to the master bedroom opened and a square-shouldered, dark man stepped into the circle of light.

Sipping the vodka drink, she said, "Well, *Señor*, it appears our Mr. Cruz does not accept instruction with good grace. Watch him. See that he follows the instructions I gave him."

The dark man frowned slightly, putting Gwen in mind of ancient Mexican carvings she had seen. They were called . . . Warrior-Priests? She watched him mull over the conversation he'd eavesdropped on and reach a decision. He smiled grimly, then left to follow their troublesome associate, leaving Isendamer with her thoughts. They weren't happy ones.

Warrior-Priest. The title suited the Colombians' operative very well and she trusted neither him nor his employers. They'd never been completely happy dealing with Este Corp.

and were always trying to insert themselves into business that was no concern of theirs. They were due for another lesson and she didn't have time for it.

***

The night was cool and windy. It had drizzled all day and the observation deck was virtually deserted as BC cautiously pushed the door of the stairs open. He cocked his head against the wind and listened. Two — no — three heartbeats aside from the resonant thud of Galen's behind him. No sign of Borgia's scent, but that was faint even to another vampire and the wet, oily pavement *could* effectively block it. With Galen close behind, he stepped into the open air.

Off in the far corner of the rooftop, a couple locked in a fervent embrace. He smiled to himself. No wonder he had difficulty separating them into two. Now, where was the Lone Ranger?

In the opposite direction, of course. He indicated the heavily muffled figure to his companion with a quick gesture. Galen responded with an almost imperceptible nod and moved off.

He watched his partner melt into shadows, avoiding the brightly lit patches, marveling once again at the grace and stealth with which the big man moved. Gae was taking no chances, either, insisting they both wear protective vests and carry weapons. He didn't mind the vests per se, he was thoroughly sick of being shot, but there was a question whether the armor could stop arrows. Oddly enough, he didn't feel threatened, although truthfully, he didn't perceive a threat from Hernandez until it was too late. Still, he was calm about being here, and in spite of the rational arguments he'd presented to Galen, his major motivation for being in the rain on this Thursday night was curiosity. He sneaked a peek at his watch. Galen was probably in place, so he strolled toward the heavily overcoated man.

There was something familiar about the figure — *could* it be Borgia? The build was similar. He sniffed the air and froze as he caught the clear smell of fear on the wind. If there was fear, the man who waited was not Borgia. He tried to close his nose to the scent, but it trailed in almost tangible tendrils from the lone figure leaning against the railing in front of him. The enticement wrapped itself around his mind, urging him to spring. He fought it down. He'd fed again before their assignation, and was glad of it. The conflict with Stallings had sparked the Hunger, so that now, it lurked below the surface, unwilling to be sated by beast's blood. The raw human emotion confronting him on the rooftop was nearly impossible to ignore when the Hunger was roused.

These were the times when his nature hammered home the fact that he *was* first and foremost a predator. From the corner of his eye, he saw Galen step toward him. Silently, he thanked his friend. Gae was getting *very* good at recognizing trouble, and going out of his way to avert it. Concentrating on Miller and their joint purpose for being there, he shook off the Predator and once more became BC Peale. Squaring his shoulders, he resumed his approach.

As BC neared, the man whirled, right hand buried in the pocket of his bulky overcoat. Recognizing his visitor, the man visibly relaxed, and though the hand remained out of sight, whispered, "Peale. Holy Mary, I swear you Nosferatu dudes move quiet."

Intrigued, BC glided to the rail. "Eddie Michalson."

Materializing on the opposite side, Galen firmly gripped

the gun hand into immobility. "Right the first time, partner, and last I heard he was workin' for your would-be Daddy."

Eddie muttered through gritted teeth, "Guilty on both counts. Hey, Miller, I dropped the piece when I recognized the kid. Could ya let go the hand before ya break somethin'?" Confidence returning, he straightened his tie. "Saw you boys on the cable news. Looked pretty good. Didja come in to help with urban renewal . . . or mebbe some other explosive situation brought ya the Big Apple?"

Galen's smile gleamed in the half-lit darkness. "From the way you phrased that, I suspect you have a few ideas on that score."

Michalson nodded smugly. No need to confess he hadn't figured it out until thirty minutes before. Trouble was, it was *so* simple, and looking for hidden complications, he'd completely glossed over what was staring him in the face. "I figure you guys been tapped to cover these hits on my people. Prolly wasn't too hard to link 'em to me, an' once that connection was made — bingo! You two had preprinted plane tickets to the Big Apple. Tell me I'm wrong."

"You're not wrong."

Suddenly, the bluster was gone, and a shudder unrelated to the stiff breeze wracked the stocky body. A touch of fear-scent returned, as he all but whispered, "But do you know who's behind it?"

"No." Peale treated Borgia's lieutenant to a close scrutiny. "But, I think *you* do, and it scares the hell out of you. You don't scare easily, Eddie. Want to give why?"

Suddenly defensive, Eddie answered, "Damn straight, I'm scared. You'd be, too, if you knew Gwen Isendamer."

Peale started involuntarily. "Isendamer?"

Eddie turned all his attention onto Peale. The kid seemed to understand; that could be very good or very bad. He asked cautiously, "Does that mean you *know* the psycho bitch?"

"No, I merely know *of* her, for which blessing I'm very grateful. Remember, we have a mutual friend in Maeve Donal. Maeve is a woman not easily frightened, but Ms. Isendamer evoked a similar response in her."

Miller spoke, his quiet rumble cleaving the damp air, "Yeah, I heard her talk about it, too. Anyone that particular lady finds disturbing worries the hell out of me, too."

Glancing at his shadowy companions Eddie said, "Okay, that makes it a little easier, but I hope you guys got time, 'cos this is gonna take a while."

He began his story, and soon neither of his listeners were aware of the damp wind any more. As he concluded, the chunky man looked up into the long, pale face beside him saying, "Findin' out it was you givin' him grief in Chicago got to him big time, kid. The things he's been doin' since then? Well, let's just say the Boss ain't been actin' as smart as he usually does."

"Like coming to our flat the night he killed Mick Marquez."

"Yeah. I'm real sorry about Marquez. He was an okay guy — for a cop — and killing him was unnecessary, but that's the kind of thing I'm talking about. Like I said, findin' out about you was the worst thing coulda happened."

Suddenly, Peale pivoted. "Are you insinuating *I* was responsible for Mick Marquez' death?"

Eddie rushed to placate him; the last thing he wanted was a pissed-off vampire in his face. "*No*! I'm not sayin' that. Geez, don't take things so personal, kid! Sure, the Boss is being screwier than usual because of you, but that sort of thing was always there. This just brought it to the surface more is all."

Peale swung away and gripping the railing tightly, muttered, "Sorry, I'm—"

Galen interrupted, "We're *all* upset — about one thing or another, so let's let it slide. That was a very interesting tale, Michalson. But I doubt you're the kind of guy who'd ask us to freeze our asses off on a rooftop for a bedtime story. What gives? Major shit has hit the fan before and you haven't yelled for a cop. Has something else happened?"

Eddie grimaced ruefully in the darkness. "Y'might say that, yeah." Almost involuntarily, he told the rest. About Borgia wounded and incoherent. About Gwen's near success in gaining her desire to become a vampire. He finished in a hushed tone, "I swear, the Boss was so far gone, he'd'a done it! I tell ya, Gwennie was sore when I butted in. She vowed vengeance on me and mine right there, an' a couple days later my people in the Apple started dyin'. You draw your own conclusions, but mine say it's the Ice Empress' revenge an' I'm number one with a bullet."

Unexpectedly, a gloved hand shot out, grasped a handful of coat and pulled the smaller man face to face with a very agitated Peale. "Gwen Isendamer wants Francesco Borgia to make her a vampire?"

Eddie goggled. "Yeah! I jus' said so, didn't I? She's always on about it."

"But . . . she's *insane*!"

"You catch on real quick, kid. You mind puttin' me down before ya make any other earth-shattering observations?"

BC let Michalson drop to the gravel before Galen could intervene. When he spoke, his voice was so quiet, it was almost carried away by the wind. "I'm okay. I'm not losing control again. I'm simply more horrified than I thought I could be." Turning toward his uneasy companions, he explained, "My statement about Isendamer's sanity isn't as simple as it sounds. You see, it's difficult enough for a person who can *reason* to deal with vampirism. When one first awakes after being changed, old perceptions are subtly altered. They've heightened — not to mention the appetites that go along with it. No matter how one attempts to control or hide it, there's always that element deep inside that threatens to — *wants* — to go out of control. Keeping a firm grasp on reason allows a reasonable grasp on humanity, but a person without that faculty of *reason* . . . ."

Abruptly, Galen felt a chill deeper than the reach of the wind. He'd seen his laid-back partner lose it a couple times and come real close a few more. He got the drift and it was an ugly one. He asked Michalson, "But, you say Borgia's refusing her?"

"Yeah, usually, but the Boss wasn't thinkin' that night — that was the whole trouble. He knows what she's like. So do I. That's why I'm scared. That's why I'm talkin' to you guys. Look, she's over the edge completely now. Killing always turned her on before, but. . . ." Drawing a wad of documents from inside his coat, he handed them to Miller. "I put her stuff in there with the dope on the Chicago operation. You can read it for yourself, but I wouldn't advise doin' it over dinner. I ain't exactly scared to die, but I *am* scared of Gwen Isendamer. That's why I hadda talk to you two special — you understand what I'm sayin'?" He could see they did. He added, "That ain't the worst part, though. I think she's plannin' to take out the Boss, too."

Borgia's scion chuckled wryly. "I wish her luck if she tries."

"It ain't funny, kid. Do ya really want to bet on who'd come out on top? If by some chance it was Gwennie, I think we'd all be in for it. Especially you. You shoulda seen her face when she found out the Boss already had a kid. She wasn't lookin' ta send ya a candygram, believe me.

"Look, things are goin' sour with the corporation, too. The Boss has been lettin' things run themselves and the machinery is startin' to shake apart at the seams. The Colombian guys never liked dealin' with us, and some of our contract operators are startin' to think they might do better in business for themselves. Okay, I know it's your business to shut down operations like ours, but believe me, the way it's goin', it'll blow apart by itself. That'll create a lot more problems than it'll solve. Trust me on this, I know what I'm talkin'."

***

Brendan Grant whistled appreciatively, then shuffled to the next page. Three pages later, he asked in a hushed tone, "This stuff is hot. Where did you get it?"

Galen chuckled, "Sorry, man, you know we can't divulge a source like this one."

"Can't blame an information junkie for trying! I'll enter this into the net and see what pops. I'll let you know as soon as I get anything."

BC grinned evilly, flipped deeper into the stack, and indicated a line. "You might start with this."

The computer jockey stared at the words for a few seconds before he whistled appreciatively. "You have the name of the parent corporation!" Splitting an evaluation between the pair, he grinned. "Do I smell RICO brewing? Wait, no need to answer. Those twin smug glows tell all." Bending back to the keyboard, Brendan happily tapped keys until the pair gathered their coats. "Hey, guys, you aren't going already, are you? Once I get this stuff running I'll have several hours of sitting on my thumbs to look forward to. Can't you stick around a little while?"

BC asked, "What about your on-line stuff?"

"Just got off. Nothing much happening in cyberspace right now, anyway. Bunch of folks asking after you, though. You kind of dropped off the grid when you transferred here. People wanted to know what happened."

BC groused, "Don't have a lot of access to a computer, do I? The one I was using is gathering dust in Chicago, and the only ones I can use are here are at SIHQ. Tried that the other night, and Uncle Joe just about went into orbit."

"Why not buy one? I mean a tablet or something. Yeah, they're kinda pricey and you have to pay for service, but that way, as long as there's access, you can log on from anywhere."

Peale thunked his head against the door frame. "Of course! I'm an idiot. Thanks, Bren — I can't fathom why I didn't I think of it myself."

"From the looks of this, I'd say you've been too busy," Grant said, thumbing through the notes. "By the way, if you're interested, I can give you the locations of a couple places. They have good prices and good technical support after purchase."

Galen pulled a chair over and dropped carefully into it, stretching his legs out in front of him. "Sounds like it's gonna be a while before we head back, so I'm gonna take a load off. Damp weather always makes my legs ache like blazes. Hey, partner, why don't you call Stallings and tell him where we are? We're so late now, a hard copy might be the best protection we can get short of a tank."

BC squealed like a stuck pig, "Me? Why me? You merely annoy him. He *hates* me." He returned Gae's unwavering glower, then acceded wearily, "Oh, all right! I'll ring him up, but I'll also ring Stroud and Taylor. They'll be stopping by the digs tonight, and we'd better let them know of the impending vaporization. Someone will have to inform the next of kin where to scrape up the remains."

Galen grunted, "Sounds like a plan."

Breathing curses on former athletes, BC rooted for his phone, but Brendan proudly slid a paperback-book-sized object from under a pile of printouts and colorful takeout menus. "Use this one. I guarantee it's a secure line. I picked it up at the Buffalo Hamfest last week. You won't *believe* the things this does! It's programmable up to eight hundred numbers, has front and back cameras, apps to track astronomical events, GPS—"

Peale stared at the device in his palm. "Whoa, Bren! That's all real amazing, but what buttons do I press to get it to make an ordinary phone call?"

Galen sat up with a suddenness that startled them both. Waving a garish pink rectangle of card stock, he demanded, "More importantly, what buttons do we press to get these people to deliver this dinner for four to this address?"

FIVE

The Sentry International Transient Agent Hostelry was originally constructed in the mid-nineteen-thirties as an upscale residential hotel. Stepping into the bustling activity of the lobby through the bronze and glass entry, Taylor rubbernecked like he'd never seen it before. For all practical purposes, he hadn't. When he'd entered these doors the previous evening, he had been so dog-tired, anything after leaving the gruesome murder scene was recalled as a gray blur. The foyer was spacious, the charm and style of its origins still clinging to it — at least in the lobby. Some enterprising architect deserved kudos for skillfully melding the necessary modern technology and period decoration. The poor sod was probably sacked instead. He had yet to encounter a bureaucracy that appreciated art in any form.

Did the elegance reach as far as the living quarters? Doubtful. Probably didn't even in the original incarnation; left to the resident's discretion, like as not. Considering other hostels he'd seen, the furnished apartment assigned to his colleagues probably had all the charm of a Motel Six. Maybe less. The lobby's registration desk had been gutted, and fitted with high-tech surveillance monitors. It was there he found Stroud, lounging against the art deco façade, conversing with the one element he remembered from last night's visit. He grinned and called out, "Hey, Elaine! What's a nice girl like you doing in a chickenshit outfit like this?"

The Security Chief rolled her eyes. "I wondered when you were going to get around to noticing me, Detective Taylor. Girion tells me you're headed up to call on the Bobbsey twins."

"Yeah. They're expecting us, but we can wait if they aren't back yet."

Frowning, she said, "They're here. Got in five minutes ago, but don't expect to find them happy and ready to party. Word is that Uncle Joe reamed them thoroughly — twice."

Stroud winced. "Oops. That's not good; any idea what it was about?"

Elaine shook her head. "None. That rarely gets out unless Herr Kapitan wants to make an example of somebody, but from the guys' reaction, it was more unpleasant than usual. Multiply that by a double dose and it ain't pretty."

Glancing at her partner, Stroud saw the goofy expression that said he was preparing to waste a little time on inter-agency relations. Smirking, she pushed away from the counter. "I'll run on up to let them know we're here and see how they're doing."

Taylor sneered amicably. "You mean you'll run on up and see if you can find out what the dressing-down was about."

Sneering back less amicably, she veered away from the elevator, and per habit, hit the stairwell. The stairs emptied at the far end of the hall, and she took two strides toward the apartment before stopping, head tilted quizzically. Angry voices filtered to her, and the loudest was distinctly BC Peale. Interesting. She'd only known him twenty-four hours at best, but even in the face of the royal screw-up at Kennedy, his calm had remained unruffled. What could Stallings say to upset the cool Brit that much? A few steps closer and jumbled sounds resolved into words; she listened without remorse.

***

BC howled, "Twice in one night! *Twice!* Okay, so he's pissed — so am *I*! This ludicrous shit of mandatory debriefing at eight thirty in the morning and mid-afternoon? Why not simply sentence me to ninety minutes in a tanning bed and be done with it?"

Galen's voice was harder to hear, but moving closer, she heard, "At least there's a reason this time. . . ."

"Y'mean other than the kindness of Uncle Joe's heart? All right. I know Colonel Black is only back in town for a short stint and has to board a plane for Washington D.C. before seven. But *he* knows . . . ."

"Yeah. The part that pisses me off is how Stallings is constantly accusing us of going over his head to the Colonel. Neither of us have ever spoken to the man."

"It's a thought, though."

"Uh uh, pard, I haven't tried to pull strings since I signed onto this outfit. I don't intend to start now."

"The big difference there is that you signed on. I was drafted! I've never liked Stallings' type — *ever.* If I hadn't run into so bloody many of them over the years, I'd happily cling to the illusion they only existed in books and bad TV."

"Look, the guy is an asshole — everyone we've met so far agrees to that, but calm down! Taylor and Stroud are gonna be here soon and this doesn't solve anything."

"*Calm* . . . ? Galen, if I don't let off steam here, I swear, I won't be able to help tearing Stallings' throat out next time." An open palm cracked on a tabletop, as Peale continued, "The cretin has my *uncensored* record! He should understand why I work only at night!"

"Maybe the guy is illiterate and can't read the dossier."

A pause, then an unmistakable grin crept into his voice, "Then again, maybe he *does* understand and just has a new Dust Buster he wants to try out."

An exclamation of disgust burst from BC, "GOD! What an awful image!" He chuckled in spite of himself, adding ruefully, "Reminds me of that dream about your mother and the vacuum cleaner. Why ever did you tell me about it?"

Taylor bounded out of the stairwell. "Y'know, Elaine's fun to talk to. Maybe later I'll ask her to dinner or something. Could be she'll ask me—" He broke off in amazement as Girion whirled and shushed him.

Beckoning him nearer, she whispered, "They were having a shouting match about Stallings. I didn't want to interrupt."

"Wanted to hear what they were saying, more like. You only became a detective because it gave you an excuse to be nosy." Grinning malevolently, he brushed past her and rapped on the door.

The sharp raps jolted through Galen like gunshots. Alarmed, he turned to find the vampire similarly paralyzed. The preternatural probing was almost visible, then BC suddenly dropped onto the divan, announcing sourly, "Told you someone would call the cops."

Taylor and Stroud? Had to be. His mind raced to recall what he and BC were saying just before the knock. Tanning beds and Dust Busters. Wonderful. One of these days they'd remember not to yell at times like that. Sure. BC was over two hundred years old, and he hadn't learned yet. That didn't bode well for Galen's learning curve. Hand on the latch, he made an instant decision to admit the anger, but avoid the details. Flinging the door wide, he said, "Oh, good, the cops are here. Officers, please convince this homicidal maniac that killing Stallings isn't justifiable assholicide!"

BC insisted, "It is!"

Arms folded, Girion considered with profound gravity. "Nope. I'm afraid BC has a point. I can even go so far as to say that Captain Brannaugh would support the decision."

Taylor nodded. "Give you an ironclad alibi at the very least." Dropping into an armchair, he added, "Elaine told us about your love trysts before we came up. You got our sympathy. Joe Stallings isn't an easy character to deal with. He's not still on about the press snafu, is he?"

BC said bitterly, "That and . . . well, let's say the words 'Special Needs' are not part of Uncle Joe's vocabulary." Visibly shedding the dark mood, his familiar aplomb returned, as he said, "We've got drinks setups and more types of snack food than I knew existed out in the kitchen. Anyone care for anything?"

Plopping purse and jacket into her partner's lap, Stroud volunteered, "I'll give you a hand. I may not be a very domesticated animal, but I can open chips."

He swept a bow, and held the swinging louvers wide for her to precede him. He then opened an overhead cabinet, displaying a staggering array of bottles.

She blinked. "Holy shit!"

He chuckled. "Don't look at me. These were here when we took possession. We figure the last agents housed here must have been real party animals. Housekeeping's not on the ball, either, but considering the short notice and the fact these were only supposed to be overnight digs, no surprise. We've found the most amazing things under the couch and in the back of the closets." Gesturing toward the table, whose top was crowded with bags from a local grocery, he added,

"We're the coffee, sparkling water and crisps crowd here."

Enthusiastically pouncing on the bags, she dug packages out, exclaiming, "Oh, good. I'm starving, and if I drank anything alcoholic, I'd nod out during the confab. Got any ice?"

Dark blue eyes dancing, he withdrew a huge bag of commercially made ice from the freezer. "Of course we do. I think Galen likes more ice in his glass than he does drink."

As he set a mismatched collection of glassware on the counter, Stroud enjoyed his spare and elegant movements until unexpected guilt prodded her to admit, "We . . . Okay— I — kind of overheard what you and Galen were saying just before we knocked."

He didn't turn, but kept rinsing dusty glasses in the stainless steel sink. Too casually he corrected, "Don't you mean shouting? It would have been difficult to miss unless one were stone deaf, I'd imagine. Good thing we've no neighbors."

Although he gave no outward sign, she knew he was embarrassed and still upset. She understood, she'd feel the same if anyone overheard one of her high volume bitch sessions with Taylor. Nervously, she said, "Look, BC, we don't know each other, and it's really none of my business, but if it helps, Taylor and I know how you and Gae feel. We've had our share of disagreements with higher-ups, too. It seems to be a law of the universe that if you're different, you get flak. If you're *good* and you're different — well, you have to be even better." She screwed her face into a quizzical frown. "I don't think that came out right . . . did it make sense?"

Facing her at last, he laughed. "Yes, it made sense, and

thanks. I apologize. I'm being flip out of self-defense. I've had this sunlight thing for long enough, I should be used to how others react to it by this time. Especially people who don't want to admit such things exist. . . ." Trailing off, he cocked his head and listened to the low buzz from the outer room, then remarked, "Oh, good. Gae has started telling Taylor about what we got tonight."

"Chewed out?"

"Aside from that. We got a fantastic break; seems our news coverage was a blessing in disguise. An old friend from Chicago recognized us and contacted us with some juicy stuff on the Borgia operation."

Oozing interest, she hopped onto the counter, and absently filched chips from the bowl. "Old friend, huh? Was he in a position to have something good to offer?"

Intent upon filling a glass with cola, he answered vaguely, "Could do. His name's Edgar Michalson. Ever heard of him?"

Stroud choked, sprayed masticated corn chip into her hand and squealed, "EDDIE MICHALSON?"

Laughter erupted from the front room. She coughed, covered her mouth and grabbed the glass from him, wheezing, "Holy Mother of God, BC! Don't do that kind of thing to me. You know Eddie Michalson? How?"

BC turned thoughtful as he handed her a paper towel. "That's a long story."

She wiped her face and nodded. "I understand. None of my business."

His intensity stopped her mid-wipe, as he replied simply, "Not right now, anyway." Before she could kick-start her brain for a comeback, he continued, "Y'know we're going to be playing mix and match partners when we get started with the surveillance thing on Michalson and his people. Think maybe you and I could team up for the first salvo?"

After a few beats of continued immobility, Stroud resumed her wiping. "Sure. Why not?"

Grinning, he hoisted her down from the counter and gathered an armload of bowls. She followed bearing more munchies, and found Taylor and Gae hadn't been completely idle. The round dining table had been re-situated under the light in the center of the room. Elbowing aside a stack of thickly stuffed report folders to make room for the food, she said, "That looks weighty."

Galen patted the folders affectionately, "Treat these with respect, Sergeant Girion. This is the collected wit and wisdom of Edgar Michalson with annotation by the noted scholars, Brendan Grant, Byron Peale and Galen Miller."

Lifting eyes from rapt perusal of his copy, Taylor asserted, "It'll never make the New York Times Best Seller list, but cops'll love it."

The next hours murmured past with a comfortable sense of common purpose. Stroud loved this part. It forged a sense of belonging that, even though from a large family, she'd never experienced anywhere else. This sense of fraternity was one of the attractions that police work held for her.

A staff psychologist once postulated that her many failures with long-term relations stemmed from the lack of affection in her family background and the double-edged sword of desiring affection, yet not knowing how to return it. The theory went that, in joining the police force, she achieved a high level of male companionship with few of the normal risks. The normal (and more personal risks) were replaced with risks on a professional level. He'd then gone on to ruin the session by blatantly suggesting she'd do better to have a relationship with a *different* type of professional, one better equipped to deal with her underlying difficulties. Rat's ass. Anyway, his observations struck uncomfortably close to the mark and she found them popping up in her mind at odd times. In fact, she was having difficulty with them now.

Her eyes slid to where BC leaned over his notes, long fingers twined in the thick hair now escaping the ponytail he'd worried through their conference. The instant attraction she'd felt for him was bewildering. Yes, he was handsome, exotic and a cop; three things guaranteed to get her attention, but this was unlike anything she'd experienced before.

Arching his back with a small groan, the object of her scrutiny cradled his coffee mug between his hands and caught her looking. He smiled at her, then scowled at the mug. "It's gone cold again. I tend to forget it's there while we're working." Standing, he added, "Suppose I better trot back and warm it up again. Anyone want anything while I'm out there?"

Receiving negatives, he ducked through the swinging doors and Stroud heard his movements as he popped the coffee into the microwave for the fourth time that night. Odd. He spent more time with his hands wrapped around the cup than actually drinking from it. As a matter of fact, she couldn't remember him taking a drink at all. He sipped at it, yes, but the level of the liquid didn't drop measurably. Oh well, as slim as he was, he was probably one of those people who governed their intake no matter what the food or drink was. She'd have to use her ski machine less if she adopted that philosophy. Nah. She liked pizza too much.

BC returned with his reheated mug, tired eyes raking the

paper-strewn table. "Honestly, if I'd known how much paperwork this kind of job entailed, Gae, I'd have packed up and escaped to Europe as soon as you tried to recruit me."

Galen snorted. "Why do you think I didn't tell you? Anyway, you'll like it better when you get your toy computer. I know you: as long as you have a keyboard in front of you, you're a happy camper."

Stroud, thumbed through her folder. "I'm a pretty happy camper now, but it's strange there *still* isn't much about the Big Cheese. The stuff on Isendamer is fantastic, especially in light of the murders this ties her to. The tacit admissions from Michalson are almost as valuable, but — where's the main guy? As the head of Este Corporation, he has to be playing a role other than signing paychecks and death warrants."

A shadow flitted across Peale's face, unnoticed by any but Taylor, who was reaching for the almost empty ginger ale. As he watched, the look hardened to something entirely different as the Englishman muttered, "He's expert at signing death warrants."

Brows knit ominously, Galen added, "The bastard's even better at being invisible. Even Seattle's Wunderkind is having a hard time with this one. Brendan said he'd asked for a couple more days to search, but it looks bad.

"This whole thing started with simply trying to find out who this guy was. For a while, we thought it was a group of people using one name. We know better now; we've seen the creep in the too-solid flesh, but aside than that we have zip.

"What we know isn't much and it goes something like this: he is currently residing at an unknown location in

Canada, stands about five-seven, has a stocky build, black hair with a funny white streak on one side. He appears to be an Italian national and Borgia may well be his family name. He killed one close friend, disposed of one looney tune, and lots of people are very afraid of him. I think I'm one of them, but I still want a piece of him when we nail him."

Stroud looked to the other agent, who stared into his cooling coffee as if the aromatic depths were a magic pool holding all the answers. She'd never seen anyone so somber. The depth of Gae's wrath and the voluble BC's reticence tipped it. The NYPD contingent would do a little poking around on their own before they met again. Taylor's preoccupation promised there'd be no arm-twisting needed for him to go along. Topping off her flavored mineral water, she returned to her open notes.

***

Carrying two bedewed bottles of Australian lager, Taylor emerged from the bomb crater identified as his kitchen by the vaguely recognizable hulks of stove, refrigerator and mound of dishes marking the location of the sink. Plunking a bottle absently on the refuse-strewn end table, he paced energetically, the unconscious finger-combing of his wild mane doing little to improve its chaotic waves.

Stroud burrowed into the comfortable couch, sipped the cold brew, and blissfully watched the familiar mannerism. Strange how utterly at home she felt in this place that was by turns cluttered and scrupulously clean depending on his mood and the workload. Little things like putting dishes in the dishwasher and picking up dirty socks took a back seat to worrying every piece of information out of every piece of evidence connected with a particular crime. Once the case was solved or otherwise put to bed, Taylor emerged from his thought-world and noticed the mess with horror. He then embarked on a whirlwind of cleaning jokingly referred to as a 'Tidy Wave.'

The unusually high level of clutter bore mute testimony to the unbroken chain of priority cases dropped on their plate lately. The resident genius hadn't had time to come out of his clouds and notice the mess. They'd been promised leave once the SI operation was closed, but that was a familiar song, and one that assumed they'd *close* the SI case.

It didn't require much deduction to see she'd been forgotten. At that moment, Tyler Taylor'd be hard pressed to name the planet he was on. She swigged again from the bottle and grimaced. Lager might be her partner's beverage of choice, but as she told BC, alcohol after a hard day made her sleepy. Yawning hugely, she attempted to deposit the beer on the coffee table, but the surface was covered with identical empties.

Resigned, she collected bottles and clinked into the kitchen, reflecting on Taylor's preference for bottles and scorn for cans unless nothing else was available. Then he drank with a vague air of distrust, like the aluminum might mysteriously pollute the contents. With quick, sure movements, she drew a trash bag from the box under the sink and chucked in the detritus of more weeks than she wanted to count. Taylor would get his shorts in a twist that she'd cleaned up, but this looked to be a strong coffee session and she was determined to find the coffeemaker.

An hour later, she emerged, the doors swinging closed on the humming dishwasher's second run of the evening. She stood behind where Taylor bent over the computer keyboard. After several brow-furrowed minutes trying to decipher the techno-babble flashing across the screen, she shrugged and plunked a mug of steaming black coffee onto the paper-strewn desk by his elbow. She said, "Taylor, you didn't bring me over here to clean your kitchen. Would you mind talking to me and telling me what we're doing? I think it's only fair since all I can make out on that screen is that you're downloading something from SINet and when they drag you away for hacking into their system, they'll take me with you."

He stretched, noticed the hot drink, and sipped it gratefully. "I am not currently Tyler Taylor, I am Byron Peale. I logged onto the SINet using his handle — I've heard it from Prometheus often enough. I was a little worried about the password, but '1984 Harley' did the trick. He has amazingly high clearance for a new agent."

"He'll be pissed."

"How will he know? I haven't messed with his e-mail and I've strictly avoided doing a newscan. Unless Brendan is on, and I doubt even *he* will be on-line at this insane hour, BC won't notice an extra logon."

"Okay. Good on the what, now let's work on the why. I have an idea, but tell me what's cooking in your head."

He stared at the rapidly flowing data until she feared he'd hypnotized himself. Just before she resorted to pinching him, he said, "Personally, I have good feelings about both BC and Gae. They're good cops — we know that from their record and the way they work together — but they aren't telling all they know."

Grunting a graceful assent around a mouthful of coffee, Stroud agreed, "Don't have to be a genius to see how carefully they pick their words, but would we do differently in their place?

"Probably not. They don't know any more about us

than we do about them, so there's no reason they should trust us. Nevertheless, things are hotting up all around us, otherwise Michalson would *never* have contacted cops for a meet." He shook his head. "I get the uncomfortable feeling that time is getting real short on something big. If we wait for the guys to learn they can trust us . . . well . . . we need to get it ourselves before the lid blows off into our faces." The machine beeped happily and he tapped more keys, initiating another cascade of data, then mused aloud, "I believe Brendan in how hard it will be to find anything on Borgia, so it would be futile to start there. I'm trying to sneak in the back way by tracking what Galen and BC did in Chicago and using Michalson and Isendamer for flag strings."

She grinned. "Sure, Dr. Taylor. What ever the hell *that* means."

"It means we need more coffee . . . what did you say about the kitchen?"

***

She was becoming accustomed to the music. She still didn't *like* all of it, but neither did Byron or Jump. This piece drifting up from the smoky club below was very pleasant, though, and one of the pieces she liked best. Come to think of it, the last one was, too. Ah, the gentle machinations of Jump Veron were revealed. Such a benign little man, and so very different from the one she and Jasmine sought tonight. So many new friends. Like Byron, she enjoyed being around people, but for so long, she'd closed herself off from their society. Too long. She'd forgotten how much she enjoyed working with others. Once again, Mother was right: she kept to herself too much. Once Francesco was sorted out, she'd visit her mother in Ireland. The standing invitation was getting a smidge dusty, but no less sincere.

Skeptical when Jump first proposed it, she was now grateful for Jasmine's assistance. At first, Francesco's severe injuries and emotional turmoil brought his defenses to a nadir. Later, as his retreat to his northern wilderness compound calmed and healed body and soul, it became harder and harder to scry him. Then, when Captain Nelson moved Byron to New York and increased the geographic distance between fledgling and sire, Francesco regained strength nightly, making Jasmine's added power *very* necessary.

Frowns drew coppery brows into a hard line. Francesco's regained power wasn't her only complaint against the reassignment. She'd struggled to find Byron again, and being separated arbitrarily grated, making it difficult to cope with being cooped up. At least he phoned regularly. Last night, he'd chattered like a child with a new toy about a 'big break' he and Galen had gotten. She didn't pretend or particularly want to understand this agent business, but she enjoyed his enthusiasm. They'd shared like that when they were lovers. . . .

Thrusting those thoughts aside, she prepared the braziers for her spell. She'd think about Byron later. Her current concern was Francesco. With his strength returning, she needed all her concentration to spy on him, and was determined to succeed. The others thought her afraid of him — and she was. She'd be a fool not to be, but far above fear blazed anger. At what he'd done. At what he'd tried to do. Anger was a flawed emotion and the strongest spells were cast in an absence of emotion, but she was unable to purge herself of it. Instead, she made her anger a conduit; a dart with which to seek out her target and pin the spell to him. It was irrational for Francesco to conclude she and Byron were colluding against him and his retaliation was extreme, to say the least. He wasn't thinking with his usual clarity. Why, when he'd locked her in those humiliating stocks, he was *surprised* she refused to speak to him. His erratic behavior was troubling. The whole affair was.

More troubling was that *both* Francesco and Byron showed themselves to be far more powerful than she'd suspected. Byron shouldn't have been able to defy his sire's will as he had. The thrall Francesco exerted was so powerful she'd felt it even on the floor above. Such a pull should have resulted in more than a momentary and quickly quashed urge to assist his injured sire. Byron walked away from it. Jump joked about it, saying Byron worked under what he called the 'Gilligan Effect': if he believed he could do something, his ability to do same increased exponentially.

She could sense Jasmine growing restless. Her new friend was right. It was time to begin. Leaning forward, she lit the incense and fanned it into the air around them. Murmuring in her birth tongue, the incantation to begin the scrying contained the unorthodox phrase, "Watch yerself, Francesco, I'm comin' for ye."

***

The stag's body was cooling rapidly. Soon, the other predators and the scavengers would move in. He sensed them now, hovering at the edges of the kill site.

Francesco Borgia caressed the magnificent beast a final time before he rose to his feet. It had been a hard chase and a good kill but . . . something was lacking. Like the elk the previous night, the bloodmeal helped, but nowhere near as much as the human kill that first night. True, his injuries were much improved compared to then, so the regeneration wasn't as obvious, but the blood of beasts simply didn't seem as restorative as the blood of men.

Spreading his hands into the brilliant moonlight, he examined them critically. Yes. There was healing taking place. He could almost see it happening, but it was taking so long. Much longer than anything had ever before. He wondered how Byron was faring—

Abruptly he and his scion were face-to-face again, the two of them locked in a desperate struggle. Out of nowhere, something dark splashed across them both, the burning emulsion spattering him and his scion's handsome face as well. Black and red against ivory— A wave of dizziness overtook him and he gripped a tree to steady himself, the suddenness of his grasp shattering bark beneath his hand.

After a moment, the pine forest stopped spinning and he straightened with difficulty. Fury as hot as the clinging potion surged in place of the previous vertigo. This was all Byron's fault. It was the boy's associates who got in the way of what was his right as sire to take. Maeve deserved a good deal of blame, too. Had she not bound him to her wrong-headed request, he would have taken the boy from the first. He could have trained him — molded him. Taught him to be the predator he should be.

No. He squared his shoulders and stood straighter. He would not go down that path. It was senseless to rail against that which he could not change. Not at present, anyway. That path led only to madness and unreasoning anger. Now was the time to heal and to find balance again. There would be ample time to reclaim that which was his right. He glanced at the sky. His time this night was waning, though; dawn would break soon. Already fingers of gray combed the eastern horizon. Turning, he sprinted toward the compound and his hidden sleeping chamber.

***

The accordioned plastic ink injector burbled as black bubbles oozed around the steel needle and burst, adding another layer of sooty freckles to her already besmirched hand. Stroud swore fluently and dropped the refilled printer cartridge onto the stained wads of paper toweling littering the tabletop. Vigorously scrubbing her fingers with a moist towel, she exclaimed, "The damned thing is as full as I'm going to get it, Taylor. I still don't see why you insisted on printing all this stuff out. It's thicker than the Manhattan phone book!"

Shuffling the papers, the blond man answered absently, "It's easier to read this way, and you can take the copy home while I keep the files." Abruptly, he lifted a still-damp sheet and said, "Hey, look at this! The Vampire Vigilante's activities were a lot more extensive than even the tabloids knew."

"Yeah, I saw that. I also saw the SI operatives in Chicago were calling him the Lake Shore Robin Hood and why. That donation to the Policeman's Benevolent fund was truly warped. I loved it!"

"Yeah, me, too. Hmmm. From the forensic reports on the victims, it's easy to see where they came up with the vampire thing."

"That *is* an awful lot of blood unaccounted for. I wonder where it went?" She gulped queasily. "You don't suppose the guy actually *drank* it, do you?"

"This from the woman who likes her steaks rare enough to moo. Seriously, though, stranger things have happened. There are a lot of odd beliefs about blood, even in so-called civilized circles. I heard of one case—"

She interrupted, "I don't want to hear about that right now. It's late and we've got enough to do without delving into your enormous store of Strange-But-True Tales of Forensic Medicine. Save it for the station, when you can gross out Sergei and the others."

Taylor leered. He had much better stories to gross out Detective Petrovich with. People with delicate sensibilities didn't belong on a homicide squad, but they did provide much-needed amusement in a job devoid of humor. He skimmed Galen's interminable accounts of stakeout attempts and sympathized. Police work mostly consisted of that stuff. The only place stakeouts had any glamour was on TV. In reality, they were the definition of boredom. He flipped forward in the document, then said, "Things picked up when BC joined the investigation. Looks like it was really Galen who recruited him, too. Roughly the same time the good material starts surfacing, BC goes from 'informant' to 'Special Agent Peale.'"

Stroud mused, "That explains a couple of his comments about being drafted when he was yelling about Stallings."

"That was before I got there."

"Yeah. Y'know, I can't get some of the things he said out of my head — they were very odd. Then again, he was *really* mad. If someone overheard one of our bouts, they'd be pretty baffled, too." She paused as another thing struck her. "He was also bitching about his medical files. Are they here? Maybe you can make something out of them about this light thing he has."

"You just want to make sure you won't catch anything if you go into a clinch on tomorrow night's stakeout."

Snarling with exaggerated venom, she lobbed a crumpled

page at him. "Creep. I brought it up because BC seemed to think it was important."

"Okay! We don't have them because I couldn't get into the medical section. It was in an entirely different location and I don't think Special Agent White Fang has the clearance for *that*. We'd need Prometheus himself to get in the SI medical base. I got a lot of good tips picking his brain the other night, but this is his area of expertise, not mine." Noting her frown, he added, "As far as I can see, the closest we can get to that is the litany of injuries those two have incurred in the line of duty."

"A bunch, huh?"

"Let's say they appear to be accident prone. Says here they were in the lakeside weapons cache explosion earlier this year."

"*In* it? No wonder Gae had that reaction to Rattner."

Taylor nodded. "He got pretty banged up and BC dragged him out of it." He flipped more pages. "OUCH! Looks like BC took a faceful of glass splinters while extracting a material witness — one Ms. Maeve Donal — from Borgia's evil clutches."

Stroud cringed in sympathy. "SI must have good doctors. There isn't a mark on him now! When did this happen?"

Taylor looked at the dates, then furrowing his brow, leafed back for re-read. Curiosity aroused, Stroud leaned forward in expectation. When Taylor got that look, it meant something wasn't computing in the professor's brain. A goodly number of their big breaks were preceded by this behavior.

She demanded impatiently, "You've found something. What is it?"

Mutely, Taylor handed her the sheets and pointed out

two lines in the text. "This can't be right, Taylor. If it were, he'd still have cuts healing, especially this one across the forehead . . . the date must have been recorded wrong."

"Maybe. It happens." He grinned suddenly. "Maybe you and BC can compare scars to relieve boredom. From the looks of this, it could be a close contest."

Smacking the hefty printout into his chest, she announced, "Okay, that's the last innuendo I have to allow according to our partnership agreement. I'm going home alone and I'm going to go to sleep in a cozy bed and pretend that I'm a normal person."

He followed her to the door. "No way! That was a clear sexual jibe — I still have at least three innuendos left for the twenty-four hour period."

His smile evaporated as he flipped the latch behind her. He powered up the monitor, and scrolled through the glowing words. Jokes aside, something about the whole mess troubled him. He felt there was a crucial piece of data missing that, when provided, would make all the other pieces snap together into a cohesive picture. After another hour of searching, that key remained elusive.

Clearly, the discrepancy centered on Peale. It wasn't the so-called allergy, although it did pique Taylor's interest. He'd give a lot to get into the medical files, but he didn't feel that was where the answer lay. It wasn't the man himself or the mutual spontaneous attraction between BC Peale and the vivacious Sgt. Girion, either. That was worrisome, and Stroud *did* pick some real losers, but BC read as an okay guy.

No. He kept coming back to where Peale officially joined Sentry; curiously, it was around this time that the Lake Shore Robin Hood's activities ceased. When the fact that Galen suddenly started making progress with Peale's assistance without using drastically different tactics was factored in, it made a very unbalanced equation.

Could BC have been a Borgia operative who switched sides? That would explain knowing Michalson, but what was the connection with the Vampire Vigilante? No, that didn't work. Borgia was an appallingly heartless and unscrupulous character. Peale didn't fit the profile for a Borgia employee — especially one high up enough to be able to render such assistance to SI.

Besides, the man harbored a fierce hatred for Signor Borgia. So did Miller. Was it because their friend Lt. Marquez was attacked and killed by Borgia himself in Miller's own apartment? That was enough, but BC's reactions included horror and — something else he couldn't put a name to. The man actually went paler at the mention of the druglord's name and for Peale, that was going some.

Realizing with a start that he'd read the same paragraph three times and didn't understand a single word, he concluded he was tired. Scrubbing the back of his neck with his palms and shutting down the system, he turned to see the sun streaming through his unshaded windows. He'd lost track of time while he was reading. Again.

He stood, turned off the ineffectual desk light and stretched. Had he reached any conclusions? Sort of. It was hardly scientific, but he had confidence in both of their new colleagues. Stroud did, too, or she would never have kibitzed with Peale in the kitchen like she did tonight. Glancing out the window at the lightening sky, he amended, *Last night.*

Most of the time, he trusted her people-sense better than

his own. Deftly drawing the blinds to shut out the rising sun, he wandered off in search of his bed. Last time he'd seen it, it was somewhere in the vicinity of that big pile of newspapers. He was really going to have to clean the place up soon.

***

Sun streamed in the window at the SI hostelry, too, and Peale had gone down over an hour ago. Galen, though, wasn't ready to sleep. He fretfully paced the confines of the tiny living room several more times, then snatched up his cell phone and punched in his mother's number. It was early in Chicago, but he suspected she'd have been up for quite a while.

"Galen! I'm so glad to hear from you, but somethin' tells me you haven't been to bed yet, so there must be somethin' wrong."

Galen cradled his forehead in his hand, grateful that his mother couldn't see how tired he really was. He'd have a cup of her herbal sleeping concoction steaming in front of him in a flash. "Right as usual. I've been trying to call Fiona on location in Tunisia and I keep getting shunted aside by some dense girl whose first language is *not* English. My phone bill's gonna look like the national debt figures at this rate. Is Fi mad at me for going public with Sentry and using this ditz as a firewall or something? Won't even let me talk to the kids and I know there aren't any messages being taken. Besides, what I need to talk to Fi about isn't the kind of stuff Joe Stallings will appreciate being put onto a message pad."

"No, Honey, she's not angry, she's just busy. I got a letter from her yesterday. You probably got one, too, if your mail ever catches up with you. She been callin' this the 'Movie From Hell.' Nothin' is goin' accordin' to plan and the production is over time and over budget. What do you bet she gave a do not disturb order that this assistant has taken too literally?"

"That's probably it, and I'm sorry to hear she's having trouble. She had such high hopes for this shoot. Anyway, I've been trying to let her know about the move to New York. I suppose I could write her, but I'd rather tell her. Like I said, Stallings has a thing about written information."

Jasmine gasped, "You thinkin' you won't be back home before she finishes? How long they plannin' to keep you there?"

"Wish I knew, Mama. This case has been stop-start from the beginning, and hasn't changed since we got here."

"There's somethin' else botherin' you, child. What is it?"

He didn't want to answer. It made him feel like a five-year-old running to mamma about a schoolyard bully, but it came bubbling out, anyway. "It's this Stallings thing. He doesn't believe in vampires and goes out of his way to tick BC off, then I'm caught in the crossfire. BC's in a foul mood because of Uncle Joe and Stallings hates me because he sees me as taking up for my mentally ill partner. Worst of all, we were supposed to be reporting directly to Colonel Black when we got here, but he's been busy abroad. . . . Sorry. I'm too tired. I ought to just let you go and hit the bed."

"I know you're tired, but this is serious. Augustine has been worried for both of you, and that worries me. It isn't good if you two are fightin'."

"Not exactly fighting, but I guess we're both prickly. It could be worse, though. I think if BC didn't have his family at Belridge to call and let off steam, I wouldn't want to be in the same city with him, let alone the same apartment. Not that he's telling them what's going on. Talking to his family just seems to calm him somehow — especially Miriam."

"Have you talked to that Nelson boy about any of this?"

"No way. While I'm here in New York, I'm strictly out of his jurisdiction. Besides, he has enough to worry about with Borgia's Chicago operation blowing itself apart on a semi daily-basis. Mick's death . . . it was God's grace Emily Hu was there to step into the gap. . . ."

He paused and Jasmine Miller leapt into the opening, "You got that herb tea I sent you?"

Here it came. "Yes, Mama."

"Good. You brew a cup and go to bed. The tea will help you relax. You promise me you'll do it."

"Okay, I'll do it, Mama."

SIX

Two identical red vinyl folders on the desks bore identical labels reading *Project Smokehouse* met Galen Miller as he entered the small office assigned to him and Peale. Tossing his jacket over the back of his chair, he spun the folder closest to him around and opened it. Inside were re-ordered and retyped copies of Eddie Michalson's information from the previous night. *"You can take the man out of the CIA, but you can't take the CIA out of the man."*

He dropped into the chair and grew serious. Yeah, Stallings loved melodrama, but in reality, Borgia did have a lot of spies in a lot of places, and nobody knew where. Yet. Code names were real cloak and dagger stuff, but if cloak and dagger kept Eddie — oops *Smokey* — safe for a while, he was all for it. They needed to keep close tabs on Michalson and everybody else on that list. If anybody hiccuped, SI wanted documentation. That was the sad truth of it. Unfortunately, when this was suggested to Eddie, the conversation rapidly devolved into an argument. Didn't like it. Didn't want it. Wouldn't put up with having the cops hiding under his bed. Tough. This was way too important for a hands-off approach. Eddie had painted a target on his back. No way would they let him stand at the end of the shooting range without some kind of protection.

He skimmed the data, satisfying himself that it was all

there. It was maybe a little drier for the translation, but they could live with that. The telephone on BC's desk buzzed. Puzzled, Galen hesitated a moment before stretching across to answer it, "Sentry International. Special Agent Miller speaking."

"I almost didn't recognize you, Gae. Won't they let you answer 'Yello' on company time?"

"Miriam!" Miriam Peale was one of Byron's favorite "cousins" among the current crop of Peales; now he understood why his partner's extension rang. The chair creaked dangerously as he reclined. "I'm real glad to hear from you. BC said he gave you the new office number."

"He did." She hesitated, then said, "I was calling now because I knew he'd still be down for the day. How is he, Galen — I mean really?"

"I don't—"

"Don't tell me you don't know what I mean. Both of you have been going through a rough patch lately and I'm not just talking about poor Lt. Marquez. Byron won't to talk about it, I was hoping you would."

Galen sighed, leaned elbows on the desktop and worried his close-cropped hair as Miriam continued, "Look, Byron called me from a crime scene at three a.m. to warn me about an upcoming news story. He sounded tired and distressed then and you've *both* sounded strained since. Everything I saw on the news looked so horrible. Please, I need to know. Did you get in a lot of trouble?"

He sighed and shook his head against his hand. "Yeah. We got our heads snapped off pretty good, but it wasn't anywhere near as bad as it could have been. Look, Miriam, it isn't that I don't want to talk about it. I don't like doing it over the phone — even a secure line."

"Fine. Tell me over dinner, then."

"What?"

"I'm in New York. I flew in this morning on a buying trip for the Peale Galleries."

"Really? BC didn't tell me you were coming."

"That's because he didn't know. I wanted to surprise you boys and it sounds like I succeeded. I hope it's a pleasant one."

Several minutes later, he sat staring through the blotter, wearing a bemused expression. Maybe the day was going to turn out pretty good, after all. With Miriam here, Peale's mood was bound to be better.

Now if they could just do something about Francesco Borgia. They *all* owed that rat's assed bastard a debt of grief. BC more than most. Miller couldn't come close to understanding what his partner was feeling, but it must be profound and painfully ambivalent. BC loved being a vampire. He'd partied through the centuries, making friends, making music and enjoying the hell out of unlife. All that changed when he'd learned who his sire was. Since then, a more troubled side of his nature had become decidedly pronounced. He wasn't suicidal. They wouldn't have to put him on sun lamp watch or anything like that, but he was nowhere near as carefree as when Galen first met him.

Reaching across the desks again, he snagged BC's prized possession, the photograph of the present-day Peale family. Cradling it, he regarded the oval face of Miriam Peale with speculation. Her unannounced arrival gladdened him more than he'd have credited. Maybe she'd be the remedy for the black mood *both* of them were struggling with.

***

Joe Stallings hovered in the hallway. The raw emotion flashing across Special Agent Miller's face since the telephone call ended made him feel voyeuristic. Opposed as he was to personal calls at the office, he'd ignore this one. After all, Special Agents Miller and Peale had just dropped what promised to be a major coup for SINY and his SpecOps corps on his plate. Maybe, those agents were originally SIChi property, but they were *his* people now.

On the one hand, though, Michalson's intel was deeply disturbing, especially the revelation that there was at least one mole in his own garden. Secrecy became even more important in light of that. The one up side was that it gave extra weight to his request for wiretaps on the principals. Those requests had been granted in record time. The downside was that it posed problems in selecting the surveillance teams through normal channels. To compensate, he'd shrouded the whole operation in heavy black and hand-selected the teams assigned to the targets on Michalson's list. Correction. *Smokey's* list. Let his colleagues poke fun at his covert procedures, but anything he could do to throw a wall around his most important informant in the history of the office was going to be utilized. Now, if said informant would stop kicking and screaming, everything would be good to go.

Smokey's refusal was exactly why he was hovering outside this particular cubicle at this particular time. He'd already delivered assignments to the rest of his handpicked agents; now he was planning to personally bestow the plum assignments on his new team. They'd be responsible for the top names on the list, Eddie Michalson (Smokey) and Lance Baer (Boo Boo). He smiled remembering how Lance Baer's last name had inspired the code names, his private bit of humor. He figured if Smokey would tolerate anyone's assistance, he'd tolerate Special Agents Miller and Peale's. After all, they were the ones he'd first contacted.

His smile broadened. They now had enough evidence to justify property seizures! That satisfaction almost reconciled him to the sight of the empty chair at the desk opposite Miller's. Almost, but not quite. Smile vanishing, he cleared his throat and stepped into the room. "Where's Peale? Colonel Black is expecting you both in his office in ten minutes — didn't you two understand his flight was rescheduled?"

The previously mobile face went deliberately blank as the bulky man leaned back in the chair to regard his commanding officer. "We understood it, sir, but Peale's not here because the sun's still up. Captain, not to be bullheaded, but I know for a fact that they sent you the whole medical workup on him. The reason for his not being available in daylight hours was there."

Stallings fidgeted, then asked in a hushed voice as if he was uttering something obscene, "Miller, you can't possibly expect anyone in the twenty-first century to believe that your partner is a . . . *vampire?*"

"Yes, sir, I do, and not because it would humor BC or me, but because it's true. It's also not because it would make working together easier — although it would. I understand the difficulty. BC does, too. Two hundred years ago, he didn't believe in vampires either. Maybe there's something you'd find convincing?"

Miller's sincerity was unmistakable and Stallings was too taken aback for a reply. Galen continued thoughtfully, "Maybe if you saw him rise for the night?"

Unreasonably chilled by the suggestion, Captain Stallings

dropped a thin sheaf of papers on the desk. "We can discuss this at another time, Miller. These are your new orders. There's also an update on the case status. You'll probably have time to skim them before you go up to meet with the Colonel in his office."

Galen sighed imperceptibly. "Sure thing, sir. I'll get right on it."

***

"I hope you won't be insulted if I admit that I never saw you play. I never was much of a contact sports fan. Golf and tennis were always more my speed."

A grin split the nonetheless familiar face as Galen Miller firmly shook Colonel Black's hand. "Actually, sir, that comes as a relief. You have no idea how often people want to relive moments from a game that they remember better than I do. Half the time I was too busy with a million other things to pay attention like the folks in their living rooms could."

Miller seated himself and Black was amused to note how the big leather armchair suddenly seemed miniaturized. "I've known Jim Nelson for years, and he assures me you're one of the all time greats — and he means more than football." Not allowing the sudden flush to become words of deprecation, he continued, "I knew Mick Marquez, too. I want to let you and Peale know how sorry I am; it was a horrible loss. It must be especially hard on Peale for a number of reasons. He's had to have suffered so many losses through his time. . . . How's he taking it?"

The Special Agent looked thoughtful, then said, "He says it's something you never get used to. I guess if you ever do, there's something wrong with you. He took Mick's death pretty hard. The circumstances . . . well, there's more than a little guilt there, sir."

"Guilt? Why?" The distinguished face beneath the silvery hair held confusion. "Because his sire was the killer? That's senseless. I understand he did all he could to prevent it, even to the point of endangering himself."

The big man visibly expanded as he relaxed. "BC's gonna be relieved to hear that. We were afraid we were gonna have the same trouble—" He broke off with a start. "Forget I said that, sir. Please don't think I'm complaining."

"Not a problem, Agent Miller. I'm already aware of what Joe Stallings thinks." Black waved his concern away. "Hardheadedness can be a strength or a weakness — in this instance, it's a weakness and one Joe will come to regret."

As the agent relaxed again, he continued. "That plays into the reason I pushed a meeting with you two tonight. I wanted to reassure you that I have no complaints with either of you. The work you've done so far is impressive." He looked thoughtful as he added, "I've known Jim Nelson for a long time. If he tells me one of his special agents is an authentic vampire, I believe it. It never occurred to me that Joe's doubts would cause so much trouble. It should have, and in light of that, I'm more sorry than ever I have to leave before he arrives tonight. Please assure him he has my support. I'm looking forward to meeting him. The background data Jim sent indicates a truly remarkable character."

The corner of Miller's mouth quirked. "He's a character, all right."

Black chuckled and leafed through the thick pile of papers crowned with the *Operation Smokehouse* folder. "Looks like I'm going to spend the flight reading; too bad it isn't a longer one. I won't have much time for reading when

I hit DC." Pausing over a page, he observed, "It must have been a tremendous shock to find that Francesco Borgia was his sire after knowing nothing of it for so many years. How is he dealing with that?"

"He's a little touchy about it, but he's okay."

"If it were me I think I'd be more than 'a little touchy.'"

It was clear, Miller was choosing his words with care. Understandable. No agent worth his salt wanted to throw his partner under the bus.

At length, Miller said, "I'm not going to deny that he was real crazy at first, Sir. Completely batshit panic crazy. I think he's managed to slide it to a back burner for now until he can figure out how to come to grips with it. He can be pragmatic about that kind of stuff, if you give him time."

"I see. Borgia doesn't seem to be taking it as calmly. How is this affecting the investigation?"

Miller paused again, but this time Black could almost see the data being evaluated before he allowed, "From what Michalson said, the jury's still out as to whether Borgia himself knows the answer to that one. Right now, he seems to be simply reacting."

"What about this business about Borgia wanting Peale to act as a spy in SI? Mind you," he said hurriedly, "I don't *suspect* Peale. I simply want to know if we have to worry about further approaches."

To his surprise, the big man grinned happily. "We had a recorder going through the parabolic mike when that hit the fan. BC was madder than a Sox fan when the Cubs win! You oughta get a copy of it, it's great. I thought he was gonna jump the guy right then and there. The — uh — incident with the launch brought an abrupt end to the meeting. But no, I don't think even Borgia would mistake that answer for anything other than an unequivocal no thank you."

Black winced at the oblique mention of Maeve Donal and silently thanked his lucky stars she'd remained in Chicago. He liked Jim Nelson, but better Nelson than himself dealing with that particular wild card. He wanted to start small — like getting used to a vampire before moving on to witches with explosive tempers.

Moving to safer topics, Colonel Black lifted the *Operation Smokehouse* folder and said, "Getting our friend to turn informant was a real feather in your caps. The information he's given us already has brought us ahead light years. Agencies all over the globe are going to turn back flips for this!" His brow furrowed as he continued, "It's worrying, though, that he told you there were Borgia people in the SINY offices. We knew there were leaks; that kind of thing happens everywhere. It can't be helped. But an actual spy network . . . I'm impressed they couldn't get anyone into the Chicago offices."

The celebrated face clouded. "We're new there, give us time."

Black glanced out the window. As much to break the thick silence as for information, he asked, "Will Peale be here soon?"

"I doubt it," he replied. "He had a couple errands he needed to run before he came in — and as far as he knew, he wanted to avoid this meeting. He's very good at avoiding unpleasant things. I tried texting him to let him know it's cool, but I suspect he has his phone turned off."

Nodding, the Colonel switched subjects again. "How are your accommodations at the hostelry? That's a fairly new undertaking for us. I understand there have been a few glitches?"

"Can't complain," Miller shrugged. "We were only supposed to be overnight guests, so the apartment we got was pretty bare of equipment. Since the thing at the airport blew the hell out of any hope of cover, we've put in requests for a few things, but . . . I'm afraid Special Agents are considered prima donnas as a whole by the regular folk. As *visiting* Special Agents, we're worse. We're sort of on the bottom of the *bottom* of the priority list."

Black bent to scribble a note. "I'm aware of that problem, too. It's an aspect of the usual interdepartmental jealousies found anywhere. If someone could find a way to neutralize that, they'd have businesses worldwide beating the door down."

Galen chuckled. "To quote Detective Sgt. Taylor, 'If ya got people ya got assholes.' Like I said, we aren't complaining. The suite is nice — especially considering all the extra shit with the inside room they had to whip up for Peale on such short notice. They did great there."

"I'm glad you mentioned the detectives. It was Joe Stallings idea to tap those two for liaison officers. I don't know if they've told you, but they were approached for recruitment right after we were chartered here in the states. Dr. Taylor was . . . shall we say, especially negative. Joe is still smarting. It might cheer you to know it shocked the blazes out of him when you four hit it off."

"Two of us especially. I think Girion and Peale are working up quite a chemistry," Miller said.

"Oh? Does she know about his condition?"

"No, and I think it bothers him that he can't be up front about it. He admits it isn't prudent to say anything until we've worked together a while, though."

"Be careful. In my opinion, those two are the best

damned detectives working on the force today. They'll figure it out on their own soon enough — bizarre nature of the concept notwithstanding."

Handing Miller the note he'd written, he said, "Give this to Gilly on the way out. She'll make sure you have your requisitions filled by tomorrow. I've put a priority on a land line and an answering machine. You two need a message base. Peale can check it as soon as he rises."

They stood together. Brian Black was a tall man; Miller towered over him. Black said, "I've got to run, now. With the moles in our front yard, perhaps we'd better put a hold on further communication until I get back." He hefted the massive sheaf of text, adding, "Besides, I'm not *that* fast a reader and this has the look of a *War and Peace* experience."

Galen smiled, his hand engulfing his chief's. "You think it's bad to read, you shoulda lived it!"

***

"If you're practicing stealth, partner, get rid of all that leather and lose the chains off the boots. I heard you creaking all the way up the hall."

BC Peale entered the room warily. "Glad to see you're in one piece. What did the Lord High Executioner want? To further correct the aberrant thinking of us poor deluded peons?"

Galen laughed. "Nothing like that. The Colonel just wanted to go over the Michalson stuff — and to meet us, but he had to be on a plane thirty minutes ago. By the way, Black is friends with Jim, so we don't have the same problem we do with other guys I won't mention."

Peale slid out of his leather duster and dropped his backpack onto the floor by the desk. "That's a relief. I don't know if I could take much more skepticism."

"I hear you," Galen said. He pointed at the folder on BC's blotter, "Those are our new orders. You guessed right on one count. We have to split up and pair off with Taylor and Stroud for stakeouts later tonight. But you'll be surprised to find that we're being trusted with the well being of Eddie Michalson and Lance Baer."

Peale skimmed the printed sheets and smirked. "Correction — Smokey and BooBoo. I feel like I've stepped into a Len Deighton novel."

"*And* Uncle Joe managed to get the nod for wiretaps on all our principals."

"That could prove useful."

Feeling a couple tons lighter, Peale plunked into his chair. He'd been very afraid Black would prove a doubter, too. Had that been the case, it might have become necessary to cut ties, become someone else again and hit the road. The prospect was not welcome. He liked his bulldozing partner and, in spite of everything, liked the job. Additionally and more embarrassingly, he was even *more* relieved that he'd still be working with Stroud Girion.

There he went again, acting like a besotted schoolboy. At his age, he ought to be better at coping with relationships. Still, he looked forward to pairing up with the two officers for the stakeouts (*Can't somebody come up with a different term?*). He made a show of studying the sheets in the binder, then after a moment, asked, "So, what else did the Colonel say?"

Galen sat back, watching emotions flow across his friend's face. They appeared to be mostly dark and worried ones. It would be a good thing to see some happy there. That was sure to happen when he learned that Miriam was in town. Making a snap decision to keep Miriam's presence a surprise, he said simply, "Tell you what, I'll give you a synopsis over dinner tonight. I felt like kicking back before we got down to work and made a reservation at the place around the corner — the one with the live music? We can talk, you can listen to the music and I can get a decent steak."

The vampire replied, "Sounds okay to me. When do we head out?"

From the residual ruddiness of Peale's cheeks, Miller suspected his partner had already fed; probably at a stock pen, where he could drink his fill with no one the wiser. With the tension at the offices, he'd needed to do that more frequently than usual. Galen glanced at his watch. "We got stuff to do here before we can run. Hey! The Colonel did tell me a good one today. Did you know that Stroud and Taylor were approached by recruiters for Sentry International right after it was chartered?"

"No, but if you tell me next that Taylor disemboweled the recruiting officer, I won't be amazed at *that*, either."

"Not far off." Galen laughed out loud. "The way Col. Black put it was, 'Taylor was especially negative'. Apparently, that's why they were chosen as our liaison officers, Uncle Joe still has hopes and someone in NYPD brass thought they were pulling a funny by putting our teams together on this. Joke's on them, I guess." He scrutinized his partner trying to gauge *how* big a joke, but elicited only puzzlement.

"What?"

"Ah, never mind. We'll talk about that stuff later, too. We'll have the things we've requisitioned for the apartment by tomorrow night. Col. Black's pushing it through. Says he wants you to check the answering machine first thing when you get up in case anything important comes up. You know, for those times when your phone gets mysteriously turned off?"

Peale at least had the decency to look sheepish. "Y'mean like today?"

"Exactly what inspired him."

"Pretty good idea . . . OH! Machine!" Unzipping the backpack, he drew out a matte black object roughly the size of a standard piece of paper and approximately a quarter inch thick. He shoved it across the desk to Galen. "The new tablet! Turns on with that little button up top. Most functions are accomplished by jabbing things on the screen with your finger. Even you ought to be able to work that."

Miller powered it up and ruefully compared the size of his fingers with the size of the virtual keyboard that popped up. "Yeah, but the keyboard on the screen is teensy. Good thing you'll be the one mostly using it. I think I need a size larger."

BC laughed. "It has USB plug-ins and a docking port here. You can plug a mouse and a keyboard in if you want — not that you don't play the cracks on a regular keyboard."

Galen sneered. His partner blissfully ignored it. "I got one of those little wireless printers, too, but I left it downstairs in the Harley's saddlebag. I figure it'll be safe there — if anyone rips it off from the Sentry garage, we're in worse trouble than I thought."

"Too true." The dark face sobered. "Not to wreck the mood, but the day had a down side, too. Stallings and I kind of mixed it up soon after I got in."

BC winced. "About me again?"

"Yeah. I'm afraid I got a little overheated and suggested if he didn't believe the official documentation, maybe he'd like to be there when you get up."

The vampire recoiled. "I don't know how I feel about that. I know Stallings is supposed to be one of the white hat crowd, but — well, he raises my hackles."

"I hear ya. If it was me, I wouldn't like it, either. It was the first thing popped into my head. If it makes you feel any better, I don't think Uncle Joe cottoned to the idea. Maybe he really believes, but is too stubborn to admit it to anyone. Himself included."

Galen watched his friend weigh the concept. Galen did understand. BC was at his most vulnerable in his dormant state. It was disconcerting enough to waken and find a friend watching him, but an adversary?

At length, BC said, "If a better solution doesn't present itself, that might be the only way. We've got to do *something*. I can't take his attitude much longer. He's going to push until I blow, then we'll all be sorry." He reflected for a moment. "Anyway, I regret missing Brian Black. Sounds like it went well, and I love the idea of the message machine. Maybe a blinking red light will remind me to check it. I never seem to remember to check the ones on my mobile."

"Do tell."

Peale ignored him. "Had I known the Colonel was on our side, I'd have postponed buying the tablet and rushed right over. I might have just been able to catch him."

"Yeah. Hey, let's get this piddling shit done and get to dinner before we run out of time. Our bear-watching stint begins at nine o'clock and I don't want Taylor and Stroud to beat us to the apartment. If they hit the fridge and find all those bottles of beef blood behind the beer, that'll be kinda hard to explain."

***

Galen zeroed in on the lithe figure lounging in a plush chair across the waiting room. There was no mistaking her, even at that distance. Apparently, she was thinking along the same lines as she scanned the throng at the reservation book. With elegant grace, she bounded across the carpet to wrap him in an enthusiastic hug. Laughing at his surprise, she released him and said, "Don't look so surprised, fella, I'm Miriam Peale and you *couldn't* be anyone but Galen Miller!"

He grinned delightedly. "Right the first time."

She searched beyond him. "Where's Byron? Isn't he coming?"

"He's on his way. I left him parking the car. It was too easy: offer BC Peale the opportunity to operate a motorized vehicle and he'll do anything you want without question. I doubt if he'd have been quite so cooperative if I told him who was meeting us for dinner — *I'd* be parking the car. With all the unpleasant surprises we've had lately, I thought it was high time for a nice one."

As soon as they were seated at a comfortable accommodation for three, she gazed over at her companion. "It's nice to finally have a face to put to the voice — aside from the Sports Illustrated covers and it was hard to see much through those big helmets."

"Looks like I had the advantage, then. I've seen your picture almost every day. BC takes it everywhere he goes."

"Really? He can be so sweet, when he wants to be." A shadow crossed her face. "I suppose I have to mention the news story again. The kids caught several versions on tape. They've been playing it enough to wear out the machine, determined to get a better look at you and the lady Stroud that Byron's been talking about. They love it, but I confess, all I could think was that it gave new meaning to blown cover. We're not on the phone now, so tell me the truth, did you two get in a lot of trouble?"

Galen looked pained. "Not as much as we were afraid of and it had a *few* unexpected side effects. A couple of them came close to making it worthwhile."

"I gathered it was rough; Byron sounds bad on the phone. That's what made me come myself. It was originally supposed to be my assistant — I *hate* speaking artsy-ese."

"Considering how much hell he's been catching lately, I don't wonder he sounds bad. He's not used to the stops and starts of police work — hell, I've been at it longer than he has and *I'm* not used to it."

She slipped out of her jacket and plopped it over the back of the chair before he could rise to assist her. Watching her easy grace, he was overwhelmed by her resemblance to his partner. He'd wondered if BC's dancer-like movements were a manifestation of the vampirism, but apparently not. Magnified by it, maybe, but it seemed to be an inborn Peale quality. Miriam straightened and caught his look. Leaning forward with a hauntingly familiar sparkle of curiosity, she said, "What is it?"

The mahogany skin darkened as he stammered, "You're very like him . . . I mean physically . . . I . . . Oh, hell!"

"Don't worry. It's a proven fact that Peales share a lot of characteristics," she said with an also familiar evil grin. "Wait until you experience the lot of us together. It's a sight that's been known to make brave men weep!" With a sudden squeak, she ducked behind the menu and whispered, "Byron just came in. He's talking to the waiter."

With devilish nonchalance, Galen joined her in perusal of the menu.

Amused, Galen watched his confused partner mouth the words "The Miller party?" then follow the headwaiter across the crowded restaurant floor. He could also tell the precise moment Peale noticed there was a lady at the table, because he entered charm mode about half-way there. His expression of utter surprise as his cousin leaped up showering him with hugs and kisses, was priceless.

He didn't find his voice until he was seated and the headwaiter was nearly back to his post. "Galen Miller! You knew about this all along, didn't you?"

"Sure did!" The big man nodded happily. "Been planning this all day and the look on your face was worth it! It's the quietest you've been all night, too. We'll have to see if we can repeat the experiment later."

Miriam leaned forward into his line of vision with a laugh. "I'm happy to see you, too, Byron!"

BC shot his partner a final glare, then, all smiles, pointedly turned back to his cousin. "But, I *am* happy to see you, Miriam. When the maitre d' said 'Miller party' I merely thought he was commenting that Galen is big enough for at least two people. I never expected he actually meant we had a dinner companion. How long are you here for and is anyone else with you?"

"I'm here for ten days and all by my lonesome — so it looks like it falls to Miller and Peale Escorts, Inc. to keep me company." She winked at Galen. "If that's acceptable with the proprietors, that is."

Galen beamed. "If I may speak for the vice-president and myself, the way things have been lately, it's more than acceptable — it's a pleasure! Did the charming client have a specific venue in mind?"

"Well, since this is both business and pleasure, I have quite a few art shows I have to look in on — both daytime and evening — and while I adore art and artists, I always like to have real people with me as a touchstone for reality." Her smile gentled as she turned to Byron and concluded, "However, I might *also* be amenable to being dragged to someone's smoky old jazz clubs, providing he and I can have a long talk first, someplace where we don't have to shout."

Byron ducked guiltily. "Oops. Is it *that* obvious I have things on my mind?"

Galen hooted with unreserved laughter. Miriam gave him a broad grin and said, "Like a Times Square billboard, Byron!"

SEVEN

The office was pitch dark after the brightly lit hallways they'd just left. Stroud Girion pressed her back against the doorframe, blinking to adjust to the sudden gloom. It didn't help. Although she understood the necessity for this subterfuge, she hated it. She felt more like she'd entered a duck blind than a surveillance post across from Eddie Michalson's downtown offices. She also couldn't bring herself to refer to a no-nonsense career criminal as "Smokey".

Michalson had been spending a lot of time at his offices of late. He'd even pulled several all-nighters; this looked to be shaping into one of those. Lighting in the listening post was dim or nonexistent aside from small, flexible book lights clipped to the edges of the desks where the agents took notes, stared at monitors and listened to audio feed from bugs and taps. Stroud's eyes were taking a long time to get accustomed to it. She stepped away from the wall and immediately smacked painfully into the corner of a desk.

One of the Sentry agents sucked air in sympathy. "Sounded like that one hurt. I always crack myself on that damn desk when I come in. Never fails."

The other agent chuckled. "Yeah. Watching Eagan do the pratfall thing is the most excitement we've had today. We been here since two this afternoon and all Michalson has done so far is scream at people. Scream on the phone, scream face-to-face, scream out the door — better be careful or he'll scream himself up a heart attack."

Peale's breath ruffled her hair as he whispered, "One of the benefits of my sunlight intolerance is that my eyes adjust to darkness very quickly. Let me find you a chair." Taking hold of her arm, he gently guided her around unseen obstacles and sat her down on a chair-shaped patch of blackness. Swinging her backpack to the floor, she said, "Thanks. I'll just stay put until I can see. It'll save wear and tear on the furnishings."

She passed several minutes leaning back with her eyes shut listening, to the murmured instructions about the log books and wiretaps. Tentatively opening one lid, she found she could make out shapes of darker dark scattered around the room. The tiny lights at the console looked terribly bright. The aroma of brewing coffee snared her and she followed her nose to a machine gurgling in a corner. She poured a cup and sipped at the strong brew, enjoying the warmth seeping through her near-frozen hands — and watching Peale limned by the book lights as the two agents showed him the equipment.

They'd ridden over on the Harley and, although the days were getting warmer, the nights were still chilly and she felt it to the bone. She was also still feeling her arms wrapped around BC as he threaded through traffic. Embarrassment warmed her face as she realized just how much she'd enjoyed the solidity of his body under the leathers and how the memory of it was affecting her. She took a big swig of the bitter coffee, grateful for the covering darkness. Collecting herself, she joined the others at the console.

When the other agents were gone, Stroud opened her pack and filled a desktop with sandwich fixings. "Okay, we got whole wheat bread, Swiss cheese, turkey, roast beef and a really killer salami from this deli down the block from Taylor's place." Digging around in a side pocket, she produced a handful of small plastic packets. "And any kind of condiment you're interested in, I'm sure we got it. I think we even have a packet or two of Duck Sauce lurking in here."

"Impressive."

Opening the bread sack released a yeasty-sweet aroma into the room, as she asked, "What'll you have?"

"Um. Nothing, thank you."

She whirled in mock fury, "After I slaved over a hot deli counter, you're not eating again? Are you on some kind of special diet, or are you just trying to make me feel guilty for pigging out?"

"I suppose you'd call it a special diet. You see, I'm not eating because I can't, unless I want to be dreadfully sick. It's all related to the chemical imbalance that gives me problems with sunlight. I can't tell you all the medical stuff, I don't understand half of it myself, but I know the things I have to do to stay healthy — even if they strike other people as odd. What it boils down to is that my body won't tolerate solid food. I take my meals in liquid form."

"Oh, man! All this other stuff must be giving you hell, then. I'll put it away—"

"No, don't do that. I've had this condition for a long time now and I'm quite used to it. You're hungry and I had my evening meal before we came out. I'll be fine for quite a while on that. I'll just nurse my coffee and chat."

It took a considerable amount of cajoling and threats to finally convince her to eat her own dinner. While she was building her sandwich, he turned back to the surveillance equipment, ostensibly checking the monitors while inwardly cursing himself for lying to her. The urge to tell her the truth was so strong, it was astonishing. But that wasn't the worst of it. There *was* something he wanted, but not here and not now. He couldn't really trust himself, anyway. Dammit! He'd fed heavily earlier in the evening; he shouldn't be getting so aroused — except what was arousing him wasn't exactly that kind of hunger, was it?

He turned his attention completely to the console to dilute his awareness of her. It didn't work too well. Maybe Galen was right. . . .

The wiretap console crackled to life, mirroring the ringing of Eddie Michalson's telephone. BC picked up his pen and filled in the time field on the logbook, then stood with the point hovering over the blank line as Eddie picked up with his usual abrupt "Michalson."

The pen clattered from Peale's fingers as the caller greeted Michalson and the world tilted. Stroud's fingers dug into his arm. He could feel the concern rolling off her like steam as she demanded, "BC, what's wrong? You better sit down. . . ."

He waved her off. "God help me, I know that voice." Grabbing his cell phone, he called Stallings' private line. "This is Special Agent Peale. We have Francesco Borgia on the line with Eddie Michalson."

***

"I am happy to say that Gwen has met with success in Louisiana." Borgia's voice was strong and classical music played softly in the background. Eddie smiled to himself. This was a good sign. The boss hadn't listened to his music since the trouble in Chicago started up. If he needed extra resolve not to mention the kid, that did it. "Glad to hear it, Boss, though I'm real surprised that jerk listens to anything other than his own ego. You callin' her up to Canada now?"

"Alas, no. Like you, she distrusts the man and fears the turnaround may be of a temporary nature. She wished to stay close, to observe."

"Me and Gwennie don't see eye-to-eye on a lot, but I respect her judgment on stuff like this. This guy's bad news, Boss. The faster we cut this operation loose, the better I'll like it."

The chuckle rumbled across the line sounding even more like the old Borgia. "Again, you both agree. With such independent advice, I cannot but follow it. We will close it down as soon as the last shipment is in our hands. There is no sense in not accepting the merchandise, since it has already been ordered."

"Maybe so, but I think we oughta start puttin' a lotta distance between us and that southern-fried loser right now."

"Consider it done, Edgar. Now for less pleasant subjects. I wish to extend my condolences over your recent losses. I hope you can locate the perpetrator and exact retribution quickly."

Eddie wanted to shout that the perp was precious little Gwennie. After a silence he hoped Borgia didn't notice, he said, "Yeah, me, too."

Borgia didn't say good-bye. He never did. He ended conversations by just hanging up. After the final click, Eddie eased the receiver back into the desk unit, then stood, fingers drumming lightly on the plastic, feeling the tension of his two bodyguards, Matt and Lester, like heat on his back.

At length, he sighed and ordered, "Okay. Spit it out."

Matt ventured, "How come you still ain't tellin' him it's Isendamer knockin' our people off?"

Eddie wheeled and jabbed a finger at him. "You got proof?"

The big man fidgeted uncomfortably. "Well, no."

"Then what good would tellin' Borgia do? Get me proof and I'll nail her icy ass to the wall."

Lester frowned. "Why don't we just nail her, anyway?"

Eddie took his time lighting a cigar. Puffing blue smoke into the air, he smiled pleasantly. "Who say's I ain't?"

***

Francesco Borgia swung toward the compact disk player and jabbed Verdi up a few notches. He then reclined in his desk chair, eyes closed, letting the music flow over him in an attempt to calm himself. It was useless. Verdi stood no chance against the endless loop playing in his head of his conversation with Michalson. It simply was not possible that Edgar was unaware Gwen Isendamer was behind the assassinations. Of course he did. If he didn't have the sense to know this, Borgia would never have hired him.

Frustration rose at his mortal lieutenants. Why did they consistently fail to grasp the overall scheme of things as he did? As Byron did? He smacked the palm of his hand against the leather arm-pad of his chair. Why was the child so unreasonable? With his son at his side, he would have little need of Isendamer. Byron had a wonderful head for business when so inclined, he'd more than proven that in the past. Some of his ventures in the late eighteenth century were marvels to behold. Unfortunately, Byron was still upset at the way things went awry in Chicago—

No! He broke off the train of thoughts, pressing shaking

hands to his temples. No sense in losing his grip again. It was just such a slip that led to Miguel Marquez' death and caused Byron's alienation. The boy could be so foolishly sentimental.

Maybe sentiment was infectious. He was behaving just as foolishly toward Gwen especially in light of her rapidly deteriorating condition. Truthfully, her behavior in Chicago unnerved him even more than the unexpected appearance of his fledgling. If he didn't eliminate her soon, she'd work her way up through the ranks of the New York operation and deprive him of Edgar Michalson. *That* couldn't be allowed, but how to do it? Draining her was out of the question. Her personality and will were strong and once taken in, would prove hard to squash. He shuddered and veered way from those thoughts.

Gwen must be eliminated from a distance, then. Perhaps he should let Edgar have the pleasure . . . no, she was his responsibility. It was his place to remove her. A slow, delighted smile spread across his face. Yes. The silver bullets — what delicious irony. To slay her still-human body with weapons meant for his own kind. The same ones that had nearly taken the blood of his blood from him before he knew it.

* * *

If the street in front of the SI hostelry was busy when Miller and Peale arrived, the usually quiet lobby was an anthill.

Galen Miller stopped just to one side of the brass and glass revolving door to take in the chaos. "Wow. Looks like we don't have the place to ourselves any more. Any idea what this is about?"

"None at all." BC Peale shook his head in amazement. "If there was a memo, I wasn't a recipient, either." He smirked up at his companion. "This looks like a job for a linebacker. You part the crowd, I'll follow."

"See, I told you, you only get it wrong when you're pissed about something." Miller snorted and started bulling his way toward the elevators.

As they threaded past the knot of people at the main desk, one of the desk clerks, who had been engaged in conversation with a man, pointed in their direction. The man looked over his shoulder and called out, "Hey, Special Agent Peale!"

Peale stopped as the other man shouldered through the crush, smiling and with hand extended.

"Oscar Baker, out of San Diego. A bunch of us just shipped in for a series of seminars, so it looks like we'll be neighbors for a while. Artie over at the desk tells me that big hog I saw in the back is yours. It's a beautiful machine! How's it run?"

BC grinned. "Gets me where I want to go."

Galen knew he was doomed as the two launched into a detailed discussion of horsepower, torque, CCs — the exact stuff that bored him to tears. Folding his arms, he rested his shoulders against a marble column with a stifled groan. All he wanted to do was soak in a tub of steaming-hot water, then crash for a year or two. The only good thing was watching the trouble fall away from his partner. BC became more animated as he spoke to the other agent about riding, seeming much more the person Galen had first met.

Were any of them from SIChi any different? Everything in Chicago had happened so fast — like a flurry of body blows. BC seemed to be affected by it more than anyone else, growing more taciturn with each new punch. He'd gotten even twitchier since hearing Borgia on the phone . . . *Ah, hell,* Miller thought, pushing away from the pillar, intending to mumble excuses and stumble back to the suite alone.

Before Miller could say anything, Peale wound up the conversation. Tossing a promise over his shoulder to show off the bike at a later date over his shoulder, BC took his leave. Galen gratefully fell into step with his partner as they continued to the elevators, where a largish group surrounded by luggage waited for the car.

Galen stifled a yawn. "How can anyone talk so long about a machine? It's just a motorcycle, man! To hear you and Baker go on, a person'd think you were talking about a woman!"

"Not *just* a machine, Gae, a Harley-Davidson Softail." BC's grin widened. "There's a lot to say about it."

A female voice from behind them exclaimed, "Hey! You're the one who owns that Harley back there? Cool!"

Galen rolled his eyes. At least they were only going three floors.

Several groups got off on their floor, but the women who were chattering with BC about the motorcycle had several more floors to go. Galen was thankful for that. He turned to find BC already at their apartment door with his keys out. "Hey, you weren't in such a big hurry before, what gives?"

"I just realized I need to make a phone call."

***

It was unusual for the telephone to ring so early in the evening. Maeve turned the Caller ID box to read the screen, then picked up with a delighted, "Byron! You're early! Jump is still downstairs."

A rueful laugh, then, "I know. I was calling to talk to you."

Something in his voice pulled her up short. "Something's gone horribly wrong. What is it?"

"Nothing's gone really wrong, just . . . we got a bit of a break tonight. We were watching Eddie Michalson's office and Borgia called him. We got a fix on his position in Canada."

"And . . . ? Byron, what you're telling me is good news. Why do you sound as if somebody died?"

He paused and she could picture him looking over his shoulder, then he lowered his voice. "God, Maeve, I heard Borgia's voice over those headphones and the world turned on its ear. It was so intense, I almost blacked out."

"So that's why you sound so shaky! And no wonder."

"What do you mean 'no wonder?' This is ridiculous! I can't even hear the bastard's voice without my knees turning to water. What's wrong with me?"

"There's nothing wrong with you. Francesco's your sire; it's just your nature at work on you."

"Nature."

Good. He was getting angry now. She knew how to deal with an angry Byron. It was the insecure and frightened Byron that threw her. "Yes. Nature. You heard Francesco, got shaky — then what?"

"Huh?"

"Very articulate, M'love. Let's try again. You said you 'almost blacked out,' meaning you didn't. What *did* you do?"

"Oh. I made sure the recorder was rolling, then called Stallings."

"Of course, you did. Byron, believe it or not, you're doing remarkably well against the bloodbond. I've talked to Mother about it and she was impressed. She said most fledglings would have just rolled over and meekly followed their sire away." She burst out laughing. "You screamed back and threatened to punch him."

Byron made a disgruntled noise. She smothered her laughter and continued, "What it boils down to is that you're each too pig-headed to give in to the other."

"Pig-headed? Your mother called me pig-headed?" In the background, Maeve heard Galen guffaw, then (slightly muffled), "You shut up!" Galen laughed harder.

Maeve placated, "She used the phrase 'strong-willed.' *I* said pig-headed." Before he could snap back at her, she added. "And please stay that way, Darlin'. It's your best defense against him."

EIGHT

"Peale? PEALE!"

Special Agent Peale started visibly. "Oh, sorry, sir. My mind was elsewhere. You were saying?"

"Elsewhere is one way to put it. I'm surprised the whole building didn't hear me just then." Captain Stallings switched off the wiretap playback, cutting Francesco Borgia's voice off in mid-word, and viewed Peale critically before continuing, "If Francesco Borgia frightens you so much, Peale, perhaps we should remove you from the case."

Peale grinned. "I think you misunderstood my preoccupation, sir. I'm not afraid of Signor Borgia." He added silently, *Quite the contrary, I was busy practicing being* not *afraid.* Next to him, Miller shifted uncomfortably. BC ignored him, giving Captain Stallings his full attention.

Stallings regarded him thoughtfully before continuing. "I was saying that Borgia's presenting Michalson with a bonus of tickets to a Broadway show this week presents a few surveillance problems. Do you have any ideas how to overcome this?"

"Oh, is that all?"

"You sound very sure."

"Well, I'd have to call in a few favors here and there, but . . . yeah, I can handle it."

Stallings made no reply, but continued to regard his

special agent who was now the picture of self-assurance. Finally, he said, "Very well, gentlemen, take care of it, but I want the full plan detailed and written out on my desk by morning."

Galen waited until they were back in their cubicle before asking, "You sure you're okay? You looked pretty shook for a minute there."

"Nonsense! I was hardly shaking at all."

Galen laughed. "Okay, I'll lay off. How about you fill me in on this big plan of yours?"

BC looked blank. "Plan?"

"Aw, shit! You were bluffing."

"Oh, *that* plan. Well, maybe just a little." Seeing the impending explosion, he added hastily, "Hey, it's no big deal. I'll come up with something." Suddenly, he dived for the desk clock. "Oh, geez. Is this right? I should be picking Miriam up right now. She's gonna kill me!"

He turned and fled down the hall, then disappeared into the stairwell, leaving Galen shaking his head.

***

Their table looked directly down onto the stage where the band was entering to hearty applause from the club's patrons. Miriam looked up from her surprisingly good chicken marsala and over at Byron. She frowned and nudged him. "Hey, fella, the band's down there, not in that glass."

He grinned sheepishly.

She sat back and commented, "Someone's preoccupied tonight."

"You're not the first to make that observation."

"What's wrong? If you hadn't had such good commentary on the prints in the art show earlier, I'd have thought you weren't paying attention to anything at all."

He ran nervous fingers through his ponytail. "I'm sorry I'm such bad company. I've got a lot on my mind."

"Not so much bad company as much as periodically absentee. Is it the investigation?"

"Partly. Partly personal."

"Ah. Stroud Girion."

"Oh God. Everybody knows — and thinks it's a hoot. All except Galen. He thinks it's dangerous."

Miriam smiled. "Maybe it is dangerous, but you've never gone for anything else. I forget which family member made the comment, but it's true, 'Byron is only interested in women who can hurt him. If they can kill him, he's enraptured.'"

His grin was rueful and slightly embarrassed. "That's only true up to a point. Besides, I was attracted to Stroud long before I knew she could kill me with her bare hands." He was suddenly very serious. "No my problem is that I want to level with her about . . . Things, but. . . ."

"You're afraid to?" She spread placating hands at his incipient protest. "Okay, maybe afraid is too strong, but it's a little beyond nervous, don't you think? What does Galen say? Never mind, I can guess. What does your friend, Jump Veron, say?"

"He tells me to be patient. That's not something I do well. It's especially hard because I'm not real sure what Stroud's feeling. I mean, what if I'm making more out of friendship than is really there?"

Miriam's brow furrowed. "You can't tell what she's feeling? I thought. . . ."

He gave a short, bitter laugh. "Stroud Girion's got barriers up to make Maeve envious."

Miriam watched him fidget with the drink; there was something else gnawing at him that he didn't want to put words to. She thought she knew what it was. Finally, she leaned over and gave his arm a squeeze. "You won't hurt her, Byron. You're not that kind."

He looked up in surprise, then chuckled. "I keep forgetting Peale women are psychic. It always gets me into trouble."

She grinned over her drink. "Not psychic, just familiar with how Peale men look when they're thinking deep dark thoughts. You'll be fine. Now relax and listen to the music. You dragged me in here for a specific group and I believe they've been playing for the last five minutes and you haven't heard a single note."

Snorting in derision, he turned his attention to the stage. It didn't do to disobey the women of his clan. Maybe that was why he was attracted to strong women — correction — "women who could hurt him."

After a moment, Miriam leaned back into him. "Ummm, Byron. If this is a jazz group, why is that man is playing a banjo?"

***

BC absently tugged at his bulky ear protectors as he watched Stroud sweeping up spent brass and remembered Joseph Stallings' red, screaming face. He snorted in amused disgust. Stroud would not be flattered by the association. He couldn't help it, though. Stallings had been irate that the requested detail of his surveillance plan wasn't waiting on his desk as ordered. He'd have been even unhappier had he known it wasn't even started. BC didn't tell him that, though. What he'd *said* was that there'd been a few holdups and that the report would be on Stalling's desk as soon as he cleared the

last hurdles. That was true — up to a point. The main holdup
had been at the hands of the ticket agent. Holdup was an
appropriate term, too, although he preferred highway
robbery. He had the tickets, though, and they were legit.
They'd also been the proof Stallings needed to calm down
and back off.

The other holdup was was efficiently collecting her empty brass.

He could almost feel those valuable bits of pasteboard
radiating heat from the billfold in his hip pocket. Galen and
Taylor were taking their turn at the range's firing line now
and their addition to the din in the place was deafening him
even through the protectors. Maybe he'd better wait until he
and Stroud were once again in the soundproofed booth
beyond the range. . . . Dammit! He was putting it off again.
What the hell was wrong with him? He crouched down and
helped her scoop the empties into a box and pointed to his
ear protectors then to the door. She grinned, picked up the
box and followed him through.

He pulled the protectors off with undisguised relief and
tossed them onto the small table built into the wall. Stroud
laughed and tossed her own on top of his, then set to sorting
the brass into keepers and trash.

She said, "You really hate those things, don't you?"

He shrugged. "Lesser of two evils, I suppose, but I've
never liked things muffling my ears."

"You really should consider reusing your brass. It's much
cheaper than buying new rounds all the time."

He grinned. "Too lazy, I think. It's much *easier* to buy
new rounds all the time."

"At least you're honest — tell you what, how about you
buy the supplies and I'll reload for both of us?"

"Watch out or I might take you up on that." He paused and looking strangely uncomfortable, glanced out the window into the firing range before continuing, "Hey, I have something I wanted to ask you about before Gae and Taylor finish up."

She stopped sorting. "That sounds ominous. Go ahead."

"Not too ominous, I hope. I landed tickets to the Friday performance of 'Phantom of the Opera' and I wondered if you might like to go."

"I'd love to. Friday? Yeah, I can get Friday."

His smile returned. "Dinner after?"

"Sure! On one condition."

The smile dimmed as he asked suspiciously, "What's the condition?"

"That we discuss the case over dinner."

The smile brightened several kilowatts. "I think we can manage that."

***

The throb of the fishing boat's engine was all but swallowed up by the expanse of sea and night sky as the pilot idled closer to a buoy in the Gulf waters. One of the three men aboard strapped on an aqualung and plunged over the side. The third, a dark man, leaned after him, peering into the black waves as if he could penetrate them by force of will, and see what was happening below.

Presently, the diver broke the surface and spat out the mouthpiece, calling, "It's here."

He grabbed hold of the boarding ladder, pulled himself up part way, then heaved a line heavy with large plastic-wrapped bundles strung along it onto the deck of the boat. Over the next several minutes, the only sounds were the slap of waves against the sides of the boat, the labored breath of the men, and the solid thump of wet packages against the deck.

The pilot looked on impassively as the dark man bent low over their cargo, then rose with a smile that flashed in the darkness.

"*Bueno*, that is all of it." This said, he pulled a pistol from under his jacket and fired one shot into the forehead of the diver, who was hauling himself over the railing. The man jerked spasmodically, then dropped back in to the waves and sank.

The pilot launched himself from his chair, screaming, "Goddam! What in hell did you do that for?"

Unconcerned, the dark man reholstered his pistol and bent to stowing the bundle. "The gentleman was with your DEA. To allow him to return with us would have been folly."

"DEA!"

"Yes, *Señor*, and now I suggest you stop shouting and begin steering us back toward land. We have little night left and I do not relish bringing our catch home in daylight."

"But. . . ."

The dark man whipped around. "Do it. Now."

The pilot sat back down and with shaking hands, turned the boat toward the distant shore.

***

If that was BC, he was disgustingly on time. *Damn him*, she thought, dabbing finishing powder at her nose. Leaning out of the bathroom, she bawled, "Be there in a sec!"

Scowling at her reflection, she inspected her 'urban camouflage.' She rarely wore clothes this elaborate or this much makeup, and it always made her self-conscious. Smacking off the light, she hobble/skipped toward the front door forcing her feet into high heels as she went.

It was BC.

"Hope I'm not too early. The cabbie I hired seemed determined to qualify for the next Indy 500 speed trials. The demon still awaits downstairs — *if* we deem it safe to travel with him."

She gleamed impishly. "Not the Harley?"

"Alas, no. I thought we'd want to look presentable by the time we reached the theater. *However*, if you insist, it'd be safer than the cab. . . ."

Guffawing, she swept up her purse and brushed past him into the hall. As she shot the deadbolt, he leaned forward, murmuring, "You do look lovely tonight, by the way. I like your scent; White Shoulders, isn't it?"

Just as she wondered if he'd kiss her, he straightened with a suddenness that startled her. Turning, she found him a step or two away, wearing an odd expression. He collected himself and smiled sheepishly. "Sorry, I didn't mean to be so forward."

Tossing the keys into her dinky evening bag, she said, "Don't worry. I'll let you know when you get too forward. Right after you regain consciousness, I'll tell you all about it."

His easy humor returned before they reached the stairs. She remained silent, surprised at how much she'd enjoyed the brief closeness, and realizing she'd not only been wondering if he'd kiss her, but hoping he would. His reaction was puzzling if amusing and she twitched a smile at his archaic apology. Who under seventy used the term 'forward' any more, for God's sake? BC was like that, though: a mix of things and you never quite knew what was going to surface next. Tonight he leaned toward the formal side. Not *that* much different from when they were at work, but subtly . . . yeah. She kind of liked it.

Stroud urged, "C'mon, your cabbie from Hell won't wait forever — he may have already changed into a puff of brimstone and disappeared."

"He'd never do that; I haven't paid him yet. Best way of binding that type of demon I've found."

Laughing, she grasped his lapel and dragged him along. "We better take the elevator, I usually use the stairs, but I don't want to chance it in these shoes."

"I can carry you, if you like."

"You might regret those words, Peale. By the end of the evening, I may make you do just that!"

***

The high-heeled shoes pinched like a sonuvabitch, but didn't rub as badly as she'd been afraid they would. Good thing. She hadn't even considered the possibility when she got impatient waiting for traffic to move again and insisted they walk the remaining blocks to the theater.

"It's only a little farther. You can kick them off when we get to our seats and no-one will be the wiser."

She halted, stared at him, and pulled a wry face. "Are you a mind reader or am I limping that badly? I thought I was doing pretty good."

Peale grinned, "I think the moaning and cursing gave it away. Do you *still* want to walk to the restaurant after the show? I know! Let's see if this helps."

Drawing her out of the flow of pedestrians, he plunked her onto a stone ledge. Before she could refuse, he had her shoe off, working the leather between his hands. Embarrassed, she scanned the crowd, but as usual, the New York passersby had eyes for nothing but where they were headed. Snatching at her pump, she demanded, "BC Peale, what *are* you doing?"

He ducked out of reach. "I thought it was obvious. I'm working the leather to soften it. This is where it was rubbing, right? Don't worry, this will only take a minute. I have a lot of experience working with leather."

The ludicrous Handsome Prince and Cinderella on Broadway made her avert her eyes trying to stifle the guffaw threatening to burst out. But turning her head didn't help, because it brought a previously unnoticed expanse of plate glass into view. Even there, in its slightly grimy surface, she could see the pedestrian crush and herself on the wall. Her smile froze, then morphed into a perplexed frown. BC wasn't there. The cool touch of his hands sliding her shoe onto her foot broke the spell and she turned away from the impromptu mirror.

He said, "There. Your ankle is a bit bruised, so it might still hurt, but let's walk on and see if the softer edge helps."

Accepting his offered hand, she stood, mentally shrugging off the inconsistency. The glass was at an odd angle. That could cause an optical illusion. Magicians did that kind of thing all the time. She rejoined the pedestrian traffic, saying, "We'd better hurry — at least *I'd* better. God only knows what you'll pull off me next if I don't."

He fell in beside her, laughing. "Perish the thought! I prefer privacy for anything higher than a shoe — usually. By the way, I was on-line with Prometheus last night, and he uploaded more stuff from Aladdin. This time it was dear little Gwendolyn's life story. A truly frightening individual."

Half-listening, she absently agreed, but in spite of willing herself not to, her eyes kept seeking reflective surfaces. BC kept not being there, regardless of the angle of the glass. When she looked back, he was giving her a searching look. Rousing herself, she lied, "Sorry. It's Isendamer. When someone who was abused goes so wrong, you think you understand. I mean you can't, really, but you can get an idea . . . but Isendamer's someone who's had only advantages."

He saddened. "I know. No matter how often I see this kind of aberration, it's always sick-making. The concept of someone taking *enjoyment* from such behavior . . . very little can prepare the sensibilities for *that*."

Struck by the vehemence of the statement, she forgot the troubling non-reflections and elbowed him. "Hey, this is supposed to be a date not a wake. Maybe insisting we bring work along with us wasn't such a good idea, after all."

His instant smile in the glaring theater lights wiped away all traces of the former mood. Sweeping a hand toward the glittering façade, he announced, "Too late at any rate, m'lady. We've arrived."

Later, strolling to the restaurant, she made a conscious (but not altogether successful) effort not to watch for her escort's reflection. Each failure brought a growl at her own silliness for allowing imagination to run away with her. It was those *stupid* tabloid articles Taylor downloaded last night combined with Brannaugh's lousy jokes about the Vampire Vigilante. She almost wished BC's trick with her shoe hadn't worked so well. If her foot still hurt, she could have kept her mind on things other than reflective surfaces.

Branding her suspicions medieval, she thrust them aside, shunting her attention to the restaurant's tastefully decorated interior . She'd never thought to see the inside of this place unless someone committed a murder in the middle of the dining room. The place even *smelled* expensive. She didn't know how well-heeled BC was, and frankly didn't care. The abandon with which he'd spent money all evening made her uncomfortable. She held silent until the waiter served the sumptuous dinner (ordered from a menu with no prices on it), then blurted, "BC, we need to talk about tonight."

He flinched. "You aren't enjoying it, are you?"

"Oh, I'm enjoying the hell out of it, but that's beside the point. This has been very expensive."

"Money isn't a problem. . . ."

"That doesn't matter — it makes me uncomfortable having you fete me like this. I'm not used to this, BC. I'm just a cop from a not too secure middle class background. It's a treat to order takeout Thai. This is all very dazzling, but I don't think I like being dazzled."

"I'm sorry, it must seem like I'm out to bowl you over with extravagance. It wasn't my intention. I like doing things for people I care about and money doesn't mean that much to me."

She softened. "I figured that out, I've seen you buy things before, but I wasn't the sole recipient then. You have to promise that I get to decide how we spend the next date"

His relief was almost comical, and he was working hard not to let it show. "That's all? Of course! What did you have in mind — and when?"

Eyes dancing with mischief, she said, "An intimate evening at the firing range. Our next night off."

He grinned. "Again? But we just went. All right, but since you got to choose the date, I get to choose the 'conditions.'"

She gave him a suspicious look. "What conditions?"

"We go to a jazz club afterward." At her ambivalence,

he chided, "Hey, if I have to spend the first part of the evening abusing my ears, I want something to soothe them later. Besides *you* got to choose the conditions tonight. We were supposed to talk about business over dinner — even though we aren't doing much of it."

Pulling a wry face, she replied, "I know. I feel silly sitting in a classy place like this calling two grown men — powerful ones, at that — 'Smokey' and 'Boo Boo.'"

"I feel silly calling them that at all! Especially seeing how I've never been particularly fond of bears. But I have a confession to make. You may be off duty, but I'm not. Be casual, but take a peek at the booth in the north corner."

Nonchalantly sipping her wine, she slid her gaze toward the indicated booth. She discovered Edgar Michalson viciously tearing into a steak. He wasn't happy, and she doubted it was a problem with the quality of the meat. All outward aplomb, she returned her glass to the table and her gaze to her tablemate, saying in a strangled voice, "You bastard! You love doing shit like that to me."

"Odd, I believe those sentiments are surprisingly parallel to those of our ursine pal, who was sitting two rows in front of us at the show, by the way. Honestly, I don't know why you're both upset. We're doing our duty as we enjoy an evening together and *he* is reassured we're on the job."

She shot him a scowl as she dug into her own dinner. The aromas rising from the plate had steadily coaxed mild hunger toward full-blown demand. Again she frowned at the small salad he'd ordered. "Are you sure that's all you want, BC? You need more than that."

He replied, "Please don't let my difficulty interfere with the meal. I like to smell good food and it's a pleasure in itself to see someone enjoying what I can't manage."

Too hungry to lodge a meaningful protest, she attacked her meal, happily discovering that the food justified the restaurant's reputation. BC maintained a light, entertaining banter, and though she delighted in the conversation, she discovered herself watching him with a certain fascination. As the waiter cleared the plates for the coffee, she realized why. He'd pushed his salad around on the plate, but hadn't taken so much as a mouthful. He'd played with his wine glass, too, lifting it several times, but the level of the rich red liquid hadn't dropped. Shit. Sometimes she wished she were in a different profession. She was always watching everybody all the time.

***

The kiss outside of her place was as warm and fierce as it was unexpected, but he responded enthusiastically. She pulled free of his embrace and studied him with an indefinable something lurking in the depths of her eyes. Suddenly, the hallway became quite confining and the blue pulse beneath the smooth skin of her neck tugged seductively.

Taking an awkward step back, he stammered: "I . . . I'd best be going."

She didn't move, but replied evenly, "Yeah, I'll see you tomorrow." In a beat, she was inside, and he heard the latch snick shut as loud as a gunshot.

Stepping out of peephole range, BC wilted against the wall, praying for strength to tackle the stairwell. Finally deciding additional strength wasn't forthcoming, he pressed the elevator button. The car arrived empty, and he descended in thankful solitude. The desire to return upstairs, to her apartment, to *her*, acted on him like a physical pull. Several hours had passed since he'd fed, and hunger made him vulnerable to the arousal spawned by her kiss. No. Returning was far too dangerous. If only she knew the truth . . . all evening, he longed to confide exactly what his 'condition' was. He wanted to trust her, but it was too early. Besides, what would he say? Lean over during intermission and whisper, *"Enjoying the show? By the way, have I told you I'm a vampire?"*

He winced at the absurdity as the elevator deposited him in the lobby. It *was* too soon, no matter how attracted he was to this lady — or for that matter, how attracted she was to him. He jogged down the stone steps to the waiting cab, and fishing out the fare plus a sizable tip, said, "Thanks for waiting, but I don't think I'll be needing the taxi after all."

The driver pocketed the cash with a knowing leer. "I thought it'd end up that way, buddy. That's a great lookin' woman ya got there."

BC smiled, reinforcing the assumption. He headed to the stairs, veering off as the cab disappeared into traffic. First to find someplace warm and crowded, then to feed. If memory served, there were several bars not far distant. Remembering his evening wear, he wryly observed that it wasn't often he actually fit people's common image of the vampire.

Enjoying the joke, he strode through darkened streets toward the brightest lights.

***

The night air was still and heavy. To the west, clouds gathered with the threat of a storm before daybreak. No! He was too close to brook failure now! He dropped his gaze to the leaf-littered forest floor. Well, so be it. The hunt might have to be abbreviated, but there would be pleasure enough in the final kill — the final healing. He was almost whole as it was.

Examining hands and forearms in moonlight as bright to him as the noonday sun revealed few scars remaining. Those that lingered were faint and he had to look hard to find them. The regeneration was almost complete. Stalking a beast this night would be a waste of his time. This would require more than a simple beast.

Becoming as still as the surrounding trees, he stretched his senses to their limit . . . searching. . . .

He found nothing. There was life surrounding him, but not the life he required. It was too much to hope fortune would smile, as on that first night when he found the perfect prey almost on his own doorstep. That had been more than fortuitous, because the weakness was full upon him. He'd been almost as rocky as on his first night as a vampire. It had taken a full kill to steady him then, too.

A breeze riffled the leaves at his feet and brought with it a hint of the scent he was searching for. He followed it, tracking it through the hollows until, in the distance, like a lone star, he saw the light of a campfire. Senses stretched again. Only a single heartbeat. Soon, Francesco Borgia would be whole again.

***

The kiss gave her three very important pieces of evidence.

One: his body temperature was *very* low.

Two: either he could hold his breath for a long time, or he *wasn't* breathing, and:

Three: she enjoyed it too much for comfort.

Forcefully lobbing her evening bag at the sofa, she kicked off the pumps and allowed the anger at BC and herself to build. Centuries ago, her suspicions could be forgiven for lurking in the back of her mind, but this was the twenty-first century, dammit. Men have walked on the moon and peered into the secrets of the atom, for chrissakes. She was an idiot for thinking— No. She wouldn't even dignify the thing by saying the word.

Dropping alongside the discarded purse, she drew her cell phone out and jabbed a speed dial button. It rang once at the other end. At the preoccupied hello, she snapped, "Taylor? I need you here right away, and yes, I know what time it is and you just got off Boo Boo duty, so you weren't asleep, anyway."

Over the click-whir of his computer powering down, Taylor ventured, "Okay. Do I get to know what's up?"

Suddenly, the fury fled, leaving her fatigued and vulnerable. Her reply was little more than a whisper, "I think I need you over here to tell me I've finally gone insane."

"Right. "Be there in twenty max."

***

Taylor was there in fifteen and let himself in, armed with a pack of beer and a bottle of whiskey in case it was as serious as it sounded. From the hysterical edge to her voice, his money was on the whiskey. It had been two years since he'd heard that tone, the night she called from the hospital with the news that her grandmother had died. Her grandmother had raised her and molded her into the woman she was today. The loss left her adrift, alone — and frightened. He wondered what happened between Stroud and Peale to trigger this. It had to be major, Stroud Girion was one of the toughest ladies he'd ever known.

She slumped on the couch, hunched over a dark drink,

unmindful of her evening finery and makeup that did nothing to hide the bruise-like smudges under her eyes. He opened himself a beer and sat quietly to one side, waiting. Best to let her set her own speed. Rushing her would only spark the volatile anger he sensed underlying the upset.

He didn't have to wait long. After a few beats of heavy silence, she began to speak with a frightening calm. The account was coldly laid out like a line of evidence cards pinned to their office board, the observations linked with incisive intuition as accurate as her target shooting. Listening with outward detachment, his inner thoughts raced from dismay to elation. There hadn't been time to share his offbeat deductions, yet here they were coming from *her*. Her voice quavered perceptibly only once — as she detailed the final kiss. The following silence vibrated as she waited for him to either burst into laughter or call 911.

He did neither. Instead he asked, "I take it you've reached your own conclusion, Detective Sgt. Girion. Mind sharing it?"

Feigned calm shattered, she plunged off the sofa and started frantic pacing. "My 'conclusion' is crazy, Taylor. I won't *say* that word — it's that damned tabloid crapola—" Breaking off with a sniff-gulp, she pointed toward the whiskey bottle. "Is that Jameson? Oh, good. All I had in the kitchen was Brannaugh's damned dark rum. I hate rum."

Taylor handed over the bottle, and leaned back, steepling his fingertips with an infuriating pedagogical air. "OK. Let's see what we have: Only works at night. Claims to have an allergy to sunlight. No reflection in mirrors or mirror-like surfaces. Doesn't eat solid food. Claims to take his sustenance in liquid form, yet is never actually seen to take a drink." He glanced at her over his fingertips. "Better make that 'never seen to drink normal beverages.'"

Ice crunched viciously, and he covered a satisfied smile. She was getting pissed at him. Agro he could deal with, angst was another thing entirely. He continued, "Cold skin, and he might not be breathing . . . ." He chanced a peek under his lashes and found her glaring fixedly at the oriental rug at her feet. He asked, "Heartbeat?"

Burning gaze unwavering from the offending throw rug, she said, "I don't know. I couldn't tell through the coat."

Laughter burbled up. He didn't check it, instead, he threw back his head hooting helplessly. Stroud loomed dangerously over her convulsing partner. She'd halfway expected to be laughed at, but now that it happened— *"Dammit, Taylor, don't laugh at me*! I'm serious about this!"

Sobering with difficulty, he wiped his eyes with the back of his hand. "Sorry, I wasn't laughing at you. I couldn't help thinking that if *I* were a vampire, the last thing I'd do was date a detective, no matter *how* beautiful she was!"

Dropping limply into her seat, she spat, "You said that word."

"Detective?"

Threatening to come off the couch again, she warned, "Taylor. . . ."

He swigged his beer, then said, "Remember the great Mr. Holmes. 'When you have eliminated the impossible, whatever remains, however improbable, must be the truth.'"

"The great Mr. Holmes is as fictional as Dracula! I didn't need you to come over here to quote popular Victorian literature at me."

Smacking his bottle down, he demanded, "Then what *did* you need me here for? Did you want an opinion based on the facts as we know them, or did you merely want assurance that BC Peale is slightly balmy and you *aren't* falling in love with a guy who fits the profile of a mythic vampire?"

Damming tears behind tightly closed lids, she breathed, "It's that obvious. I bet the guys in the squad room are having a great time with this."

Dropping beside her, he kneaded her shoulder. "It's not obvious to anyone else — except Brannaugh, and it's his job to notice stuff like that. Look, you and I have been living in each other's pockets for five years now. We ought to know each other pretty well by this time."

Though tears still glistened in her lashes, she was back in control when she lifted her head and looked him in the eyes. "Okay, so what's the plan?"

He grinned. "That's my girl! I knew it would take more than being enamored of a suspected supernatural creature of the night to flap Stroud Girion for long." At her incipient wrath, he scooted away and raised his hands. "I surrender! I was trying to lift you from your morass of woe. You think better when you're pissed off than when you're sobbing."

"Well, it worked. You have ten seconds to tell me your take on this. One. . . ."

"I arrived at the same conclusion last night, but for the life of me, I don't know what to do about it other than wait and watch"

"BC was the Lake Shore Robin Hood, wasn't he?"

Noting her use of the lesser of his two titles, he agreed, "It certainly looks that way, but after working with him, I can't help thinking there's more to it than we know. It goes a long way to explain the half-truths we got from him and Galen about the Borgia stuff, though. D'you think maybe Borgia found out BC's dark secret and that's why we're getting hate-fear reactions about the guy?"

"Mmmm. It would also explain why those two got hustled out of Chicago and onto our turf without much warning."

"Yeah. I've got 'Smokey' surveillance coming up tomorrow night, and unless I miss my guess, Gae'll make certain I'm paired off with BC. Considering, he may be trying to protect you . . . BC didn't try anything tonight, did he? You know . . . try to hurt you in any way?"

Eyes flashing, she stated firmly, "NO."

"Sorry. I didn't think so, but I had to ask. Look, we'll see what happens tomorrow night, then take it from there. Whatever happens, they're *both* damn good cops."

She examined him over the rim of her glass with wry amusement. "Was that supposed to make me feel better?"

"Yeah. Didn't it?"

It was Stroud's turn to dissolve into helpless laughter. The release of pent-up emotion felt more refreshing than a shower.

***

"That's your extension again."

"Thank you, Galen, I noticed that." He scooped up the receiver. "Sentry International, this is Special Agent Peale."

"Byron, I'm glad ye've not left yet."

"Hi, Maeve. You *do* realize this makes your third call this hour?"

"Oh, shut up and let me finish. I've been keepin' tabs on Isendamer as well as Francesco. I just scried for her and she's not in Louisiana any more."

"She— Well, where is she?"

"I don't know, you dolt! That's what I'm sayin'. All I can tell you is that she isn't anywhere near where she was last night. If you want more specific information, you'll have to give me some time to cast again."

"Look, let me transfer you to Stallings. He's still in his office—"

"You call Stallings, *I'm* going to start another spell. Besides, you have such a charming way with the good Captain, it's so much more fun to have you handle it!" She hung up.

He glared at the now-dead receiver. "Doesn't she ever just say good-bye like a normal person?"

Galen said, "What was that about? You look like someone just steam-rolled your Harley."

"Isendamer has left Louisiana and Maeve isn't certain where she is. Ms Donal is leaving me with the happy task of telling Stallings."

"Better you than me, Pal."

Peale's snarl became a grimace as his telephone rang again. "Probably Maeve with specific instructions on how and when to tell Joe Stallings what. I wish she'd bloody well call him herself." He let it ring once more before answering, "Sentry International, Special Agent Peale speaking."

Instead of Maeve's lilt, his eardrums rattled under a pure Big Apple assault. "You tapped me! Goddammit, you *tapped* me. You weren't supposed to do that, kid."

"Hi, Eddie. Calm down—"

"Calm down, my ass! This is as civil as you're gonna get from me, asshole! You tapped me! No other way you could be in that restaurant last night — betcha were at the show, too, weren't you?"

"Eddie, it was a *date*, okay? I do that, too."

"With Detective Sergeant Stroud Girion of the New York Police? I don't think so, kid. Even you aren't that stupid. Or does she know what you are?"

"We're trying to protect you, Eddie. We ran the stuff you gave us and we agree with your assessment about Isendamer."

"Oh, well that's different. I feel warm and fuzzy all over, now. Look, kid, you tell your people to keep their distance from me and my people from now on. Got that?"

"No can do, Eddie, I just got word from Maeve Donal that Isendamer is on the move. Any guesses where she's headed?"

There was silence at the other end. BC tried again, "Look, you might want to let your boss know."

"Lissen, Kid, if you're so hot to tell Papa about Gwennie's sidelines, you better call him yourself. He'd love to hear from you, I guarantee it."

BC winced at the final click, then dropped the receiver into its cradle, grousing, "*Nobody* says good-bye anymore."

Gae drummed the desktop with his pen. "Well, that was real smart. Tell the target before you even tell the commanding officer. Uncle Joe is not going to see much humor in that."

"Tough."

"Yes, it is tough, Peale."

Miller and Peale swiveled toward the voice. Joseph Stallings stood in the doorway white with anger. "Just when did you intend to let me in on the secret of Isendamer's whereabouts?"

"I was about to tell you about it when Michalson called, sir."

Galen nodded. "He was, captain, that's the truth."

"Fine. You should know that our surveillance team just reported that Michalson's people are busy moving everything out of the office."

BC winced. Stallings leaned onto his desk and hissed, "You had just better hope like hell he's going to a location we know about, mister. Regardless, he's your responsibility from now on — yours and Tyler Taylor's. Maybe with Sgt. Girion out of the way you can keep your mind on the job." He jabbed his finger in the silent agent's face. "This is a *real* job for some of us."

As Stallings stormed back down the hall, BC fell limply into his chair and looked over at Galen. "Damn."

Miller shook his head. "Hey, don't expect sympathy from me. I'm with Stallings on this one."

"What?"

Galen stood and snatched his jacket. "Better move your ass, we have to meet Taylor and Stroud in fifteen minutes. I'll give you the honors of explaining why Michalson did a bunk."

"How in hell was I supposed to know Eddie'd go off like this?"

"I don't want to talk about it. Now are you coming or are you going to drive yourself?"

***

It was cold, but Gwen Isendamer tore along the road with the convertible top down, enjoying the wind whipping her hair and face. She took one hand off the steering wheel to caress the small black plastic box bouncing on the seat next to her. Soon. She took a tight curve at high speed and reveled in the rush as the little car fought her control and laughed aloud as she gained the straightaway again. *What will it be like,* she wondered, *to take a curve like that on the motorcycle, clinging to Byron Peale?* They had so much in common, she could hardly wait until they could be together. Would it be as instantaneous a bond as it had been with Francesco? She'd know soon enough. Regretfully, she slowed as she neared her destination and caressed the small black box again. Ah, well, business first, pleasure later — and wasn't it so nice that some business was a pleasure?

***

Crime was paying pretty well for Eddie Michalson. His place outside town was too small to be called an estate, but still very nice. Taylor wriggled against rough tree bark, and scanned the well-manicured lawns with the night glasses. Their hill commanded a clear view of the house and grounds, but was far enough from the orbits of the neighborhood security patrol to prevent an awkward encounter. It was also colder than the ninth circle of Persian hell. Damn. Hadn't anyone told the weather it was summer now?

Checking his unusually laconic companion, he wondered what to do about the uncharacteristic spate of silence. Okay, so BC screwed up. Everyone did sooner or later and no harm done here since Eddie headed straight for his private residence. Probably didn't realize the authorities knew about it since it was purchased under a pseudonym. Anyway, he didn't think that was quite enough to cause the massive friction he was witnessing. Whatever the cause, the fallout was so bad that on the drive over, BC hardly uttered a word unless prompted. Shivering suddenly, Taylor huddled over the meager warmth of his insulated coffee mug, wishing to God Eddie had been more ostentatious in his choice of homes. Just then, he'd have killed for a nice, cozy carriage house to slip into.

Thoughtfully studying BC's silhouette curled around his own cup, Taylor resumed his inner struggle with the concept of vampirism. Intellectually accepting it as a bizarre, but logical bottom line for a specific set of data was one thing — accepting it emotionally was another. Stroud preferred the insanity plea, but his training said this man was not mentally unbalanced. Troubled, yes, and more so tonight than usual, but not insane. That left one option: there were such things as vampires and he was currently sharing a cold hilltop with one. He ached to fire questions until he could think of nothing else to ask. That was *not* an option, though. Not here, not now. Anyway, BC was so steamed about whatever went down between himself and Galen that tossing a large packet of unpleasant surprise on the bonfire would be a real bad idea. Still, he had to do something, the silence was making him nuts. Hoping he sounded calmer than he was, he began, "So, was Gae all over you about getting involved with my partner or what?"

The oval smudge of Peale's face snapped sharply around and Taylor held his breath, enduring the scrutiny. At that moment, he'd have given a lot to know how *well* he was being scrutinized, but he kept quiet and waited. BC stayed quiet, too, but the tilt of his head gave the impression he was thinking over how — or whether — to answer. Finally, settling back against his side of the tree, he groaned. "You, too? Good thing I'm not a conspiracy buff, or I'd think you, Uncle Joe and Galen arranged this beforehand."

Taylor grinned in the darkness. "Thought that was a big whack of it. No worry, I won't add any agro. As you're discovering, partners sometimes get over-watchful, but Stroud and I generally don't interfere with the other's romantic life." He took a swig of his coffee and continued, "Stroud is one helluva lady and the best friend I've got. Contrary to rumors past and current, our relationship is *not* as intimate as reported. We only tried that once. Talk about a disaster!

"It began with a candlelight dinner and ended with us standing on opposite sides of the bed, stark-o, shouting at each other about a case. Finally, we saw how absurd it was (in other words laughed hysterically), got dressed, popped a couple beers and watched movies on cable. It was stupid, but I think it made us better friends."

"You're getting at something, Taylor. Pardon me for being obtuse, but what?"

"I'm saying as long as Stroud's happy, I'm happy. Oops, I didn't mean that the way it came out — I'm not going to threaten to break your legs or anything like that."

This elicited a quickly smothered guffaw. "I'd be more afraid of that from the lady herself."

"Too right there, Mate!" Taylor joined in the muffled enjoyment, then sobered. "Seriously, what gives with you two?"

Peale considered. "I can't speak for her, of course, but I like her very much. It's been a long time since I cared for someone in this way."

Taylor wondered *how* long 'a long time' was and was fighting the urge to ask when Peale nudged him and whispered urgently, "Hey, look over there."

Taylor looked, but even with the bright moonlight, only saw shadows flitting across Michalson's roof. He grabbed the night glasses, but was still twiddling the focus when Peale's grip tightened. "I make six. All in black and all carrying weapons. We better call Stroud and Gae, then haul ass down there."

Taylor activated the cell phone and Galen answered before the first ring finished. Words tumbling over themselves in urgency, Taylor said, "Gae, BC says six guys in black carrying weapons just showed up on the roof of Michalson's place."

BC pulled his .45 and checked the clip. "They're dropping a rope to Eddie's bedroom balcony. I'm moving now." Riveted on the house, he hesitated. "Huh! They're running back the way they came . . . why . . . ?" In sudden horror, he broke into a run, shouting over his shoulder, "Oh *GOD*! Taylor get off — ring Eddie! Tell him—"

Gwen Isendamer's signature fireball lit the rolling lawn with a stark light and the accompanying roar shattered the peaceful night.

***

"*It's like nothing happened down here.*" Taylor observed on his flight through the strangely untouched foyer and up the staircase. At the top of the stair, he saw BC kick open a partly sundered door and race through.

Following his proxy partner into the wrecked room, he pulled up as rain spattered on his cheeks. Abruptly, he realized the 'rain' was from a ceiling sprinkler system that survived the blast and was now capably doing the job for which it was designed: quenching flames. Fire still ruled along an interior wall where the sparking remains of a large-screen TV defied the overhead shower with a spectacular pyrotechnic display. The track lighting hadn't fared as well and the sparking flames provided the room's only light.

Taylor quickly saw he could do nothing for the two bodyguards. They'd apparently been standing right by the French doors when the bomb went off. Michalson lay under the strewn cushions of a virulently green velour love seat that had been lifted by the shockwave and tossed against the wall. Blood covered every visible part, but Taylor was at a loss to tell whether it was Eddie's or from the ill-fated henchmen.

BC reached Eddie first, and flipping the love seat aside, bent over the motionless body. Face contorted with rage, he said, "He's alive, but just. DAMN! Screwed up again! I *knew* Isendamer's MO. I should have been watching for a bomb."

Taylor tossed him the phone. "Don't blame yourself, we *all* had the data. Call for backup and emergency teams, willya — not that every alarm system in the area hasn't dialed everyone possible. I'll see what I can do for our mate, here."

Swallowing his anger, Peale took the phone, then winced as a surge of static popped and faded. Snapping it closed, he swore violently. "I'm getting electronic interference, probably surges from the television. I'll kick the plug loose and see if it helps."

"NO! Don't go near that shit! With all this water about, you'll get your ass fried and I can only handle one casualty at a time. Go over to the balcony — or what's left of it, and try from there."

Amusement tugged at BC's mouth in spite of the surrounding carnage. "You're the doctor."

Cutting the sparking wreckage a wide berth, Peale stepped over the remains of the French doors, and stopped cold at the sight of a silenced rifle barrel pointed squarely at his breastbone. On autopilot, he dropped the phone, and leaped forward, slapping the evil-looking suppressor aside. Soggy acoustical tile spattered the combatants as the weapon emptied into the ceiling over the intended target's head. The would-be assailant kicked off the outside wall, attempting to swing out of reach. Eyes outlined by the slits of a knit ski mask widened as his opponent moved with inhuman speed to seize the collar of his black bodysuit and haul him inside, line and all. The sniper dangled long enough to utter a cry of unreasoning terror before his chest exploded with a spray of blood and gore.

A searing trail followed the bullet as it smashed through the sniper, then Peale's own ribs. He fell backwards with the body of the sniper sprawled across him. The tantalizing scent of fresh blood slammed into his already his reeling senses with a force greater than the bullet's.

The bloodscent was lost in the jolting wash of cold water as hands hauled him backwards and tore at his jacket. The red mist cleared and the alarmed face of Tyler Taylor swam into view, demanding, "Where were you hit? Eddie's shocky, but he'll keep, tell me where you're hit."

The inhuman rage faded as realization of what happened lent strength to push the screaming Hunger aside. He struggled up and away from the probing hands. "No. No, I'm not hit, I just got knocked down when the other guy was scragged. Take care of Eddie and get him out of the line of fire. I'll get downstairs to see if I can stop his murderous friends before they get away."

So saying, the bloodied agent drew his pistol, and jacking a round into the chamber, sprinted into the hallway. The sound of his passing was drowned by spattering water and the wail of fast-approaching sirens. The detective stared after him in shaken awe. Taking deep deliberate breaths, Taylor commanded his mind back to the job at hand and checked Michalson. He was well out of range where he was, and Taylor preferred to leave the task of moving him to the sure-to-be-arriving EMS team. Wary of snipers, he crabbed over to snatch the soggy cell phone, then darted back to cover. Reassuring himself the phone still worked, he called Gae and Stroud.

PART TWO

"I have seen something else under the sun:
The race is not to the swift
or the battle to the strong,
nor does food come to the wise
or wealth to the brilliant
or favor to the learned;
but time and chance happen to them all."

~~ The Bible Eccl. 9:15 (NIV)

"It ain't over 'til it's over."
~~ Lawrence 'Yogi' Berra

ONE

The sound of a horseman turning off the main road cut through the splash of the water. Collapsing against the lichen-covered masonry, Byron Peale cursed his luck at losing strength on such a heavily used thoroughfare. He'd just ignore it and pray the rider would pass without using the watering trough. The hollow clop of the animal's hooves grew louder and angled for the fountain. Soul railing within, he kept his back resolutely turned toward the unwanted company and his wet handkerchief firmly pressed to his face. The scent of the surging blood of horse and man penetrated the mossy odor of the water. The dual pulse pounded at his sharpened senses in a seductive rhythm that was becoming increasingly difficult to ignore. With a supreme effort, he wrenched the overwhelming thirst under control and concentrated on the cold wetness against his face. Concentrate . . . it was no use. The horseman dismounted and approached, each step bringing the tantalizing scents closer. Fear-tensed muscles strained against bone, as he willed the man to water his mount and be away.

A pistol's cylindrical hardness pressed into his ribs. Bewildered, he looked up into a highwayman's mask. He tried to make his shocky brain work — no joy — the man was too close and bloodscent filled his senses. The bandit laughed, as from the end of a very long tunnel. "Well, well, one of the illustrious Peales out alone on a dark night. The black sheep of the flock, too. Let's hope you haven't drunk up all your gold, Byron, or I'll have to kill you. Ah, I think I'll do it anyway!"

The pistol roared. The ball tore through his midsection and he slammed into the retaining wall in back of the trough—

Muffling a cry of pain, his head flung up as the Colonial Philadelphia street dissolved into a resolutely empty mirror reflecting only the institutional washroom of the New York Sentry Hospital. It was fever that resurrected the long-ago night — likely a form of delirium. He gulped back panic and his rising gorge; it wouldn't do to vomit again.

Not that there was much left to come up; he'd used up most of his earlier feeding in the night's activities. The violent retching brought on by injury and shock had doubtless cleared whatever was left — as if he wasn't light-headed enough. Another spasm swamped his resolve and he heaved again into the lavatory. Spent, he dropped to his knees, hot forehead pressed against the cool porcelain of the fixture. He rinsed the telltale scarlet stains down the drain. Shakily pulling himself to his feet, he leaned against the sink, swabbing a cool compress over his forehead and throat. It helped a little.

If only there'd been time to tell Gae he'd been shot, but getting Eddie into the care of the SI docs was the priority. *He'd* survive, but it wasn't a sure thing about Eddie. What scared him most was that Tyler Taylor, resident genius, saw him take the hit. True, he'd backed off after BC insisted the bullet missed, but still. . . .

He'd absented himself far too long. Better don the mask and get back to the others, Taylor was suspicious enough, lingering would only make it worse. He checked his makeshift bandages, wincing at the angry, torn flesh beneath them. At least the bleeding was slowing — but, maybe that wasn't so good. If he wasn't careful, he'd slip into dormancy. No, he didn't want to think about the consequences of *that*. Willing himself to walk normally, he zipped his thankfully undamaged jacket over the paper toweling and flipped the latch on the washroom door.

***

Taylor's abrupt request of a detour to Richie Tsu's medical lab made Stroud tighten her grip on the steering wheel. Mentally holding her breath, she asked, "What's this about?"

"Sounds like you've got a pretty good idea it's about BC. You're right. I saw him do some amazing things tonight and. . . ." He held up a sealed evidence bag in the intermittent dark-light as they passed under street lights, then continued, ". . . that shooter didn't miss. I saw it with my own baby blues, this slug passed right through him. I retrieved it from the carpeting when he ran after the gunmen. Unless I miss my guess, he's pretty badly hurt — he ought to be on a slab in the morgue instead of hogging the gent's and trying to act like he's all healthy and everything. This landed in wet carpet, but there ought to be enough blood and tissue on the little nasty for tests."

Stroud had seen far too many shootings in her career, and swallowed hard at the images Taylor's story called up. "Doesn't he know you saw him get hit? I mean, that's a pretty big thing to hide."

"You don't know the half of it! I *saw* the wound before he pulled his jacket over it. He swore blue that the bullet missed, and he just got splattered with the mess from the other guy. I let him think he convinced me — it would have been a waste of time to do anything else. Eddie was stable, but I still didn't want to hang about arguing the issue with a stubborn vampire."

"You said that word again."

"After what I saw tonight, I think we're gonna be saying it a lot from now on. I want to run my tests, then we'll discuss what to do, okay?"

She didn't answer, but stared straight out the windscreen, hands white-knuckled on the wheel.

He pressed, "Is that okay with you?"

Stroud drew a deep breath before asking, "Does Richie know we're coming?"

***

Francesco Borgia railed against Heaven for this latest blow. Too soon! Outside his study, his dismissed henchmen buzzed in tones pitched so as not to disturb their employer. Few of them understood his nature and none understood fully. That was the way he wanted it. They were all wondering who would fill the spot vacated by this violent passing. The answer was simple, but would have baffled the debaters — nobody.

There was no one in the current organization capable of filling Edgar Michalson's position. Behind his purposely vulgar and untutored camouflage, Edgar hid a sharp mind and intuitive grasp of human psychology. That intuition also gave him understanding of Borgia's not-quite-human psychology. This, coupled with a healthy respect for his employer — respect Gwen Isendamer sadly lacked — brought him closer to true friendship than Borgia had experienced with a mortal in centuries.

DAMN DAMN DAMN you, Gwendolyn Isendamer! He wished he could crush her now. Sadly, her special business talents would be more necessary than ever for a while. Getting the corporation back on track would be simple enough, but he'd need to replace Edgar. That would be the hard part. Then and only then could he administer the justice she richly deserved.

He paused. According to his source, Edgar died in Sentry International's medical facility. Why there? There were hospitals and emergency centers much closer than the SI facility. Ah, but they all were 'civilian' operations. That begged the extremely interesting conclusion that Sentry agents were on the scene before anyone else. *How* much before everyone else? There was no help for it, he'd have to contact his man in Joseph Stallings' department. He didn't want to play that card, but he needed the whole story before he acted — at least as much of the story as he could get without bringing Eddie back from the dead.

You've won this round, Gwen, but I shall see to it you do not win the game. He wondered where she was. Her passionate hatred for Edgar would demand she be close at hand to witness his death, but there'd be little chance of catching her out. Gwen used cell phones almost exclusively so she could be next door and still claim to be in Louisiana. He hated that. He cursed her and the madness that nudged her into more and more rash acts.

If only Byron . . . NO! No time for his own personal madness. He'd regained so much balance, he could ill afford to lose it now. He called Gwen's number. The electronic connection trilled and was cut off sharply as a drowsy-sounding Gwen picked up. She always slept soundly after a kill.

Mastering his anger, he said, "Cara! I shall need you in New York. I have had the most dreadful news."

***

"Oh, God! Not Eddie, too. Who is doing this? Certainly, Francesco. I'll hop the first flight north and have *Campo della Ferrara* opened up and ready for you. Is Carlo at the house? Then I'll instruct him to be waiting when you arrive. Good-bye, Darling." Gwen Isendamer turned away from the telephone, stretched luxuriously and laughed with delight. "Oh yes, and Eddie, too. Whatever *will* we do without him?"

Her laughter was cut short by a nervous tap at her door. At her command, Tony De Luca entered and approached her desk. She was too elated to notice his mood. "Ah, Tony. It went swimmingly! I've just been on the phone with Mr. Borgia— Where's Vinny?"

De Luca squirmed under the icy glare. "Um. Vinny didn't make it back, ma'am."

She froze momentarily. "Was he captured?"

"Oh, no ma'am. I know your rules on that an' I took care of it myself."

Her elation fled and she all but fell into the armchair behind the desk. "What happened? When I left, everything had gone according to plan."

"Well, the hit went fine, Boss, you saw to that, but right after that everything went to hell. We was pilin' in the van to leave an' Vinny was doin' the final check when he radios and says 'Hold the phone, I'm about to make her Highness a very happy lady.' He went back and we waited. Then Vinny got pulled through the window by this other guy into Michalson's room. There wasn't no other way, except to shoot through Vinny and into the other guy. Vinny died. The other guy got up."

"Got up?"

Tony blanched and nodded. He knew she wouldn't like that part.

"No one gets up from a direct hit from a high-powered rifle."

"Honest, Ms. Isendamer, the guy got up. He just got up and came tearin' down the stairs after us — like some kinda goddam ghost!" He blinked hopefully at his boss.

She was not smiling.

***

What he saw upon entering the VIP waiting room made Captain Stallings pause, then hurriedly latch the door behind him. Special Agent Peale was collapsed into a chair in an apparent faint with an agitated Special Agent Miller attempting to disrobe him. Catching sight of a spreading red stain on Peale's shirt, he demanded, "What's going on here?"

Peale stirred and Miller straightened. "Captain, this punk just informed me that the sniper actually hit him at Michalson's place tonight."

Stallings jolted. "Good God, man! Why didn't you say something earlier? I'll call the doctor!"

Peale tried to sit up, but instead nearly slid onto the floor. Miller caught him, reinstalled him in the seat, and answered sourly, "The idiot was waiting until Girion and Taylor left, but the doc sounds like a real good idea to me. Maybe the guy Dr. Klotski sent the records to?"

With a visible effort, Peale rallied. "No doctor — please. I'd rather not put up with the hassle of explanations right now. All I need are some real bandaging materials. These institutional paper towels have such large wood chips in them, I think they're doing more harm than good.

Swearing with a vehemence that surprised Stallings, Miller

ripped Peale's shirt open, revealing a blood-sodden pad crisscrossed with white first-aid tape.

BC grinned weakly. "Nicked the tape in the emergency room. They had so many rolls and were so concerned with Eddie, I didn't think anyone would notice."

Wordlessly, Miller peeled the tape back with a delicacy unexpected from hands so large, lifting the scarlet mass to reveal the damage it concealed. Peale winced as the wad thudded unceremoniously into the trash can, then said, "I will need more blood, though. I was sick, too."

The DSOI stretched forward for a better look and blanched. "That looks like it went straight through!"

Peale sat up a bit more and nodded. "In this case, looks aren't deceiving. I was lucky, though, it missed my jacket. It isn't that I'm tired of repairing and replacing them — well — I am, but I was able to zip it up and convince Taylor I wasn't hurt." He added faintly, "Maybe I should have just kept acting okay. It hurts worse now that I admitted it's there"

Miller stopped plucking paper fragments out of the wound and asked sharply, "Taylor saw this?"

"No, I got it covered over in time." Peale hesitated, then stated more firmly, "I'm sure of it."

Joe Stallings' mind rebelled. This man had taken a fatal wound over an hour ago . . . oh. He decided quickly. This was a secret and he was good at keeping secrets. It wasn't the first secret he'd kept that he wasn't completely comfortable with, and it wouldn't be the last. He cleared his throat and said, "You'd better be right, Peale. Tyler Taylor is one of the most intelligent people I've ever met. If he wasn't completely convinced by your charade, he won't rest until he learns the truth. Believe me, the fact that *most* rational people don't believe in vampires will be a mere a hiccup for his brand of logic. Stroud Girion isn't be trifled with, either."

Peale grinned, revealing unnervingly sharp and visibly lengthening canines. "You're the third person to offer that warning, and it sounds like you don't lump yourself in with 'most' any more, sir."

Miller also noticed the lengthening canines. He stood quickly. "I better see about getting that blood, Captain."

Stallings stopped him. "No, stay with Peale. I'll have better luck rounding up the necessary things . . . unless . . . ." His voice trailed as he studied the languid vampire.

Galen followed his gaze, then smiled. "It's okay, he doesn't do friends." Sneaking another look he amended, "But maybe you better hurry anyway. Looks like he's fading and I don't relish the idea of trying to carry an apparent corpse out the back door of a hospital."

Mustering a laugh at the macabre but humorous image, the DSOI fairly bolted into the hall. As the door whispered shut behind him, he heard Miller asking, "*Third?*"

"Jump."

"Oh."

TWO

His lips, as they brushed her throat, were cold as ice, but she welcomed their caress. Soon he'd take what he needed. Then, once he was replenished—

A hand gripped her shoulder and shook it vigorously. She lunged upright, to find herself on a rumpled gurney in a smelly laboratory. Instead of the indigo eyes from her dream, she found the piercing and slightly amused cornflower blues of her partner.

"That must have been some dream. I kind of hated to wake you up," he said.

Dragging stiff legs off the gurney, she grumpily rubbed circulation into the arm she'd lain on. It *was* some dream. They *all* were. She'd been having steamy dreams about BC Peale several times a night since their theater date. Well, okay, since before that, but they only took on vampiric overtones since that night. Regardless, she wasn't about to tell Taylor. Instead, she yawned. "What'd you find out?"

"Nothing that we didn't expect to."

"Well, *that's* edifying. Such as?"

"The blood and tissue on the slug are human, but they react unlike anything I've ever come across. I woke you because I'm ready for the final test." At her cranky and sleep-besotted glower, he elaborated, "The sun came up about a half hour ago. I want to take the remaining sample outside and see what happens."

Girion peered dubiously at the tiny blot of pinkish goo in the container. "There isn't much there."

"I know, and absolutely nothing might happen. Humor me."

"Let's go."

Outside, they found a low concrete wall bathed in the full morning sun. Taylor set the glass dish on the gritty surface, removed the lid and waited. At first nothing happened, then the sample bubbled, smoldered, then rapidly reduced to the consistency of ash or dust. They stared at the remains in silence, then Taylor clapped the cover back over the dish and slipped it deftly into another evidence bag.

Watching her partner zip the bag, Stroud murmured, "I think we better get back in there and clean everything real good before Richie or any other folks begin arriving for work."

"And I'd better destroy my notes."

"No. Keep them for a while. We might need them when we talk to Galen this afternoon."

"Before sunset."

"Exactly."

Taylor gave a massive yawn and stretch.

Grinning, Stroud took his arm and towed him back into the building. "After you've gotten some sleep, that is."

He vigorously scratched his unruly honey-blond mane and said, with a sleepy grin, "You're the doctor."

***

The tiny gray mouse vanished in a puff of cyber-smoke as a particularly sneaky cat pounced between two blocks and nabbed him from the rear. Galen Miller smacked the tabletop and growled, "Damn! Thought I had that closed off."

Clicking away the offer of another game, he shoved the tablet aside and took a swig of coffee. Pfah! Cold again. A sharp rap at the door headed off a tirade about sadistic vampires who thought it was hilarious to get innocent people hooked on stupid computer games. Bestowing a final glare of disgust at his cold, milky drink, he stomped to the entry.

He'd scarcely identified the visitors, before they pushed wordlessly past him. Staring after the pair in astonishment, and taking in the twin dark looks, closed the door firmly and exclaimed, "Well, do come in! I wasn't expecting you guys until later tonight. What brings you out so early?"

Taylor hung back, maintaining a careful distance from Miller, but Stroud paced the middle of the room, splitting her glare between Galen and the short hall to the bedrooms. Uncertain which behavior disturbed him more, Miller glanced from one detective to the other. "Okay, guys. You better tell me what gives."

Stroud pivoted and demanded through clenched teeth, "*We'd* better tell *you*? Where is he?" Gesturing down the corridor, she continued, "Is he down there? Left or right? I'd guess right. Left would be the outside room — too hard to block the windows."

Galen eyed Stroud with a mixture of understanding and misgiving. She was dangerously close to hysteria — well, different people reacted differently to learning that vampires were real. He answered carefully, "Yes BC has the inside room, but you won't be able to talk to him right now. He's sleeping, and when he goes down, he's impossible to wake up."

From behind him he heard, "I *bet* he is."

Stroud started down the hall, asserting in a flat voice, "I want to see him."

Taylor startled Miller by diving around him and darting after her. Clearly whatever plan they'd worked up before coming, this wasn't it. That didn't matter, he couldn't let them go down the hall. A few swift steps brought him between Stroud and the arched opening. He spoke gently, "That won't be possible, Stroud. He locks his door. Let's sit down and talk this over."

She evaded his hands as he tried to guide her to the couch, sidestepping to get past him. "Then I'll have to kick the door in."

Taylor called sharply, "I think that would be a bad idea, Stroud."

Raw fury blazed as she rounded on her partner. "You, too?"

"We wanted to confront him, not kill him, remember?"

She froze, then, seeming to shrink into herself, buried her face between her clenched fists and began to sob into them. "That bastard!"

Taylor shrugged. "We know about BC."

"I figured that out. Maybe you better get her settled on the couch — I'll round up something strong to drink. I think we need it. Unless. . . ." He shot an uncertain glance down the hall, then looked questioningly at the tall Australian.

Taylor assured, "That part's over, and it wasn't the plan in the first place. She's more upset than I thought she was."

Nodding abruptly, Galen ducked into the kitchen, and reemerged carrying a tray with tumblers, a bottle of amber liquid and a bowl of ice. Placing it on the nearest table, he gestured uncertainly, and said, "Didn't know if anyone wanted ice."

Taylor said, "She does."

Stroud, sobbed openly and clutched at the glass. "She doesn't!"

Taking his own drink, Taylor launched into a step-by-step account of their side investigation. He finished by saying, "So, if I hadn't been suspicious beforehand, I would have flat out freaked when he took that bullet. As it was, I was pretty wild. Of course when he came up insisting he wasn't hurt, I didn't say different — if he'd been a normal guy, he wouldn't have been standing at all, and my Ma taught me never to argue with an injured vampire . . . how is he, anyway?"

Galen laid the neatly scribed notes on the table and replied resignedly. "He was in a lot of pain, but he's real good at hiding it — for a while, anyway. We patched him up at the hospital, and got him a couple units of blood, but the moron waited so long to tell anyone he was hurt, he tossed the first one. Just to be sure, though, we stopped off at the stock pens by the harbor before we came home."

Stroud sipped at her tumbler, then leaned forward to top it off again. The lady made a fast comeback. Momentarily perplexed, she asked, "Stock pens? Why . . . *oh!*"

Taylor poured his own. "Beef on the hoof, I assume. That's interesting. Any kind of blood will do?"

"It has to be a mammal — you should hear him talk about the time he was so desperate, he tried a fish."

Stroud looked horrified. "Yuck! He *didn't?*"

Snickering, Galen nodded. "Not successfully. I can't tell you how good it is to be able to talk about this. We been busting our brains trying to figure out how to tell you the truth." Turning to Stroud, he added, "He especially wanted to tell you."

She nodded and dropped an ice cube into her drink. When the catch in her throat didn't dissolve, she nodded more firmly and vigorously swished the ice around in the glass.

Galen continued, "We weren't sure how you'd take it, though — especially in view of the trouble we were having with Stallings."

Taylor perked up. "Were? Is the past tense significant?"

The big man nodded again, this time fighting a smile. "Shoulda seen his face. Too bad it took Peale getting shot to convince him, but I do have to cut the guy a little slack. 'Your new agent is a vampire' has a little more negative impact than 'your new agent is a diabetic' or something." He paused ordering his thoughts, then said, "Look, it'll be simpler if I start at the beginning like you never heard it before, and we'll get to other stuff as it comes up. Now that you know about BC's condition, a lot of things are probably clearer than before. A lot hinges on believing in vampires." Pausing again, he glanced at his watch. "I'd better get to it before he gets up, too. It's kind of personal and he gets pissy if he has to talk about it."

Taylor asked, "Y'mean like his relationship with Borgia?"

Galen jumped like he'd touched a live wire.

Stroud frowned at her partner. "What are you talking about?"

Taylor gestured widely. "Hey, I told you I was a deductive genius, didn't I?"

Later over a table littered with chip crumbs and empty soda bottles, Galen finished, ". . . and I couldn't very well walk up to you guys at the airport and say, 'Hi! I'm Galen Miller and this is my partner, the Undead Stalker of the Night!'"

The familiar accent came from the short hallway behind them, "Why not? You've all but done it before."

They swiveled as one. BC, clad only in jeans and the bandage around his middle, leaned in the archway, regarding them with open uncertainty. Try as he might, he couldn't sort through the flurry of emotion bombarding him. Stroud was especially hard to read, and her heart gave a peculiar lurch when she heard his voice.

He crossed the room and fell sullenly into a chair, drawling, "Gave myself away last night, didn't I? Lost my temper and got stupid. I'm bad at that."

Taylor grinned widely. "Nah, we suspected long before that. Charlie Chan say, 'undercover vampire should never date pretty detective.' Seeing you take that hit was simply another piece of accumulated evidence. Talking of that, d'you want me to take a look at that tonight?"

With a sidelong look at Stroud, BC said, "Why not? I kind of want to know how it's healing anyway. I suspect not that well. I was pretty badly drained, and by the time I was able to feed, I was headed for shutdown. That never bodes well. The wood chips in the cheap-o paper toweling didn't help, either."

He stood with arms held out as Taylor removed Galen's handiwork, then frowned at the revealed wound with a dissatisfied grunt. Taylor eyed the wounds front and back, then asked doubtfully, "Are you trying to say *this* isn't healing well? This looks like it happened days ago, not just last night."

"Well, for me it isn't. As much blood as I had last night, this should be half gone by now. It depends on what made the wound, though, I don't get true infections and if the weapon wasn't wooden or silver — or not so wide as a church door like this one — I'm usually fully mended by the time I go down next dawn."

Fascinated, the forensic specialist bent again to probe the injury with skilled hands, then straightened and announced,

"Looks fine to me! Granted, my area is forensics, but considering our mate here, I think that's on the money. Where are the first aid supplies so I can get this escapee from a Roger Corman film rewrapped?"

Standing, Galen said, "They're in the bathroom. You get that while I rustle up more munchies. I warn you, Taylor, the stuff is in the bathroom cabinet and you might have to dig a little. BC calls it 'Fibber McGee's closet' and after hearing what that meant, I think he has a point."

Taylor sprinted down the hallway, calling over his shoulder, "Gotcha! I'll stand back before I open it. If I'm not back in twenty minutes, send for the K-9 unit."

With a start, BC realized he was alone with Stroud. Glancing nervously toward her, he found her sipping her drink, eyes thoughtful over the rim of her glass.

Lowering the tumbler to the table, she remarked, "Subtle, aren't they?"

Even with fewer emotions in the room, she was hard to read. Her scent, mixed with the whiskey, insinuated enticingly through his defenses and, urged on by his healing body, fanned the nascent pangs of Hunger. Breaking eye contact, he folded himself into a seat. "I don't blame you if you're angry, but whether you believe me or not, I was trying to work out how to tell you about — well — all of it."

"I know. Galen already told me."

"This changes everything — it usually does. You're probably ready to drag me into the sunrise by my—"

She leaned forward with an intensity that silenced him. Though he felt her eyes locked on him, he didn't dare raise his to meet them as she said, "When I first found out and right after I got here, I wouldn't have given good odds for your survival, but Galen explained a lot to us — to me. I'm not mad any more. I'm not sure how I feel. Let's give it time, okay?"

His eyes slid to her face as he treated her to his slightly lopsided smile. "Sure. Time's something I have a lot of."

Contemplating her melting ice, she said, "I also need to tell you how sorry I was to hear about Francesco Borgia. It must have been horrible to find out he was your vampiric father." He frowned, but remained silent. After a moment, she said, "It's a shame nobody gets to choose their parents."

He sat forward. "Oh, but I *would* have chosen my real parents. They were good people. I never knew my father, although I would have given anything to have done. He died just after I was born. My brother, Charles, took over as head of the family then. We were very poor and he was all of nine years old. . . ."

Watching his warm half-smile of memory as his words trailed off, she found herself both reluctant to intrude on his thoughts and even more attracted by this display of his gentler side. Dimly a chime of memory was struck by the name Charles Peale, but she was unable to dredge up anything other than it had something to do with Sister Alicia's history classes.

She probed, "How old are you?"

He looked a little pained. "I'm around two hundred-sixty."

Wow. Even though she'd expected an answer along those lines, hearing the words came as a shock. She had a lot of thinking and research to do. Hmmm. She owed Sister Alicia a call . . . that ought to be a good place to start.

Reinspecting him, she found him gazing steadfastly at a

point on the carpet, handsome face carefully arranged in a neutral expression. It was like he was preparing himself to be hurt. How strange. Did he feel so strongly about her, or was it something else entirely? She couldn't deny she felt a strong attraction to him. Taylor accused her of falling in love — maybe — what was wrong with that, anyway?

She hummed thoughtfully. "Okay. I've always had a thing for older men."

He burst out laughing and relaxed into the BC she'd become familiar with. "Thank you. I can't tell you how that eases my mind. However I hope you'll forgive me if I don't spring forward to enfold you in a tender embrace. Y'see I woke hungry and if I say you smell wonderful tonight, it might not be a compliment."

"Oh!" She faltered momentarily under the unexpected and disturbing statement, then recovered by arching an eyebrow and shaking her finger in a passable imitation of Reverend Mother. "We're *still* gonna talk, mister. I want time to chew this over *and. . . .*"

In a quicksilver move, she smacked her palm solidly against the swinging kitchen door, eliciting a pained "Ow! *HEY*!!" from Galen, who eavesdropped directly behind it, then continued sweetly, ". . . More privacy. My place. I have tomorrow night off — I'm fixing chili. *You* better get dinner beforehand."

THREE

Nothing had changed other than her perceptions. Objectively, what would she think if she stumbled unknowing onto this scene? Probably, '*Wow, I hope that guy getting the first-aid doesn't put his shirt on real soon.*'

Who'd know the injury being tidily bound should have been fatal and that one of the four plastic cups contained cow's blood rather than cola? Squishing the giggle-urge, and profoundly grateful vampires weren't telepathic, she looked again, and saw little to raise an eyebrow. Maybe she was rushing things, or maybe simply becoming comfortable with the idea of what he was faster than she'd expected. Whichever, there were definite advantages to a relationship like this.

The telephone at her elbow rang stridently, and from the kitchen, Gae sang out, "Whoever's closest, grab it. It's probably Uncle Joe making sure BC's resting and not out partying."

Yeah, Stallings *would* do something like that. She answered using her business voice, "Peale and Miller residence." Her expression changed and she responded, "Why yes, it is, but . . . ."

BC grinned, and apologizing to his erstwhile medic, hurried to the phone.

Stroud handed the instrument over with eyes narrowed. "It's your friend, Jump. What have you been telling him about me?"

"Nobody has to *tell* Jump Veron anything." Taking the receiver, he enthused, "Hi, Jump! I hate that I'm missing the jazz festival this year and listening over public radio just isn't the same — depress me, tell me how much I'm missing."

"The festival is as wonderful as always, *mon ami*, and if this were a social call, I would have many amusing things to share with you, alas, it is not so."

"That sounds ominous. Hit me."

"Maeve has left Chicago."

"Oh. When?"

"No idea. I was all day at the Festival downtown, me. I come back to the club early because I feel something wrong and *POOF*! She is gone, leaving only the note to say she has been transferred and cannot say where."

"Transferred by who? Sentry? D'you think they're sending her here?"

"I feel yes to all, and I do not think she is so happy right now. If she is, indeed, headed your way, she will seek you out." He chuckled. "Perhaps you should get the other woman out of the way before she arrive, eh?"

BC rolled his eyes. Jump could never resist ribbing his friend about his love life. Voice dripping with sarcasm, he said, "Thanks, oh great Swami, whatever would I do without your sage advice?" Sobering, he asked, "Seriously, though, have you called Jim Nelson?"

"*Non*, I think me, it is bes' I call you first. I am not so sure Captain Nelson would tell me anything. However, I think if she head your way, you should know."

"Thanks, Jump — this time, I mean it."

A familiar too-rich perfume reached him before frantic the pounding sounded. Taylor moved toward the door, but

BC shot out a powerful hand to hold him back. Punctuating his action with a warning head-shake, the vampire spoke into the telephone again, "Jump, Maeve's at the door now. I'll call you back later, okay? Bye."

Galen poked his head through the swinging doors from the kitchen and winced. From the side of his mouth he told the detectives, "Remember the witch I told you about? Ladies and gentlemen, let the fireworks begin." Pulling back inside, his murmur was barely audible, "I better get another glass . . . and a flak vest. . . ."

Peale rushed past the puzzled detectives to fling wide the door.

Maeve rushed past him, slammed the door, locked it behind her, and threw her arms around him. "Not that lockin' the door will keep them long. Oh, Byron, I'm so glad you were here. I was afraid you'd be out—" Catching sight of the bandage, she pulled back. "—oh, what's happened?"

He'd been prepared to be angry, but the depth of her agitation concerned him. He guided her toward a chair, saying, "We can talk about what happened to me later. Right now, I think you need a drink, then you can tell us about what happened in Chicago."

For the first time Maeve, noticed the man and woman standing just behind Byron — who slapped his forehead and said, "I'm a ditz with no manners. Maeve Donal, permit me to introduce Detective Sgt. Tyler Taylor and Detective Sgt. Stroud Girion of NYPD. And, before you ask, yes, they know everything." He turned and called, "Hey, Gae! We'll need another glass out here!"

"Gotcha covered. Even got Irish whiskey in it already." Galen pushed through the swinging doors extending a tumbler toward the new guest. The hand she took it with shook; concerned, he crouched beside her. "Hey! You okay?"

She smiled. "I'm fine, Galen, just a trifle peeved." Taking a sip of the whiskey, she eased back into the cushions. "Thank you. After the day I've had, this is most welcome."

BC leaned across the back of her chair. "Okay, you've got your breath back. What gives?"

"I apologize for the dramatic entrance, but I slipped away from my 'escorts' thanks to the crowd in the lobby and fair flew up the stairs to get here before they could stop me and lock me away again. That Captain Stallings of yours is a right beast."

"Finally, the seminar crowd comes in handy." Gae chuckled. "Don't blame Stallings on us, though. He was here before we were. Your note to Jump said you'd been transferred — was that Uncle Joe's doing?"

Maeve looked blank. "Uncle . . . oh! Uncle Joe as in Joseph Stalin. Very appropriate. I wish I could tell you what happened, but I honestly don't know! I was restin' up to scry against Francesco this evenin' when up pops Emily Hu, saying that orders came through to move me to the New York hostelry. She said she hadn't been told why. I believe her. She wasn't even supposed to let me leave the note, but I sneaked it when she was out of the room — conveniently out of the room, if you see what I mean."

Galen nodded. "Em's good people."

"Any bets whether this is in response to last night's little do?" Peale said.

"Wouldn't surprise me," Miller said. "Lots of shit's been hitting lots of fans since we put out that Michalson was murdered."

"No!" Maeve paled. "Not Eddie!"

Recognizing genuine shock, BC hastened to reassure her, "It's okay, Eddie isn't really dead — but he is seriously hurt. We simply put out the story he'd been killed for public consumption. For Borgia and Isendamer, mostly. We think Isendamer was behind the assassination attempt."

"I understand," Maeve said, recovering her composure. "Now I think it's your turn to tell *me* what's happened."

Tyler Taylor perched on the arm of the sofa. "The short of it is that Michalson's home was bombed last night. They sent in a sniper afterward to make sure there were no survivors. Fortunately for Eddie, BC and I were already there, so it didn't work quite the way they'd planned."

"Sniper?" She looked up at Byron who still leaned on her chair. "Is that how you got hurt? Protectin' Eddie?"

"Sort of," he said with a negligent shrug.

Stroud lounged in her corner of the couch, largely ignored and for once, happy as a little clam about it. So this was the woman who sicced Francesco Borgia on her ex-lover? Interesting that BC still trusted her. Maybe what burned between them wasn't completely snuffed out? Oh, well, that could wait. Rousing herself, she interjected, "I agree that it sure looks like Isendamer is here. That makes me wonder one: Where is she now? And two: Does Borgia know what she's been up to?"

BC shook his head. "We can't be absolutely sure, but from the sound of the tapes we've gotten from SI Canada, Borgia's in the dark on this."

The telephone rang again. BC grinned at Galen. "Your turn."

Galen groaned. "Three guesses who it is. We'll all get it." With that, he punched the speaker phone button. "Miller. You're on speaker"

"Miller, this is Stallings. I trust Ms. Donal can hear?"

Maeve said, "I can hear ye just fine, Captain Stallings."

"Uhh, good. The apartment directly above the one you're currently in is yours. You can pick up the key at the desk, whenever you're ready. Your luggage is already up there. I trust this will be satisfactory."

"As satisfactory as anything has been so far."

Stallings paused. "Good, then. Are the NYPD liaisons there?"

Peale slid a glance at Maeve and whispered, "Surveillance cameras. They were probably following you as soon as you hit the stairs." Then, louder, "Everyone is here, Captain."

"Well, people, our ruse worked. SI Canada reports that Borgia took off for New York in a chartered jet ten minutes ago. I'm already at the office. I want all of you here in thirty minutes for a preliminary briefing, then we'll hit the field." With that, he hung up, leaving only an amplified dial tone in his wake. Galen silenced it with a jab of the button.

Slipping into a fresh shirt, BC told Stroud apologetically, "From the sounds of this, we'll have to postpone tomorrow night."

She grinned mischievously. "Not if I can help it, Mister."

The bantering familiarity didn't escape notice and Maeve's eyes narrowed.

Peale pulled his motorcycle jacket on. "I guess we'd better get started for the office, then." He glanced uncertainly at Maeve. "Unless you want to freshen up before we go?"

"Thank you, Byron, but I'll go as I am. I, for one, would prefer to get this over with as soon as possible."

***

With a sick, sinking feeling, BC Peale realized where he'd seen the man who met the private charter from Canada. He was a Sentry Agent. He was in procurement; not a special agent, but high enough in Stalling's department to be a shock. As the pair passed him for the main terminal, his sire seemed preoccupied. Good. During his wait he'd become morbidly convinced Borgia would stroll casually over and say, "Good evening, Byron. My car is waiting." Worse, he was terrified he'd be powerless to stop himself from simply following his elder out and into the night.

Fear outvoted relief. They were well down the concourse before he thumbed two short bursts on his transceiver. He followed, relying on his enhanced senses to keep them in view. After all, that was the reason he was tapped as the inside spotter in the first place.

Borgia headed for a cluster of seats near the entrance, then sat so he could watch a limousine being loaded outside. He motioned the Sentry mole to the opposite chair. The elder vampire steepled his fingertips, regarding the human agent before him. "Now, Myre, what do you have for me?"

***

They were parked behind a subcompact and a limousine, when their radio hissed and Stroud Girion's voice crackled, "Scratch the exit. He seems to be heading for a stand of potted palms by the window."

Galen craned at the window opposite their unmarked car and gawped as the familiar form sank into a chair, motioning someone else into another. Alarm became anger as Miller spat, "Copy that. He's practically in our laps. I recognize the other asshole, too. John Myre; he's Sentry, but it looks like he's playing both sides of the fence." He replaced the communicator on the car seat and resumed his vigil. "Peale knows him, too. He's probably having a shit-fit in there."

Taylor expanded his scan for a nonexistent passenger to include the window. "I take it the short guy with the white streak is our Borgia, then. There's BC and you're right, he doesn't look happy. Not comin' too close — don't blame him, there. Took a lot of guts coming *this* close to the old man after what happened the last time."

Gae snapped a photo with his cell phone while pretending to make a call. Caution was supreme here, with Borgia staring straight at them. Too much activity would spell the worst kind of trouble. Suddenly Borgia's demeanor changed and his formerly roving eyes riveted on Myre.

"I wonder what the grass said," Taylor commented. "He's got Borgia's undivided attention. I'd give a lot for a laser mike right about now."

"No you wouldn't. Peale can see the damn laser — the whole beam, not just the contact spot. Borgia could, too."

***

The double agent squirmed in front of the plate glass. He'd risked everything coming tonight, but Borgia paid well, and that new house was costing beaucoup bucks. True, the palms shielded him from the terminal, but conversely, he couldn't see out, either. Aw, what the hell, unless someone at SI had a crystal ball, there was no way anyone could know he was here. Relaxing, he said, "For starters, your guy ain't dead. Somethin' big went down last night, but the Special Agents they imported from Chicago have things sewed up tight. On toppa that, we got Joe Stallings givin' the CIA treatment to the whole Special Ops branch. Clearance ratings an' all that shit. You wouldn't believe what I hadda go through to get what I got."

Borgia shifted dangerously and interrupted so softly, BC had difficulty hearing over the background noise. "These agents from Chicago, what are their names?"

Myre looked blank. Of all the questions he'd expected, he never thought that would be high on the list. "Ummm. Galen Miller and BC Peale. Why?"

"Answer questions, do not ask them. Continue," Borgia snapped.

"Uh, right. Anyways, it's on accounta Stallings' cloak and dagger stuff that what I got is sketchy. It boils down to somebody blew up your guy's house last night but Peale was there and pulled him out. They put out the story it was a gas leak and that the guy died. That's it."

Amazingly, Borgia leaned back and chuckled deep in his chest. After a moment, he waved a dismissive hand at his spy. "Go. You have done well. You will be paid in the usual manner."

The man sped away in such haste, he almost collided with a tall red-haired woman standing next to the newsstand.

***

"Stone the crows! Hey, Myre is leaving in a hurry — just about ran Stroud down. It's gonna hurt like blazes to let that guy stroll outta here."

"Yeah, but we know where the sonuvabitch lives and we got hard evidence now. He won't fly far."

The principal target remained seated, apparently lost in thought, his amusement never fading. Moments later, the uniformed chauffeur, previously busy loading expensive suitcases into the limousine just ahead of them, stood in front of the glass. Catching the preoccupied vampire's attention, he signaled toward the car. Borgia nodded curtly and rose.

Taylor put the automobile in gear and said, "Lady Luck's ridin' with us tonight! They're right in front of us and it looks like showtime. See Peale anywhere?"

Galen scanned the throng as Borgia stepped into the waiting car. "Not a hair. But considering Peale's ability to disappear when he wants to, that's no surprise."

The limo glided smoothly down the drive. Taylor gave it a short lead, then eased out to follow.

With an ear-splitting grate of metal on metal, the sedan lurched and bounced under the impact of a small, but rapidly moving shuttle van. Roaring in inarticulate rage, the detective kicked open his door and advanced on the shuttle driver who was yelling for somebody to call a cop.

Taylor flipped open his ID and snarled, "Too late, I'm here."

As the shuttle driver backpedaled, Gae exited the sedan. Pounding the hardtop in frustration, he watched the limousine melt into traffic.

"You'll have a hard time explaining fist dents to the motor pool, Gae."

Whirling toward where his wryly smiling partner leaned on the wrecked car, Galen growled, "The whole night's setup just got screwed royally, what do *you* have to smile about?"

His partner's smile twisted as he answered seriously, "The limo that just left? *I* wasn't in it."

Galen stared, then glanced to where Stroud was intervening between the shuttle driver (hysterical), airport security (unhappy seeing the foursome again) and Taylor (livid). With sudden resignation, he dropped his head onto his arms and said, "You got the phone, partner. You'd better call this in before Security does."

"Oops. Right." He pulled out the device and dialed.

***

As the gates of *Campo della Ferrara* swung solidly together behind his limousine, he relaxed into the plush leather cushions and inhaled the fresh scents of his woodlands. This was the one place in the modern world where he felt truly at home and at peace. Sadly, he couldn't recreate the soaring spirit of *Casa d'Este*, the place he had been *truly* at home. The absence of his beloved sister and brother-in-law left a gap that could never be filled. He could, however, recreate the physical beauty of the palace, and although the flora and fauna of *Campo della Ferrara* were different from those of his native Italy, he felt he'd succeeded rather well.

With a pleasant jolt, he recalled that buying the land at the heart of this estate was why he had been in New York when Maeve summoned him to Philadelphia in 1780. He'd created his home and his son at the same time, and as they sprang from the same soil, both shared a wild beauty. He relished the symmetry.

Both were capable of surprising him, too. Though he'd been informed of his son's presence in the city, he was astonished beyond words to see the boy emerge from the same door he'd just used. The child must have been close, yet he'd sensed nary a whisper. Then, the boy ambled over to the automobile collision that first attracted his attention. There he stood beside Galen Miller, who angrily gestured toward his own departing limousine. How did they know? Ah, yes. Maeve. He'd sensed her magical presence several times lately.

While the scene was amusing, he wondered what they hoped to accomplish. Regardless of their original aims, they'd certainly identified one of his highest operatives in New York Sentry. No matter. He owed the boy for Edgar's life, and a paltry spy was of little import alongside that. Edgar's survival gave him more latitude in handling Gwen — and he *would* have to do something soon. The woman's madness was becoming uncontrollable. Allowing personal dislikes to interfere with business when that business was reaching its ultimate goals was inexcusable. She'd failed this time, but only because Byron and his companions had thwarted her. He did not intend to give her a second chance.

It would be as difficult to replace Gwen as Edgar, but now he had the luxury of choosing his own time and circumstances. *Perhaps,* he thought, *when the time came, his son could fill her position. Certainly, Byron did not possess her uncanny business acumen — who did?— but he had a capable mind.*

"We are nearing the house, Signor."

Carlo's voice crackled over the speaker, rousing him, giving him time to compose himself as the limousine rounded the curve of the drive and the sprawling mansion hove into view. He dreaded the day he'd have to replace Carlo. The man's ability to anticipate his employer's moods and his sense of timing were invaluable. It was almost enough to . . . *no,* he chuckled to himself, *Byron is enough of a handful for any father.*

As expected, Gwen ran down the stone staircase, all tears and hugs as he stepped onto the terrazzo. Knowing the hypocrisy behind it, the display doubly sickened him, but he suffered it for Carlo's sake. No sense in arousing her anger at the chauffeur by causing a humiliating scene in front of him.

Safely inside, he pushed her away. "*Basta*! I will have no more of this until you have told me why you left New Orleans without notifying me."

Her surprise was unfeigned. "But, Francesco, you asked me to come."

"No Cara, I have learned you were already *in* New York. Why did you not tell me of this, eh?"

Stricken eyes wide over crumpled hankie, she was silent. Borgia could almost hear her mind racing. He had a pretty good idea what her intentions were, but she could never admit them to him. Not without revealing her hand in the attack on Edgar.

After a moment, she spoke, a convincing catch quivering in her voice. "Oh, darling, I wanted to surprise and please you, but then this horrible thing happened to Eddie and. . . ."

Rummaging in the briefcase resting on the hall stand, she produced a photo clipped from a newspaper. Thrusting it into his hands, she said, "Here. It was in the New Orleans paper and I rushed up here to see if it was true. I thought Eddie might know something — you know how he is . . . *was* about the news."

He stared at the grainy image of his child. Reading the accompanying text, he again marveled at the boy's ability to dumbfound him. He'd not seen or heard any of this — but then, there was no one in Canada who knew of Byron's existence. If Edgar had seen it, he'd be inclined to investigate thoroughly before passing the information on, especially in light of his employer's recent problems.

He became aware of Gwen watching him. The intensity

of her scrutiny made him want to take a step back.

She said, "I'm sorry it happened this way, Francesco. I so wanted to be able to bring you and Byron together. Under the circumstances, I haven't made much headway. I didn't want to bother you with it until I'd spoken with him . . . Byron, I mean." In the face of his continued silence, she added, "I was worried when I saw the television coverage. I wondered if you saw it, since it made the international cable networks. I kept my fingers crossed you wouldn't until I could check it out."

So, it was televised, too? Edgar never missed a broadcast; he must have known. Curious . . . more curious is the way darling Gwen skirts the issue of speaking to Edgar. Did they talk? Possible. Aloud Borgia snapped, "*Basta*! Now is not the time for this, I have not fed this evening and have suffered a very long flight with the scent of mortal blood filling my nostrils. We will discuss this after I have sated my hunger."

Leaving her open-mouthed in the foyer, he ascended the stairs to don more comfortable clothing for the hunt.

The woods were cool and lush, but even their pleasures and the insistent Hunger couldn't drive the things he learned from his thoughts. It was certain Gwen called this vendetta against Edgar for what she perceived as ruining her best chance to become a vampire before they left Chicago. He wasn't so delirious that he missed the angry voices from the next room. He owed Michalson for averting a calamity — giving a psychopath like Gwen Isendamer the power of a vampire could be called nothing less.

On the other hand, if this story about the arms shipment were broadcast on cable, Michalson, the self-proclaimed

'News Junkie,' would have seen it — and recognized both agents. *Edgar, Edgar! What game were you playing? I cannot believe you knew my son was in this city and did nothing about it. I wonder what you've done?*

Yet, Byron was close at hand when you needed him most. This is also interesting, but I cannot know the reasons for it until I speak with one — or both — of you.

Pausing his preternaturally silent progress, he cast a speculative eye toward the brightly lit house nestling majestically in its formal gardens. Amusement tugged the corners of his mouth. Abruptly, he threw back his head and roared laughter to the sky. Whatever Edgar was about, it was certain that Gwendolyn was going to *hate* it. Still chuckling to himself, he continued deeper into the wood, where the scent of a stag blotted out all but hot, pulsing blood and the chase.

***

In spite of the warm night, a fire blazed in the hearth Francesco Borgia leaned against. He surveyed the room again, enjoying the feel of it as much as the warmth of the fire. He'd owned this property for over two centuries under a diversity of names, spent a great deal of time here, and decorated it to reflect the luxurious drawing rooms of his native 16th century Italy. This study was his especial favorite, where even the lighting was designed to as closely approximate candlelight as possible. Over the years, he'd acquired the surrounding woodland, assuring that his closest neighbors were a comfortable stretch away.

The flush of fresh blood and the exhilarating chase still shaded his perceptions toward pleasure. Tonight's quarry, a magnificent stag, had eluded him with such grace and power, he was more and more minded of his scion with every step.

In the end, the analogy struck him so forcefully that, when he'd run the beautiful beast to ground, he'd been unable to slay it. Instead, he sated the Hunger, soothed the animal's fear, and released it back to the wood.

Strange. The only other person able to affect him like that was his sister, Lucretia. Thinking of that oddly dichotomous pair, Lucretia and his scion, suddenly made the opulent refuge he'd built seem empty and chill. How she would laugh to see him grow maudlin over his willful progeny.

The thud of Gwen's pumps on the carpeted staircase lifted his eyes from the flames and his mind from the past. There was much to do and little time to do it; he could ill afford to let emotions rule as they had recently done to disastrous effect.

She hesitated outside the study, heart pounding fit to break her ribs. Was she finally afraid of him? If so, it was more than time — it was too late.

***

Dressed in tasteful black with a string of matched pearls at her throat, she crossed to where he frowned into the fire and hovered, searching his face with wary eyes. He didn't seem angry as before. Rather more melancholy than angry, but then, this place had a way of bringing out that side of him. Odd how he missed his family so much. They'd been dead for so long and she didn't miss hers a whit. Francesco said that would change when she'd been as he for so long, but she doubted it. Her brother was an insufferable prick and her parents, selfish, aging jet-setters. Killing them was not only a pleasure, but a social service. No, she wouldn't miss them. Ever.

Had the excuse for slipping into New York passed muster? He hadn't commented, but he'd also not given the clipping back and she didn't see it anywhere in the drawing room. She also hadn't found it in his suitcases when she'd unpacked them while he was hunting, so he must have taken it into his private chamber.

"I unpacked your things myself and told Carlo to turn in after he got the fire going," she said. "It's been a long day for everyone, and I thought it would be nice to have time alone."

He remained silent. The reflected flames dancing in his eyes and on his hair made him look even less human and more exciting than usual. Not knowing how to read him, she continued, "Rest assured, nothing will fall too far behind because of this. I don't have Eddie's rapport with the hoi palloi, but I can easily assume his duties."

Rousing himself from the leaping flames, he responded flatly, "*Buona*, Gwen, I'm certain he will appreciate it. No doubt he will thank you in person, when he's mended enough to return to us."

The statement didn't make sense. She said, "I don't understand — Eddie's dead. He won't be back unless you . . . but you promised *me!*"

A slow smile spread across his face. "Ah, that would be your first thought, would it not, *Cara Mia*?" Then, to her profound dismay, Francesco Borgia laughed. *Laughed*! Finally, wiping away tears of merriment, he said, "*Gracia, Cara*, I needed a release. No, I have not made another fledgling! I doubt Edgar would accept if ever I offered."

"Then, I'm confused, Francesco. Eddie died from injuries sustained in a natural gas explosion. Don't tease me, Francesco, please."

He caressed the marble mantlepiece's satiny surface,

enjoying its warmth as she had seen him do countless times before. This time, though, there was something in his manner that made her want to lunge and shove him into the flames.

As if sensing her thoughts, he stepped away from the fireplace and said, "I'm afraid you have incomplete information. According to *my* sources, Edgar was badly injured in the explosion, but was pulled alive from the wreckage by my own Byron. As a result, Byron and his colleagues were able to save his life and spirit him away, out of the reach of further harm."

Fighting nausea, she stared wide-eyed, struggling against a fuzzy blackness edging into her vision. She'd never fainted, and refused to give him the pleasure of seeing her do it now. He'd deliberately maneuvered her into this position to waylay her. That was obvious. What was not obvious, but far more important was: what did he know, and how did he find out?

As she slowly lowered herself onto the divan, her vow to resist swooning was nearly forfeit. *Oh god! That was Byron Peale at Eddie's place.* No wonder Tony was so adamant he hadn't missed — he probably didn't. Too bad Tony wasn't still around, so she could tell him he'd used the wrong term. Byron Peale wasn't a *ghost*.

She became aware of Francesco hovering in charming concern. He cradled her hand and said, "But I did not intend for the good news to come as such a shock! I should have broken it more gently, no? I must get you a brandy to calm the effects, *Cara*."

Sadistic bastard. Collecting her wits, she pulled her hand from his grasp and laid it on his arm. "No. I'm all right now; it's just hard to take in at once . . . your informant was certain? Where have they taken him?"

"That was unfortunately too well-kept a secret to discover, but we will learn soon. But, as you see, Edgar's good fortune now allows us to concentrate on more pressing matters."

Luckily, he didn't seem to require a response, because she was utterly incapable of delivering one. So, her rival for Francesco's affections rescued her rival in business — this time. She'd never missed before and the failure rankled. Perhaps her error lay in relying on others to do a job she was better suited to. Perhaps. Regardless, she'd rectify the error.

Francesco was again staring into the flames and speaking almost to himself. "So, *Cara mio*, my son is not only here, but once again taking an active hand in his sire's affairs. This time it was to the benefit, but next time? Who can say?"

Deciding the drink sound like a good idea after all, she poured herself a large one, but nearly dropped the glass when he murmured, "I must discover Byron's lodging place. It should not be difficult, even though he knows I am here."

Smacking the glass onto the rolling bar, she cried, "Francesco! What are you *saying*? You can't be intending to go straight over there . . . not after . . . ."

He was at her side in an instant, smiling and stroking the soft curve of her cheek simultaneously reaching out to soothe her roiling emotions. "Have no fear, Gwen. I do not intend to repeat the Chicago fiasco. I will wait — to do as our injured associate terms 'lay low' and see what the boy is up to. However, I must know where he is staying so our people can watch his movements, yes? Our time will not be wasted. There are many other affairs that command our attention. Edgar's mishap has left much to be attended to and I will have especial need of your peculiar understanding of the business world to cope with it."

So saying, he strode to the desk and flipped the latches on his attaché, an action so familiar, she grasped it like a life preserver to pull herself back to rationality. This was business. She could deal with business.

***

Stroud sat in her favorite easy chair, hugging blue jean-clad legs to herself, resting her chin on her knees. A very defensive pose. He wondered if she realized it. BC wriggled into an even more comfortable position on the far end of the couch. All the better to prove he wasn't about to spring on her and tear her throat out — well, to tear her throat out, anyway. The jury was still undecided on the springing part.

She unfurled and ventured, "I really don't know where to start. I've spent all day reading books about vampires and each one says something different than the last. I'm confused."

"Tell me about it! When I was first changed, my brother, Charly, and I found the same thing. As time passes, I'm discovering some of it's right and some of it's pure bullshit — at least for me. After encountering Francesco Borgia, I'm wondering if vampirism affects each one a little differently." He grinned. "Fact is, I've been like this for better than two hundred years and I'm *still* confused."

"But you're dead from sunrise to sunset?"

"I prefer 'dormant,' but yes. Before you ask, no, I can't turn into a rat, bat, mist or any of those other things."

Stroud's eyebrows shot up. "How'd you know I was going to ask that?"

"Everyone does. Charly was convinced I could do it if I

just tried. We spent weeks 'thinking foggy thoughts.' All I got was a headache."

Laughing, she asked, "That reminds me! Did Charles really give Rachel Brewer an hour to accept or decline his marriage proposal and pull out his pocket watch to time it?"

BC blinked, "I wasn't there, but Rachel told it the same way and it was *such* a Charly thing to do." He paused. "You've been doing your homework."

Stroud grinned and thudded a stack of books onto the coffee table, then shoved them toward him. "I told you I've been reading all day. You have a fascinating family."

BC lifted the over-sized book from the top of the stack and smiled with pleasure at the reproduction of Charles' family portrait. "I love this painting."

"So do the historians. It's in every text I saw on the Peales and most about the Revolution and Colonial period."

"Too right. I feared something like that would happen. That's why I insisted Charly paint me out. He was most annoyed."

Brow knit in puzzlement, she slid onto the couch next to him to see the cover better. "Paint you out . . . oh! The big space in the middle!"

"Yep. When he first blocked it out, he put me right there. When he pulled it out to finish it in 1808 or thereabouts, I'd been changed for several decades. My perceptions had changed, too. We had a pretty good row over it."

She was suddenly acutely aware of his nearness and looked up to find him staring at her. He bent to kiss her. She let him and toppled back onto the cushions, pulling him with her.

The book slid unnoticed to the carpet.

FOUR

"Mama, it's seven a.m., there has to be something wrong." Gae tumbled out of bed prepared for the worst.

His mother chuckled. "You're overreacting, child. I just wanted to let you know I got a telegram from Fiona. She's on her way to Chicago."

"Shit. Where's she gonna be next? I gotta let her know I'm in New York. They're bound to stop over here."

"She's gonna be in transit, Gae. You won't have much hope of catching her. I'll just let her know when she gets here."

"Man, she'll go ballistic."

"It will be fine. You tried to let her know. It's not like you left Chicago just to ruin her visit. Besides, now she and the children can stay in your apartment."

"Uh huh."

"Galen Samuel Miller, trust your mama. It'll be fine."

As he hung up, he mused, "I trust my mama, but I *know* my ex-wife."

He groaned and stretched. Too much adrenaline flowing to go back to sleep, now. He might as well head for the kitchen and rustle up some breakfast. He padded down the hall and stopped abruptly in front of BC's open door. The bed was empty.

"Oh shit."

He scrabbled for his cell phone, and realized he'd left it beside his bed. A few strides brought him to the living room phone. Hands shaking, he punched in Stroud's number. She answered groggily and his words came out in a rush. "Stroud, he's gone. I knew I shouldn't let him run around alone right after Borgia got into town. What time did he leave last night?"

Awake now, she said, "Whoa, Gae! Slow down. Run that by me again, okay?"

Miller took a deep breath. "What time did Peale leave your place last night?"

"Ah. It's okay, Gae, he didn't leave."

"Everybody keeps telling me everything's okay. That's makin' me nervous. He's still there?"

"Yeah. I put him in the bathtub."

"Bathtub."

She continued with great patience: "Yes. The bathroom is an inside room and in the tub, I can pile blankets—"

He made an exasperated noise. "Do me a favor. When he rises tonight, tell the asshole that I'm enrolling him in Message Leaving 101. Night course."

***

Stroud rolled over and tried to get back to sleep, but it was no use. Galen had a point, Borgia being back on the scene made for special circumstances and they really should have given him a call. The trouble was, that required *thinking* and thinking was definitely not what they were doing last night. She groped the floor for her robe and found it under the bed where it had been kicked, then headed for the bathroom. It would have to be the shower at work this morning since her tub was in use. Grinning wickedly, she pulled back the blankets, enjoyed the view, and let them drop back with a sigh.

"He can call it dormant all he wants. Sure looks dead to me."

***

Peale skidded through the front door and raced down the hall pausing only to toss his jacket onto the couch. "Be back in a sec, Gae. I've got to throw on some fresh clothes before Miriam gets here and I'm dreadfully late."

Miller didn't look up from his magazine. "Dennis Brannaugh's on his way, too."

BC stopped and turned, still unbuttoning his shirt. "Yeah? How come?"

"Been trying to locate someplace named Campo della Ferrara, the one mentioned in the Isendamer material. I think he has some maps and stuff."

"Stroud didn't tell me about that."

"Maybe because she didn't know. Seems her phone wasn't being answered last night when he tried to call."

"Oh. I didn't know she turned the phones off. Look, Galen, I know I should have called."

"With Borgia on the loose in the same city as you?" The big man carefully closed the magazine. "Why should you let anyone know where you were?"

"*Huh* uh!" Peale whirled, jabbing his finger at his partner. "All of you knew Stroud and I were together last night. I'll own up to being an airhead and forgetting to check in, but don't lay that other shit on me!"

"Goddammit! Stallings is right, you haven't been paying attention to a single thing since you first laid eyes on Stroud Girion."

"Don't be so cryptic, Special Agent Miller," the vampire

said folding his arms across his chest defensively. "If my relationship with Sgt. Girion gripes you, just spit it out."

"You're gonna get yourself or somebody else killed. If that sniper had—"

"Had what? Gotten there before Taylor and me? Then Eddie would be dead. If you're saying I'm not a policeman, big surprise! I told you that when we met. Even Mick Marquez never tired of pointing out that I'm a musician, not a cop."

Miller flung the magazine aside and sprang to his feet. "Don't you *dare* bring Mick into this."

***

Miriam Peale smiled at the stocky, sandy-haired man who held the door for her, then shouldered her way through the crowded lobby toward the elevators. The big man was right behind her. The cars seemed to be crawling along making extended stops at every floor.

When the lift finally arrived, the doors opened, emptying a crowd fit for the Marx Brothers' famous stateroom scene. At length, only she and the sandy-haired man were left. He smiled, got in and held the door open, asking, "What floor can I getcha?"

"Four, please," she said, and stepped in.

He punched the button and let the doors slide shut. "Looks like we're headed the same way, again." He paused and said, "I'm Captain Dennis Brannaugh of the NYPD. Please, don't think this is some kind of come-on, but I feel like I know you from somewhere?"

To his surprise, a delighted smile lit her face. "You're Captain Brannaugh?" She held out a slender hand, saying, "You don't know *me*, but you know my cousin, Byron. I'm

Miriam Peale. Are you headed up there?"

He shook the offered hand. "Yeah. If the elevator ever makes it there. This conference has the place packed to the gills and I think the thing needs a rest." As if in answer, the car shuddered to a halt and the doors slid back, revealing a crowd of agents waiting to enter. Brannaugh stepped out and held the door back until Miriam had exited and the crush of agents had entered.

"So it's business tonight?" Miriam asked as the doors closed and the elevator shuddered on its way again. "I was just about to ask if you'd care to join Byron and me at an art show. I have three tickets through the Peale Gallery and Galen begged off because he has to call Chicago."

Brannaugh was a bit nonplussed. To his dismay, he heard himself saying, "It's only partly business. I mostly wanted to get a better look at your cousin."

"Byron?" Realization lit her face. "Ahhhh! This is about Sgt. Girion. Am I right?"

"Uhhhh — I'm sorry," he backpedaled. "I don't normally get this nosy, but Stroud Girion doesn't usually get this stuck on a guy this fast, either." He reddened. "Sorry, I didn't mean for it to come out that way."

To his relief, Miriam Peale laughed. "It's okay, Captain, Byron's pretty stuck himself."

"I kind of gathered that." He turned the corner and came to an abrupt halt. "What the—?"

Miriam peeked around him to find a small knot of agents casually milling around in the hall listening to— "Oh, good lord, that's Byron. What in the nine hells are they fighting about *now*?"

She bolted around Brannaugh, but he caught her arm.

"Do they do this often?"

"I'm afraid so." She sighed. "But it's been worse lately."

He nodded and bulled through flashing his badge. "Okay, folks, show's over. Just pretend you're all adults and go on about your business."

At the sight of the shield and the mobile brick wall wielding it, the group vanished in various directions.

Miriam opened the door with her own key, then followed Brannaugh in.

The Captain stepped into the living room, growling. "You two! Break it up *now*!"

The startled combatants turned toward the command. Miriam stepped around Brannaugh and shook her head helplessly. "Do I even want to know what this was about this time?"

***

The little silver car raced through the twilight, swirling gravel dust behind it. Francesco would rise before she got back, but she didn't care. If she'd stayed in that Renaissance mausoleum one moment longer, she'd have exploded. Either that or set fire to the place. She'd love to watch it burn — and Francesco with it. His attitude had changed since that rotten night in Chicago, when he'd lost control and killed Miguel Marquez. Then *Eddie* got between them just when he was going to change her. *Damn you, Eddie Michalson! Why won't you just die?* She pounded the steering wheel and screamed her fury to the lashing wind.

Damn Francesco, too. Last night, all he could talk about was 'poor Edgar', and had all but accused her of making the hit herself. Well, so what? She'd like to see him prove it. She'd like to see anyone prove it, for that matter. Only Vinny and Tony could have possibly linked her to any of it, and they weren't going to be talking to anyone without a Ouija board ever again.

Well, time to switch candidates. Switch vampires, at any rate. Driving into New York for the day had been good cover. It had given her time to visit her *pied á terre* to write and mail a nice little note to Byron Peale. She'd sent the message straight to the New York Sentry International headquarters. It was a waste of time to wait and find out where he was staying and she understood that Sentry had snapped up Francesco's nasty little spy as soon as he'd returned to his home the previous evening. With that interference out of the way, it was so much simpler to send a direct message. She could extend a personal invitation and no one but she and Byron would be the wiser.

***

Joe Stallings scowled at the maps tacked to the wall. Dusk was falling and the overheads needed to be turned on. He didn't notice. He wasn't really looking at the maps, anyway. Why, with all the resources at his disposal, was he drawing as many blanks as Denny Brannaugh at finding that damned place? That was bad enough, but it was worse when he found Brannaugh's footprints on data he had just found, himself, dammit. He took a big pull at his coffee, and spat it back with a grimace. Cold again. Cold, just like the trail to Borgia's estate, this *Campo della Ferrara.*

Suddenly noticing it was getting dark, he wondered how long he'd been staring at that damned map. Too long, by the look of things, and it had been a big waste of time to, boot. Well, with luck, they could remedy that. Sentry International had one resource that NYPD didn't: Byron Peale.

With another sour look at the stale coffee, he headed to the break room to get a fresh cup, flipping on the overhead lights as he went. If only there were some way to use Peale as bait — he didn't care who bit, Borgia, Isendamer — *anyone*. They'd be bound to make some headway with that. The trouble would be getting Peale to cooperate.

***

Byron Peale came awake knowing he wasn't alone in the apartment. He should have been. Galen always went to the office in the early afternoon, leaving him to follow later on the bike. Straining his hearing to the limit, he caught only muffled movement, the intruder was too far away for a heartbeat or a scent.

He rolled off the bed and pulled on his jeans. Reaching for the boots, he decided against them; the heavy, decorative spurs made too much noise. Slipping his hand far under the mattress, he withdrew his pistol and checked the clip. "Secure" Sentry apartments notwithstanding, some of the people he'd encountered over the centuries made him reluctant to take chances. He'd let his guard down in Chicago and look where that landed him.

Easing down the short hall, he pressed against the wall and listened again. The heartbeat he could hear now definitely wasn't that of his Bunyanesque partner. It was lighter and quicker. Quiet sounds came from the kitchen. Whiffing the air, he caught the puzzling aroma of milk and cinnamon. An intruder making a snack?

Firming his grip on the pistol, he crossed the tiny living area in three long strides and kicked open the swinging louvers. Diving and rolling, he came up into the prescribed crouch with his pistol leveled at the intruder.

Maeve Donal threw herself against the cabinets with a piercing screech. The spoon in her hand splattered his face and bare chest with hot milk from the pan on the cooktop. Mute seconds of shocked silence passed between them before he stood, unloaded the weapon and stuffed it down the back of his jeans.

Maeve used the intervening moments to muster her considerable fury. Inhaling deeply to slow her pounding heart, she advanced on him, wooden spoon clutched like a club.

"I suppose you think this is funny, Byron Peale? Sneakin' up on friends that mean you no harm and scarin' the life out of them?"

His eyes widened. "Sn—? I think it's about as funny as someone breaking into my apartment to fix an evening snack."

She indicated the pistol with a scornful gesture. "Usin' a key isn't a break-in and just what d'ye need *that* for? You're a vampire. Ye have no need for a weapon."

"Sometimes, it's useful to keep to a distance." He grinned maliciously. "You should know all about that."

"Fine way to treat someone who was concerned enough about you bein' alone all day she took the time to come down and protect you," she said turning to assault the milk with the wooden spoon.

"Protect me? This is a high-security apartment building! Who — aside from you — is gonna come in here and bother me?"

"Francesco Borgia."

Good God, she was right. If anyone could get past SI's defenses — "Wait a minute! Francesco Borgia is as likely to be up and about during the daylight as I am!"

She smiled coquettishly. "But it had you goin' for a minute, didn't it? Just proves you're worried, whether or not you want to admit it." The smile faded as she glided solicitously toward him, grasping the closest towel. Gently wiping milk droplets from his skin, she said, "Really, m'love. How can these people who claim to care about you go off and leave you when you're dormant? Maybe they don't understand how vulnerable you are then the way I do."

Suddenly tired, he saw where the scene was leading. He felt like kicking himself. He'd known Maeve long enough, he should have seen it coming. Taking the towel out of her hands, he dragged a chair away from the table, and straddled it, regarding her sadly over the back.

At length, he said, "Every time I think this is settled between us, it pops up again in a different guise. I've said it at least a hundred times in at least as many ways, but I'll try again: what we had together died with my mortal life back in 1780."

Anger stiffened her back, but she didn't pause pouring steaming milk over a dollop of honey in a stoneware mug. "Don't you mean when you *walked out* on me in 1780?"

He shook his head pensively. "No, not then. It didn't happen until later, not until I woke in your cellar."

Milk splashed the counter as the pan smacked down. "Meanin' what?"

He paused before answering. She wasn't going to like what he said, but it had to be out. "Meaning that I was still in love with you after I walked out, Maeve. When I told you that I needed to think, I was being as truthful as I knew how to be. The emotions were so intense, it terrified me. I had no idea what to do next — especially since the only thing I could think of scared me worse than how I felt."

She treated him to a wary gaze, as if he'd finally gone mad.

"The following weeks were absolute hell," he continued. "Everywhere I went, there you were, too. It was maddening! I was finally coming to realize that it was actually because *I* kept going where *you* were when someone very, very strong dragged me into an alley and killed me."

She turned away sharply and busied herself cleaning up splattered milk. After a few moments, she said quietly, "I'm sorry about chainin' ye to th' wall. I was only tryin' t' keep ye still while I told ye what had been done. Frankie wasn't certain how coherent you'd be when you first rose and ye *do* tend t' chew the scenery when you're upset." She turned and challenged, "Why are ye tellin' me these things? It's been unsaid for more than two hundred years, why now?"

"Because I've been thinking about it a lot lately and someone I trust insists that friends are up front with each other."

"Doubtless that flame-haired minx."

"Actually, it was Galen." He smiled at her own thick, red-gold waves, "Although, I do seem to have a penchant for redheads, don't I?"

Wrong move.

Swinging the wooden spoon, Maeve flung herself at him cursing fluently in Gaelic. Leaping back, he caught her arms, but not before she'd dealt him a sharp whack alongside the ear with her makeshift cudgel. Swearing, he flipped her around so as to have the snapping teeth aimed away from his face.

Pinning her solidly against himself, he yelled, "Dammit, Maeve! This insane — what are you trying to accomplish, anyway?"

She sagged against him and, although still clearly angry, began to weep.

***

Joe Stallings was pleased with the account of ex-agent John Myre's arrest, but his eyes kept straying from the trio of listeners to the clock on the far wall. He was saying: "The minute Myre saw the warrant, he started to spill and hasn't stopped, yet. We have three more of Borgia's moles in our cages now; unfortunately, Myre didn't know all the operatives. Michalson was very restrictive in what he allowed each person to know, so it looks like we're back to waiting for Eddie to recover enough to talk to us. Let's hope he does.

"It's too bad Peale couldn't call in the identification earlier . . . ." Peevishness engraved a line between his eyebrows and he abruptly demanded, "Where the hell is Peale? The sun went down almost an hour ago; what's holding him up *this* time?"

Miller, whose eyes were straying to his wristwatch with increasing frequency, answered, "I don't have the slightest idea, Captain. He sometimes loses track of time. It isn't like him to do a complete no-show."

"I'd be interested to know what his concept of time *is*," Tyler Taylor mused. "Since he's for all intents and purposes immortal, does it seem slower or faster or . . . I dunno — different somehow?"

Joe Stallings drummed his fingers on his desk in a tattoo of irritation. He sometimes wondered why he wanted these brainy types on his team. "Right. Sgt. Taylor, since you're apparently in a cogitative mood, maybe you'd give us your take on Gwen Isendamer. She's apparently at the bottom of a good deal of the fertilizer hitting the blades. What can we tell about her?"

The blond detective frowned. "I'm better with a postmortem

than a psychological profile, but it looks like Isendamer's mental state is deteriorating. If it weren't, it's doubtful she'd have overtly attacked Michalson. Further, if what Ms. Donal believes is true, Isendamer was acting in a manner she knew to be against Borgia's wishes. This would indicate he's losing his hold over her. Eddie Michalson felt this, too. If it's true, it's only a matter of time until she rebels and attempts to usurp and destroy Francesco Borgia, himself."

"Wait," Stroud objected "According to Michalson, Isendamer wants to become a vampire more than anything else in the world. No way she'd make a move against Borgia until she got her wish."

"Of course she wouldn't," Taylor said. "Unless she knew of the whereabouts of another vampire."

Miller's mutter cut the resulting silence. "Shit. That one was so obvious, I think I didn't *want* to see it."

Stallings shifted uncomfortably. "Is it possible that she could have made contact already and Peale might not have mentioned it?"

"Not a chance," Miller said emphatically. "That woman scares the willies outta him. You should have seen his face when Michalson told us she was trying to get Borgia to change her. No, if she'd approached him, we'd have heard the shriek all over town."

Stallings nodded. Ever since he saw that gaping wound through Peale's body, he'd unequivocally believed in vampires (Peale in particular). The notion of a supernatural operative (Peale in particular) still made him nervous, but he'd grudgingly come to admire the way the Chicago team meshed. Their methods of procuring information frequently took on the annoying aspect of pulling twenty-pound rabbits out of baseball caps, but they'd proved themselves trustworthy. If Miller claimed his unnerving partner would report an approach by Gwen Isendamer, he did not doubt it was true.

Sgt. Taylor said, "This puts a new complexion on things, though. Maybe we ought to ring him up to see if he's left. With Borgia back on stage and considering what happened in Chicago not too long ago, it's entirely possible something could have happened."

Miller's brow furrowed and Joe Stallings pushed the secured landline phone toward him.

***

Fuming, Maeve Donal flung herself onto the couch in her own apartment. Nothing had worked the way she planned. Not only had Byron managed to shunt aside her advances, but he'd also extracted a binding oath from her with very little difficulty. Worse, her proposal that their truce should last only as long as the case itself was met with a devilishly hearty 'done!' She could have wrung his glorious neck. He always could worm what he wanted out of her. In all honesty, she was angrier with herself than with him.

Perhaps what she was most upset about was the fact that, even with all that had happened, her loyalties remained divided. Yes, she still had a deep love — call it passion, if you will — for Byron. A passion he once shared. However, long before she met Byron Peale, she'd shared a similar passion with Francesco Borgia. That passion had cooled, morphed and solidified into an abiding friendship. Francesco was an older, more powerful vampire and had proved a valuable ally on many an occasion. Until now, anyway. His recent behavior puzzled and frightened her. He'd always been impulsive and impetuous, but never before erratic. That was new. The venom he'd aimed at her when he held her hostage at his hunting lodge in Wisconsin was also new. It must all be linked to Byron's sudden reappearance. It had to be.

If they'd only talk to each other, come to an understanding, surely Francesco could regain an even keel. Sadly, both were too angry to even consider reconciliation. Especially if the suggestion came from her. It was a pity. They shared so many interests, she'd first hoped they could become friends. That was so long ago. Now, her fervent wish was to keep them from destroying each other.

She loved Byron with all her heart — not to mention the physical desire. They hadn't been intimate in a long time and she missed it, but tonight, he'd almost been in her arms again. Gray eyes hardened to angry flint at the thought of Stroud Girion, the woman who doubtless had what she desired. Well, the blackguard had always been a fast worker.

Hands clenched into the sofa cushions, she railed inwardly against the almost physical bonds of her oath that prevented her from taking action against the mortal woman. Rationality clamored and all but knocked her in the head for notice. She was missing something important. What was it?

She replayed her first evening at the hostelry. Of course! In her anger toward the female half of the police team, she was forgetting the male counterpart. Tyler Taylor. When he spoke, she felt power surging through him. It appeared to be largely latent and Sgt. Taylor seemed blissfully unaware of it, but it marked him as a potentially powerful mage. It was remarkable that he was unaware of it.

For that matter, nobody seemed aware of it. Such power wasn't easily contained. Perhaps it manifested itself in an unconscious manner aside from his extraordinary intelligence. Hmmmmm. Extraordinary intelligence that matched his good looks. A wicked gleam lit the heart-shaped face. Perhaps she should bring his latent power to his attention and offer her expertise by way of training? The noisome oath didn't forbid an offer to help, did it? Two could play the jealousy game as well as one. Yes. That had definite possibilities.

***

Peale gingerly fingered the lump raised by the wooden spoon. Dammit! He was an idiot. He should have seen what Maeve was up to as soon as he'd entered the kitchen. Was he being deliberately obtuse in an attempt to avoid the problem? Fat lot of good that ever did.

It didn't help that combat seemed to be a natural state between the two of them. That had been true even when he was human. Back then, though, the argument would usually end in a fierce interlude of love-making. Not indicative of what would be called a healthy relationship in today's parlance. In any parlance, actually.

Maeve must have known he was alone in the apartment. Why else would she have come in before he rose — without her signature perfume, to boot. Most likely, she'd figured an argument would end in the well-established pattern. It might have, too, if Miller hadn't been so adamant about keeping the 'fridge stocked with flasks of fresh beef blood — Jump Veron jokingly called them "Bloody Elsies." At the peak of the row, when her scent triggered vivid memories of ardent flesh and hot, piquant blood, he'd felt his canines extend. He'd grabbed an Elsie. As usual, it was flat and he didn't like cold blood, but it sated the Hunger and allowed him more control. They'd wound up sitting at the tiny kitchen table, chatting companionably while she sipped her reheated milk drink and he nursed his flask. The illusion of innocuous domesticity in the scene amused him to no end.

Pissed the hell out of Maeve, though. A slow grin spread across his face. Knocked her guard down, too. Well, knocked it down enough that he'd managed to get her to promise not to cause any trouble with Stroud Girion until their investigation was complete. He couldn't hope for more than that. Truthfully, he was pleased he'd gotten that much.

As soon as she realized what she'd said, she'd stomped off declaring she had scrying to do. Fine. That was why she was there in the first damn place.

He did feel for her, though. As hard as it was for him to fathom why, she had counted Francesco Borgia as one of her closest friends. What the elder vampire had done to her shook her confidence more than she wanted to let on. Well, the events in Chicago hadn't done much good for any of them, had it? Not even Borgia, himself.

He gulped the last of his Bloody Elsie and grimaced. Damn things just didn't age well. Best to stop on the way to the offices and grab a bite. Probably still have to be cow, though. No time for — *time!* Indigo eyes slid toward the clock by the couch, then squeezed shut. He was late. No. He was *epically* late. No doubt the ass-chewing would also be of epic proportions.

Grabbing his jacket and keys, he bolted for the door. It was just his luck that his mobile went off before he'd even reached the hall.

FIVE

Francesco Borgia carefully placed the sheaf of paper atop the other sheaves cluttering the expanse of his desk and smiled. He never ignored kismet. If he had, he wouldn't have lived long enough to become a vampire, considering the unpleasant propensities of certain members of his notorious clan.

So, the lovely dark-haired woman Byron was entertaining at the nightclubs was another Peale. Miriam. An attractive name.

Her hotel was five-star, although she was rarely there. She spent most of her time at art shows, Sentry headquarters, or the boy's flat. Seldom alone, she was usually accompanied by his son, Miller, or both. From the hours she passed at his flat, she certainly knew Byron's secret.

Shuffling the photographs, he nodded approvingly. His son shared his taste for beautiful women. There was, of course Maeve, but this policewoman, Stroud Girion, was fascinating. Byron was having quite an affair with her. He chortled, wondering how Maeve was taking it. Badly, one hoped. He flipped to another photo.

The Peale woman was exquisite. Her sloping shoulders, graceful neck and oval face framed by dark chestnut hair were worthy of a Renaissance Master. The intelligent eyes were quite alluring, as well. It was decided. He'd pay his son another visit. Purely social, of course, to meet and welcome a charming member of his fledgling's mortal family. Care must be taken to avoid the previous errors, although, they couldn't have been foreseen by anyone barring an oracle.

It was an admirable time for a *tête-à-tête*; should he bring gifts? Certainly for the lovely Ms. Peale. A piece of art, then, since she was an art dealer from a family of artists. Frowning, he tapped blunt fingers on the glossy photos, contemplating his son's strong family feeling. That could prove a double-edged sword.

He knew all about family. The Borgias had very strong ties. However, given the history of his scion's remarkable family, it would be essential to break its influence upon him. By all accounts, Byron had been a rake and a bit of a scoundrel. Best to appeal to that side of his nature and eliminate the family's stabilizing influence. Once he gained the upper hand, he must be the young one's only family.

That brought up another matter. Lifting a multi-paged legal document, he peered critically at the small print. Typewriting was an improvement over the alternately crabbed and spidery handwriting of older documents, but the language was just as cryptic. Possibly, these papers were premature, but he wanted it seen to while the legal staff was at *Campo della Ferrara*. The exorbitant fees they charged for coming to the estate at night meant little to him. There was plenty more where that came from. What was unbearable was the undercurrent of superior long-suffering over the whims of their eccentric client. No, better to have the paperwork done, and surprise the child later. It could always be rescinded if things didn't work out — but of course they would. Between *them*, blood would tell.

He signed the document with a flourish.

***

The scented note with the tasteful script letterhead read:

> Byron, darling,
>
> Please excuse the familiarity, but I already know so much about you, I feel we are old friends. Perhaps we can meet in person and share a drink soon. The number above is my private line. Call me anytime.
>
> Yours,
> Gwen

Joe Stallings regarded the agitated agent looming over his desk. He said, "Sit down and be calm, Peale. It isn't like we weren't expecting her to approach you."

Peale did as requested — the sitting part, anyway. Calm was another thing altogether. "What now, Captain? I'm certainly *not* going to ring her up."

"No one expects you to," Stallings said with a placating gesture. "It would only be useful if we could locate her phone that way. Considering Isendamer, she'd never have given us the number if it would help us find her. Probably got some sort of relay or — whatever — set up. I'll get the tech guys on it, though. We might have enough of a case against her, to swing a warrant."

Relieved, Peale leaned back into the chair.

Joe sat back, too, drumming his fingers thoughtfully against the desk. What he wanted most of all was to trap the tiger — err — *tigress*. If he could use a slightly dead stalking horse for bait, he'd do it without a second's hesitation. He doubted Peale would go along with it, though. What he really couldn't figure out was why someone as powerful as

Byron Peale would actually fear this woman. Sure, she was a lunatic, but still. . . .

"Just get back to work, and forget about this," Stallings said. "You're liaising with Brendan Grant to compile the list of properties associated with the Este Corporation for seizure under the RICO statute?"

"Yes, sir. I am. We're making excellent progress."

Stallings shook his head helplessly. "I'm damned glad *you* can talk to him, Peale. He's one of our best computer people, but I can't seem to pass the time of day with him."

Peale's demeanor reverted to a reasonable facsimile of normal as he grinned, saying, "The first thing you need to remember is, 'Mr. Computer is your friend.'"

His superior officer arched an eyebrow in a very superior way.

***

The quartet was hot and the club was dark, but not as smoky as Miriam had feared — thank you, New York anti-smoking ordinances. She sipped her drink, studying her mismatched escorts, who were engaged in an animated discussion about (of course) music. Byron was waxing eloquent about time signatures and rhythm, while Galen remained doggedly (and quite deliberately) unconvinced.

Smiling contentment to nobody in particular, she thought about the Belridge diaries entrusted to her as the family historian. The stories they contained repeatedly illustrated Byron's love of people and propensity for making friends. She wondered how normal this was for one of his kind. Probably not very, but since he was the only one she knew, there wasn't enough evidence to form an opinion.

This particular vampire also had a talent for accumulating

exceptional people. She'd enjoyed dinner the night before with Tyler Taylor and Stroud Girion. Unavoidably, that reminded her of Maeve Donal. She was ambivalent about the Irish woman.

After she'd pried the whole shamefaced story out of Byron, she had to acknowledge that Maeve's anger was justified. The retaliation was a bit extreme, though, no matter how much Miriam enjoyed the results. On the other hand, maybe her perspectives would be different if she were a sorceress born in the fifteenth century. *Wow! What a train of thought. If anyone tapped in on this, they'd lock me up for sure.* Anyway, she had her fingers crossed that Maeve and Byron could patch things up enough to become friends. She wanted so badly for him to have *someone* he wouldn't lose. It must be hard to lose people you love time and time again.

The amiable debate continued as Galen snorted, then launched a counter argument about dissonance. She'd taken an instant liking to this soft-spoken giant whose conversation quickly gave lie to the phrase 'dumb jock.' It pleased her that the mercurial Byron had such a solid friend. Movement drew her eye as a stocky man drew a chair to the vacant side of their table and seated himself.

The stranger settled comfortably and beamed upon the small group. The animated conversation died in mid-sentence as the handsome newcomer fixed Byron with a gaze and said in a deep, resonant voice, "*Buon noche, figlio mio.* I trust I have not arrived at a bad time."

Her companions' expressions were frozen in mingled incredulity and anger. Their guest ignored this, spanning the table with the smooth movement of a striking snake, he seized her hand in a startlingly cold clasp. Pressing her fingers to equally cool lips, he smiled engagingly.

"Forgive the improper introduction, *Signorina* Peale. I am Francesco Borgia, Byron's father. Since I learned of your arrival, I have been anxious to meet the most charming member of my son's . . . American family."

Horrified, she wrenched free, but Borgia's smile didn't waver. Addressing his fledgling, he asked, "Byron! Have you no words of greeting for your father?"

Byron's mobile face set in a mask of contempt. "Were my father here, I would greet him warmly. Since it's only you, we can dispense with the formalities. What do you want?"

The brittle tension between the combatants shattered as their attentive waitress came to take the new patron's order. Grinning wickedly and sweeping a heavily ringed hand toward the tumbler of amber fluid in front of Byron, the elder vampire said, "I will have the same as my son."

Byron stiffened, then, as the girl retreated for the bar, hissed, "You are *not* my father, and I resent your insistent claim to the title."

Borgia tsk-tsked, and including Miriam and Galen in a wide sweep of his arms, remarked sadly, "Children can be so impertinent, don't you think? Although, I understand Jasmine and Drew are quite well-behaved. I congratulate you, Mr. Miller. But alas, I fear young James is very like my Byron — he must be a trial to a conscientious aunt. Perhaps it was the influence of his globe-trotting mother? Now, with the other children? They are young. I am certain you can mold them marvelously."

Miriam snapped her teeth shut on an angry retort as the

waitress returned. Borgia paid her with a generous tip, and the girl treated the three handsome men at the table to a dazzling smile before hurrying back to her duties with a final, envious look at Miriam.

Gauging the waitress to be out of earshot, Galen bristled. "You got a lot of gall coming here, Borgia. I think BC was more polite than necessary, considering all you've done. What *do* you want?"

Borgia twirled his glass negligently. "I have told you, I wished to meet the charming Ms. Peale, but also I wanted the opportunity to express my sorrow for the tragic death of your friend, Miguel Marquez."

Byron gaped at him. "Sorrow? Man, in case it's slipped your mind, *you* were responsible for his tragic death."

"*Ammesso*. I admit guilt. What happened in Chicago was regrettable. I can only say for myself, that I was gravely wounded and unable to think clearly."

Intent on Byron, he felt more than saw Miller tense. The big man's voice was dangerously close as he growled, "Do you expect us to just let you stroll in here and out again after all you've done? Mitigating circumstances or not, you are responsible for the death of a very good friend of ours. That doesn't even take into account the other pending charges of a moderately international nature."

Borgia executed a gracefully eloquent gesture. "I cannot answer charges I know nothing of, but as to Lt. Marquez? Would that I could change history. I remember nothing of the battle but pain." Appealing directly to the sullenly silent Byron, he explained, "My instincts gained the upper hand and I could not stop what occurred. Byron, you must know what I am speaking of; have you never been so injured you lost control?"

The younger vampire flinched, and with inward satisfaction, Borgia recognized guilt. Without missing a beat, he insisted to the table as a whole, "Since you have mentioned it, Signor Miller, I must also admit to anger. I have this evening learned that the American government has seized certain of my assets, although, as a legitimate businessman, I cannot understand why. Many of my European assets have been frozen per the same request. I would ask my son why this has been done."

Byron quirked a smile. "Legitimate businessman? That's a laugh. How many legitimate businessmen deal in narcotics, d'you suppose?"

Borgia sighed. "I will not honor that with a reply, Byron. I did not come here tonight to argue over business. I came to spend time with my son and his friends." Looking around the table, he frowned. "Such a shame the lovely Ms. Girion and her partner had to meet with the FBI people tonight. Ms. Girion has so quickly become such an important part of your life, I should have enjoyed meeting her, as well. I trust you have finally made her privy to the health condition you inherited from me?"

The mention of the detectives reignited BC's anger. "I've had the nasty feeling I was being watched. Thanks for confirming it."

The ancient nobleman raised placating hands, "Please, please, *figlio mio*, do not be angry that I wish to know those that are close to you, for they are also important to me. Calm yourself. Maeve warned me of your quick temper. I see she did not exaggerate — how is she, by the by? After our last little disagreement, I do not feel comfortable telephoning her to ask, myself.

"I trust she is enjoying herself since she has able to engage in her beloved 'shopping.' She prefers New York to Chicago, although I confess that my people and I lost track of her until recently. I compliment you on your excellent methods in concealing her. I don't suppose you'd care to reveal . . . no? Alas."

Silence again.

"Please!" Borgia said expansively. "I am not such an avowed enemy! Have I not also been of assistance? Did I not remove that irritating Hernandez fellow? He nearly succeeded in destroying my son! I should think you'd be glad of his demise."

Byron's head jerked up with fury. "If you think I'm going to thank you for that, you're farther out of your fucking mind than I'd imagined! The only thing you accomplished by killing that poor insane bastard was getting me blamed for it! Jim Nelson nearly dragged my ass under a sunlamp before I could explain I didn't do it!"

Borgia winced at the language. "I never intended for your associates to reach this conclusion." Before his table-mates realized what he was doing, he'd again ensnared Miriam's hand. Holding it immobile and stroking it lightly, he smiled into her face. "Have consideration for the lovely lady in our midst. Such language is unsuited for a gentlewoman of breeding."

Anger warred with fear as she tried to — and realized she couldn't — extract her hand from the viselike fingers. Looking up in surprise, she met him eye-to-eye and felt him insinuate into her mind, attempting to pacify and bend her to his will. The contact ended abruptly, and she caught herself against the table, reeling from the onslaught.

Byron's right hand was clamped around Borgia's wrist and his left covered Miriam's protectively. "I will not permit this. If you persist, you will have to deal with me first."

Francesco smiled condescendingly. "What may the chick do to hinder the hawk?"

Byron's reply was a glower of barely suppressed rage.

Borgia continued in the same tone, "You must recognize there is little you could do should I decide to act, be it to kiss an exquisite hand or to visit your refuge at Belridge. I am your sire, and whether you like it or not, there are certain privileges that go with that."

Byron stiffened. "I should have thought the mighty Francesco Borgia above base threats. Surely, bringing innocent children into this is unnecessary. Displaying your knowledge of intimate details is a contemptible ploy to alarm us."

With a flush of pleasure, Borgia said, "Ahhhhh. The haughty eighteenth century gentleman on his dignity — yes, the aristocratic blood is dilute, but it is there. Excellent. A worthy son of the house of Borgia."

In the semi-darkness, Miriam saw Galen reach for something inside his shirt. Hands swift and unobtrusive, he pulled a small, cloth bag from inside his shirt. A slight tug and a silver chain snapped and wrapped around his fingers like a shimmering silver snake. Outwardly calm, he placed the hand containing the object on the table and slid it closer to the malevolent vampire.

Francesco Borgia was locked in a glaring contest with Byron when he suddenly stiffened and glanced at Galen's hand moving closer and closer. The nobleman recoiled and his face contorted. Insane fury blazed, then, with an effort, he resettled his suitcoat and all trace of passion was gone. To Miriam, it was as if a demon had suddenly appeared at the table opposite her and just as quickly disappeared, as if humanity was a thin veil that had briefly slipped aside, then back again. She shuddered and moved closer to Byron.

Mustering shredded dignity, Borgia straightened. "Very well played, *figlio mio*, I concede this round to you."

Disbelief drowned anger on the younger vampire's face. "A game? This *is* all just a sport to you, with real human beings as the gaming pieces, isn't it?"

"Blood of my Blood, do you not realize that it is you and I who are 'real' and the rest are merely as cattle to us? *Comprendi, caro?*"

Standing, he gently stroked his scion's hair, ignoring the convulsive jerk at his touch. "*Arrivederci.* We will talk again, my son." Leaving stunned silence in his wake, he exited as he had come, his stylish figure disappearing into the smoky crowd.

Shuddering violently, Miriam gulped the remains of her drink, wishing it were stronger. Tentatively, BC reached out to his trembling cousin, then hesitated, eying Galen's white-knuckled fist and the silver chain wrapping it. "I didn't even know you had that with you." He pulled slightly away. "I don't blame you for keeping it near. I haven't exactly been the most stable or pleasant flatmate of late."

Before Miriam knew what was happening, Galen had grabbed her cousin's shoulder and hauled him over until they were nose-to-nose. When he spoke, Galen's voice was low, but deliberate. "I'm only gonna say this once, so you better get your head wrapped around it right now. You. Are. Not. Like. That."

BC was too stunned to respond. It didn't matter; Galen wasn't waiting for an answer. Fist safely engulfing the tiny bag and chain, he jerked a thumb toward the door. "I said this before and I'm gonna keep on sayin' it: *That* is a disgusting reanimated corpse that was likely never a human being to start with." The gesturing paw swung around and thudded emphatically into his partner's breastbone. "*You* are a pain in the ass, but you're one of the good guys and probably the only decent thing that slimeball ever did — and it wasn't even *his* idea in the first place. Do you understand me?"

BC stared blankly at the enraged face inches from his own.

Galen growled, "You better start nodding that granite block of yours, or I'm gonna rip it right off your shoulders."

Peale, eyes wide with awe, and certain the threat was not idle, nodded vigorously.

Galen thumped the tabletop, physically deflating as his rage subsided. Draining the beer, he screwed his eyes shut and inhaled deeply three — four times, palpably pulling himself together. Looking slightly gray, even in the dim light, he announced he was going to call Stallings, then disappeared for the lobby.

Byron's eyes were still locked on the hulking figure long after Miriam could no longer make it out against the gloom. Taking his cool fingers lovingly in her own, she observed how different they were from those of his sire. Yes, they were cold, but there was . . . *something* different. She whispered, "He's right, you know. The only thing you have in common with Francesco Borgia is a mutual associate, and an incident in a Philadelphia alleyway."

He snorted derisively. "You forgot to mention the minor detail of the blood that makes me as I am. As *he* is."

"I believe Galen already gave the prevailing opinion on that particular aspect. You're lucky to have a friend like him!"

Smile curving one corner of his mouth, he replied: "Oh, absolutely. If it weren't for Galen, I'd actually have to go out and make *enemies* to rough me up."

"Byron. . . ."

Untouched drink cold between his palms, he furrowed his brow and closed his eyes for a moment. She could almost hear the thoughts racing through his head. At length, he said, "I appreciate the faith you both have in me. I hope I'm deserving of it. As family historian, you ought to know that I'm notorious for disappointing people."

Laughing, she said, "You're right, as family historian I know all about what you deserve, but we love you anyway." Ignoring his grimace, she glanced toward the bar. "Oops, here comes the server."

The girl approached the table cautiously. Hitching her tray under her arm, she advanced with trepidation. "Will either the older gentleman or your other friend be returning?"

Miriam watched in amazement as Byron's demeanor changed back to his usual affable self. The waitress relaxed visibly as his dark blue eyes fixed on hers, and he replied lightly, "The older gentleman will most assuredly *not* be back, but the large fellow will return momentarily and likely require another equally large infusion of beer."

Making a note on her pad, the girl swiftly collected the untouched drink and the empties, started away, then paused. Turning slightly she said softly, "I know it ain't none of my business, but I'm real sorry about what happened. My old man rags on me somethin' awful, too, so I kinda know what it feels like. Just don't let it bug ya."

He smiled. "Thanks, I'll try not to."

Duty done and comfort dispensed, she sped off for the cold ones and didn't see the smile fade as she left.

After the beers arrived, BC's gaze kept turning toward the doorway that Galen had gone through. Miriam tried unsuccessfully to draw him into conversation until she said, "Look, Gae will be all right. I'm sure Borgia is far away from this place by now. Besides he took that little bag with him. Whatever it was, our chum didn't care much for it."

BC raised an eyebrow and through a quirky grin, explained, "It's a charm. Galen's mother is quite adept at making them. You're right, though, Borgia won't come too near it by choice. According to Mama Miller, he's more affected by their power than I am. She says it has something to do with Borgia being evil and me merely being naughty. Even so, it'll be a long time before I forget my first up close and personal encounter with one." His face sobered as he repeated, "I didn't even know he had it."

Catching the hurt behind the words, she mutely rubbed his chill fingers between her warm palms. She knew, when they tensed slightly, that Galen was back. She looked up as Byron asked, "So what's the verdict? Uncle Joe give any orders?"

The muscular giant flumphed into the protesting chair and snatched up a full bottle of beer. "Sorta. He asked why we didn't call earlier. I think he wanted to bust Borgia's butt right here in the nightclub."

"Oh, that would have been cool."

"Yeah, seems since we aren't undercover anymore, anything goes." He fidgeted with the beer bottle, picking at the label with a thumbnail, then said, "Hey, Peale? I'm real sorry. I got kind of rough there."

Peale waved the apology away. "Francesco Borgia is noted for bringing out the best in people."

Gae insisted, "Still, it's my fault about the charm. It came in the morning mail and I just kept forgetting to tell you about it. The note from Mama and Jump said I was to wear it for occasions like tonight's little shindig."

BC nodded, but remained somber.

Galen flared again. "It was for Borgia, not you. God *damn*! You can be such a—"

BC grinned. "'Pain in the ass?'"

"You got it, partner. Oh yeah, speaking of asses, Jump put a PS on the note with the amulet and specifically instructed me to tell you there isn't much can be done to help *you* against Big Daddy, so he says (and this is a quote) '*Guardez votre* butt.'"

BC broke into laughter.

Galen said, "Must be good, wanna share?"

BC composed himself and replied: "Not enough time now, it's a looooong story, but it's been years since I heard that phrase. Trust Jump to use it when it would do the most good."

***

"Really, you two! I'm flying back to Baltimore in the morning. What difference will it make if I spend one more night in the hotel by myself?"

"Maybe not much, but by the time your morning flight takes off, Francesco Borgia will be safely dormant." Gae shifted his grip on the suitbag slung over his shoulder. "Unfortunately, so will BC, but we can't have everything."

BC deposited a suitcase and unlocked the steel door to their SI apartment, saying, "I'll settle for having a nice boring remainder of the— Oops."

Galen crowded in. "Oops? What oops? I don't like oopses, Peale."

With a curt gesture for his companions to stay put, Byron entered the apartment, and stood motionless in the living room, straining every sense. Finally satisfied that he was alone in the flat, he advanced on the dinette, and the items that had sparked his alarm. Sharing the tabletop with his tablet computer were a heavy vellum envelope and a beautifully wrapped package.

Not wishing to disturb the items yet, he tilted his head to read the legend scrawled across the paper in a distinctive, elaborate hand. It read:

'Edgar Michalson, Sentry Medical Center.'

Ice formed in the pit of his stomach as he carefully removed the tiny card tucked under the gift box's ribbon to read his cousin's name in the same hand. Before he'd even scanned the note, he knew whose writing it would be.

Ms. Peale,

Our meeting was a delight to be long savored. Let us hope our next encounter will not be so volatile.

Sincerest regards,
Francesco Borgia

Sensing Galen behind him, he handed the card over his shoulder. "The other appears to be a card for Eddie. My only wonder is that he didn't deliver it in person."

By the light from the open doorway, Galen read the short message, then eyed his partner with alarm. He leaned forward and whispered, "Could he still be here?" Grimacing, he declared in a normal tone, "Riiiiiight. Like he couldn't hear me or wouldn't be waiting on the sofa. Pardon a brain damaged ex-jock. Five'll get you ten Artie Li didn't see a soul go by the security desk."

"No bets, but check anyway."

Both men flinched as the overhead light flicked on. Miriam shut the door firmly. "You guys might be nocturnal animals adapted to the dark, but I need light. What's the big deal, anyway?"

Somberly, BC placed the package and note into her hands. "With love from Frankie. Still feel safe staying alone in your hotel room?"

"No. And I'm not convinced about this place either, but it looks like we're stuck regardless." She eyed the pretty package in her hands warily. "Are you sure this is okay?"

BC shrugged. "Big bangs are Isendamer's trip, not his. He may be an arrogant sonuvabitch, but this is strictly a gift. I'm not sure what he's trying to accomplish, but for now, he's making nice."

Watching as his cousin gingerly removed the wrappings, he mused silently, *Emphasis on for now*. Underlying message received and duly noted. If you can walk into a block of high security flats like this, what chance have I to protect my family from you? Or Galen's family, for that matter? Anyone?

The disgusted clunk of the telephone receiver pulled his attention back as Miller announced, "No surprises. Other than Miriam, no recorded non-Sentry personnel have come through. Sounds like I lit Artie's tail, though. He's going to have all the security tapes reviewed ASAP. Hey, what's in the box?"

Miriam stared into the cushioned depths in mute awe, then slowly and carefully, lifted a tiny object. "A new piece for the museum in Baltimore, although I don't think that's what the giver had in mind. It's a miniature portrait of a lady. Sixteenth century Italian, unless I miss my guess."

BC examined the vibrant image of the coyly smiling young woman. "Considering your expertise, not to mention the source, I would say your guess was on the money. Which museum? The Museum of Art or the Peale Museum?"

Exasperation brought her around to face him. "Byron Cyrus! You really have to ask?"

He grinned impishly. No, he didn't, but it was more fun that way.

Clearing his throat pointedly, Galen said, "Hate to put a wet blanket on things, but this stuff didn't walk in here under its own power — one of us has to call this in to Uncle Joe. And may I point out that *I* made the last call?"

"All the more reason for you to make this one, too. After all, this isn't a separate incident, it's more of an update."

"I knew you were gonna say that. I'll just make the call from my room so Joe's screaming won't disturb your delicate sensibilities."

Watching the broad-shouldered back retreat toward the bedrooms, Miriam said, "That was mean, Byron."

"Yeah, but effective."

Reverently snugging the painting back into its cushioned box, she straightened and stood looking at him appraisingly. Suddenly, she pulled him into a fierce embrace, saying, "Come here, you vile creature of the night! I need a hug. You do, too." Releasing him, she tossed her jacket onto the couch and turned toward the kitchen. "I'm going to get a pot of coffee brewing. Something tells me it's going to be a long night."

Byron followed her into the kitchen and leaned against the counter, watching as she found what she needed.

Measuring coffee into the machine's filter, she sighed, "I wish I could get something for you, too. I think you need it even more than either Galen or me."

"I'd hoped it didn't show," he answered with a rueful smile. "We vile creatures of the night are supposed to be inscrutable. Anyway, I'll grab one of those despicable Bloody Elsies. They're foul, but apparently, to my body, blood is blood — no matter how cold."

"Maybe I could try to warm it in a pan of water like baby formula?"

He shrugged, "It's worth a try, I suppose."

Filling the carafe, she assured him over the noise of the water, "You don't have to stand guard, Byron. Go on back with Galen. By the time you're done filing your report or whatever, I'll have things well in hand here." Ignoring his patently dubious expression, she insisted, "I'm not afraid to be alone. You said yourself that Borgia is making nice and what *I* said at the club still goes: he's far away from here by now."

Face stubbornly set, he remained at his post.

"Uhhhh *huh*!" Flipping the switch on the machine, she methodically rummaged through the drawers. With a cry of triumph, she withdrew the small wooden spoon from where BC had jammed it behind the towels and pot holders, spun, and waved it sternly under his nose.

He sprang back and yelped, "*Hey*! No fair using wooden objects."

"Your mother's journal entries heartily recommended this method of behavior modification for you even in pre-vampire days. Glad to see it still works."

Byron was incredulous. "*Mama* said *that*! Oh, she *never* would!"

Miriam chuckled. "Not in those words, but the intent was the same. Now get back there and do your cop thing, or else."

He vanished, and through the still-swinging partition, she heard his muttered commentary on the tyranny of Peale women through history.

Self-appointed sentinel gone, she allowed her front of strength to disintegrate, although, with Byron's abilities, she doubted the pretense succeeded for anyone but herself. Long-denied shivers burst to the surface as she leaned heavily against the stainless steel sink, pressing wet a paper towel to her throat. Well, maybe he could tell she was frightened, but there was no way in hell she'd let him see the depths of her fear. In his present mood, he was as likely to believe he was the cause, rather than his soul-chilling sire.

Poor Byron. His reaction to Borgia was so primal. Certainly, discovering that the being responsible for his creation was a creature of such evil would be shattering, but was there more? Did the sire actually have such power over the child, especially after so long a time? Whether or not the actual power was there, Byron believed it was, and that belief could make it happen.

***

Galen waved BC into the room as he spoke into the phone: "Yes, sir, we'll have a report on your desk by sunrise, and I'll be sure to pass on what you said to BC. He'll appreciate it, I know." Hanging up, he turned to his partner, saying, "Stallings is calling Baltimore to request an unobtrusive surveillance of the house at Belridge ASAP."

"You're right, I appreciate it. I don't think it will help, but I appreciate it."

The only response was a noncommittal grunt as Gae added, "Plus, he's on his way over. He wants our written statement . . . well, you heard. But, he wants to talk to Miriam in person. By the way, we were completely justified for bringing her here under our protection. He would have done the same thing if he'd been in our place."

"Oh, *that* makes me feel wonderfully better. Dammit." He frowned, then said, "I suppose it's Stallings' way of saying 'nice work,' but I still find it grating. Well, Miriam's preparing for an all-nighter, anyway. She's currently in the kitchen fixing the largest, strongest pot of coffee known to mankind. I'm instructed to fetch you when we've finished here. If I return sans Miller, she'll lay me out with the deadliest weapon used by Peale women from time immemorial — ye Wooden Spoon."

Galen was grateful for the laugh. "Sounds lethal, both the spoon and the coffee. Lead on —. oh, wait." Digging into his pocket, he produced the charm with a 'Ta Da!' flourish. Involuntarily, BC stepped back from the swinging silver, as Gae pointed at the object. "I don't think much of surveillance, either."

Peale nodded in sudden comprehension. "Excellent idea, but may I suggest that we phone Chicago and see how many more of those Jump and your mother can whip up on short notice?"

"God, you're right. We got your family, mine, Taylor

and Stroud . . . I wonder if we should get one for Maeve, too."

"Nah. Hey, D'you think they can work one up *against* Maeve?"

Galen chuckled. "Probably, but they'd never give it to you."

SIX

He'd chosen this club because nobody knew him here. Tonight he wanted to make like Greta Garbo and be alone. Without even having to resort to vampiric leverage, he'd wrangled his favorite spot, a booth tucked in the back, well away from the center of activity. In spite of all factors being in his favor, he was having a remarkably hard time thinking about anything. That wasn't true. He thought about plenty of things. The trouble was, he kept arriving at the same place. It wasn't a pleasant place.

Twirling the snifter, he watched viscous cognac bead and run down the sides of the glass. Good-byes were distasteful to him. There'd been far too many of them over the centuries, and Miriam's recent return to Baltimore had left an aching void. He missed her, even though she was no longer safe around him.

Was she any more safe at Belridge? Certainly, SI had posted guards at the house and on the grounds, but the elder vampire had easily bopped in and out of the SI high-security hostelry. The surveillance video was chilling. On the recordings, Francesco Borgia strolled casually past Artie Li as if invisible. To Artie, he was. Borgia was plainly unconcerned about the cameras — except to keep his face hidden from them. No doubt, the idea was to prevent any usable photograph being taken. Grim satisfaction curved Peale's lips in the dim club lighting. A bit too late for that. Borgia should have considered that before he took an artist from a family of artists as his fledgling. The sketch he'd made after their first encounter at the Wisconsin lodge was quite a good likeness, if he did say so himself. That drawing was now being sent to Sentry International posts worldwide. Interpol got it, too.

The satisfaction was fleeting. One unpleasant thought looped endlessly through his brain: nobody was safe from this evil thing and it was *his* fault.

Clearly Borgia had no intention to leave his unwilling fledgling alone. The thinly veiled threats toward his family and friends and even Maeve were plain as an engraved tombstone: "Join me, or I'll destroy you an inch at a time."

No. Human guards would be no help if Borgia decided to make good on his threats, no matter how good or sophisticated their equipment was. He had more faith in the potent little charm Miriam had worn home. He wished there was a way to get one for each member of the family, but there wasn't time. Maybe later — if Borgia *gave* them a later.

Maybe for the good of all, he should simply accede . . . NO! Good Lord! How could he do that? Besides, that would give the bastard even more power over him and make his loved ones more vulnerable than ever.

Borgia must be destroyed.

There. He'd said it — or thought it — and that made it real. It had hovered over him like the sword of Damocles for quite some time. Now that he'd faced it, there was a lot to do, and a very short time to do it. He'd have to be careful; if Galen realized what he was planning—

"I can't make up my mind which of you is sexier, the elder or the younger."

He'd only heard the voice from a distance before, and it had lacked the enticing intonations then, but he knew beyond a shadow of a doubt, and by the crawly feeling on the back of his neck, whose voice it was.

"Good evening, Ms. Isendamer," he said. "Forgive me for not asking you to join me."

Gwen Isendamer smiled fetchingly, sweeping her thick, pale hair back away from her face. She was a remarkably beautiful woman, but even with several feet of distance between them, he could feel the dark twisting of her mind. The strength of this impression made him wonder how she could pass unnoticed through humanity. Deviance this extreme must surely strike alarms in even the most unperceptive person.

She cooed, "Gwen, please, and I'll call you Byron. So glad you dispensed with all the 'have we met' rubbish. That's so tiresome, and I think we know each other pretty well, don't we?"

Uninvited, she slid sinuously into the booth and leaned into him. "Naughty boy," she said. "I had the devil of a time finding you."

"Yet, here you are."

"Yes, here I am. How lucky for me that your motorcycle is as distinctive as its rider."

Note to self: take a cab next time. He drew away. "What *is* it with you people? Do you have an objection to my having a quiet evening out, or is it my taste in music you dislike? If it will keep you at bay, I'm willing to take up opera."

"You never called me."

"You noticed."

"Francesco is very angry. You weren't nice to him last night."

"Did he send you here to tell me that? I thought you were a bit high-priced for a messenger service."

Eying him levelly she said, "Francesco doesn't know I'm here. I came because I wanted to talk to you."

"I'm beginning to think I need to hire an appointment secretary to handle all the people who've suddenly got the desire to chat with me."

"You *can* be rude!" She bristled, smoothed it over, and smiled silkily. "Good thing I like incorrigible men. You fascinate me, Byron. I came to offer you an interesting evening. Don't worry, I know your appetites and I'm more than ready to accommodate them. My car is waiting; I have a little place. . . ."

"You fascinate me, too, Ms. Isendamer — your scent, your accessories: Chanel and Semtex, so unique. And that adorable little pistol in your handbag. Can you give me a reason why I should put myself in closer range of what are undoubtedly silver bullets?"

Her face went hard as she spat, "Pig! I went to the trouble to look you up and offer you an intimate evening and this is how you act! I see why Francesco is angry with you."

Wait wait wait, Stupid! He was doing the same thing he'd done at the first meeting with Borgia. Okay, so the woman gave him a massive case of the creepy crawlies. If he blew this opportunity, Stallings would drive a stake through his heart. Slowly. Under a sunlamp. Also, in light of his decision concerning Borgia, having Isendamer pleasantly disposed to him might not be a bad idea. Was it too late for a change of tune? Scrubbing his face with his hands, he said, "Ms Isendamer . . . ."

"Gwen."

I'm going to be sick. "Gwen. Please understand that I'm finding all this attention overwhelming. For so many years, I was essentially alone. Now, I'm surrounded by people who want to 'get to know me.' It's a bit unsettling."

She smiled sultrily and reached to stroke his face. "Well, I *said* you were fascinating."

He didn't flinch at her touch, but it took every ounce of the willpower he had to stay seated and submit to it.

She leaned across the table. "Look, this place is so noisy . . . let's head to my place, where we can talk more privately."

He smiled at her, his mind racing for a way to refuse and not make her mad again, when a persistent vibration buzzed inside his jacket. *Saved by the mobile.* Smile turning rueful, he withdrew the device and held it up for inspection. "Duty calls — or at least my mobile does. As you see, even my kind are tied into the information super-highway these days." He stood. "They have rules against mobile phones in the club. I'll have to go outside."

"We'll both leave. You can call on the way to my place. I have the most marvelous. . . ."

"I don't think that's a good idea: it's . . . my office calling. You know, Sentry International?"

The unwelcome information sank in. She peevishly tossed her hair, saying, "I'll wait for you here, then. I'm not finished with you and I haven't given up hopes of an enjoyable evening." She downed his cognac, then smiled up at him seductively. "You can get it back later. In private."

Mentally, he swallowed hard, then hurried for the exit. She sat tight, apparently secure of his return. He didn't like the smell of that. Loping straight for the door, he sneaked a peek outside. Three burly types were staking out his Harley and a sporty silver European car parked next to it.

Back to the wall, so as to keep both the entrance and the terrible trio in view, he raised his cell phone and punched redial on the number from the Missed Calls list. In spite of what he'd told Isendamer, he hadn't recognized the number. Still, he wasn't too surprised to hear Galen's voice.

"You must make a hobby of sitting on telephones, Gae. What are you trying to hatch?"

"Very funny, pal, I'll make a note to laugh later," Miller said. "I'm at the hospital. Our friend is more or less back with us. You better get over here at warp speed; he keeps fading out."

"That might prove difficult, but I'll get there as fast as I can — I gotta ditch someone — *several* someones."

***

He'd never liked hospitals. All his mortal life and for long years after, they were places of doom. To be sent to hospital was usually to be sent to die. It was no longer so, but centuries of ingraining didn't change easily in a few short decades. He followed the white-coated orderly through halls that reeked of antiseptic and the disturbing underlying smells the chemicals couldn't mask. Two men in SI Security uniforms flanked the door he was led to. One stepped out as they approached. The orderly jerked a thumb and said, "This is Special Agent Peale. They're waiting for him in there."

The guard accepted Peale's ID, grunted, then resumed his post. Though the way was clear, BC stood indecisive as the disquieting scents from the adjoining room filtered through. Stallings was most prominent, probably standing closest to the door. Galen was there, too, but most disturbing was the scent of the patient, faint, and altered by painkillers. Under the glare of the guards, who no doubt wondered what this guy's problem was, he stepped in, grateful to find the sickroom lighting dimmer than the white brilliance of the hall. Privately astounded at the number of tubes and wires connecting the bruised body to innumerable bags and machines, he smiled and said, "Hi, Eddie! Sorry it took so long, but I had to leave my bike at the nightclub and slide out through the alley. I don't have to tell anyone what hell it is to get a cab this time of night."

Eddie laughed weakly. "Yeah, Miller tol' me; hadda ditch yer date, huh? Maybe ya should send her a box of chocolates on me t' make it up."

BC looked thoughtful. "I'm not sure I want to make it up, but you might want to send her something, Eddie, though not chocolates, I think." Glancing toward his commanding officer and partner, he explained, "It was Gwen Isendamer. Young, white, single female psychopath seeking to have meaningful relationship with younger vampire."

Over the others' muttered exclamations, Eddie's heart leapt alarmingly. Peale shot forward for the emergency call button.

Eddie regained control and, smiling weakly, waved him away. "S'okay, kid. I ain't croakin' you can leave off the panic button." The drawn face became reflective. "Maybe we do need a panic button, after all. If Gwennie's makin' her big move now, it's all gonna hit th' fan fast an' hard. She was bound t'do it sooner or later. Th' Boss'll have his hands full with this — an' don't you think he don't know what she's up to. He can read her like a first grade primer."

Stallings said, "Then there's no time to lose. Any idea where they'll be, Michalson? You can save us a lot of time by telling us now"

"Yeah, an' I'm sunk, anyhow," Michalson said with a faint shrug. "I getcha. Yer best bet is the Boss's estate about an hour north o' th' city, *Campo della Ferrara*. It's on the river. He always stays there when he's in this part of the country. He's owned the place for somethin' like two hundred years and it's the only place I ever heard him call home. He even keeps his master files there. If ya can get in, I'd say ya got 'im dead t'rights." He paused with a grin toward Peale. "No pun intended, kid."

Stallings ignored the comment and leaned in. "What kind of security does he have?"

"There ya got a problem. The joint's a fortress. He don't keep a lot of guys around, on account of him likin' t' hunt in the woods there an' not many in the organization knowin' about the boss's condition, but he's got the place pretty well wired. You plannin' to make a social call?"

The question and answer session lasted about an hour. More precisely: lasted until the nurses poking their heads into the room progressed from disapproving noises to open threats. Stallings reluctantly closed his notebook and shut off the recorder. The information looked valuable, but time would tell. Time would also provide another debriefing since Michalson was conscious and talking. This ball was going to roll. Collecting his things, Stallings gestured for Miller and Peale to follow, then left.

Whispering a quick explanation to Galen, BC returned to the bedside. Eddie's condition had steadily worsened as they spoke and he couldn't hide his concern.

"Thanks for the help, I can't say it'll make things easier, but at least we'll know what to expect." He hesitated. "What about you, Eddie, you gonna be okay?"

The characteristic sound of disgust was so close to the old Michalson, the vampire was partly reassured. "Okay? Depends how ya define okay, I guess. I'm finished in th' business, no matter what. Even if I get outta this bed, Gwennie won that part of the match, anyways."

"How so?"

Eddie stared at the monitors. "I gone state's evidence, ain't I? Nobody's gonna know for why, they'll just see I fingered my associates. Even if I tried t' explain my boss was a five-hundred-year-old dead guy whose girlfriend was a psycho bitch assassin who wanted to be a vampire, too. Then I add that the arresting cops were an ex-football star and th' Boss's three-hundred-year-old kid? Hey, I'm lookin' at either a high-rise headstone or rubber walls the rest of my life."

"Two hundred-sixty-three."

"Huh?"

"I'm only two hundred-sixty-three."

The invalid fixed him with a stare. "You're real weird, kid."

**

Dammit! Peale was right. He did play the cracks even on a regular-sized keyboard. As he backspaced over the typo, his partner's extension rang. He heard the pleasant voice answer, "Sentry International. Special Agent Peale speaking . . . oh, hi. Yeah, well, I told you who was calling, didn't I? I got called away."

Miller sighed and tried to shut out the distraction. He had fifteen minutes to finish the damned report, although why Stallings *wanted* a report when he'd been right there was far beyond him. It was some new form of torture. Yeah. That was it. Maybe he ought to get in touch with Amnesty International.

A paper wad sailed over his monitor and bounced off his forehead, landing in the middle of his keyboard. He clenched his teeth. Of all the juvenile — snatching it, he wound up to hurl it back with compounded interest only to find Peale having a panic attack. The pale man was even paler than normal and frantically waving a notepad with ISENDAMER scrawled across it.

Surreally, Byron's calm, cultured voice continued, "No, I can't tell you what it was about. Classified, and all that."

Miller swiftly punched in the Captain's extension. It was picked up almost immediately, "Stallings."

Hand cupped over the receiver, Galen whispered, "Captain, we need a recorder rolling and a trace on Peale's line. He's talking to Isendamer."

"Now? Good God! I'll get on it."

Giving his partner the thumbs up, Miller settled back to listen. Peale was literally tearing at his hair, about to have a stroke, but if you closed your eyes, you'd never know. His voice was smooth and his conversation light. If the situation wasn't so deadly serious, it would be hilarious.

Peale said, "No, I've got to be here tonight. Pretty much all of tonight, if you want to get right down to it. I doubt I'll have time for another club for a while. Yeah, the Blue Note's great. . . ."

Stallings appeared at the door and Peale looked at him hopelessly, saying, "No. No way I can duck out, even for a show like that."

Stallings nodded vigorously. Peale shook his head vigorously. "Yeah, I'm sure. Maybe another time? Yeah, me, too. Talk to you later, okay?" The phone was dropped into the cradle and his head dropped into his hands, spilling long hair over his fingers.

Stallings stalked to the desk, bellowing, "Dammit, Peale! We could've had you wired in twenty minutes. Whatever possessed you to turn down a meet?"

Peale met Stalling's eyes. "Not. Tonight."

Stallings blinked. He deflated against the door frame. "Okay, it probably wouldn't be good to look too eager, anyway. The next time she calls, though — she *will* call again, won't she?"

Finger-combing his hair back into place, Peale said dully, "Oh, yeah. She'll call back. Probably several more times tonight. She's in the city without Borgia looking over her shoulder. Her words."

Brightening, Stallings rubbed his hands together, "Great! We'll keep the tap going, then." He started out into the hall, turning hopefully, almost pleading. "If you change your mind. . . ."

"I won't." Peale's head went down into his hands again. Stallings returned to his office muttering about lost opportunities.

The silence left in his wake continued until Miller asked softly, "Uh, BC, you didn't . . . uh . . . *push* . . . a little there, did you?"

"I dunno. Maybe a little."

"Thought so."

Peale's head snapped up. "Well, what would you have done?"

"Probably the same thing." He tossed a hair pick onto Peale's blotter. "Hey, man, you're a mess. Better get cleaned up. If your girlfriend sees you like that, she might call it off, then Stallings will break down and cry."

Peale snatched a comb from his own pocket and attacked his wild mane in silence.

"Seriously, you oughta get an Oscar for that performance," Galen said with a note of admiration in his voice.

"Stuff it."

***

The limousine stood out like a neon sign in the hostelry's parking garage. He backed the motorcycle into the reserved slot, turned off the engine and waited. Something deep inside lurched when the rear door swung open and Francesco Borgia stepped onto the pavement. Gloved fingers tightened on the handlebars as he fought back the urge to fire up the engine. He wasn't sure if it was to run the approaching figure down or flee. Maybe both.

As if aware of the thoughts, the elder vampire stopped a safe distance from the motorcycle.

"Good evening, Byron," he said. "Please, dismount and we will talk."

The words resonated through every fiber of his being. He felt his grip loosening, then, with a surge of will, he clamped down again, more firmly than before. He kept his voice even as he said, "I don't believe I want to do that."

Borgia's fists worked at his sides. Peale braced for an outburst, instead, the elder vampire calmed himself. "*Please.* Talk with me, Byron. Only talk."

"Look, I've had a really bad night. . . ."

"I have made a polite request. Do not make me ask again," the stocky man said through tightened lips. Byron could feel the elder straining for control as, he was sure,

Borgia could feel his own struggle to keep it.

Hands dropping from the grips, Peale heaved a sigh. "Oh, okay."

As BC strode away from the bike, Borgia bowed with exaggerated courtliness. His voice dripped sarcasm as he said, "*Grazie*. Sometimes, my son, you try my patience."

"Don't mind if I do, you must come over and try mine sometime."

Borgia paused in confusion, then nodded in sudden comprehension. "Ah! A joke."

The Groucho quote had put the elder vampire slightly off-balance. *Thank you, Mr. Marx.* Aloud, he said, "Yes. I've been waiting years to say that. What did you want to talk about?"

"Not here. This is so public. Get into the car and we will talk as we drive."

"I definitely don't want to do that. I like public."

"But we have so much to talk about. You have done very well on your own, but there are still many things to learn. Things that only I can teach you." He gestured toward the still-open limousine door.

"This isn't edging around to a 'join me on the Dark Side and we'll rule together' bit, is it? If I were you, I wouldn't even try that one on, you're no where near tall enough."

"Byron, I tire of your flip attitude."

"Oh, trust me, I'm exhibiting one of those survival traits. I'm not getting in that car with you."

"Why not?"

"Because if I get in, I won't be coming back."

To give him credit, Borgia didn't try to deny it, but finally gave way to his anger. "Get in that car."

"No."

"Come. With. Me."

The words drew him. His sire's power surged through him compelling him to move forward to the waiting car. Anger rose against the pull, giving him strength to step back, closer to the hostelry's entrance. Anger also gave force to his words as he said, "Don't try that again."

Turning on his heel, he stalked deliberately to the building.

From behind him, Borgia commanded, "Come back this instant."

He didn't turn, but kept walking. The stairwell entrance with its tiny keypad lock seemed miles away. "The conversation is over."

"One week, Byron. I will give you seven days to reconsider. After that, we shall see how strong you are against me. Who can say what might happen to the lovely Ms. Peale or the sensual Sgt. Girion?"

"Don't make threats." BC turned slowly and looked his sire square in the face. It was a calculated risk, but he held the depth of his emotion before him like a shield. "They may not have the effect you think."

Borgia slammed the door to the limo and the big car roared away. He watched it vanish, then sagged against the building. "Well, waddya know? I *can* do it."

***

Stroud Girion's warm, firm touch cut through his funk and brought him back to his surroundings. Her bedroom always surprised him with its Spartan, almost masculine trim unexpectedly punctuated with feminine touches and crowned with glass cases of shooting medals and citations. Portrait of the lady herself.

Beside him, Stroud said, "Hey! Where the hell were you? It must have been a couple million miles away. I almost had to punch you to get your attention!"

"Not miles," he said with a smile. "Decades. The war council we had tonight with Brannaugh and Stallings? The last time I saw that kind of mapwork and split second planning was World War II — maybe. I wouldn't want to make any bets on it."

"You ain't seen nothin', yet! Wait until the SWAT briefing. Hey! Wanna make a date for after it's all over tomorrow night? I can put a reserved sign on your pillow."

"Sure." Rolling over, he kissed her throat and settled down to watch her pulse. He wanted to see that vibration continue for a long, long time. She let him lie in companionable silence for several more moments.

Finally, she blurted out, "I know about Borgia. I mean what happened in the parking garage — about what he wants from you and the threats he made."

Her comment was akin to touching him with a red-hot poker. He pulled away and swung his legs over the side of the bed. "Ah. The Galen Miller News Network, I suppose."

"Yeah. He called today and told Taylor and me about it." She scooched over and wrapped her arms around him. "Lie back down, I'm not bitching at you. I know you hate to talk about him — but you *won* this round."

He turned more toward her. "Won? Glad to know that. I would never have guessed that throwing up and having the shakes for two hours were signs of victory."

Stroud shook her head and said firmly, "You walked away."

"He threatened everyone I hold dear."

"Look at me, BC. I'm not worried — afraid, yes. I'd be

stupid not to be afraid of someone like Francesco Borgia. But I'm not worried." Springing up, she padded over to the armoire and took a box of bullets from the top shelf. Returning to the bed, she opened the box and held the contents out for inspection. He recoiled at the ranks of silver domes.

"I had three cartons made up," she said. "I even took them to my priest and had him bless them. He thought I was going off the deep end, but he did it, anyway." Closing the cardboard lid, she placed the box on the bedside table, saying, "That box is yours. If you wear your biking gloves when you load, you should be fine."

He stared at the box, unsure how to respond.

She came around and looked deeply into his eyes. "I'll load them for you if you want. I don't want you to get burned on them. They're strictly for the bad guy."

He lifted the box gingerly, but aside from a somewhat different weight, and a business card for a police equipment supplier taped to the top, there was nothing remarkable about it. Looking at her over the card, he knew she'd guessed his plans. Of course she would. It was what she'd do. "I think the gloves will work fine. Thanks."

"Don't mention it. Just be sure you survive." Abruptly, she was on the bed again, leering wickedly. "Hey, stop worrying about that creep and get your mind on what's important."

He didn't resist as she pulled him down to her.

She grinned. "After all, if we waste all night talking, like we did last time, you'll end up spending the day in the hall bathroom again. That could be bad because I don't know the Vietnamese to tell the cleaning lady 'Please ignore my dead lover in the bathtub.'"

***

The angry voices were audible even before the elevator doors slid back. He lingered in the hallway trying not to hear the words. No joy. Even without vampiric hearing, he'd be able to hear the thunderous diatribe. Not that shutting it off out here would do much good, since his apartment was the combat zone. Wincing, he gave silent thanks that the last seminar attendees had gone home the day before, leaving Gae and himself alone on the floor again. He prayed the ceiling and floor were soundproofed better than the walls. He doubted it. He could picture Maeve curled into a comfortable chair in her apartment upstairs, hanging onto every word. The woman did love her dirt. The one good thing about it was that he wasn't one of the combatants for once.

Come to that, who *did* the other voice belong to? It was a woman, and it was familiar. . . . Oh. Fiona Miller, Galen's ex-wife.

Eying the elevator with open longing, he dismissed the possibility. Retreating downstairs was out of the question. He'd seen Elaine snatching at the house phone even as he entered the lobby. Likely giving Galen warning that he was on his way up. A roommate alert, as it were. At the time, he'd wondered about Elaine's nervous urgency and Artie's twitchiness. Now he understood it completely. Too bad they hadn't seen fit to give *him* an ex-wife alert. He sighed. Chances were, Gae told them not to, in some sort of desperate bid to keep him from heading for the hills. He snorted in amusement. Imagine him as the cavalry.

Oh well, the point was moot. Where could he go, anyway? Sunrise was an insistent hum growing ever louder on the edge of his consciousness. Pausing, hand on the latch, he flinched as Fiona shouted:

"Don't tell *me* it wasn't that bad! Your mother told me you were nearly killed! And did you tell me about it? No! You let me find out about it from your mother. Again! Why is that, Galen?"

"Because I wanted to avoid a scene like this one," Galen answered. Byron could feel his frustration right through the door. "Mama didn't have any business telling you and the kids, it was only an accident that she found out—"

"The same kind of accident where I discovered you were in New York instead of Chicago? Do I have to rely on the news to let me know where my children's father is, now?"

"Don't give me that! I left enough messages with your staff to fill a filing cabinet. Don't blame me if you didn't get them. Check my phone bill, if you don't believe me. Maybe you need to hire more competent people instead of throwing shit at my head!"

That seemed as good an entrance cue as he was likely to get. Fixing his face in a pleasant expression, he flung open the door, calling, "Good morning! I trust I'm not arriving at an inopportune moment."

Miller appeared to teleport to his side. Clamping Peale's arm, he pulled him into the apartment, hissing, "About damn time you showed up." Galen's face struggled to achieve a smile as he turned back to the woman standing, arms folded, in the middle of the living room. "Fiona, this is my new partner, BC Peale. BC, this is my ex-wife, Fiona Mitchell-Miller."

The handsome woman in the heavy brass jewelry released her anger to smile warmly, stepping forward to give his hand a firm shake. "Hi, BC. I knew who you were the moment you came through the door. My Mother-in-law showed me the tape she'd gotten off CNN."

Oooooh. That was bad. His smile became rueful. "Not one of my more shining performances, I fear."

"Maybe not," Fiona said with a pointed look at her ex-husband, "but the plot was riveting. I'm sure we'll get to know each other better over the next few weeks, so, if you'll excuse me. . . ." She plucked a nylon grip from the floor, announcing, "Since Gae doesn't seem inclined to do it, I'm going to put this away myself."

With a flip of beaded braids, the stylish figure retreated down the hall and disappeared into Galen's bedroom.

Peale watched her progress, and turned to Miller, wild-eyed. "She's planning on staying here? 'Few weeks'?"

"Calm down," Galen whispered. "She's only staying here for what's left of tonight; there was nothing I could do about it. You'd better get back to Stroud's."

"No can do! Even if I *could* get over there before the sun rose, she's got her maid service coming over today and— Oh, God. What about the Elsies in the 'fridge?"

"Geez. I hadn't thought about that. Look, there's only six of 'em. Chug what you can and dump the rest. I'll get her into a hotel tomorrow. Don't worry about it."

Miller sprinted after his fuming ex, leaving Peale staring down the empty corridor. Hugging the box of special rounds against the heavy leather of his motorcycle jacket, he absently fingered the business card, then eyed the kitchen doors. Maybe the Elsies weren't such a bad idea. He was probably going to need the extra sustenance — and body armor. Definitely body armor. He glanced down the hall toward Galen's now-closed bedroom door. The body armor might even come in useful for the Borgia raid.

SEVEN

Galen Miller awoke to the smells of brewing coffee and frying bacon and the sound of women's laughter. Sounded like Maeve. Wonderful. He sat up and groaned. Sleeping on the couch never used to leave him this stiff. Oh, well. Fi would get checked into a hotel first thing this morning and he'd have the bed back tonight. Pulling on his ratty terry cloth robe, he padded in the direction of the voices and the aromas.

As he pushed into the kitchen, Maeve grinned over her coffee cup. "Oh my! Look what the cat coughed up."

Fiona looked up from her cooking and laughed. "Quick, give that man some coffee."

Galen sneered and poured a mug for himself, sipped it, and said, "Good morning, ladies. I don't know which surprises me more, Maeve up this early or Fi being domestic."

"Hmmph! Early, is it?" the Irishwoman exclaimed. "Mid-afternoon, more like."

"It's morning to me."

With an exaggerated sniff, Maeve rose and rinsed her cup out at the sink. "Fiona may have to stay here and be insulted, but I don't. I have an afternoon in the shops ahead of me and I intend to enjoy it." She brushed past Galen with a grin, but turned at the door. "Fiona, are you sure you wouldn't like to go with me? There are some lovely sales."

At Fiona's head-shake, she shrugged and took her leave.

Fiona laughed as the door closed. "I shudder to think what her idea of a sale is."

Galen took the seat Maeve just vacated. "Been having a nice chat with our local branch of the IRA?"

"Galen! Maeve is a nice person and your mother specifically asked her to come down and say hello." She brandished the bacon-greasy turner warningly. "I see that look. Don't even think about saying what you're thinking about saying."

He laughed and held up his hands in surrender. "Okay, I won't. I suppose she was giving you the rundown on our continuing soap opera?"

"I'll say! And here I was, wondering if BC was gay."

Galen choked and sprayed coffee. "What? Why the hell did you think that?"

Hesitating, she glanced toward the swinging doors. "Can he hear us? I wouldn't want to insult him."

"Good time to think about that, but no — he'd probably just laugh, if he did. The medication he takes knocks him out completely for the day. Don't expect to hear a peep out of him until nightfall."

"That must be hard for him," Fi said, sympathy flooding her eyes. "Have the doctors tried to do anything for the condition? Has he seen any specialists?"

"Nuh uh, Fi, you're trying to change the subject. Why were you thinking Peale was gay?"

"The stereotypical stuff, I guess. He's so good-looking and never been married." She paused for a moment before adding, "Then, you two guys sharing an apartment . . . ."

Galen puzzled for a second before the penny dropped.

"Hold on, there! You were thinking BC and I . . . I don't believe I'm hearing this from my own wife!"

"EX-wife."

"Mother of my children, too," he said drawing himself up in mock indignation. "I bet you were one of those prudes casting aspersions on Bert and Ernie."

"Galen Miller!"

Unable to keep a straight face any longer, he guffawed and pounded the table. "Aw, man, Peale is gonna roll on the floor!"

"Don't you dare tell him about this." She smacked a heaped plate onto the table. "Here, eat your breakfast and shut up."

"If you want proof I haven't changed . . . ," he said, giving her a sidelong look. "BC *is* out like the dead. All day long."

She abruptly turned back to fill her own plate. "Gae, don't go there."

"What? I was just . . . ."

"Let's just drop it, okay?" She sat down and stabbed a fork into her scrambled eggs.

Confused, Galen watched her maul her food in silence, then said uncertainly, "Sure. Whatever you say, Fi."

***

Francesco Borgia jerked angrily away from Gwen Isendamer's embrace and stalked behind his desk, putting the massive expanse of gleaming mahogany between them.

She stared after him in unfeigned confusion. "Darling, what's wrong?"

He busied himself stacking papers into his briefcase. "I am not in the mood for such foolishness tonight."

"Foolishness? Francesco, I was only going to kiss you. You never used to mind that."

"Be that as it may, we are finished here." The case snapped shut. "You may go now."

Ivory cheeks flushed with pink fury, she spat, "I will not be dismissed like a servant!"

"Then how will you be dismissed? I wish to be alone, I cannot make it plainer than that."

She slammed out of his study. He heard her pelt up the stairs and into her rooms. Sighing, he spun the rheostat back down to candlelight level and fell heavily into his throne-like desk chair.

He handled that badly, to say the least. In his defense, it had been only an hour since his remaining Sentry International spy had called to tell him about the rumors of her approaches to Byron. Approaches his own watchers had not reported. He didn't need to wonder at that silence. Gwen was extravagant with money when it meant getting what she wanted, and it seemed she now wanted his son. The men would be seen to. Gwen would be seen to, as well. If only he didn't need her for now.

His thoughts were interrupted by his private telephone. It had brought nothing but bad news lately. He lifted it. "Yes."

The whisper was hoarse and hurried, "This is Verhoff, again. I just got wind of a raid on someplace called *Campo della Ferrara.*"

Borgia was stunned to immobility.

The voice prompted, "Hello?"

"Yes, yes, I hear you. When does this happen?"

"There's a real tight lid on it, so I dunno for sure. Best I can tell, it's soon, mebbe tomorrow sometime. The DEA and ATF are gearing up for it, too."

"You have nothing more specific?"

"Not yet. Let me nose around some. I'll call back when I know more."

Still in a state of shock, Borgia let the telephone drop back into its cradle and sat, staring unseeing at the roaring fire in the grate. No doubt he had Gwen to thank for this, too. Her clumsy machinations against Edgar had sent out shockwaves that could not go unnoticed. There was nothing for it. He'd burn all records and eliminate Gwen immediately. Let them find nothing but ashes and her lifeless corpse.

He'd have to go to ground briefly. He could contact Byron later. Pinning the telephone to his ear with one shoulder, he pressed both Carlo's extension and the button to release the catch on a secret drawer. Carlo could easily pack the limousine without alerting Gwen and the other men. Carlo picked up and as he spoke, Borgia withdrew an automatic pistol and a pair of gloves from the hidden compartment. Pulling on the gloves, he deftly loaded the weapon with his special parting gift to Gwen Isendamer. Silver bullets.

***

Duster tails flapping like leather wings, BC Peale skidded into the office almost two hours late. Watching the entrance, it occurred to Miller that his friend had been a little too mysterious about his pre-raid plans. He'd just said he had to "buy a few things" and disappeared soon after sunset. Unfortunately, the Fiona Fiasco had kept Galen way too busy to worry about it — then.

Three fully loaded clips thumped into the middle of Galen's blotter.

BC said, "Here, you might want a few of these, too. Stroud gave them to me last night."

Looking from the clips to the black leather gloves covering his partner's hands, Galen picked them up and examined the rounds. They were awfully shiny. And silvery. He said, "You missed the SWAT briefing, but so did Stallings, so you're cool. I almost thought you weren't going to make it."

"Nope. There's no way I'd miss this party. Just had a couple things to pick up," Peale said absently.

"Yeah. So you said."

Hip-perching on the edge of the desk, Peale pulled two weapons out from under his coat to check them. He'd augmented his beloved .45 with two brand new Mini Uzis and the black gloves stayed in place as the vampire ejected, examined and re-slotted the machine pistols' expanded clips. Two guesses were one too many for what kind of rounds those clips were filled with.

Trying to lighten the mood, Gae remarked, "Man! The way you came flying in here, you looked like some kind of pulp fiction avenger. If you start talking about evil lurking in the hearts of men, I'm outta here."

The vampire smiled mirthlessly as he slapped a loaded magazine home into his .45 and slipped it back into his shoulder holster.

A chill passed through the ex-linebacker as he watched his partner methodically check a Velcro strip on his coat lining that was dotted with more ammo. He had enough to fight a small war.

"Did you have any trouble getting Fiona into a hotel?" BC asked lightly, apparently unaware of his partner's apprehensive silence. "I saw her things were gone when I rose."

"No, we got her registered pretty fast, although I don't think she's finished reaming me a new bodily orifice. Once she finds out why I couldn't take her to dinner tonight like she wanted, she's gonna go ballistic."

BC grinned. "Maybe we should have convinced Fiona to go shopping with Maeve this evening — I didn't tell *her* what was up, either."

"Good idea. Uh the *last* part, not the first. The less Maeve knows about this raid, the better off she'll be. She still hasn't reconciled to the fact that Borgia has to be stopped. Been friends too long, I guess." He sighed heavily. "As to the other part, I don't think I want Maeve and Fiona too close together, either. The way Fi's feeling right now, I'd be afraid we'd end up sharing daytime accommodations."

"It's that bad?" Peale's grin faded. "I could tell she was pissed, but . . . God, Gae, what does she want? You're already divorced!"

"What it comes down to is she's scared I'm gonna get killed. She says it's for the kid's sake, but I think Mama has her so worked up that what happened to my Pop is going to happen to me, she isn't thinking straight."

Gilly McGillicuddy popped her head into the cubicle. "We're ready to rock 'n' roll, fellas. Glad you decided to join us, Peale."

"Let's go, Partner," Miller said, giving Peale a companionable swat on the back. The contact, however, brought Galen a fresh and deeper chill. Under the leather, lurked the distinctive bulk of bulletproofs. Ordinarily, he wouldn't have been surprised. SI flak jackets had been issued right after the SWAT briefing. But BC hadn't been at the briefing. He determined to keep close tabs on his slippery partner tonight. There was bound to be trouble enough without Peale going all Lone Ranger on him.

***

The limousine idled so smoothly and quietly, it was sometimes hard to tell it was running. It was also nearly packed. In a few moments, he could let *Il Padrone*—

Snick

Carlo Umberti slid his eyes toward the small sound and froze. Straightening slowly, he laced his fingers behind his head.

***

Gae wanted to talk. He knew that. It was probably about flak jacket. BC had felt the big man tense when he'd felt the armor through the duster. It was probably a blessing, then, that buying the vest and the Uzis had made him miss the briefing, since he didn't want to talk about it. Keeping other agents between himself and Miller on the way out to the estate took some doing.

He waited now outside the mansion in a deceptively peaceful formal garden. It was a beautiful place. One that, sadly, would soon witness violence, but that was a choice its owner had ensured a long time ago. To his right, he felt Galen fidgeting, awaiting the signal to storm the veranda and burst through the French doors into the salon. He'd make sure Gae got through before he did. If the big guy saw him break from the main group and slip down the corridor, he'd be sure to follow and that would be far too dangerous.

Michalson said Borgia's favorite room was the study, so Peale had memorized its location on the maps. The room was on the side of the house that overlooked the river, with a small corridor connecting it to the salon. The NYPD team was responsible for cordoning off the river road, so he'd have a few minutes before his police colleagues got there. A few minutes were all he needed. Better it should be all over by the time Stroud appeared on the scene.

At the signal, the concealed mass of humanity burst into the open and surged over the moonlit lawn. He hung back until the invaders encountered the first group of defenders. He used the shouting and gunfire to cover his detour, ducking into the narrow passage off the salon. Gunfire clattered again as he entered the study; and was muted suddenly as the padded door swung shut behind him.

Borgia was alone in the room, busily throwing papers onto the fire. There were too many, and they weren't burning well. Intensely dark eyes flicked up to see who entered, the ugly black German pistol in the elder vampire's hand automatically leveled at his visitor's middle. Eyebrows lifted in surprise as he registered the intruder's identity and he paused, the pistol wavering slightly.

Aside from the weapon, the library setting was so absurdly normal, the younger vampire felt a hysterical giggle bubble up. He squashed it and surprised himself at the steadiness of his voice as he said, "Good evening."

The sound of his own voice startled him. It broke the spell that held the elder, as well.

Borgia carelessly placed his weapon on the corner of the desk and resumed destroying documents. "I haven't time for you now, Byron."

Peale stepped closer, causing his not-quite sanguine sire to spook slightly toward the pistol. Noting the move with satisfaction, he said, "I've come to kill you."

Borgia looked up from the fire in disbelief, then laughed as if his scion had made a particularly clever joke. "I don't think so, fledgling. I made you; I can destroy you."

In a movement so swift, even Byron had difficulty following, Borgia had the pistol and popped off two quick shots that took the slender man square in the heart. Dazed and ears ringing from the explosions, he slid to the floor, realizing that Borgia had not been totally unprepared. Even through the armor, he could feel that the slugs were silver.

Good. That made what came next easier.

Shaking his head at the youngster's folly, the sire turned away, never seeing the fledgling spring to his feet with Uzis blazing. Byron's bullets were silver, too. He caught the Italian in a crosscut pattern, firing and firing until the weapons began clicking instead of jumping. Deafened by the automatic fire, he watched Francesco Borgia drop to his knees, then slide to the floor onto his face in a din of hellacious silence.

At the end, he looked . . . surprised.

Edging closer, he flipped the body over with his foot and saw, to his dismay that his loads had too much power. Most of them had passed right through. The blessings did their job, though. The ancient nobleman was in pain, probably dying, but he couldn't take the chance. Body forged of brittle ice, he knelt beside the bloodied form and tore aside the clothing covering the neck.

Forcing his fangs to extend, he unwillingly bent to finish the job in the only way he knew how, when impossibly,

Borgia's eyes flew open. The sire's powerful hand locked onto his scion's throat. Peale had a vague impression of increased G-forces as the elder leaped to his feet, dangling the younger man like a kitten. Peale felt his larynx crush. In desperation, he kicked at the bands of red across his captor's front. Borgia's mouth opened wide in agony. He released his hold, letting the younger vampire slide to the floor.

Relegated to passenger status in his own body, Peale rolled out of range on pure instinct. The same primal force drew him to his feet, reeling, his throat on fire where the crushing fingers had been. He watched as from a distance as he launched himself, grabbed the white forelock and yanked the head back. Blood filled his mouth. Borgia's blood. The wrongness of the taste revolted him, and he gagged, but he kept drinking. A roaring stronger than a roomful of Uzis filled his ears. He felt himself engulfed in blackness, being subverted somehow, losing himself in the force that was Francesco Borgia — then he became aware of sharp blows raining on his back.

Pain freed him from the engulfing personality — allowing him to come back to himself. Borgia's body slipped from his fingers. He vaguely felt the weight sliding to the floor against his legs as he turned toward the blows. It was Gwen Isendamer, wielding a reddened fire poker. He could see her mouth gaping as she screamed at him. The incongruous notion that, considering Isendamer, he should probably be grateful he couldn't hear flashed through his brain.

As Borgia hit the floor, she lost interest in Peale, dropping the poker to snatch wildly at the falling body. He was intensely grateful for that, too, because his legs had suddenly gone all jellied inside, and everything else began to violently spasm. He tumbled to the floor a few feet away, his face even with the staring eyes of his sire.

Borgia had a funny, dusty kind of look. He seemed to dissolve as Isendamer clutched at him. He was trying to make sense of it, when Galen Miller's face came between himself and the movie. Strong arms lifted the jelly off the floor and guided it to the door, the useless Uzis vainly striving for attention on either side.

***

Even in the chaos of the running gun battle, and probably because he was expecting it, Galen quickly realized he was Pealeless. Swearing, he stepped out of the flow of law enforcement bodies and made his way back to where he'd last seen his partner. That turned out to be adjacent to a dark, narrow hallway. At the sound of muffled automatic gunfire, Galen had bolted down the side passage. He'd kicked the padded door open at the end of the corridor, hit the carpet, and rolled up, weapon braced and ready. He needn't have bothered. Nobody was paying him the least bit of attention.

He reached his partner's side at the same moment Isendamer clutched frantically at Borgia. In shock, he watched as the woman's hands passed through the Italian vampire as he disintegrated into ashes on the oriental rug. Beside him, BC knelt unseeing, covered with blood, shaking like high voltage was passing through his body.

Staring at ash-covered hands, Isendamer collapsed beside a bloody fireplace tool and screamed incoherent obscenities at them. It didn't take a lot of study to realize the woman wasn't merely hysterical. The insanity that had been previously hidden now poured from her, most of it directed at Peale.

It suddenly became a very good idea to get out of there. Sharing a room with Isendamer in that state wasn't a healthy hobby for *either* of them. Police medics could be dispatched to deal with her later, but gauging from the commotion filtering through from outside, he had little time to lose. The backup teams would break in at any moment, and it would be hard to explain Peale's injuries. Keeping a watchful eye on the raving woman, he crouched in front of BC, and called his name.

The vampire's response was vague, but there was recognition in his eyes — that was a relief. Then Galen saw the trickles of blood oozing from both ears. Idiot. He should've known better than to fire automatic weapons in a closed space without ear protection. Whatever else was wrong with him would have to wait. Miller hauled Peale to his feet and steered him for a door at the rear of the study, hoping like hell that it actually lead somewhere.

Peale was all but a dead weight as they stumbled down the gloomy passage. Galen was careful not to bump his cumbersome burden into the paneling of the narrow passage. Last thing he wanted was to leave a trail of blood-smears.

The corridor emptied into a huge, well-equipped kitchen. Apparently, Borgia took his mortal hirelings' well-being into account and saw to it that the other people sharing the house had three meals a day. The room was currently unoccupied. There were doors on the far side of the kitchen. Miller made for them in hopes of finding a place to stash his injured partner while he looked for Taylor and Stroud. He especially wanted to find Taylor. He wasn't sure what a doctor could *do* for Peale, but he'd feel better if someone with medical knowledge took a look at him.

As they passed two huge, stainless steel sinks, Peale suddenly grabbed at the edge of the nearest one. Pulling himself toward it, out of Miller's grasp, he heaved, sending a violent gout of dark red into the basin.

"Oh geez." Galen gulped and looked away until the retching stopped. When he looked back, he found BC draped weakly along the steel rim, shaking worse than before. Galen turned on the taps, sending the red mess swirling down the drain. Byron's face was a mess, too. Galen wet a wad of paper towels and wiped the spatters away. This seemed to calm the injured vampire considerably.

"C'mon, man," Miller said, hauling his partner up by the armpits. "We gotta get you outta sight. Listen to me, talking to the idiot who shattered his own eardrums with a matched set of Uzis."

Dragging Peale along, he opened doors as he went. The first was a dark stairway leading down. The second was a good-sized pantry. Perfect. The kitchen was equipped to cook for the hordes, and accordingly, bought in bulk. Leaving BC propped against the doorframe, Galen shoved a huge bag of flour over onto the floor, coughing and waving at the white fog arising from its impact. Next, he spread some aprons across the bag and sat Peale on it, making sure he wouldn't slide off. Closing the door behind himself, he went looking for the detectives.

He didn't have to look far. He found the two creeping up the hall he and BC had just come down. Relief upon sighting friendlies was mutual.

Securing his weapon, Taylor asked, "Where's BC? We haven't seen hide nor hair of him since we got here. We saw you slide out of the fracas in the front of the house and followed as soon as we could. The way you were acting, we thought you might need a hand."

"You thought right," Galen said. Jerking his thumb toward the pantry, he added, "I got Peale stashed back there. He's hurt bad, and I think you oughta look at him, Taylor."

"He's hurt?" Stroud caught her breath. "Did it happen back there? That room we just passed though looked like the bombs had hit it."

Eying her thoughtfully. Did she know BC was planning to take care of his sire on his own? Peale said she'd given him the silver bullets. He answered simply: "He mixed it up with Borgia one-on-one."

Once inside the pantry, Taylor's face darkened seeing the limp body sprawled on the sacking. Crouching alongside, he probed with practiced fingers.

Stroud's composure slipped as she calculated the damage. She'd seen a lot of corpses in her homicide career, and this looked like one of the worst. Pistol sliding smoothly into its holster, she asked shakily, "A-are you sure he's not really gone this time?"

Galen answered carefully, "If what I saw when Borgia went was any indication, I think he's still with us. The guy shriveled up before my eyes. When Isendamer grabbed at him, he just kinda sifted away."

Taylor's head snapped up. "Borgia's dead? You saw this?"

"Yeah. I saw it," Miller said. "Not likely to forget it any time soon, either." A frazzled memory circuit suddenly completed. "Shit! Isendamer! I was so concerned about getting BC the hell outta Dodge, I left her sitting by Borgia's ash pile screaming obscenities at us. Was she still there?"

Stroud registered alarm. "In the study? Didn't see her

and she couldn't have passed us in either hall. Come to that, I didn't see an ash pile, either, just a lot of blood."

She was talking to thin air, because Galen had bolted for the porch off the kitchen. Following, she caught up with him as he flew down the steps and hit the gravel path, bellowing for whoever was on duty in the yard. Pelting down the path behind the steamroller-like figure, she vaguely caught the sound of a motor catching and turning over.

As they rounded the landscaped bend, the path disgorged on a low dock. An unlit speedboat tore away, and sped out into the river throttles open all the way. Only one person was silhouetted against the reflected moonlight, and the pungent odor of gasoline on the water told the fate of the other craft that had been moored there.

Miller's rage ripped the air. "Shit! SHIT! **SHIT!** *Why* wasn't anyone covering those damn boats?" With disgust, he wrenched his phone out of his jacket pocket.

Stroud smacked a mooring post and swore. "What a cock-up! This is gonna take forever. I hope Taylor can hold the fort until we get this under control."

***

The damage pattern across Peale's back puzzled Taylor, until he remembered seeing a bent and bloody fireplace poker lying on the study carpet. *Yes*, he thought, probing a deep gouge where the flak vest had shredded, *even the best flak vest can only take so much punishment. Whoever lit into him did it with intent to do the most damage possible.*

He nearly flung his insensible patient to the floor, as a meaty paw gripped his shoulder. He wheeled to find Dennis Brannaugh sadly regarding the lifeless form sprawled over the unbleached, unsifted, all-purpose examination table. The

Captain said sorrowfully, "Sorry, Taylor — losing a friend is hard. God, this is gonna crush Stroud."

Shit. Resolutely, Tyler Taylor stood, and carefully wiping thick blood off his hands, said, "Captain, you'd better sit down. I've got a really long and *really* crazy story to tell you."

Brannaugh started to reply, but instead, recoiled with mouth gaping, as impossibly, Peale's corpse flung itself up and tried to stand. Swearing, Taylor swung around and caught the maimed body before it slid to the floor.

***

Fifteen minutes later, Stroud and Galen returned to the kitchen and the sight of Dennis Brannaugh holding a semiconscious Peale up beside the kitchen sink. Taylor acknowledged their arrival, as the captain flopped his burden down into a convenient chair.

Wetting a cotton towel under the faucet, Taylor gestured toward a crumpled mass of dull metal on the table. "That's one disaster averted. We found two silver slugs flattened out against the bulletproofs. Good thing he was wearin'. His back's a mess. The fireplace poker, from the shape and size of the wounds. Ripped right through the armor in places. We haven't been able to ask him about anything since his eardrums are burst and his larynx is crushed." He shook his head and wrung out the towel. "Good job he's already dead, or that would have killed him. He's in deep shock, though — no surprises there."

Brannaugh shifted his stupefied gaze from the impossibly still-moving corpse to the tall Australian. He muttered, " Sgt. Taylor, one of us is crazy, but the jury's still out on which."

Galen and Stroud exchanged glances. They knew

Brannaugh would have had to be told about BC sooner or later, but they'd both been counting heavily on later.

Galen cleared his throat. "Will he be able to talk to Colonel Black when he gets here in maybe thirty minutes? He's headed our way and wants to debrief all of us on site."

Brannaugh nodded toward a radio unit on the table. "We heard. That's why we dragged the kid out here. Easier to clean him up this way."

Taylor methodically swabbed blood off Peale's face with the dampened towel. "Half an hour? I dunno. He's healing pretty quickly, though. At the rate he's going? Hour, maybe?"

Stroud moved to her lover's side, and taking another towel, gently wiped down an arm.

"I think the smell of all this blood isn't helping — his canines are fully extended and don't show any sign of retracting," Taylor observed.

With a small sigh, BC relaxed into Stroud.

Taylor grinned. "If that's any indication, he'll be back with us sooner than I thought. Y'might get your thirty, after all."

A sputter of disgusted amusement burst from Captain Brannaugh. He thumped Galen in the chest. "Regardless, you and me better back get to Uncle Joe. He's stuck in front directing the wrap-up, and fit to be tied. If we don't put in an appearance soon, he'll likely have warrants sworn out on all of us." Brow furrowed, he watched the trio by the sink. "If nothin' else, we can buy Dracula Junior more time to pull himself together. Maybe those kids are a perfect match. She's murderous, but he's dead already, so it don't matter. Might save the rest of us a lot of grief."

EIGHT

"Ah, Special Agent Peale," Colonel Black said as he strode across the room with his hand extended. Peale gripped it for a solid handshake as Black added, "I don't know if you're aware of it, but I'm originally from Philadelphia. Your family is legendary there."

"Depends on who you're talking to, sir." The errant member of the clan grinned. "Some might call us infamous."

Black chuckled, but before he could respond, a commotion in the foyer turned all heads toward it.

"Ma'am! *Ma'am!* You can't—"

"Don't tell me what I can and can't do, ye officious little man."

"Ma'am!" The chief of the forensic team backed into the room while trying to block Maeve Donal from entering. He was failing miserably.

With a cry of, "Byron!" she ducked around him and darted straight for the group by the love seat.

Defeated, the tech appealed to his superior officers, "I'm sorry, sirs. She showed up as we were leaving and just piled into the van."

"Not your fault, Dr. Schwarz," the colonel said, shunting him toward the crime scene. "Greater forces than the head forensic pathologist of SINY have been bowled over by this particular lady."

The pathologist looked ridiculously relieved, thanked the colonel, then he and his crew fled to relative safety of the destroyed and bloodied room next door. Black noted with silent amusement how the entire team gave the redhead a wide berth. Truthfully, he didn't blame them. For someone so physically tiny, she was a force to be reckoned with. She'd even done a good job of steamrolling Joe Stallings. That took some doing. Personally, he'd hoped to postpone the pleasure of meeting the notorious Ms. Donal a little longer. That choice seemed to have been taken out of his hands. At present, though, she was Special Agent Peale's problem, and to give the woman credit, she seemed genuinely concerned.

"What happened m'love? I know ye've been hurt. I felt a terrible pain in my head like somethin' burst." She looked around as if suddenly seeing her surroundings for the first time. "One of those pathology people told me this was Francesco's estate, where—"

Her words broke off as she stared past him through the open door and into the study beyond, where ash smudges were being taped inside a roughly human-shaped outline on the oriental carpet. "What is that dreadful little man sayin' about remains, Byron?"

"It's just what it sounds like, Maeve," Peale answered quietly. "Francesco Borgia is dead, once and for all."

She searched his face. "Byron Peale, tell me this was none of your doin'." Her gray eyes grew wide at his silence.

Just as suddenly, the Irish woman's eyes narrowed and her back grew ramrod straight. Colonel Black followed her gaze over Peale's shoulder to see that Sgt. Girion was walking through the study with a forensic specialist, retracing the path she and Sgt. Taylor had taken earlier.

Remembering the fiery retaliation from the Chicago division's rescue operation, Black hastily stepped forward. "Excuse me, Ms. Donal?"

Startled, she whirled to face him. Bruise-like smudges marred the creamy skin under her eyes. To his surprise, he realized she was trembling. "Ms. Donal, I'm Colonel Brian Black, the head of the United States branch of Sentry International. I understand your shock, but please don't be angry with Special Agent Peale. He was acting in self-defense."

She remained silent, but the pain in her eyes was eloquent.

***

Halfway across the room, Dennis Brannaugh could see Brian Black struggling. The guy was a good cop for an Ivy League type — if you could call what Black did being a cop. Whatever. It was still law enforcement. Larger beat, but the same basic idea.

Well, he was a cop, too. The plain vanilla kind with none of the bells and whistles, and like other cops, one thing he was unhappily used to dealing with was people in pain. No matter how you labeled what happened in the study behind him, never mind the method or how officially clean the action was, somebody died. Pure and simple. Somebody died, and that always left someone else, somewhere, hurting. Black might be able to parley with heads of state and be at ease in multi-cultural settings that would drive Brannaugh batshit, but the guy was out of his depth in the face of a grieving woman.

With an inward shrug, the burly policeman stepped forward, saying, "Hey, folks, I understand Sgt. Taylor has located the coffee machine. Seems to me the lady might could use a cup."

Taking her faint nod as permission, he slid a brawny arm protectively around her shoulders and herded her toward the doorway. Off to the side, Stroud Girion stood, watching the techs comb the study carpeting. He got her attention and motioned her over. She took a step forward, saw who he was with, and balked. He motioned more forcefully and guided Maeve into the hallway. Stroud fell in behind them. The Detective Sergeant didn't look very happy about it, but that was tough.

They didn't take the straight route to the kitchen. Instead, Brannaugh steered them along a circuitous path in an effort to give Ms. Donal a chance to walk some of the shock off. Any extra time it gave Detective Sergeant Taylor to finish clearing the bloody scene the forensics techs would never see was gravy. Peering through the swinging door at the end of the big dining room, he assessed the scene beyond before pushing through. To his relief, Tyler Taylor was doing exactly what he'd advertised, manning an industrial-sized coffee maker.

Leaving Maeve in Stroud's care at the scrubbed table, he crossed to where Taylor was puttering. The detective had used his time well; there was no sign of their earlier frantic triage.

Brannaugh sang out, "Three cups, Henri, clean ones if ya got 'em."

Taylor jerked his head toward the pair at the table and asked quietly, "Is that a good idea, Captain? Relations have been strained between those parties for well-known reasons."

"Maybe, but I want to keep an eye on both of them. The Donal woman took Borgia's death slightly better than a two by four against the side of the head, and Stroud's hiding it pretty good, but she's been twitchy since she saw her boyfriend all banged up. Can't blame either of them."

Taylor nodded. Handing Brannaugh two steaming mugs, he picked up two more and followed the lumbering figure back to the clean-scrubbed table.

As they approached, Maeve spat, "Stroud Girion, y'knew what Byron was thinkin', didn't ye? How could you let him? In so doin', ye may have doomed him, as well! If you really loved him—"

"Ms. Donal, if you want to fight over BC, you're shit out of luck." The detective's eyes were icy. "I don't fight over people. BC is twenty-one — to say the least. I don't like people messing with my life, so I don't mess with anyone else's. Yeah, I admit it. I love him, but I haven't put a brand on him. Last time I had the opportunity to look, there wasn't one from you, either."

Standing so abruptly her chair fell over, she stormed out the back door. Brannaugh sighed, nodded Taylor toward the Irishwoman, then took his pair of mugs outside in pursuit of his best lady detective. This was serious. In all the years he'd known her, he'd never heard her use the L word.

***

Taylor watched the pair disappearing into the night beyond the door with mixed emotions. Part of him wanted to follow, but the more logical part knew the Captain was more suited to the talk that was going to have to happen out there. Righting the chair he sat down and set a steaming cup of black coffee in front of the trembling witch. He couldn't tell if the shakiness was from grief, anger, or a dangerous mix of both.

Aloud he said, "Drink that. If it doesn't kill you, it might make you feel better."

Donal didn't move, but sat still, eyes closed and fists clenched white-knuckled in her lap.

He pushed cream and sugar toward her and tried again. "It's a little known fact that Aussie-made coffee will even remove warts — not that you have any — I merely use it as an illustration."

Suddenly, she was sobbing. "No matter what Francesco had done t'me, he was still my friend, don't you see? I loved him. I love — loved both of them."

The detective was nonplussed. He was never good at emotional scenes. He always let Stroud or Brannaugh handle them. After a moment, he reached out and gave her hand a hesitant pat.

Just as suddenly as the tears began, they stopped. Sniffing, she pulled away and dabbed at her eyes with a paper napkin. "I'm sorry, Taylor, darlin'. I'm a tad bit hysterical. Give me a minute and I'll get m'self together."

Taylor watched her compose herself. He couldn't stop himself from asking, "What did you mean a few minutes ago, that Peale may be doomed? What did he do that was so bad?"

"He drained Francesco, didn't he?"

"It appears so—"

"I knew it." She jumped to her feet and paced, crumpling the paper napkin in her fist. "I knew it as soon as I laid eyes on him. Oh, the *idiot!*"

She sat down again and gulped some black coffee, visibly struggling against more tears. At length, she said, "I suppose there's no way ye could know. For that matter, Byron himself might not know. I don't know the details, but Francesco once told me there were dire consequences if one vampire drained the blood of another."

"That could mean anything," the detective said sitting back thoughtfully. "When did he tell you that? What were the circumstances?"

"It happened a long time ago." She took a deep breath and released it in a half-laugh, half-sigh. "Unlike Byron, Francesco is — *was* very territorial. That's why he got so upset at first in Chicago. When we were livin' together as lovers in Italy, another vampire moved into what he considered his domain.

"He was furious. He sought his rival out and they fought. It was terrible, Francesco won, then dragged the other outside and did . . . well, let's just say he did everything he could to ensure the dawn would find the poor wretch. However, he stopped short of draining his blood, even though this seemed t'me the surest method. When I asked why, he said, 'In such an event, only the strongest of wills can prevail.' He refused to tell me anything else. Shortly after that, I moved out. He didn't follow."

"Holy shit," he breathed. After a moment, he asked, "What if he . . . lost the blood?"

"Lost it?" She asked in confusion. "He was sick?"

"According to Galen, pretty violently."

Painted fingernails absently tapped along the side of her mug as she considered. "I don't know. I wish I did, but Francesco was notoriously secretive about his nature. I would imagine it would help, but there seems to be more involved than just blood. It involves the will in some way — Francesco's will was very strong."

"Yet, BC was able to give him the shove but good on several occasions."

"Yes, he did, didn't he?"

Taylor stared into his own cup for a moment. "Okay, I'm not trying to start trouble, but maybe Borgia wasn't the only one who wasn't forthcoming enough."

Gray eyes narrowed. "Meanin'?"

"Meaning that maybe BC would have known better, if you'd shared more of your knowledge with him in the first place."

Fists clenched against the tabletop, she spat, "Told ye all about it, did he?"

"Told me enough." He cooly met her gaze. "More than enough to know that you wield powerful magic. Surely, with all your ability, you can help him through this?"

Maeve wilted and he wondered if she was going to lose control again. Instead, she said quietly, "Darlin', I'm not even sure what 'this' will be. Magic does have its limits." She paused, engaged in some sort of internal struggle, then leaned across the table with sudden urgency. "The timing for this couldn't be worse, but I may not get another chance . . . there's somethin' I need to discuss with ye. It's about magic."

***

Dennis Brannaugh frequently thought that heading a squad of detectives like his ought to come with special training. In his time, he'd acted as marriage councilor, grief therapist, school headmaster and fight referee. He wasn't certain where his talk with Stroud Girion fell in that. It definitely wound up as bus boy, carting the two now-empty mugs back to the house. He stopped cold with one foot on the back step as Tyler Taylor's voice reached him through the screen door. *Add spy to that list, I suppose,* he thought, leaning in to hear better.

"No. I understand perfectly what you're saying, and I want no part of it," Taylor said. Brannaugh had heard that tone all too often. His Sergeant had reached one of his boundaries and no amount of pushing would get him to cross it.

"But, Taylor," Maeve Donal pleaded. "You must understand, you're a born mage! D'ye understand how rare that is? Y'need trainin' to properly channel that power. If not me, please let me take you t'me mother or one of m'aunts."

"Thanks, but I don't want to be any more special than I already am."

"I suppose I see your point." The Irish woman sighed heavily. "Promise me you'll at least keep the door open. Later, if you change your mind, speak to Byron. He'll know how to find me."

Gravel crunched behind Brannaugh. Stroud was finally heading in. He resumed his progress up the stair as if it had never been interrupted, making a noisy show of cramming the mugs into one hand as he reached for the door latch.

"Sgt. Taylor!" he called, opening the screened door. "Ah, good. You're still here. Better get more coffee brewing. Looks like things are wrapping up fast and cold cops want hot coffee."

"There ought to be plenty, Captain. This kitchen was set up for the masses. The coffeemaker is a restaurant model, and there are two pots ready and waiting." He looked beyond his commanding officer into the darkness. "Where's Stroud?"

"Right here." The screen opened again Stroud stepped in. "I don't know if you guys have your radio units on, but they're ready for us in the study." Glancing at the stony-faced Irishwoman, she said, "They want Ms. Donal there, too."

Letting the two women head into the corridor, Brannaugh caught Taylor's arm, pulling him back into the kitchen.

Taylor looked confused, then the penny dropped, "Ah. You heard."

"Yeah," Brannaugh said. "I wasn't trying to, but it happened. You wanna tell me just what the Donal woman was going on about?"

The sergeant looked sullen for a moment. "Nope," he said with finality. "Not until I've had a chance to figure it out myself. Might take a bit, though, 'cause I don't intend to think about it much."

***

It took some looking, but Galen Miller finally found his partner leaning in an open French door, looking out onto the moon-drenched gardens. The pale face swung around at his approach, and to Miller's relief, there was a smile of greeting on it.

"Hey, Gae," Peale said, the smile going slightly rueful. "Sorry to slip off, and leave you holding the bag, but if I had to go over what I remembered of the fight one more time, I'd go barking mad on the spot."

Chuckling, Miller took up a post against the other doorframe and breathed deeply of the garden scents. "No prob, pal. I saw you gettin' twitchy, so I covered for you when you slid toward the exit."

"Oops. I simply couldn't take being asked where Isendamer went after the fight one more time."

"Forget it. Considering how out of it you were, I'm surprised you could remember Isendamer was even there.

People are clutching at straws because no one's happy that she got away."

"Too right, there. Especially since she killed the uniformed officer guarding the dock to do it."

"At least it was quick and clean. The Ice Empress doesn't usually give her victims that much."

"Small consolation," Peale murmured. "I certainly don't envy Dennis Brannaugh's task of informing the young man's parents."

Miller grunted his assent. He didn't either — any more than he relished informing Peale that they they'd been indefinitely assigned to New York. Oh, Colonel Black gave some bullshit song and dance about 'wrapping up'. No mistake, there'd be plenty to do, but bullshit was still bullshit. He wondered if SI simply didn't know what to do with them.

Personally, he wasn't happy about staying. He'd been looking forward to getting home to Chicago. He missed it and his family. Yeah. Family. Fiona had been talking up California again. Going on about how happy they all were there and how great life was before things went sour. He recognized the signs. There was something she wanted so badly, she could taste it. He wished like hell she'd tell him what it was. Was she trying to rekindle their romance? Not if her reaction in the apartment kitchen was any clue.

He stole a sidelong glance at his partner. How Peale would take the reassignment was up for grabs. He missed Jump Veron and the Inferno, but Stroud Girion was a complication.

Screw it. He didn't like always being the bearer of bad tidings. Let Stallings take the heat. Instead, he said, "It's nice out here, isn't it?"

"Yes, although how someone so evil could construct a place of such beauty is beyond me. Maybe for much the same reason I'm enjoying it: looking out over such peace lets me forget all the ugliness for a few moments."

"How come you didn't tell me you were gunning for Borgia?"

The smile in the dim light was ambiguous, but the tone was rueful, "You'd have tried to stop me, wouldn't you?"

"Probably. I could tell Stroud knew, though. How come you told her?"

"Didn't. She figured it out just like you did. I think the thing was, she realized she couldn't do anything about it, so she tried to get me all the edge she could. Guess it worked."

They stood in silence watching the first fireflies of the season flit through the topiary and listening to the insect sounds attempting to drown the buzz of human voices by the river. Even though the operation was winding down, there were still people crawling all over the estate. Glimpses of flashlights gleamed through the trees as teams of agents searched the grounds for God knew what.

BC said, "In all the years I've existed and in all the wars I've fought in, I've never before gone into a battle with the intent to destroy one specific person." The rest was almost inaudible. "I hope I never have to do it again."

Miller remained silent. Even without his friend's special abilities, he sensed emotions boiling and muscles clenched bone-snapping taut with anxiety. He wanted badly to say something profound that would make a difference, something to relieve the pain he knew was there, but words were never his strong suit. He hoped his understanding would be evident enough to not need words.

Peale asked suddenly, "What's going on down there? I saw the forensics team leaving. They didn't seem to be carrying much more than when they came in."

"They weren't. There was an empty case by the bookshelves with a card giving a history for a Greek vase. Something about red-figures? Anyway, it looks like she scooped the ashes into that with the fireplace broom and shovel and did a bunk out the window. There was a mashed down place in the plantings and a pretty good trail of cypress mulch for a ways down the path. She didn't leave much else."

BC sniffed in bleak amusement. "Hard luck she's a homicidal maniac. She's more thorough than any parlor maid I've met. She could make a fortune at cleaning up."

The big man grinned through the grime. "Cleaning up sounds like a good idea to me. What say we find Stroud and Taylor and blow this joint?"

"Sounds good to me, too." Peale stood aside to let his bulky partner precede him.

Miller hooked his shoulder and steered him toward the door. "Nuh uh! That's how you gave me the slip the last time. I'm gonna keep you in sight from now on." He paused for effect, then asked, "So tell me, Special Agent Peale! How'd you like your first case?"

Incredulous, BC stared for a heartbeat. "Let's see, I got shot — with both silver and regular bullets, blown up, staked, shot again . . . ." A mischievous glint lit his face. "You're a mighty dangerous person to work with, Galen Miller."

***

Gwen Isendamer clutched her parcel tight against her chest as she forced herself to calmly mount the private jet's boarding ramp. The box looked innocuous in its kraft paper wrapping. Even though she was a private charter passenger, the package had been x-rayed, scanned and sniffed until she thought she'd scream. Thankfully, no one had tried to make her open it. If it were opened, the evidence inside would be enough to hang her and she'd already had more close calls than she wanted.

She'd made it out of her apartment by the skin of her teeth. Just as the cab she rode in pulled away, police cars had come to screeching halts in front of her building. She'd watched through the back window as officers sprang from their vehicles and stormed the place, then sank against the stained seat cushion in carefully concealed relief as the activity shrank to ant-size then disappeared from view. She'd had barely enough time to disguise herself, make connections with a charter pilot who wasn't too nosy, throw a few things into a bag and pack the ancient vase into a cardboard box.

Her next hurdle had been keeping her composure as she made her way to the private boarding lounge. She couldn't remember ever being so on edge. The brown wig was stiflingly hot and the foundation that darkened her ivory complexion felt like a mask. She'd almost come out of her skin when the attendant told her the jet was waiting on the tarmac. Keeping an outward calm was the key. The airport was crawling with security personnel, and was sure to get worse. It was only a matter of time before Sentry International clamped down security on all ports.

There were times the slow grind of bureaucracy was a boon. This was one of those. Soon, she'd be on her way to the west coast of Canada and, from there, a boat to Russia. Once there, her contacts could get her around customs and farther into Europe. They'd better. They'd been paid enough.

"We're ready for take off, Ma'am."

Breath catching in her throat, she turned toward the speaker. It was only the charter pilot standing beside the cockpit door.

He added, "I can secure your parcel in front with me, if you'd like."

Willing her voice to be steady, she answered, "No, thank you, I prefer to keep it with me."

Forcing herself not to hurry, she strapped into her plush seat. Belting the precious parcel into the seat next to her own, she thought, *"And you* will *be with me, won't you, Francesco darling? Always. I'll find a way."*

***

"I didn't think you'd feel like keeping our date, but I'm glad you did."

Stroud snuggled against him and he took her in his arms, savoring the warmth and scent of her vibrantly alive body. Peale said, "After everything that's happened, I need to be with you more than ever. Besides, there was no way I was going to stay at our flat tonight."

"Mmmm? Y'know you've talked a lot about how Gae feels about this posting, but I haven't heard a personal comment yet. How do you feel about it?"

"Truth to tell, I'm torn. The only bright side I can see so far is that we'll be together more. It brings me closer to my family, too, but I confess I was looking forward to getting back to the club, back to my music. Now that Maeve has decided to return to Ireland—"

She jerked in surprise. "She's *leaving?*"

"As soon as she can. She's very upset about what happened. She's trying to fight it, but she's having a hard time looking me in the eyes. It's an odd feeling. This is only the second time she's voluntarily taken leave of me. While I admit to a certain sense of relief, the circs aren't the most auspicious"

"That thing about Borgia's blood?"

He frowned and she felt him tense. "Yeah. She can bang on about Borgia not being forthcoming with information all she wants. She was just the same with me, dropping convenient facts like so many breadcrumbs. I don't know if it was to cover what she didn't know or as a measure of control. Maybe both. Maeve likes control."

"I don't think she likes me much."

"I like you enough to make up for it, don't I?"

His lips brushed her hair and dropped to her neck. She leaned into him enjoying his flesh against hers until the first playful nip.

"Hey!" Stroud pulled away and sat up. "Not so fast, fella. Do you have any idea what she was talking to Taylor about? Whatever it was has him jumpier than a toad on a hot sidewalk." Jabbing a finger into his chest, she said, "You promised you'd find out what it was."

His brow furrowed and he said slowly, "I really didn't understand a lot of what she told me, but the upshot is that your partner is a natural born sorcerer."

"A what?"

"Sorcerer." He wiggled his fingers in the air. "You know, hocus-pocus, here comes a fireball?"

"Seriously?"

"Seriously. Maeve told him about the power she sensed in him and he wasn't impressed. I gather that, for some reason, her revelation was most unwelcome."

"That doesn't surprise me. For all his vaunted intellect and the jokes he cracks about being a genius, I think what Tyler Taylor wants more than anything else is to be 'normal.' Whatever the hell that is."

He frowned. "Don't we all?"

"Not me! I like a healthy dose of abnormality from time to time." Grasping his ponytail firmly, she pulled him to her, murmuring, "Speaking of which — where were we?"

***

She didn't know where the number connected and frankly didn't care. All that mattered was that when she called and gave her information, good money came her way.

This time, the voice that answered was female. She told it, "Francesco Borgia is dead. Gwen Isendamer and Edgar Michalson are out of the picture. The field is open."

Not waiting for a response, she ended the call and slid the back off the ugly pink burner phone, removing the SIM card before she tossed it into the river. Her past tips had made life very comfortable for her. This one ought to be worth a real bundle.

www.ingramcontent.com/pod-product-compliance
Lightning Source LLC
Chambersburg PA
CBHW072056020726
47501CB00003B/614